THE ARKHANGELSK TRILOGY

TRILOGY

A Final Dawn Story

MIKE KRAUS

Contents

Copyright   v

Other Books From Mike Kraus   vii

Book 1 - Archangel Rising   ix

Chapter 1   1

Chapter 2   5

Chapter 3   9

Chapter 4   25

Chapter 5   43

Chapter 6   45

Chapter 7   71

Chapter 8   75

Chapter 9   89

Chapter 10   107

Chapter 11   109

Chapter 12   115

Chapter 13   123

Chapter 14   131

Chapter 15   139

Chapter 16   141

Book 2 - Archangel Falling   149

Chapter 17   151

Chapter 18   163

Chapter 19   171

Chapter 20   179

Chapter 21   185

Chapter 22   195

Chapter 23   205

Chapter 24   211

Chapter 25   221

Chapter 26   231

Chapter 27   241

Chapter 28   257
Chapter 29   263
Chapter 30   271

Book 3 - Archangel Triumphant   283
Chapter 31   285
Chapter 32   293
Chapter 33   303
Chapter 34   311
Chapter 35   317
Chapter 36   323
Chapter 37   329
Chapter 38   333
Chapter 39   339
Chapter 40   345
Chapter 41   353
Chapter 42   359
Chapter 43   365
Chapter 44   375
Chapter 45   391
Chapter 46   399
Chapter 47   407
Chapter 48   415
Epilogue   421

Author's Notes – April 28, 2017   427

Arkhangelsk
A Final Dawn Story
The Complete Arkhangelsk Trilogy

By
Mike Kraus

© 2017 by Mike Kraus
www.MikeKrausBooks.com
hello@MikeKrausBooks.com
www.facebook.com/MikeKrausBooks

Other Books From Mike Kraus

Final Dawn: The Complete Original Series Box Set

Clocking in at nearly 300,000 words with over 250,000 copies sold, this is the complete collection of the original bestselling post-apocalyptic Final Dawn series. If you enjoy gripping, thrilling post-apocalyptic action with compelling and well-written characters you'll love Final Dawn.

Surviving the Fall

Surviving the Fall is an episodic post-apocalyptic series that follows Rick and Dianne Waters as they struggle to survive after a devastating and mysterious worldwide attack. Trapped on the opposite side of the country from his family, Rick must fight to get home while his wife and children struggle to survive as danger lurks around every corner.

No Sanctuary

An unprecedented terrorist attack has devastated the United States. As the nation reels from the consequences of the attack, two complete strangers must work together to not only survive but to come face-to-face with the perpetrator of the attack in an effort to stop them from completing their ultimate goal.

Prip'Yat: The Beast of Chernobyl

Two teens and two Spetsnaz officers travel to the town of Prip'Yat set just outside the remains of the Chernobyl power plant. The teens are there for a night of exploration. The special forces are there to pursue a creature that shouldn't exist. This short thriller set around the site of the Chernobyl nuclear disaster will keep your heart racing right through to the very end.

Book 1 - Archangel Rising

Chapter One

PROLOGUE

Alexander peered down the narrow corridor, straining his eyes to catch a glimpse of anything that might be ahead. His breathing was slow and methodical, though he could feel his heart practically bursting through his chest. Blood fell slowly from his forehead, pooling on his right brow before dripping in front of his eye onto his cheek. The wound wasn't deep, though the smell of iron was strong. He moved his hand from the handguard of his rifle, wiping away the blood with the back of a sleeve that was already soaked through.

Behind him came the sound of dozens of shuffling feet along with the murmurs of a crowd. Alexander gritted his teeth and prayed silently, hoping that anything in the corridor wouldn't be able to hear the people behind him. His footsteps were measured and quiet, honed from seven years spent as a special forces operative. The people he was leading, though, were not nearly as skilled.

There were a few businessmen, many dockworkers, two government employees, one homeless woman, several children and family members and a few others that Alexander had forgotten about. They were all that was left of the larger group that had managed to cling to survival in the city after the day the sky had turned to flame and ash. They were the last survivors of the city.

Not that it matters in the end, he thought. *This whole world's gone mad. First half the city gets wiped out, then those… things.* He forced back a shudder, not wanting the grip on his rifle to waver. Another drip of blood came down, this time into his eye. He stopped in his tracks and lowered his gun, blinking and rubbing his eye to rid it of the blood.

The ambush came without warning, from a small metal door in the wall. Alexander had his gun halfway back to his shoulder when the metal door was forced open with one blow, striking him in the side. Powerful muscles plowed into him, slamming him into the far wall and knocking the breath from his lungs. Alexander struggled as he fell, but nothing could slow his inexorable collision with the ground. Pain lanced through his back, up through his neck and reverberated in his head. Light exploded in his eyes, and he suddenly wished for nothing more than to close them and fall asleep.

A roar came from his side, and through the haze, he realized that the attack wasn't just from one creature. Two others passed by him in the dimly lit corridor, heading for the crowd that Alexander had been leading. A scream came from down the hall as the survivors caught sight of the creatures bearing down on them. A few scattered gunshots echoed out, but Alexander knew they would be no match for the intensity of the attack.

Another roar came forth, this time from the creature that was now standing in front of Alexander. Human in appearance only, it snarled at him, light glinting off the silvered metals that twisted through its body. Hands raised for a killing blow, it came forward again to finish what it had started. Watching the creature charge him was like a light switch in Alexander's mind. A fresh surge of adrenaline poured into his veins, and the pain in his head was gone.

Alexander rolled to one side, off of the small ledge he had been thrown on and narrowly avoiding the creature as it slammed into the wall above him. The sound of metal colliding with tile and concrete was agonizing and exhilarating. Alexander felt around him with his hands, squinting through the dust and dirt, searching for his weapon. More gunshots sounded out, along with the painful squeal of one of the creatures.

Alexander grimaced. *Perhaps they'll make it after all.* The creature closest to him roared in pain, one of its arms dangling from its side, twisted and broken. It charged him again, slower this time, and Alexander knew he wouldn't be able to pull off the same trick twice. Unable to find his gun, he rolled onto his back and pulled out a black blade from the front of his vest. He strained to sit up and grasped it with both hands, raising the blade as the beast slammed into him.

The force of the blow knocked Alexander back several feet, but this time he was prepared. He rolled with the impact, falling backward while keeping his chin tucked and the blade steady. It pierced the chest of the creature as it slammed into him again. Alexander rolled back as he fell, pushing against the creature's legs with his own and sending it flying over him and down the hall. The knife stayed lodged in the creature as it went, and the once-powerful roar softened to a dull whimper before going silent.

Another scream drifted toward Alexander, reminding him that he had no time to sit still. He scrambled to his feet and stumbled back down the corridor. His eyes flicked back and forth across the floor, searching for his weapon once again. The glint of metal and sound of wood came a few seconds later as his foot collided with the gun, sending it skittering across the gravel a few feet ahead of him. Another burst of adrenaline came with the sound as Alexander realized they still had a fighting chance.

He picked up the weapon and charged back toward the group of survivors. A scream of fury escaped his lips, and he raised the rifle as he ran. A thin beam of red lanced forward from the end of the rifle, piercing the darkness and coming to rest on the silvery strands on the back of one of the beasts. It was hunched over, clawing at a body on the floor, when Alexander squeezed the trigger. Fire bloomed from the end of the gun and the sound of explosions filled the air as lead found flesh and bone.

Before the creature's body hit the ground, Alexander was already at the center of the group, scanning the corridor before and behind him for any sign of the second creature. One of the survivors pointed back at the creature Alexander had killed. Slumped over on the ground, one of its hands was still buried in the body of the second creature, which it had been mauling even after death. Alexander turned back to the survivors and raised an eyebrow.

"Who?" he whispered.

A tall man in a torn business suit stepped forward. His arms were bloody, and he limped along, carrying a pistol in one hand. "I did."

Alexander nodded. "Good—" The accolade was cut short as a shriek came from further down the corridor, in the direction the survivors had been traveling from. Howls joined the shriek, then a series of roars. Alexander felt his stomach sink.

All pretense of stealth was dropped. Alexander turned on the flash-light that was pinned to the front of his vest and pushed his way to the back of the group. Bared fangs and glistening eyes reflected off of his light. Alexander braced himself against the closest wall, ejected the empty magazine from his rifle and slammed home a new one before shouting to the group behind him.

"Run! For God's sake, RUN!"

Chapter Two

INTRODUCTION

On March 26, 2038, the world was destroyed. Virtually every nuclear bomb in existence detonated at the same time across the planet, causing widespread death and destruction. For those few who survived, the true horror was only just beginning. Instead of facing deadly radiation, they were met by a far more ominous enemy. Swarms comprised of trillions of nanobots – tiny, nearly invisible robots – blanketed the globe, killing many of the survivors and transforming others into horrifying creatures. Controlled by an artificial intelligence created by a clandestine government program, the nanobot swarms were responsible for the destruction of the planet – and the devastation that followed.

Four of the individuals who managed to survive both the bombs and the swarms were united under the most unlikely of circumstances. Each carried with them their own experiences, skills and knowledge. Leonard McComb, an engineer, was deep beneath Manhattan Island when the bombs fell. Marcus Warden, a self-made millionaire, was camping in the middle of a West Virginia forest. Nancy Sims, an accountant, was crossing the plains of Kansas. Rachel Walsh, a government scientist who had worked on the artificial intelligence project, heard her family's screams as they died.

All four were on separate paths when they met and were forced to work together while under attack. After formulating a plan, Leonard and Nancy headed west, toward Alaska, where the signature of a Russian nuclear submarine had been detected by an orbiting satellite. Rachel and Marcus, meanwhile, headed to the lab where Rachel had worked in the heart of Washington D.C. to try and recover a device that could destroy the swarms.

Though their journeys nearly cost them their lives many times over, they were, in the end, triumphant. Rachel and Marcus managed to link up with another survivor from the government lab, along with a specially designed electromagnetic pulse generator that was powerful enough to destroy even the largest swarms. Leonard and Nancy found the Russian submarine, the Arkhangelsk, and convinced the commander of the sub to assist them in their destruction of the swarms.

As the swarms built a massive structure along the gulf coast of the United States, the two groups raced to get there, knowing that each moment they delayed was another moment the swarms came closer to achieving their ultimate goal: the complete eradication of humanity. The structure built by the artificial intelligence was dubbed the "Nexus." Situated along the gulf coast of the United States, the artificial intelligence used the structure as the backbone of a computing network designed to help itself "evolve" to a new level of existence.

On April 27, 2038, Rachel Walsh gave her life to save the world. Facing down the artificial intelligence inside of the Nexus, Rachel distracted it long enough for the Arkhangelsk to rain down hellfire upon the building, destroying the AI. The fires that had signaled the end of civilization, decimated the population and brought humanity to its knees were, in the end, the world's salvation.

In the months following the destruction of the swarms, the survivors worked ceaselessly to regroup, reorganize and rebuild. As one of the only surviving sea-worthy vessels, the Arkhangelsk proved invaluable in this effort by helping to transport supplies and building materials and by acting as a base of operations during search and rescue missions for other survivors. The first concerted effort between the survivors resulted in the city of New Richmond, a few miles down the coast from where the Nexus had once stood. Survivors from across the

Americas were brought there, both by the Arkhangelsk and by teams that traveled by land.

In May of 2039, the Arkhangelsk set sail for Russia. Long months of finding and assisting survivors in the Americas had taken its toll on the primarily Russian crew of the sub, and they were eager to return to their homeland to see what remained. Only too happy to help, Marcus, Leonard and Nancy journeyed with them to assist in whatever ways they could. With a functioning city now operating along the Gulf of Mexico, they were eager to seek out other groups of survivors around the world and to assist them in any way possible.

While the threat of the AI had been destroyed on that April evening, the group of explorers were soon to discover that the dangers spawned by the swarms were still very much alive.

Chapter Three

THE ARKHANGELSK

Leonard's breath grew rapid as his headlight dimmed. He stopped crawling and slapped at his helmet a few times. The feeble light glowed brighter again in response, though it started to fade again after a few seconds. He cursed the light under his breath. His heartbeat grew more rapid, and he could feel the sting of salt on his tongue from the sweat pouring down his face.

Once again Leonard was hundreds of feet underground. Trapped in a narrow passage with no way out, he clawed his way through debris. Rebar and concrete scraped at him, tearing holes in his clothes and drawing blood with every scratch. Dust was thick in the air, thrown up by each movement forward. The air was nearly impossible to breathe, and Leonard felt his breaths growing shallower by the second as he tried desperately to pull in more air.

In the distance, down the narrow passage, Leonard could see a pale silver light. He crawled faster. The light was far, but close enough that he was sure he could make it before his headlamp gave out. A moment's worth of crawling later, he could crouch. Another moment and he could stand up. He ran through the tunnel, shrugging off his heavy tool belt as the silver light grew brighter.

He was nearly on top of it when he saw, with a gasp, that it wasn't light at all. Hundreds of silvered eyes stared at him, the light reflecting off them from his headlamp. The eyes were static and immobile, sitting sunken in their skulls. Harsh, raspy breathing came loud from the tunnel, along with the sound of bodies rustling in the darkness. Leonard tried to scream as the eyes leapt forward and the bodies began coalescing into human shapes. Clothing tattered and skin torn, they weren't human anymore. Twisted and misshapen, they were horrific combinations of flesh and metal. Abominations, each and every one.

Sharp metallic claws lashed at Leonard as he tried to get away. He tried to scream again, to yell for the help he knew would never come, but his voice refused to work. The screech of metal on bone sounded loud in his ears, and he closed his eyes, still struggling against the wave of creatures that came crashing down upon him. They tugged and pulled, jerking his legs from underneath him and throwing him down to the floor.

Leonard opened his eyes as he felt himself falling. He flailed his arms, catching nothing but air as he landed with a loud thump on the floor. Panic set in, and he began thrashing against a rough wool blanket that was dyed green and looked as though it had seen a hundred years of service. Blinking several times, Leonard slowly realized where he was. His breathing slowed, and he pulled himself up and began crawling back into his bunk, then cursed loudly as he slammed his forehead into the top of the structure.

"Shit!"

The pain finished the job of fully waking him from his slumber. He sat down on the edge of his bed and rubbed his eyes, still pulling the blanket off of himself as he struggled to get his bearings. The room was still dark, though the light from the corridor outside the room filtered in through the curtain that hung in the doorway. A deep thrumming came from somewhere underneath the floor, and he could hear gases and liquids rushing through pipes inside the walls and out in the corridor.

An alarm clock on the floor next to the bunk was the origin of the screeching he had heard in his dream. Leonard reached down and turned it off, then patted his chest and arms, breathing a soft sigh of relief at the confirmation that it was, after all, just a dream.

While it had been well over a year since he had crawled, climbed and fought his way to freedom out of the depths of the Manhattan sewer system, dreams of his time there still haunted him. He had been working on a repair order, hundreds of feet underground, when the bombs had fallen. The structure of the underground environment was radically altered by the explosions above ground, and he spent the better part of two days making his way back to the surface. Though he hadn't met with any of the mutated creatures in the time he'd spent underground, the many close calls he'd had with them after the fact was enough to make every night one that was filled with nightmares.

Wiping the sweat from his face and neck, Leonard squinted at the clock in his hand. Seven-thirty in the morning. He swore again. "Damn!" Six hours out from the Arkhangelk's first Russian port of call and he was late. He had wanted to be on the control deck before seven-fifteen, but the never-ending nightmares were a foe he had yet to vanquish.

"Damn, damn, damn!" Leonard tossed his blanket aside and stood up. He grabbed his pants – hanging from the empty bunk above his own – and threw them on. A crumpled shirt from the floor followed. He looked around the room and spotted one of his final targets. Gleaming silver and leaning up against a small desk in the corner stood an artificial leg. Leonard hopped over to it, grabbed it and then pulled out the desk chair.

The leg snapped into a small metal port directly below his knee easily enough. A soft green light on the leg glowed to life, blinked twice and then went off. Leonard stood up from the chair and squatted, flexing both legs. He had worn the artificial limb for nearly a year, but was still struggling to feel like it was truly a part of him.

A piece of modern technology that had survived the destruction of the planet, the leg had been installed by a microsurgeon rescued from the state of Washington. After offering his services in artificial limb replacement, the surgeon had been inundated with requests from the residents of New Richmond, but Leonard had been given the honor of being the first recipient. He had agreed—somewhat reluctantly—after realizing that he wasn't going to be of much use out in the field if he was using crutches all the time.

Leonard kicked at the implant with his natural foot a few times and grunted in satisfaction. The internal gyro felt off again, but he would get used to it, as he always did. He had been enjoying sleeping and walking without the leg for a few weeks while the Arkhangelsk had been underway, choosing to use crutches instead. With the upcoming mission, however, he doubted he would be taking it off for quite a long time. A pair of socks and shoes went on both feet next, then he stood up, stretching and yawning.

Bleary eyes peered back as Leonard stepped in front of his mirror. *I'm far too old for this,* he thought. He splashed water on his face and patted it dry, then squeezed a lump of toothpaste onto his brush. With a cleaner face and fresher breath, Leonard exited the cabin and headed for the con. There was a slight limp to his gait and hard flooring – like that on the Arkhangelsk – magnified it.

Out in the corridor, the sound of the engine grew louder, as did the sounds echoing in the pipes. Thick sets of piping ran the length of the corridor on both sides, branching off up, down and to the sides of the walls at regular intervals. Being set out in the open meant there was less room to walk in the corridors of the vessel, but any repairs could be easily conducted. For a craft meant to be underwater for the majority of its operating life, being able to fix problems quickly was—to put it mildly—a necessity.

In 1981, the world's largest nuclear-powered submarine was commissioned by the Russian Navy. Designed to carry twenty nuclear-tipped warheads, eight of the Akula class submarines (designated as "Typhoon" class by NATO) were planned, but only six were built. At five hundred and seventy-four feet long, seventy-five feet wide and well over forty feet tall, the Typhoon class could hold a standard complement of one hundred and sixty passengers, with room for another hundred with the help of hot bunking and a bit of uncomfortable squeezing.

Built as the ultimate war machine, they were the quietest and deadliest submarines of their day. By 2026, though, five of the original six Typhoons had been scrapped, leaving only one still in active service. Used mainly as a tourist attraction and to perform occasional exercises with the Northern Fleet of the Russian Navy, the Arkhangelsk had its last major upgrade in 2014 when it was outfitted with a more powerful set of nuclear reactors designed with a fifty-to-seventy-five-year life-span. The Typhoon class subs were designed to be first-strike weapons, capable of moving quickly and silently near an enemy and devastating them with missiles.

In early 2037, the Arkhangelsk received additional upgrades to its systems and an overhaul of its internal structure—a strange move for a vessel as old as it was. The reason for these upgrades came to light in 2038, when the Arkhangelsk was put under the command of Artem Alexeyev and sent on a mission into the Bering Strait. Ordered to sail the western length of the United States, Alexeyev's mission was called a "training exercise," though he had suspicions otherwise.

When the world ended, the Arkhangelsk was submerged beneath ice floes in the middle of the Bering Strait, protected from both the bombs and the swarms. The vessel was old enough not to show up on computerized reporting systems, so the artificial intelligence simply didn't know of its existence. Most other seafaring vessels weren't so lucky. Any that were on the surface were immediately destroyed, and those that were submerged were called to the top with falsified communications before they too suffered the same fate.

Before dying in an encounter with a swarm during a surface mission, Alexeyev left the command of the Arkhangelsk to his capable second-in-command, Pavel Krylov. After a frantic voyage from Alaska to the Gulf of Mexico, the Arkhangelsk deployed its nuclear weaponry in a staggering display. Half detonated in the air around the swarms' Nexus while the other half exploded on impact, ensuring that the bulk of the swarms were destroyed instantly, crippling the artificial intelligence in the process. Krylov's swift action ensured that the AI's final plan was stopped, and thus—quite literally—he helped saved the world.

Leonard stopped abruptly and put his hand on the wall. The deep-throated roar of the turbines in the heart of the sub had increased in frequency. He resumed his walk to the con, moving faster this time, wondering why there had been an increase in speed. A moment later, he pushed open the half-closed door to the control room, emerging into the middle of a three-way argument.

"Krylov, I've been over this with you before. I'm not staying on this ship!" The first voice was high-pitched and full of frustration. Nancy's arms were crossed, and she shook her head as the man in front of her spoke.

"Ms. Sims, please, I implore you to consider what I'm saying." A heavy Slavic accent blanketed the second voice. Commander Pavel Krylov stood across the table from Nancy, watching her intently.

"Oh, I'm listening all right." Next came a mocking tone. "'Nancy, you have to stay on the ship; it's too dangerous for you!' That's bullshit, and you know it!"

"Nancy." Marcus reached out calmly and put a hand on Nancy's shoulder. "Let's just calm down, okay?"

Nancy shrugged Marcus' hand off and turned her ire on him. "So what, you're on his side? Marcus, I'm not doing the 'staying on the ship' thing again. You know that I'm just as good as—" Nancy looked around and spotted Leonard, then pointed at him. "I'm just as good as our resident cripple! No offense."

Leonard chuckled in amusement. "None taken whatsoever. Can I ask what all this shouting's about, though?"

"Mr. McComb. Please." Commander Krylov clasped his hands together and turned to Leonard. "I believe Ms. Sims has misunderstood my intentions."

"I know good and well what your intentions are, you Russian ba—"

"Whoa there!" Leonard stood up and walked in between Nancy and Krylov. "Okay, you two. Time to take a break. Let me hear this one at a time. Krylov, you were saying?"

Commander Krylov nodded. "I was simply explaining to Ms. Sims that I believe she would be more valuable here on the ship rather than as a member of the rescue party."

"Bullshit," Nancy mumbled.

"Nancy, c'mon now." Leonard shook his head. "What's the big deal here?"

"The 'big deal', Leonard, is that I don't want to sit my ass here on the ship while the rest of you are off gallivanting about on shore. I want to be on the rescue team. Let one of Krylov's men handle the ship."

Krylov stepped closer to Nancy and Leonard, lowering his voice and glancing around. "Nancy, please understand that this isn't something I'm doing for the rescue party. Your presence would be invaluable. I am doing this for the Arkhangelsk. She needs a commander who has experience, both with the vessel and in battle."

Krylov motioned to the crewmembers seated in their various positions around the control room. "Look at them. They're still inexperienced. All they've known is here, in the ship. They've fired their guns a few times, helped to save people, yes. But none of them are leaders. You have the intuition and experience that they lack. None of them were able to assist me in arming sixteen nuclear missiles the way that you did. Besides, they look up to you. They respect you. I trust each and every one of them to do their best, but I would trust none of them with the command of the Arkhangelsk while I'm away."

Nancy's features softened as Krylov spoke. When he finished, she rolled her eyes and sighed. "Damn you, you Russian bastard." Reaching out, Nancy shook Krylov's hand, then pulled him in for a hug. "Fine. Asshole."

Krylov grinned and nodded. "Thank you, Nancy."

"Well then." Leonard clapped his hands. "Looks like I arrived just in time to help clear things up!"

Nancy laughed and shoved Leonard in the chest, sending him into a chair behind him with a thump. "Oh, stuff it. Besides, are you sure you want to go out with that leg of yours?"

Leonard feigned pain as he grimaced. "Ouch! Way to pick on the resident cripple!"

Marcus shook his head and laughed. "All right, guys, let's circle up here. We've got a lot to talk about, and we're only a few hours out."

Krylov adopted a more formal stance, shaking off the argument and levity and returning to his position as leader. He motioned at the table, and Marcus, Nancy and Leonard crowded around. A three-dimensional map projection appeared on the surface of the table, showing the location of the Arkhangelsk in relation to their destination.

"As you know, we're on course for the port city of Magadan, located on a bay of the same name inside the Sea of Okhotsk." The map changed orientation, zooming in on a three-dimensional view of the city. "The city had a population of close to two hundred thousand in 2030, but it could have as much as doubled thanks to the resources our government was pouring into the area. We don't have any more recent population numbers on board, though, so that number is unknown."

The map changed again, showing a satellite view of the area

surrounding the region. "Magadan's the only major city in the area. It served as the administrative center for the district, so any survivors in the countryside nearby would have fled to the city—at least initially."

"Which would explain the beacon." Leonard poked at a button on the table, and the map changed to show a red dot pulsating in the center of the city.

"Precisely," Krylov continued. "Mr. Landry's analyses revealed this broadcast coming from within my country. It's our number one priority to investigate and aid any survivors we encounter. While there are certainly survivors elsewhere in the region, we have to start somewhere."

Nancy rotated the map and zoomed in on the imagery of the city. "It looks like two bombs were detonated in the area. One at the southern end of the city and one in the northern. The center looks relatively untouched. How stale is this data?"

"Mr. Landry's satellite performed a pass two weeks ago."

Marcus grunted. "So it's as fresh as we'll get. What do you think we'll be looking at as far as muties go?"

"That we cannot be certain of, Mr. Warden. The mutants we've encountered in the Americas have been steadily dying off, but given the broad range of types we encountered—particularly along the western coast—anything is possible. I would venture to guess that any mutants left would be extremely hardy: protected against the frigid temperatures and well-adapted to life in the hard climate."

Marcus was about to respond with a groan when a crewmember stepped up to the table and whispered in Krylov's ear. His face notice-ably brightened, and he nodded in reply. "Put him through on speaker right away."

Krylov turned back to the table and smiled. "It looks like our call with Mr. Landry is early today. He's being patched through now."

"Hello, Archangel!" A voice coated in static blared through tinny speakers built into the map table in the center of the con. "How's everyone doing on this fine morning?"

Leonard smiled as he replied. "David! We're doing well here, aside from missing full-sized beds. How are things back at the city?"

"All good here! We had two new groups come in, ten and thirty strong. There were several farmers, and we finally found another chemist. Weather's taken a bit of a turn, but nothing we can't handle."

"David," Nancy jumped in, "that's wonderful! Any word on the search parties in Canada?"

"They've been out of touch, but I've followed them on the satellite. They're progressing along normally, so I think we're still good there. What about your mission? Have you made it to Magadan yet?"

"We're still five hours out," Krylov spoke again. "We were just starting to go over the mission details again in preparation for our arrival."

"Good timing then." The static increased momentarily, and they heard David swearing at someone before he returned to speak to them. "Sorry about that. Something about some livestock getting loose. Anyway, I have some updates for you. Unfortunately, though, none are good."

"Please," Krylov said, "tell us. Anything additional would be useful, good or bad."

"I won't have any more satellite updates for you anytime soon. Best I can do is a week, maybe ten days out. I've got it tasked over Canada right now to keep an eye on the searchers up there, then I have to do a sweep over Europe. You'll have to work off of the last data I sent you. Sorry about that."

"Not a problem, David." Leonard zoomed back in on the map to a close-up of their destination.

"Yeah, well, I wish I could do more. We won't have more birds in the sky for another three months minimum. What I can tell you is that the storm data I'm tracking over here is looking worse, so my guess is that you'll see an uptick on the squalls there, too. I don't have anything solid, but just be careful. You know how freaky the weather's been lately. The whole world is still readjusting to whatever the AI was doing to the atmosphere."

"We've encountered some rough seas, but nothing terrible. We'll keep an eye out, though."

"Good. Okay, this last one is a bit strange. I've had a couple of folks here going over the infrared imagery we took over that city of yours in detail. I know we've seen a big die-off of the creatures here in the States, but I don't think that's necessarily the case over there."

Leonard felt the hairs on the back of his neck prickle. "What do you mean?"

"There's something... off about these images. We've seen outlines of bodies lying in the streets in multiple spectrums. On the IR passes, though, we saw movement. The bodies shifted positions in between passes... or something. It's hard to explain."

"Do you think any of them are still alive?" Nancy's voice had an edge of worry that they all suddenly felt.

"I'm really not sure. There's a lot of time in between passes – several hours in some cases. Plus there were storms rolling through the area. It could have been high winds or snow, or perhaps it was survivors moving them about. We're still working on analyzing the raw data and doing some post-processing to try and pull out anything else that might be useful. If I find anything, I'll let you know."

"Thank you, Mr. Landry." Krylov looked at the other three gathered around the table with him. "Thank you all. This journey is one I did not wish to make without your help. I am grateful that you are still here."

Leonard smiled and shook his head. "What's there to be grateful for? You and your crew sacrificed everything in helping us establish New Richmond, not to mention all you've done to help bring back survivors. We're forever in your debt for that, Krylov. Don't you ever forget that."

Krylov beamed and looked down at the table again. "Mr. Landry, thank you once again. Please keep us updated with any new information you have."

"Will do, Pavel. You all be safe, and keep an eye on that weather." A round of goodbyes passed between Marcus, Leonard, Nancy and David before the connection was terminated.

"Now then." Krylov clapped his hands together. "With Mr. Landry's assistance, we now know that there may be greater dangers from the creatures than we first anticipated. This is an unknown environment, so we'll need to be well-prepared for anything we come across."

"Who else is going in with us?"

"Excellent question, Mr. McComb. In addition to you, myself and Mr. Warden, we'll be taking two soldiers to help us– Mikhail Egorov and Roman Lebedev. They're a bit wet behind the ears, but they've done well on the last few missions we've run, and I think they'll do well here."

Leonard nodded in satisfaction. "Excellent. What about weapons and supplies? Are we still planning on two weeks' worth of rations?"

"Ms. Sims and I were running some numbers on that earlier this morning. We've decided to go with ten days of rations and fill the empty space with additional ammunition and some explosives. In light of Mr. Landry's new information on the potential mutant problem, I'm convinced this is the wisest choice."

"Sounds fine. Weapons?"

"7.62 millimeter. We'll each carry a folding stock AK as a backup and a fixed as our primary. The modifications you assisted with will make the weight more than manageable, and our weapons chief finished them last night."

"No snipers?"

"I'll be carrying one, and Lebedev will assist with a second. You believe we will need more?"

"Nah." Leonard shook his head as he zoomed in on the map to highlight the destroyed areas. "We won't have a good vantage point for much, by the looks of things. We might never use them, but I prefer taking out the muties from a distance over getting up close and personal."

"Very good." Krylov adjusted the map, and a grid overlay appeared. "These," he said, pointing at crisscrossing red lines, "are the underground metro rail built into the city in 2030. The rapid expansion of the city necessitated an underground cargo storage and moving operation, but they were also used for general civilian transport." Krylov pointed at an intersection of several lines near the center of the city. "We believe here, at this metro station, is where the survivors are located. The transmission coordinates match up to this location, and it would be possible for someone with enough skills to tap into the radio tower nearby, since there are lines that run beneath the metro tunnels."

Marcus looked at the tagged location and shook his head. "How would they even survive in that kind of a place for a month, let alone a year?"

A wry smile crossed Krylov's face. "We've seen many examples of extraordinary survival in the last year. These people are tough and hardy, used to troubling times. They would have no problem digging in and finding ways to survive."

"Still though." Nancy whistled. "A year in this place? It makes the Brazilian jungle look like Disneyland in comparison."

Krylov shrugged. "They are Russian. Americans make fun of Russian stubbornness, but it comes in handy at times."

Leonard patted Krylov on the back and laughed. "Indeed it does." He turned and walked away from the table and arched his shoulders, stretching his back. "I think that about does it, right?"

"Da. It does. Please remember one thing, though."

Leonard leaned back against a nearby chair and listened as Krylov glanced between them and spoke quietly and sincerely. "These are proud people, and they will not be expecting Americans. A year spent in isolation after having destruction rained on their heads will make them afraid. When we find them, allow me to talk to them first. I will do my best to calm their fears."

"Do you think they'll want to go with us?"

"That I do not know, Ms. Sims. Uprooting themselves from their homes will not be easy for them, despite whatever they've gone through for the last year. If they choose to stay, I will respect those wishes." The three nodded at Krylov in agreement. He smiled at them again and stood straight, raising his voice for all in the control room to hear. "Very well. Thank you again, my friends."

Krylov looked as though he was about to continue talking when another crewmember ran up to him and saluted, then whispered in his ear. He nodded and walked to the periscope. "Dive Officer, bring us to periscope depth. Mr. McComb, would you care to have the first look at our destination?"

Raindrops slid down across the viewfinder as Leonard stared out across the choppy waters. The weather was dreary, with black clouds as far as he could see in every direction. Waves rocked over the front of the Arkhangelsk as she charged forward through the sea, breaking through the turbulence as though it didn't even exist.

Directly ahead to the east, off the bow of the boat, was their destination. Shrouded in rain, it was difficult to make out, but any form of land was still a welcome sight after so long at sea. Mountains drifted into view behind the clouds, covered in patches of white and green. Closer down toward the water, the shapes of buildings took form.

Stereotypical Russian design was on display in full force in the city. Tall white and grey block buildings—apartments, from the looks of them—towered high at the eastern end. Closer to the water were squat industrial buildings with different signs plastered across them. One tower stood near the southern end of the city, though it was surrounded by the debris of a half dozen more and was missing a large chunk from its edifice. The city petered off toward the north, transitioning from multi-family block units to small, single-family dwellings. The remnants of a few parks were scattered through the city, but they were difficult to make out through the clouds and rain.

The bombs had struck the city in the northern and southern portions, though they had clearly been low-yield based on the limited damage that had been done. Two rings of destruction were evidence of the damage, but—surprisingly—the center of the city had been left relatively intact. The concussion waves from the blasts had torn roofs from many of the buildings, knocked out all of the windows and sent cars, power poles, shipping containers and all manner of debris flying in all directions.

The port itself was also surprisingly intact, though most of the ships were either half-submerged in the shallow water or had been thrown out to sea. A few shipping vessels were stuck on the sand and rocks to the north and south ends of the bay, while others sat idle in the water as the Arkhangelsk navigated around them.

"Looks peaceful." Leonard stepped back from the periscope and rubbed his eyes. "Or it would, if not for the weather and the fact that chunks of the city are gone. Other than that, though."

Nancy stepped up to the viewfinder and rotated the periscope, scanning their surroundings. "What about those ships? You think there might be anything useful left on those?"

Krylov took to the viewfinder for a moment, then stepped back. "No, those are all industrial vessels, transporting raw goods. The currents must be keeping them trapped here in the bay, or else they would have drifted out into the ocean long ago."

Nancy pursed her lips in thought. "The port looked intact. Do you think we can pull up to one of the docks and go in that way?"

"I wouldn't recommend it. Underwater obstacles are going to be treacherous enough once we get a little closer to shore. It will be easy to miss something that could damage the screws or cut a hole in the hull."

"How close do you figure we can get?"

Krylov looked at a new map on the table in the center of the room. An underwater topographical map of the local area, it was changing slightly as they moved forward, updating in real time based on sonar pings that the sub sent out. "The debris field grows larger and harder to define at about eight hundred meters out. We should stop there to deploy a reconnaissance drone, then use inflatables to get to the shore."

Leonard nodded and looked at the clock. "How long till we arrive?"

"At our current speed, we'll be at the designated position in about four hours, maybe a bit more."

"Right, then. I'm going for some breakfast. Anyone else want to come?"

Leonard headed off the con with Marcus following behind. Nancy watched the pair head down the corridor before turning to Krylov and lowering her voice. "Are you sure about this?"

"About what, Ms. Sims?"

"About you going on this rescue mission. You know I can handle myself out there. I'd much rather be going than you."

Krylov smiled. "I appreciate the thought, but we are in my country now. I must be at the forefront of the mission."

"I still think there are better people than me for this."

"Nonsense. Besides, it's done. No need for further discussion. Now, if you don't mind, I think I'll join them for breakfast. Would you care to come?"

"Yeah, I'll be down in a few minutes. I want to look at these maps a little more first."

Krylov smiled and left the con, supremely confident in his decision. While there would undoubtedly be some in the crew who would initially reject Nancy's command of the boat, they were few and far between. Most knew her well and—more importantly—respected her immensely.

A few hours later, after all had eaten and were triple-checking their weapons and supplies for the trip, Nancy's voice rang out of the ship-wide speakers. "Rescue team to the control room. We're twenty minutes out."

Chapter Four

THE ARKHANGELSK

"Can't you get any closer with that thing? I thought this was your hobby way back when."

"Do you want to fly instead?" Marcus glared grumpily at Leonard, who held his hands up and shook his head.

"Hey, take it easy. We just can't see very well."

"The winds out there are insane right now. I'm lucky this thing hasn't taken a dive into the water yet."

Huddled in the corridor near a ladder leading to the surface deck, Leonard, Krylov, Mikhail and Roman were all watching a small screen held in Marcus' hand. Marcus sat on the floor, cross-legged, with sweat dripping down his face as his fingers twitched over the twin sticks. The screen displayed a live video feed from a remotely operated drone that Marcus was doing his level best to take on a slow sweep of the coastline and port. The weather, unfortunately, was not cooperating, and the drone's video feed suffered immensely for it.

Bobbing up and down, the feed was shaky and had intermittent cutouts. Each time the video paused or blinked out for a second was another time he was certain that the drone had caught a crosswind and was plunging toward the ground. Thankfully, though, his years of practice flying drones as a hobby hadn't left him entirely, and he managed to keep the craft in the air.

"I'm not seeing much at the port; I'll get in closer to the city and drop down some. Maybe I can get some cover from the wind behind the buildings."

"Careful taking it down too far," cautioned Krylov. "Our spare drone isn't operational yet."

"No pressure," Marcus whispered. The drone dove toward the ground, heading inland. The docks and scattered shipping containers gave way to larger piles of shipping containers scattered across sand, gravel, dirt and asphalt lots. Chain-link fencing still stood in some places, marking separate areas for storage of the containers before they were loaded onto shipping vessels.

"Whoa, what's that?" Leonard jabbed at the screen. "Is that— Krylov, you saw that, right?"

Krylov nodded, clenching his jaw. The movement on the screen had been brief but unmistakable. It was fast and calculated, nearly slipping by undetected as the drone went by: a human-sized figure sliding across an open doorway, wearing the tattered remnants of clothing and pockmarked by webs of reflective silver.

"Damn. I guess that's confirmed. We'll have mutants on the ground to deal with."

Leonard leaned in closer to the screen. "Can you try to get a better look at it?"

Marcus glanced at Krylov. "The closer down I get, the trickier this is going to be. These winds aren't letting up one bit."

Krylov nodded. "Do it. We must know what we will face."

The drone swooped down toward the street, staying about twenty feet off the ground. Marcus turned to look through the industrial building's front door and windows to try and get a glimpse of the creature, but the interior was dark. The press of a button switched the feed to a thermal camera view, but the structure was cold and lifeless.

"Take us back up," Krylov said. "See if you can get any hits on the thermal in a pass down the street there. We must estimate numbers if we can."

"Got it." Marcus pulled back on the left stick, and the drone rose back into the air, the view becoming shakier the higher it went. Flying directly into the wind offered more stability to the view, and he pushed the throttle to its highest setting. Black buildings whipped by below, punctuated by small, light grey patches that signified areas that weren't quite as cold as their surroundings. It wasn't until the drone had flown a full two blocks worth of distance that the scenery took a drastic change.

Without warning, the video feed began to spin. "Something's wrong!" Marcus shouted, trying desperately to regain control of the craft. "It's going down!"

"Give the controls to the craft; have it auto-hover!"

"Already tried that. It's no good! This wasn't me, I swear! The flight path was clear. Something hit it!" Marcus glanced up at Krylov, who looked at Leonard in response. Leonard's face was cold, and he felt a chill run up his spine.

The video feed shorted out for a few seconds as it hit the ground, then it flared back to life momentarily. The video had switched back to the normal camera, giving an extra dimension of horror to what came next. A dozen creatures ran at the drone from down the street, their mouths open in what was undoubtedly a howling cry of victory. Accompanying them, though, was something new. A veritable flock of animals ran alongside the former humans—and they, too, had the same appearance as the creatures.

Their eyes were gone, replaced entirely by a gleaming silver surface that reflected the light. Silver streaks crisscrossed their flesh, and large pieces of fur were missing. The majority of the smaller creatures looked as though they had once been pets—mostly dogs, with a few cats mixed in. Their mouths were also open, and Leonard was suddenly very glad that the drone wasn't transmitting audio along with the video.

The video feed went dead as soon as the pack of creatures arrived at it, leaving the five to stare at the blank screen in silence. Finally, after a moment's contemplation, Krylov cleared his throat, picked up an intra-ship microphone and spoke. "Con? This is Commander Krylov. The drone is down. There is a heavy presence of mutants in the city. We'll be sending down the recording momentarily. What's the status on the transmission?"

"Muties?" Nancy's concerned voice came through loud on the speaker. "Shit! How many of them?"

"Indeterminate. Mr. Warden believes that they brought down the drone, most likely to keep us from determining their number. We saw approximately twenty on the video feed before it went dead, though."

"That's a lot."

"Indeed, Ms. Sims. Please, what is the status of the transmission?"

"Still coming through loud and clear. Same message as before. Fifty survivors holed up in a metro station running low on food and ammo. It has to be recorded and unmonitored, because we haven't detected any changes in response to our broadcasts to them."

Krylov grunted. "Very well. Give us a moment to return to the control room so we can update our plan."

Back on the con, the group shrugged off their backpacks and leaned their rifles against the wall. They gathered around the table in the center of the room, and Krylov glanced between them. "Based on this new information, it appears as though our mission has grown more urgent—and dangerous. Any suggestions on how to proceed?"

Leonard manipulated the map to display an overhead view of the city. "Before the drone was destroyed, we saw creatures along the length of the area near the port, starting near the north end and stopping about halfway down to the south. What if we insert here, at the far northern end of the city, and deploy some inflatables to fire off flares and make some noise at the southern edge of the city?"

"A distraction?" Krylov rubbed his chin. "It could work, but not in that way. We don't have enough inflatables in working order."

"How many do we have?"

"Two."

"Hm."

"What if you insert here to the north, but instead of going into the city, you circle around and come in from the hills on the eastern edge?" Nancy outlined an arc with her finger that extended around the northern end of the city. "If most of the creatures you saw were near the port, then that area should be safer, right?"

"Maybe," Leonard said, "but we don't know. And since that was the only working drone, we can't find out anytime soon."

"What if we do both?" Everyone turned to look at Marcus, who had been standing off to the side, listening intently.

"Mr. Warden, as I said, we don't—"

"Have enough boats, right. But we have torpedoes, don't we?"

Marcus pointed at the docks at the port. "There are a couple of big ships still moored there, and I bet they'll make some noise if we hit them."

Leonard nodded as he realized the simplicity of the plan. "We'll take an inflatable into the north and loop around the city. When we're ready to head into the city proper, we'll signal the sub, and they'll make enough noise to raise the dead."

"It will work." Krylov grunted with satisfaction. "I approve."

Nancy's grin spread from ear to ear. "Making some noise and blowing something up? Hell yeah!"

Krylov smiled at her. "Very well. Rescue team, gather your gear and assemble in the armory. We have one final stop to make before we depart."

A few minutes later, in the armory, the team crowded around Krylov and watched as he opened a long black case. Inside, nestled in grey foam, was a device that looked very similar to a rifle, but with a few modifications. A thick copper coil wrapped around half the barrel, and a thin metal shield extended out where the coil stopped, directly in front of the forward handguard. A large pack fitted to where the magazine would normally go, and it had a small series of ten LEDs that were all shining bright green.

"What is this?" Leonard asked as Krylov handed him the device.

"Something a couple of our electronics experts cooked up. A short-range directional EMP cannon."

"A microwave oven gun?"

Krylov laughed. "More refined than that. And less dangerous to the user. But more or less, yes. It should stop a mutant in its tracks from up to seven meters away. Any farther than that and the results are questionable. It will also disrupt a swarm, should we happen to encounter one."

Leonard hefted the gun before putting it to his shoulder. "Feels good. What's the charge time like?"

"Only a few seconds. Each of the battery packs holds forty shots worth of charge. We only have a few packs, though, so we'll need to be careful when using it."

Leonard passed the device to Marcus, who then passed it to

Mikhail and Roman. "Nice thinking, Krylov. Better than silencers and more deadly to the muties, too. What's the spread on it?"

"Not much. A few meters at its maximum operating range."

"Is there just the one?"

"Yes, unfortunately. There are other prototypes, but none that are functional."

Leonard took the device back and gave it a final once-over. He looped the strap around his neck and cocked his head at Krylov. "Well then, let's go give it a test, shall we?"

Twenty minutes later, the group gathered at the bottom of the same ladder they had been at previously. This time, however, their expressions were far more serious. A gust of wind tore down the hatch as it opened, sending the howling rain blasting down into the corridor. Krylov, first on the ladder, winced as the cold water stung his exposed face. He squinted as he climbed upward, followed by Leonard, Marcus, Roman and Mikhail. With the Arkhangelsk holding still in the water, the boat was feeling the turbulence of the rough waters far more than when it had been on the move. A steel cable with handholds extended out of the hatch and over to the edge of the deck, where two crewmembers struggled to hold an inflatable boat in place.

Equipped with a thin plastic hull and two large inflatable pontoons, the boat was as simple as they came. Three rows of seats with ample room for gear were placed in the middle, while at the back was a single small seat directly in front of a pair of powerful outboard motors. The rescue team slowly made their way across the slippery deck, fighting the wind and rain as they clung to the cable.

Krylov entered the inflatable first, dropped his gear onto the floor in front of the rear seat and started the motors. Mikhail and Roman followed next, then Marcus and, finally, Leonard. Each of them clung tightly to their weapons with one hand while keeping another hand on their seat. Krylov gave a thumbs up to the crewmen holding the raft in place, and they let go while simultaneously giving the craft a kick away from the sub.

The outboard motors roared as Krylov twisted the throttle and angled the inflatable away from the sub. Even in the driving rain, the sound was deafening, and he was suddenly glad for the thickly padded hood of his jacket that was secured around his head. Bouncing from the crest of one wave to the next, the inflatable turned north and headed parallel to the city's dock, making a beeline for the northern end of the city.

"When is this rain going to let up?" Marcus shouted at Leonard over the noise.

"Next few hours, hopefully! At least that's what the short-range radar showed!"

Marcus groaned, both at the thought of being out in the weather for that long and the somersaults being performed by his stomach with each lurch of the boat. Ahead, through the rain and clouds, the city's shape continued to solidify. Marcus stared at the destruction and the remaining buildings, wondering who could have stayed alive for so long in such a remote place. A shiver went down his spine, though whether it was from the chill in the air or the thought of the creatures lurking in the ruins of the city, he wasn't entirely certain.

Thirty minutes—and five very upset stomachs—later, the inflatable surged onto the beach. The plastic hull crunched to a halt on the rough gravel, and Krylov turned off the motors. After piling out of the boat, Krylov motioned for Marcus and Leonard to move aside, then he directed Roman and Mikhail to pull the inflatable further onto the shore before securing it to a nearby boulder well above the high tide mark.

"This should be safe." Krylov panted slightly, trying to keep his voice low. "The storms will not reach this far up. Come, let's move inland."

With stealth being a priority, the rescue team hurried over the loose gravel and sand. After a few meters, the shoreline abruptly changed to scrubland. The brown grasses whipped in the wind while sparse clumps of green bushes merely swayed, their stature too stocky to be affected by the storm. Wearing dark green and brown military outfits, the team blended in well with the terrain. After moving a few hundred meters inland, they slowed to a halt as Krylov surveyed the city with binoculars.

To their west, along the shoreline, were oil and fuel tanks that marked the start of the port. Through the mist, Krylov could see a few small vessels at a repair dock, though all of them were rusted, and their mooring lines looked as though they could snap at any moment.

Beyond the tanks and rows of old discarded shipping containers, the land took a sharp turn to the south, where the true docks began. Those were impossible to see due to the weather, but that was the location where the drone had spotted the creatures. *And hopefully*, Krylov thought, *where they'll be staying.*

"Let's move," Krylov whispered to the group. Climbing the hill in front of them was no small task in the driving wind and rain, but they managed to scale it in less than an hour. The clouds quickly grew thick with the altitude gain, and before they realized it, they emerged from the grass into a flat rocky area filled with a couple of half-destroyed mobile buildings and the remains of the local tropospheric communication array, nicknamed "Dragon."

Capable of communicating via microwaves over hundreds of kilometers, tropospheric radio stations bounced microwaves off of the Earth's troposphere to communicate over long distances where there was no line of sight. This enabled communication over mountains and other obstacles, and made it possible to communicate over the visible horizon. Long since abandoned, most of the antennas were lying on the ground, save for one, which stood facing out over the bay.

Leonard stared at the remains of the system in awe as he realized what it was. He remained slack-jawed for a few moments, until Marcus poked him in the arm.

"Hey!" he whispered. "Let's get moving. Krylov's going to leave us behind."

The sight of the old communications system stirred Leonard's engineering spirit and made him long for the days before survival was the primary priority. Leonard gave one last look at the radio station as they continued to the east, making for the western edge of the northern part of the city. The path was finally much easier as they followed an old gravel road that was overgrown with grass and weeds. The path continued straight down a slight slope in the hill before turning into a sharp series of zigzags as the hill grew steep at the base.

Krylov glanced behind them and was encouraged by the sight of clear skies at the edge of the horizon, far beyond the bay. The rain and wind had started to let up, and they were beginning to see more details of the city ahead of them. Directly in front, down the hill, were rows of houses, while off to the left sat a few factory buildings accompanied by enormous red and white smokestacks. Most of the homes were only half-standing, a testament to the power of the bomb that had fallen on the northern end of the city.

Krylov pulled out his binoculars again and scanned the city, looking for any signs of movement. While they hadn't been completely quiet in their travel, the poor weather had apparently masked their approach, as there were still no signs of movement in the city ahead. While the sky was still clearing and the rain was letting up, the sun was beginning to set behind them, prompting Krylov to want to stop for the night.

"How are we looking?" Leonard stepped up next to Krylov and squinted at the houses and destruction beyond. "See anything?"

"Nothing moving. But I think we should stop here for the night. Take shelter in one of the factories over there." Krylov pointed at the factory buildings.

Leonard took the binoculars and scanned the buildings, then frowned. "I don't know; I'm getting a funny feeling about those things."

Krylov glanced at Leonard quizzically. "How so?"

"Look at the damage to the houses. The factories are close enough that they should be in pieces, or at least the smokestacks should. They look practically pristine, though."

Krylov frowned. "Hm. You may be right. Roman, I want you and Mikhail to scout the factory. Go light; leave your gear here. In and out in thirty."

The two Russian soldiers shrugged off their heavy packs and readied their rifles. Each man took three extra magazines. They were about to move out when Leonard held out his hands to block them.

"Whoa there, wait a second." He set his pack on the ground next to theirs, along with his rifles. He picked up the EMP cannon and an extra battery pack. "No need to be going in loud on this one. I'll take the lead while you two follow up behind. Don't fire on anything unless I tell you to. Got it?"

"Understood." Roman glanced at Krylov, who nodded his silent approval.

Leonard took off without another word, breaking into a sprint toward the factories. Roman and Mikhail hurried to catch up. The three men clutched their weapons tightly, keeping them pointed at the ground while they ran, ready to fire at a moment's notice.

The factories loomed overhead in the twilight, their shadows extending far beyond the twisted and broken fences that marked the perimeter of their compound. Leonard didn't know what they had been used for in years past, but they were silent now.

"Mikhail, you circle around with Roman. Stay spread out. I'll cut through the middle of the compound and see if I can draw anything out." Leonard had run enough missions in the last year to be familiar with the basics of a standard scouting operation, but no matter how many firefights he got into with mutants, crazed locals or wannabe bandits, he could never quite shake the feeling that he was just playing soldier.

The factory compound was quiet as they walked through, and Leonard glanced around to make sure nothing was sneaking up on him. Careful not to be too loud lest the noise carry all the way into the city itself, he cupped his left hand around his mouth and shouted. "Hello! Anyone there?"

Leonard's heartbeat picked up, and he felt adrenaline surge through his veins. He strained his ears, suddenly acutely aware of every insect's chirp and the rustle of every blade of grass in the wind. After a moment, he turned to eye Mikhail and Roman, who were crouched on the outer edge of the compound, watching him intently.

Leonard shrugged and walked toward them, away from the factory. "Guess I was wrong," he said. "If anything was here, it would have come out by now. Radio Krylov. Tell him it looks safe here."

Leonard turned and looked up at the imposing factory building and smokestacks as Roman spoke to Krylov in a hushed tone. While Leonard felt confident that one of the smaller buildings in the factory compound would be safe for the night, he still couldn't shake the feeling that something else was going on—something that involved the swarms.

You don't naturally have pristine buildings like this so close to a damage circle. Especially not when the city's filled with mutants of all shapes and sizes. The reminder that the mutants on the drone's camera had been more than just human sent a chill up his neck. A few minutes later, the sound of crunching gravel alerted Leonard to the arrival of Marcus and Krylov. The two men were panting with the weight of the extra three packs, and they were relieved when Mikhail directed them to a small building he and Roman had begun to clear out for their night's stay.

As the rest of the group laid out mats and prepared a hasty meal, Leonard stood outside the building, his cannon at the ready as he took the first watch. He chewed slowly on a piece of jerky, scanning the factory compound and surrounding land for any signs of mutants. His night vision goggles—courtesy of the Arkhangelsk's extensive armory —revealed no threats, and by the time he was relieved, he was very nearly convinced that his bad feeling was nothing more than that: a feeling.

Unfortunately, that thought was quickly squashed by Mikhail's panicked face early the next morning as he shook Leonard awake, right at the point in his recurring dream where the panic had begun to set in. Being rudely awoken turned out to be a blessing—at least at first.

"Come, quickly!"

Leonard rubbed the sleep from his eyes and dashed out of the small building, grabbing his rifle and the EMP cannon along the way.

"This way. Hurry!" Mikhail ran around the factory compound to a steel double door on the side of the largest building. The door had been forced open, and outside stood Marcus, Krylov and Roman, all watching the open door. Leonard walked up to the group slowly, feeling suddenly nervous as he saw that their faces were as white as sheets.

"What's going on?" Leonard whispered.

"In there." Marcus pointed at the open door.

"Muties?"

Marcus shook his head. "Not exactly."

Leonard pushed open the door and waited for his eyes to adjust to the dim interior. The root of the building wasn't, as he had though, in perfect condition. Shafts of light shone through cracks and small holes in the ceiling, revealing the unadulterated horror that was strewn across the factory floor.

Twisted piles of bones and flesh in various stages of decomposition were laid in neat piles across the width and length of the building as far as Leonard could see. Each pile was in a slightly different configuration, and most had discarded tools, wires, batteries, small industrial equipment and other odds and ends sitting nearby. The entire setup was both haphazard and orderly, and Leonard struggled for a moment to understand what he was seeing.

"What the hell…" Leonard muttered as he crouched down next to the nearest pile. He felt his insides churn at the sight and smell of the pile of bones—at least five people and three animals worth by his estimate—but he swallowed hard and fought against his stomach. Using the end of his rifle, Leonard turned over a few of the bones. As they clattered to the ground, Leonard saw bits of silver on the flesh and bones, along with wires and steel plates that appeared as though they had been grafted directly onto the bone.

Leonard's eyes scanned other piles, realizing that many of them contained virtually complete bodies. Some were covered in layers of steel plating, the flesh having rotted away, while others were only half-finished, the bodies appearing fresher, but with crude blades and spikes attached to the legs and arms.

"Sweet mother of pearl." Leonard stood up and backed out of the factory, his eyes wide with the realization of what he was seeing. He nearly tripped and fell when he reached the door, but Marcus caught him and held him steady. "Is that… is that what I think it is?"

Marcus nodded. "We found it earlier this morning. Krylov wanted to scout the factory, to see if we could find anything useful. We broke the lock on the door and walked in on that. I'm no expert, but it looks to me like somebody's been experimenting with bodies. Trying to augment them. Manually. Without the swarms."

"H—How many bodies?" Leonard wiped saliva from the edges of his lips and forced down another swallow, trying to keep the bile down.

"Thousands. At least. We didn't check the other buildings."

"These things were augmenting themselves? How could they be doing that without swarms?"

Marcus shrugged. "You tell me; you're the engineer."

"Christ…" Leonard turned and leaned on the side of the building, his mind racing. The discovery that the creatures in the area had been trying to improve themselves was a frightening prospect in more ways than one. Beyond the fact that the creatures would likely be better armored and more resilient in a fight, there was the fact that they still retained enough intelligence—either human or AI—to both desire to improve themselves and have the knowledge to do so.

When the AI had been defeated, most of the creatures in North and South America had died relatively quickly due to the bulk of the AI's processing power being contained within its Nexus. The rescue and exploratory missions that Leonard had been on to help build up New Richmond had encountered small swarms and groups of creatures, but none had possessed the capacity to do more than engage in a simple fight for survival. The larger threat had always been something else—either human nature or nature itself.

"Marcus. Krylov." Leonard motioned to the men, and they hurried over. "You two realize what this means, right?" He continued without waiting for an answer. "This goes beyond us. Beyond the rescue mission. If there are creatures here who are still this advanced after so long…. This is bad. Very, very bad."

Marcus and Krylov looked at each other, then back at Leonard. "What do you mean?" Marcus' voice shook slightly as he asked the question.

"I have a few ideas, but I'm really not sure yet. But the fact that we've never seen behavior from remnants of the mutants like this before means something big is up. Maybe they're adapting, trying to grow and improve themselves."

"Or maybe they just really enjoy arts and crafts and the supply store was out of paper and glue."

Leonard stifled a chuckle at Marcus' morbid joke, but was secretly glad for the break in the tension. "Come on. We should get going. If we have time after we locate the survivors, we'll come back."

Krylov nodded and called for his soldiers. "You two, you have thirty seconds to photograph as much of the interior as possible. Then we move."

The two soldiers glanced at each other in panic, then slowly moved toward the factory. "Hurry up!" Krylov snapped at them in Russian. The men hurried inside, one holding a bulky camera while the other held both of their flashlights. The camera was crude, old and not the best, but it was durable, rugged and the batteries would last for weeks, all very good traits while out in the field. It was also capable of transmitting photographs over short distances via radio signals so that the team could relay the photos back to the Arkhangelsk.

After the photographs were secured, Krylov resealed the door.

Leonard, Marcus, Mikhail and Roman watched the city carefully in the early dawn's light. There were still no signs of movement, which made the seemingly abandoned city appear even more ominous. After finishing with the factory door, Krylov stood with the group and examined the city with his binoculars. Satisfied that they were safe for the moment, Krylov pulled out his radio and began contacting the Arkhangelsk.

"Arkhangelsk, Arkhangelsk, this is Commander Krylov. Do you copy? Over."

A few seconds later, Nancy's voice came back, sounding flat and filtered by static. "Krylov, this is the Arkhangelsk. We read you. What's your situation? Over."

"No engagement with hostiles yet. Found significant signs of their presence at the factories north of the city. Over."

"Roger that, Krylov. We're standing by with the distraction. Just say the word."

"Start a countdown. Five minutes. Go on that signal. Over."

"Copy that. Five minutes. Timer started." Nancy's curt responses suddenly grew more relaxed. "Krylov, what did you find? Over."

Krylov thumbed the microphone to reply, but hesitated, uncertain of how to describe the scene. Leonard motioned for the radio, and Krylov happily handed it over. "Nancy, Leonard here. It's disturbing. Remains of thousands of bodies—probably more—all showing signs of experimentation and dissection. We've never seen anything like this before."

Krylov nudged Leonard before tapping his watch impatiently. "Sorry, I can't really explain it right now. Krylov wants us to move out."

"I, uh, understand. I guess. Timer's down to four minutes and fifteen seconds. Once you're safe, I'd like to get the full details. Over."

Krylov took back the radio. "We'll be sending along photographs soon. Out."

Krylov shoved the radio into the backpack that sat at his feet, then shouldered the pack and cinched up the straps. "Mikhail, once we get secured, I want those photos transmitted to New Richmond. Bounce them off the Arkhangelsk's systems so that they and Mr. Landry can analyze them."

"Yes, sir!"

"All right, everyone. The Arkhangelsk is going to make a hell of a lot of noise in just a few minutes. We need to get moving now. We'll make for the northern center of town and try to get as far as we can before the distraction goes off. Once it does, we'll be moving even faster. Stick close together, minimize the noise level and don't be shooting at anything unless it's a life or death situation."

Marcus, Leonard, Roman and Mikhail all nodded in acknowledgement at Krylov. "Okay, let's move." Krylov took off down the hill toward the ring of destruction at a jog. Leonard followed close behind with the EMP cannon at the ready. Marcus and Mikhail followed, with Roman bringing up the rear, his sniper rifle in hand.

The team moved quickly through the grass, scrub and brush, forgoing the gravel path for a slightly faster and more direct route. Once they reached the houses, Krylov stopped for a few seconds to check his watch. "Three minutes. Keep going!"

The bay was still visible from the rows of houses, but the level of destruction in the area made movement slow-going. All manner of timber, shingles, wiring, insulation and household goods were scattered far and wide. Nails and sharp strips of metal still peeked threateningly out of the soil and debris, ready to puncture a misplaced boot or cause a slight fall to turn into a much more serious injury.

Krylov led the way through the debris as best as he could, but the group soon found themselves spread out by several meters as they all picked their own paths through, hurrying to get as far into the city as possible. All five were panting for air when the first sign of the distraction echoed through the air.

Boom.

The sound was distant, but unmistakable – something had just exploded. Each member of the team clambered to get to a high vantage point before finally settling on a small outcropping of rocks situated next to the foundation of what used to be a small home. Down in the bay, the remnants of an enormous fireball rose into the air, accompanied by a thick cloud of smoke.

Leonard pulled out a pair of his own binoculars and looked at the scene. Water roiled around the body of one of the cargo vessels as it bobbed back and forth in the water, still rocking from the force of the torpedo's impact. As he was scanning the length and breadth of the ship, he was startled by a blinding flash of light, followed a few seconds later by the sound of another enormous explosion.

A fresh fireball rose from the side of the cargo ship, and more black smoke billowed out. Before the smoke had a chance to clear, a secondary explosion sounded out, and the vessel listed hard into the bay, sending water and pieces of the ship flying in all directions.

Krylov grinned broadly at the sight and sound coming from the bay. "She used two torpedoes. Excellent."

Marcus laughed. "If that doesn't get their attention, nothing will."

Turning behind to the east, Leonard shielded his eyes against the rising sun. "As great as this is, I'd suggest we get a move on. The sun's coming up fast, and we have a lot of ground to cover. There's no telling how long those things will stay distracted."

Krylov stepped down from the rocks and pulled out a map. "You're right. We'll want to proceed to the southwest until we reach this location." He jabbed his finger at a point near the center of the city. "This is the primary hub of the metro station. If the main entrance is open, we'll get in there. However, I suspect that it will have collapsed, either from the bombs or from the survivors."

"If they're even there."

Krylov raised an eyebrow at Leonard's gloomy tone. "You think they are somewhere else?"

"No, this makes sense. Easy access to the transmitter and all. It's just... that factory. Something felt wrong about it from the moment I saw it. And now this whole city's starting to give me the same feeling. There's something wrong here, Krylov. I think you know it, too."

Krylov folded the map and put it back in his jacket pocket. "You may be right, Mr. McComb. But what choice do we have?"

Leonard hoisted the EMP cannon and shrugged. "None. I just hope you're right about them still being there. I'd hate to be walking into an underground station that's filled to the brim with muties and nothing else."

The team set off through the destroyed houses, picking through them as quickly as they could. After clearing the neighborhood, a wide field stretched out in front of them, marking the separation of the more suburban areas from the city proper. They jogged across the field, keeping a close watch in all directions as they headed toward the piles of rubble and twisted metal of the city.

Chapter Five

MAGADAN

"Natalia?" *The man speaks in Russian, his voice shaking. "Where are you Natalia?"*

Inside the apartment, there are no lights. The deafening roar of the fire moments before had snuffed those out, and took with them the lone window of the room.

"Natalia?" The man coughs. Dust swirls into the apartment from the outside, pushed in by the wind from the explosions. It settles on everything it touches, tainting the apartment with the invisible killer brought from the sky.

The man crawls through the apartment, his eyes blinking, but unseeing. An unfortunate side effect of watching out the window the moment a bomb struck, he is blind. The shock of the experience has not yet worn off, and he is unaware of his condition.

"Natalia, please. Answer me! Where are you?" His voice is hoarse. He bumps into a table, nearly knocking it over. His wife left to buy food an hour before and has yet to return. A sinking feeling wells up inside of him, and he lies down on the floor. 'Just a rest,' he thinks. 'Just for a moment.'

An hour later, Andrew Mikhailov dies.

Three minutes after his death, Andrew Mikhailov draws breath again. His sight returns, though not as he remembers. The world appears behind fractals, like he is peering down the tube of a kaleidoscope. He feels his body jerk and twist beneath him. He stands up and peers down at himself, the movements not his own.

Around him, barely visible, silvered dust swirls. The swarm intensifies, passing through the house like locusts. It filters the air before alighting on every surface, searching every nook and cranny for the sweet nectar it so desperately needs. Radiation. The life-taker and the life-giver.

Andrew swivels around and stumbles toward the window. His mind fights against his body's movements. He tries to call out, but his voice no longer works. Clouds appear around his vision, and he feels his memories slipping away.

'Natal…' The thought is fleeting. It meant something, once. But now it is gone. Replaced by a sea of blackness that envelopes Andrew's mind. He struggles against the sea and, for a few seconds, feels like he is winning. But the sea fights back. The waves of darkness consume his senses—and his mind.

The creature stares out the window of the apartment. The nanobots carefully tear through the flesh, knitting it together into a newer, stronger form. The organism's mind struggles, but in the end, it gives in to the insatiable hunger of the swarm. They integrate swiftly, having perfected their methods through millions of repetitions.

Then something happens. Something the swarm does not anticipate. Something it does not realize has even occurred until it is over and the something becomes nothing—a part of the background noise. But in that moment, the moment the swarm did not see or anticipate or even know had happened, they themselves began to change.

Chapter Six

MAGADAN

Leonard was tired. Tired of hauling around a backpack that was too heavy. Tired of having to watch his every movement for fear of making a sound. Tired of being in close quarters with four other people and smelling their sweat. Mostly, though, he was tired of being constantly on edge, waiting for a creature to appear out of every nook and cranny that they passed.

"Where are we?" Leonard whispered to Krylov, who was in the middle of gulping down half a bottle of water. Krylov opened the map with one hand and laid it flat on his leg. He pointed to a location that was slightly closer to the center of the city than they had been an hour prior, but it was still agonizingly far away.

"This blows," Marcus whispered over Leonard's shoulder as he peered at the map.

Though the group had worked together on numerous search and rescue missions before, they had mostly stayed away from large cities. While large cities had the potential to harbor survivors in their depths, that hadn't been the case most of the time. The majority of the survivors that made up New Richmond had come from suburban and rural areas, small towns and isolated villages. People who lived away from civilization and were genetically similar due to familial connections stood the best chance at survival from both the bombs and the swarms.

Started as a clandestine government program under the purview of a mysterious figure known only as "Mr. Doe," the nanobot program's original purpose was still a mystery. Records of the program had been destroyed when the bombs had fallen, and not even David Landry—one of the principle scientists on the project—knew its true purpose. Only one man truly knew what the program had been designed for, and he had long since died.

When the nanobot's AI had gained sentience, it was only an act of sabotage from the researchers—David Landry and Rachel Walsh—that had kept it from wiping out every human on the planet. By inserting DNA markers into a "whitelist" in the core programming of the nanobots, they had been able to protect anyone who possessed those markers. Upon scanning a person to decide whether to kill them or transform them into a mutant, the nanobots also performed a DNA scan. If a person possessed the whitelisted markers, then the swarm would ignore them, carrying on as though they didn't exist.

That fact did not, for whatever reason, stop the mutants from attacking people carrying the markers on sight. Whether it was an alteration in the AI's programming upon the completion of a mutation, the fact that the mutants didn't possess the ability to scan DNA or some other reason, no one was really sure. The only thing that a survivor knew was that if you saw a mutant, you had to kill it fast—or else you'd be dead before you could pull the trigger.

"Yeah. No kidding. I hate urban fighting." Leonard rubbed his leg above where the artificial limb was attached. All of the climbing, crouching and marching over the hard ground had left his leg feeling particularly sore, and he was thankful for the brief rest.

"Arkhangelsk, this is Krylov. Please report on the status of the mutants. Over," Krylov whispered into the radio while Roman and Mikhail kept watch. The team had found a small building that was relatively intact to take a short rest in while Krylov radioed the submarine.

Marcus patted Leonard on the shoulder and whispered to him again. "Take it easy for a few minutes. I'm going to see if I can find anything useful in here."

Marcus explored the building, unsure of what he was looking for. If the last year had taught him anything, though, it was that he had to constantly be on the lookout for anything that might be of use. The building had served some sort of government-related purpose judging by the rows of desks, chairs and filing cabinets. Marcus thumbed through scattered piles of paperwork and opened and closed several drawers, but found nothing of use.

"Commander? This is Nancy. Sorry about the delay there." Marcus wandered back over to the group as he heard the radio crackle in reply.

"Not a problem, Ms. Sims. Are you able to give us an update on the mutants? Over."

"Taking a look now, Commander. One moment."

On the Arkhangelsk, Nancy peered through the periscope, zooming in on the docks. Where there had previously been no sign of movement, it was teeming with creatures. Dozens of humans and canines raced around the port, searching high and low for any signs of the source of the billowing smoke.

"The port's never been this busy, I'd say. There are more muties hanging out there now than we've seen in one place in a long time."

"Excellent. Thank you, Ms. Sims. Over."

"How are things faring for you there? Have you run into trouble yet?"

"Things are proceeding well for the moment, though the terrain is wreaking havoc on our estimated time of arrival. We'll need you to keep an eye on the creatures and make sure they stay occupied at the dock. If they start heading back into the city, please provide them with another distraction. Over."

"Copy that, Commander. We'll take care of it. Oh, and before you go, would you put Leonard on?"

Krylov handed the radio to Leonard, then stood up to stretch his legs.

"Leonard here. What's the word, Nancy?"

"Those images you all sent to David are coming through now." Nancy's tone was hushed as she spoke about the pictures of the carnage inside of the factory. "Do you have any idea what's going on?"

"I have a few ideas, but nothing solid yet. I think we're going to have to talk to the survivors first before I can get a clear idea of what's going on."

"Do you think they're trying to organize? Like what happened at the Nexus?"

Leonard held down the microphone button, but paused, unsure of what to say. "I... I don't know. As soon as I find out, though, we'll let you know."

"Dammit!" Leonard heard the bang of metal as Nancy slammed her hand against a bulkhead in frustration. "I should be with you all right now, not spinning my wheels on this boat."

Leonard smiled. "I hear you, Nance. Just stay focused and make sure those creatures don't come back into the city."

Krylov came back over to Leonard and squatted down beside him to speak into the radio. "You're doing a marvelous job so far, Ms. Sims. Please keep it up. We're counting on you here."

Nancy sighed. "Yeah, yeah. Just stay safe. Call us if you need something. If you hear explosions, that'll be us doing a bit of distracting of the locals."

"Copy that, Ms. Sims. Out." Krylov took the radio back and slid it into his pocket. He turned to face Leonard, straightening up as he addressed him. "Mr. McComb—"

"Krylov, for the love of everything holy, just call me Leonard, okay?"

"Leonard." Krylov gave a small *hrmph* as he said it, but continued nonetheless. "I'd like you to take point from here on out. You have more urban experience than the rest of us. I'll do my best to guide us, but I want you in front to keep an eye open for any dangers."

"No problem." Leonard slapped Krylov on the shoulder and smiled. "I thought you'd never ask."

Emerging from the government building on the north end of the city, the rescue team scanned their surroundings for any signs of movement. The area was quiet, with the only sounds being those caused by the wind. Moving slowly, Leonard took the lead, followed by Krylov, Marcus, Mikhail and Roman. Leonard glanced over at the map that Krylov held, and pointed to an area just to their east.

"Why don't we cut through these buildings and head for the canal? It might be easier to get through there."

Krylov nodded and tucked the map away. "It's worth a shot. I've no idea what would be built up around there, though."

Leonard shrugged. "If it's blocked, we'll come back through here and continue pushing through the debris."

Signaling to the rest of the team to follow him, Leonard took a sharp turn to the left, ducking through the remnants of a factory doorway. The roof of the building had been blown off and one wall collapsed, but the rest of the structure was intact, offering a relatively clear path to the canal.

While the canal—in actuality a small river—had once denoted the eastern edge of the city of Magadan, the building and population boom that had seen the growth of the port had also seen an expansion across the canal to the east. A great expanse of fields, farms and forest between the north end of the city and a small settlement of houses out to the east had been consumed by more homes, factories, warehouses and apartments.

The canal that had once marked the edge of the city soon became the center of the city. As part of this process, it had been widened by several meters, and the bottom was dredged, making it deep and wide enough for flat-bottom boats to traverse its length. A second canal—this one artificial—had been dug out to the western port, while the natural course of the original river continued out to the east, where a smaller port was located. The artificial canal had quickly become the primary means of transport of goods from the port to the factories in the city, eliminating the need for reinforced roads to be built to accommodate large transport trucks.

Though the destruction to the northern end of the city was great, Leonard was hoping that the canal would be clear enough that they could walk next to it down towards the center of the city. If that route was blocked, then there was always a chance that the water would be clear enough to traverse by boat or makeshift raft—though the enemy of that idea was time. They were already behind schedule, and every moment they spent walking out in the open was another minute that drew them closer to an encounter with a mutant.

The group moved stealthily through the ruins, hindered greatly by their supplies and weapons. What had started off as an easier path quickly turned sour as the level of destruction increased, thanks to a collapsed block of apartment buildings between them and the canal. The midday sun shone bright overhead, providing some much-welcomed heat, but it was also a reminder that they were getting nowhere fast. Krylov and Leonard consulted the map again, growing frustrated by the lack of progress.

"Perhaps if we cut south, around this block to the canal?" Krylov traced a potential path through the debris.

Leonard shook his head. "No, that's going to take far too long. We need to get out of this ring we're in. Once we do that, the streets should be mostly clear for us. Here, give me the map."

Leonard outlined a circle on the map roughly in line with the pattern of destruction caused by the bomb. "We're here, about midway on the southeastern portion of this. Let's just cut directly through those buildings, and by the time we reach the other side, we'll be out of it. Then we can get to the canal and be on our way, or take the streets if they're clear."

Krylov looked at the rows of grey and white buildings Leonard was pointing at. Part of the new apartment block construction to help deal with the population boom in Magadan, they had survived the blast relatively well thanks to their newer design. Older blocks, like the ones between the team and the canal, hadn't fared as well.

Krylov nodded. "Let's go."

Leonard took off at a jog for the apartments as the team trailed behind. The open courtyard in front of the block was surprisingly free of debris, making it easy to cross. Seven tall buildings stood in a shape between a circle and a rectangle, with a wide grassy area around them and in the middle. The trees and grass had long since died—replaced instead by scrub and weeds hardy enough to survive without human intervention—but Leonard could picture what the place had once looked like in his mind's eye.

As Leonard neared the apartment block, he slowed down and glanced behind him. Krylov was right next to him, Marcus was a few meters behind, Roman was next and Mikhail was in last. Mikhail Egorov was one of the youngest crewmembers of the Arkhangelsk, and not an original crewmember, either. Picked up in South America during a rescue mission, Mikhail had taken a vacation from his home just outside Moscow only two weeks prior to the end of the world.

Thanks to his genetics and being in a relatively remote area of the continent, he had survived the bombs and the swarms. Young and inexperienced, he had still managed to stay alive for a few months. When the Arkhangelsk had sailed into Valparaíso, he had been amazed to find a boat with his fellow countrymen so far from home, and he had eagerly joined the crew.

Krylov had taken a liking to the boy, and Mikhail had shown promise in the field—hence why he had been chosen as one of the additional two to join in on the rescue team—but even the commander had to admit that the boy wasn't the best when it came to stealth. It was, then, no small surprise when the young man tripped over himself as he struggled with his backpack while running across the courtyard. What did surprise both Krylov and Leonard was the louder-than-expected shot that rang out as Mikhail faceplanted into the ground.

BOOM!

In the stillness of the city, the shot was like an abbey's bell being rung in the early morning hours. It bounced and echoed off every inch of their surroundings, reverberating and carrying out farther than Leonard would have liked to imagine. Marcus jerked around at the sound, and everyone ducked, fearful of a second shot. When none came, Marcus was the first one to run back out toward Mikhail, helping him to his feet and checking him for any injury.

When they rejoined the group, Krylov hissed at him in anger. "What are you doing?! Why was your safety not on?"

"I'm sorry, sir. I don't know. I was checking my weapon when we were resting earlier, and it must have—"

"Shh!" Leonard hissed, holding a finger to his mouth. He cocked his head and strained, grasping for any sign that the sound had attracted unwanted attention. Krylov snapped his jaw closed and listened as well. Leonard, Krylov and Marcus watched each other closely, waiting for a sign that one of them had picked up on a noise. Backs against the wall of the nearest apartment building, the trio held their breaths while Roman helped Mikhail adjust his ill-fitting backpack and check his rifle for any damage from the fall.

For a few long, agonizing moments, everything was quiet. The wind picked up a few times, sending swirls of dust through the courtyard and rustling the scrub and brush, but otherwise, the city seemed completely at peace. Just as Leonard let out a long exhale of relief, the radio in Krylov's jacket crackled to life.

"Krylov, this is Arkhangelsk! This is an emergency! Do you copy? This is an emergency! Krylov, pick up, dammit!"

Krylov fumbled with the radio for a few seconds before answering. All formalities of communication went out the window. "Nancy, what's going on?"

"You have to get moving now! A huge group of those things just took off toward the center of the city. We're arming another torpedo, but it won't be ready for three more minutes. And honestly, I don't think it'll do much good anyway. They were running like bats out of hell. What's going on over there?!"

Krylov closed his eyes and put his head back against the wall. He cursed loudly in Russian before returning to the radio. "Nancy, do whatever you can to get their attention. Destroy half the port if you have to. Just buy us some time!"

Marcus looked between Leonard and Krylov. "What's the plan?"

Krylov gritted his teeth. "We keep going. The path should be clear between the buildings ahead. If it's not, we'll hunker down and try to hide, wait for them to pass. Now, let's go!"

Krylov helped Mikhail to his feet, checking his rifle closely to make sure the safety was on. With a pat on the back, he pushed the young man forward to fall in line behind Leonard, Marcus and Roman. Krylov took up the rear as they moved forward between the apartment buildings, making a beeline for the canal.

The courtyard in the middle of the apartment blocks was still, protected from the wind and blowing bits of debris by the massive buildings surrounding it. Based on the swings, slides and what remained of tables and chairs, it had once been used as a park and playground for the residents of the apartment blocks. Time had not been kind to the park, though, in spite of its protected location. The metal slides and swing sets were rusted through, and the few pieces of plastic that hadn't disintegrated and been blown away were worn and faded from the elements.

The team moved around the park on a brick walkway that encircled it, then ran down a narrow alley separating two of the apartment buildings on the opposite side of where they entered. There was still no sign of pursuers, but the knowledge that the creatures could appear at any moment spurred the team to go from jogging to breaking into a sprint.

After passing in between the apartment buildings, Leonard glanced in both directions before taking off to the left, cutting across a four-lane road and down a side alley. Here, on the opposite side of the apartment block, the destruction was less dramatic, with most of the damage coming in the form of shattered power poles, destroyed roofs and over-turned cars. The buildings were by and large intact, making Leonard glad that he had chosen the path.

As the team ran down the alley, Krylov shouted at Leonard from the back of the group. "The canal is nearby. Shouldn't be much farther!" There was no more pretense of stealth now; speed was the only directive.

After passing through and around a few more buildings, Leonard skidded to a stop as a steel and concrete waist-high barrier appeared. Stretching off to the left and right as far as he could see, it twisted and turned to follow the path of an empty canal. Confused, Leonard's eyes flicked over the area intently, wondering where they'd taken a wrong turn.

"Shit." Marcus stopped next to Leonard and Krylov, pointing ahead of them. "Is that the canal?"

"I—I don't know. Wasn't there supposed to be water here, Krylov?"

Krylov looked at his map, then turned around and checked the buildings near them, comparing their location to the map. He looked defeated as he handed the map to Leonard and nodded. "I'm afraid this *is* the canal. Or what's left of it anyway."

The scar in the earth was wide and deep, dividing the city just as it appeared on the map. But instead of being filled with water and having banks covered in grass, it was empty, with the smallest trickle of water running down the very center.

"What's the source for this, Krylov?"

"It feeds from lakes to the north, beyond the city." He shook his head. "I don't understand. It wouldn't have simply drained like this."

Leonard stood staring at the dry canal for a moment before his mind kicked back into gear. "Okay, this is fine. We can just follow alongside the walkway down into the center of the city. It looks clear enough, and there's no need to get our feet wet."

The group was turning to the right to head south and east toward the center of the city when a distant howl echoed behind them from the direction of the apartment buildings. Leonard froze and turned to Krylov.

"Any suggestions?" he asked.

The reply was simple: "Run."

Leonard had hoped that taking a water route would save time and offer an increase in stealth, since they wouldn't have to make noise walking or running down empty streets if they were floating down the canal. That was in addition to the other, more selfish reason of wanting to get off of his feet for a while. His prosthetic leg ached fiercely, and he could feel the weight of it increasing with every moment that passed. Made of titanium alloy, it was lighter than a normal leg, but after going without it for so long, he was finding it difficult to make such a sudden adjustment to having it back on.

The team broke into a sprint again upon hearing Krylov's words, with Leonard in the front. His grip on the EMP cannon tightened at the sound of the creatures' howls, though he dearly hoped he wouldn't have to find out how well it worked. Several minutes of running passed, and Leonard held up a hand for the group to slow down so they could check their location on the map again. What happened next came in a blur, with a speed so fast that the group barely had time to react.

Six dark shapes came out from a side street, their bodies low to the ground as they slipped on the grass and gravel and rounded the corner to come face-to-face with the rescue team. Having never seen mutated dogs before, Leonard hesitated when he saw them, unsure of what to do. The creatures were mutts, with bodies horribly disfigured and twisted by the same silvery metals that gave human mutants their distinctive appearance. The dogs' eyes were missing, too, replaced by sunken holes of silver. Most of their fur was gone, leaving dried pink skin in its place, though a few filthy mats of hair still clung to their bellies and upper legs.

While Leonard, Marcus, Mikhail and Roman were frozen in shock by the sight of the creatures, Krylov wasted no time. He let out a fierce shout and dropped to one knee as he thumbed the safety on his rifle and opened fire on the creatures. A crack shot, Krylov aimed for the heads of the beasts, watching in satisfaction as two skulls split open like ripe cantaloupes under his careful fire.

The sound of the shots lit a fire under the rest of the team. Marcus, Mikhail and Roman opened fire alongside Krylov, taking down two more of the creatures in only a few seconds. Leonard fumbled with the EMP cannon, releasing the safety catch and simultaneously hitting the button on the side to charge it. A high-pitched whine came from the stock of the gun, and a row of lights on the top turned green one after the other. When all six were lit, Leonard pulled the trigger on the cannon, aiming it in the general direction of the two remaining creatures.

The result was, to put it mildly, obscene. An invisible wave of energy surged from the end of the cannon and passed over the bodies of the four dead creatures and through the two live ones. Immediately, the two living creatures dropped, their momentum carrying them forward several feet. Bright sparks of white light surged from the silvery metal that intertwined their bodies, and their flesh erupted in flames from the intense heat. All of this happened in the space of less than a second, and the group shielded their eyes and stepped back.

"Holy shit!" Leonard shouted, then caught himself and glanced around, wishing he hadn't been so loud. "That was amazing! Krylov, this thing is incredible! Why didn't your guys put something like this together sooner?"

Krylov smiled and started to reply, then stopped and turned his head. Another howl echoed behind them, louder this time as it was joined by more distinct voices. The sounds reverberated in the empty canal, making them sound closer than they actually were—but not by much.

"Come on. We must keep moving." Krylov pushed Leonard forward and the team took off at a sprint, giving a wide berth to the smoldering corpses in the middle of the narrow street. The small gravel path widened as they continued, and it soon turned into a paved road with two narrow lanes. As they traveled farther toward the heart of the city, the destruction gradually cleared until things almost looked peaceful except for the distinct lack of people.

Small shops dotted the road on their side of the empty canal. First an electronics store, then a shawarma shop, then a row of buildings that even Krylov wasn't sure about. As the buildings grew larger and more elaborate, they eventually spotted a golden spire rising up ahead of them.

"That's the Holy Trinity!" Krylov exclaimed, suddenly increasing his speed. "Hurry, we must get there!"

Magadan's Holy Trinity Cathedral was an imposing white and gold building, surrounded by a tall fence and positioned across from a government building and next to the canal. The roads around the cathedral were wider, and more cars were on the streets, some parked and others stopped in the middle of the road. Krylov passed by Leonard as they ran along, taking the lead as they rounded the enormous government building and began crossing the street toward the church.

"Leonard, help with the gate!" Krylov shouted behind him as he ran for an enormous gate on the northeastern side of the fence. Understanding what Krylov was trying to accomplish, Leonard picked up his pace to help break the lock on the gate. The fence was some twenty feet high, tall enough to keep out all but the most determined mutants, and enough of a deterrent that if they could get inside before being spotted, the creatures might not even investigate the building once they arrived. With everyone out of breath and in need of a rest, the cathedral was their best possible option.

Krylov struggled against the lock with a small crowbar he retrieved from his pack. Leonard pulled out his pistol and pointed it at the lock. "Should we risk it?"

Krylov shook his head as he grunted, straining with the lock. "Won't work. Metal's too strong. Help me leverage it open."

Leonard retrieved his own crowbar and jammed it into the lock's loop, then pulled back. The additional weight was too much for the rusted lock, and it flew open, sending Krylov and Leonard tumbling to the ground. Marcus and Roman helped the two men up while Mikhail retrieved their crowbars and handed them back.

"Good work. Now get inside. You, too, Leonard. The less of us out here, the better. I will seal the lock, then be in after you." Krylov barked an order at Roman in Russian, and the man slipped his backpack off and pulled out a black plastic box, which he handed over.

Krylov took the box and nodded his thanks, then opened it to reveal a small welding kit. Marcus and Mikhail stood behind Leonard and Roman as they forced open the locked cathedral door. The group stepped inside and closed the door nearly all the way, leaving it open just a crack so that Marcus could stand watch over Krylov.

Krylov's work didn't take long, and after just a few minutes, the lock was back to looking relatively normal. Krylov kicked it a few times with his boot through the bars of the fence to make sure it would hold, then he glanced up as another series of howls echoed across the streets. They were much closer this time, and after the noise of their screams passed, he could hear the scrambling of feet and claws across gravel.

Krylov threw the welding kit into his bag and grabbed it with one hand, then picked up his rifle with the other. He ran full tilt for the cathedral and threw himself inside as Marcus opened and then closed the door as quickly and quietly as possible. Leonard, having already ascended to the second floor, crouched near a window, keeping his rifle handy and the EMP cannon lying on the floor near his feet. He kept his head low in the corner of the window, fearful of one of the creatures spotting him.

Leonard's wait to spy the creatures wasn't long. Less than thirty seconds after Marcus had closed the door, a pack of creatures tore down the road where the team had been running only a short time before. Leonard counted sixteen humans and at least a dozen canines, though with the erratic way in which they ran, he wasn't sure about the numbers. The creatures snarled, howled and screamed as they ran, their feet and paws thundering on the ground. They pushed against each other and the obstacles in their path, leaping over cars and shoving others of their kind out of the way.

The creatures, as Leonard and Krylov had guessed, avoided the cathedral entirely, flowing around the building's perimeter on both sides like a rushing river. A few of the creatures glanced up at the building, but none of them gave it more than a passing glance. Leonard let out a sigh of relief and sat down with his back to the wall, listening quietly as the sound of the creatures began to fade away.

"Psst. Hey, Leonard." Marcus was standing down in the midst of the pews, his hands cupped around his mouth as he whispered as loud as he dared. "Are they gone?"

Leonard stood up and looked through the window again, then leaned over the railing and gave Marcus a thumbs-up. "All clear." Marcus nodded, then passed the message on to Krylov, who had collapsed into a pew in the back of the church and was breathing hard. Leonard glanced out the window one last time, then descended the stairs to rejoin the group.

Standing in the middle of the Russian Orthodox church, Leonard looked around at the décor. Built in 1985, it wasn't an ancient building, but years of upgrades and changes to the interior and exterior of the building had changed it substantially from the original design. The white tile flooring on the interior had been replaced with a cream-colored pattern, and the formerly white walls were barely visible behind the detailed paintings, statues and murals that now adorned them.

A long crack ran up the side of one of the walls to the ceiling, evidence of the powerful forces that had shaken the city. Somehow most of the windows in the cathedral had survived unscathed, likely due to the fact that they were nearly three times as thick as normal glass. Whatever the reason, Leonard was glad they were there for the additional visual camouflage they provided.

"We need to contact the Arkhangelsk," Leonard said, turning around to the team. "With that many muties out there, we'll be lucky to get a quarter of a mile before they start tearing into us. And as great as that cannon is, I don't think we'll be able to take on a group like that." Leonard gestured toward the EMP cannon, and Krylov nodded in agreement.

"I don't know what—if anything—they can do, but we need to contact them." Krylov pulled out the radio, looking exhausted as he turned it on.

"Here, I'll call them. You rest." Leonard held out his hand and took the radio from Krylov, who merely leaned his head back against the wall and closed his eyes.

Leonard turned on the radio and thumbed the transmit button as he began to pace back and forth down the main aisle of the church. "Arkhangelsk, Arkhangelsk, this is Leonard. Do you copy? Over."

A crackle of static came for a few seconds, then the reply.

"Leonard, this is Nancy. You're coming through with a bit of static. Over."

"Yeah, we're in a bit of a rough spot, Nancy. Had a run-in with the creatures." Leonard glanced at Krylov. The commander's eyes were still closed, and he was too tired to care about Leonard dropping the word "over" from his transmissions.

"Is everyone okay?"

"Yeah, we're fine here. One of the soldiers tripped and had a misfire. That's what drew them to us. I can tell you one thing, though, these dogs... wow. They are not messing around. Whatever the swarms did to these things made them look meaner than the humans."

"How many of them have you seen?"

"We killed six, but there's a huge group of them that were chasing us. We're hiding inside the cathedral here near the center of town, but who knows how long it'll be until they find us."

Back on the sub, Nancy was pacing as she racked her brain to think of what they should do next. "Should we just abort? I can have a team on shore to meet you within the hour."

"No." Krylov's voice was firm. Leonard turned and looked at him as he replied to Nancy.

"Is that transmission still going?" Leonard asked.

"Still alive, strong and not responding to anything we send back."

"Then we keep going. Do whatever you can to draw their attention. These things learn and adapt, so you may need to be creative."

"Will do. Stay safe, Leonard. Arkhangelsk out."

The line went dead, and Leonard crossed the room to hand the radio back. "Thank you, Leonard." Krylov's voice was quiet. "This... means a lot."

Leonard smiled and held out his hand. The commander clasped it, and Leonard pulled him to his feet. Feeling slightly better after the brief respite, Krylov shook off his weariness and addressed the group.

"Things are not going according to plan."

"No kidding," Marcus mumbled.

"But we will continue to press forward. The Arkhangelsk will be attempting to set up another diversion to lure the creatures away. By my estimate, we are less than two kilometers from the entrance to the metro station. I recommend that we give the crew on the Arkhangelsk some time to try and distract the creatures. We can rest here until dusk, then move out under the cover of darkness."

Leonard raised an eyebrow. "Those things are even deadlier in the dark, you know."

"Yes, Mr. McComb. But their strength may be ours, as well. They will not expect us to be moving about at night. If they decide to start searching through buildings along the path where they pursued us, it will only be a matter of time before the fence and walls of this building are not enough to protect us. No, our best chance will be tonight, when we have rested and—with any luck—some of the mutants have been lured back to the docks."

Leonard shrugged. "I wouldn't recommend it, but this is your party, Krylov. It's as good a plan as any. Let's see if we can find a back room, someplace a little farther inside to muffle our sounds in case they start searching around the cathedral for us. Mikhail, break out some rations." Leonard checked the time. "Marcus, I'd like you to be on first watch. I'll relieve you in two hours."

"Sounds good."

The group moved deeper into the cathedral, eventually choosing a small office to rest in. Marcus stayed in the main portion of the building, pacing around the second story at a slow pace, keeping a close eye on the grounds around and beyond them.

Leonard didn't expect to get any rest in the small office, but he was glad to see that Roman and Mikhail had dozed off almost immediately. Krylov, on the other hand, was sitting at a desk, studying the map and writing in a notebook. The two hours passed slowly, punctuated by the occasional snore or murmur, until eventually Marcus pushed open the door and glanced inside. Leonard crept out, and Krylov followed close behind, leaving the two soldiers to their rest.

"You two couldn't sleep, huh?"

"Sleep is for the dead, Mr. Warden. A few moments of peace is all I require, and I have been afforded that. Come, before you rest, I wish to show you both something."

Krylov laid his map out on the floor at the front of the cathedral, where the last few rays of sunlight were streaming in through a stained glass window, illuminating the paper with a dazzling array of colors.

He opened his small notebook and glanced at it as he spoke, pointing to various buildings in between the cathedral and the metro entrance.

"If we traverse this path, taking care to avoid making any noise, I believe we will have an advantage against the creatures almost the whole way."

Marcus looked at Krylov doubtfully. "How do you figure that?"

"Observe, Mr. Warden. Our first stop, merely two hundred meters away, is a large factory complex that stretches for another hundred and fifty meters in the direction we are traveling. This type of factory I am familiar with; it will be easy to enter, and we can use the building as cover until we reach the other end.

"From there, we will cross the street and pass into this row of storefronts leading to the south, then again to the west. The stores are connected in the back by a series of access doors that we can pass through, again protecting us from being seen on the street."

"That's... not bad, Krylov." Marcus grinned. "Not bad at all. You have paths like this all the way to the metro station?"

"Very nearly, yes. Our principle problem, however, will be dealing with any creatures that happen to be using these buildings as domiciles, as well as dealing with any noise we may make. I think we learned from today that some members of our team can be counted on to generate a lot of excess noise."

"The creatures will be easy to deal with, if we're quiet," Leonard said. "I'll take point with the EMP cannon. It's quieter than anything else, and we can knock them out before they make a sound."

"Exactly what I was going to suggest, Mr. McComb. Excellent! Now, for the distraction... I believe that may be something the Arkhangelsk can assist with. Speaking of which, I'll radio them now and get an update.

"Arkhangelsk, this is Commander Krylov. Do you copy? Over."

"Commander? Nancy here. I was just getting ready to call you. I think we've found the answer to your distraction problem!" Nancy's voice was distorted, and Leonard could swear he heard the sound of wind and waves in the background.

"Ms. Sims?" Krylov looked at Leonard as he spoke. "What do you mean?"

"Can't explain right now, Commander! I just need you to get your asses moving. Your distraction is going to be going up in about fifteen minutes, and it's going to be loud as hell!" A great burst of static cut through, then they heard Nancy's muffled curse before the line went dead.

"Arkhangelsk?" Krylov thumbed the transmit key. "Ms. Sims? Are you there? Shit!" Krylov put the radio in his jacket and turned to Marcus. "Get Mikhail and Roman up; everyone needs to be ready to go in two minutes. Mr. McComb, help me with the front gate!"

Leonard strapped on his backpack and picked up his weapons. He wordlessly trailed behind Krylov as they exited the cathedral into the twilight evening. With the sun fully gone, leaving only traces of orange behind the buildings to the west, darkness now began to spread a shroud over the city.

The front gate was opened in seconds, and a moment later, the front door to the cathedral swung open as Marcus, Roman and Mikhail came jogging out. Krylov held his finger to his lips and motioned for them to circle around. He gave a quick whispered summary of what had transpired on the radio to the two soldiers before he addressed the group.

"I have no idea what Ms. Sims is about to do, but we need to be ready for anything. Let's get moving to the first waypoint, the factory, and continue from there. Leonard, you take point. Head that way." Krylov pointed at a shadowy structure down the road, and they took off at a sprint.

Looping around the southern end of the cathedral, the group devoured the two hundred meters with ease. Less than a minute after they started, the team was safely tucked in the shadow of the factory, watching as Leonard gently pried open a narrow metal door. After several seconds of grunting and struggling, the lock finally gave with a sharp metallic *snap*, and the door swung open.

Ducking inside first, Leonard squinted in the darkness, fearful of turning on a flashlight for not only what it might attract, but for what he might see. The piles of mutilated bodies on the floor of the factory complex was still in the forefront of his mind as he pored over what they could mean.

Behind him, Krylov did not share the same trepidations, and a soft click accompanied a bright glow that penetrated the darkness. A narrow beam of light came from directly behind Leonard, scanning the room and revealing its contents. Instead of bodies, as Leonard had feared, the factory was filled with machinery, though its purpose was difficult to determine at a glance.

With Krylov lighting the way, Leonard stepped quickly down the main aisle of the factory complex, sweeping to the left and right with the EMP cannon. Behind Leonard and Krylov, Marcus, Roman and Mikhail swept their weapons and lights across the walls and ceilings, looking for any signs of an ambush. The main floor of the factory was expansive, but the team moved quickly to the opposite end, where a wide set of double doors with large glass windows separated the work floor from the offices.

Leonard pushed gently on the right door, and as it opened, he froze at the sound. Off in the distance, a high-pitched whistle sounded, growing gradually deeper in pitch the longer it went on. Leonard stepped back from the door and watched it swing gently on its hinges, then turned to look at Krylov and Marcus. Krylov's eyebrow was raised, Marcus's brow was furrowed and the two soldiers were staring at Leonard with wide eyes, their expressions a cross between terror and amazement.

"What the hell was that?" Leonard whispered.

Krylov shook his head, then reached forward to touch the door. Before he could, the whistle sounded again, this time from a slightly different direction.

Leonard pushed through the double doors, moving swiftly into the administrative offices. There, the walls were cracked and crumbling, and the once-wide windows had been shattered. The view from the factory down into the port was limited, but Leonard strained his eyes nonetheless, trying to find the source of the sound. When the whistle blew again, it was louder, and when he finally spied the source, his heart skipped several beats.

Off in the distance, on the train tracks that passed in between the city and the docks, Leonard could make out a few pinpoints of light coming from a moving object. Though it was hard to make out any details, Leonard was certain of what the object was without a shadow of a doubt – a moving train.

"What is that?" Marcus stepped up next to Leonard, along with

Krylov and the soldiers. All had extinguished their lights before leaving the factory floor, and they pushed against each other in the darkness, struggling to see out of the window at the same time.

"That, Marcus, is one of your favorite things in the entire world."

Leonard turned to Marcus just in time to see the man's face freeze in a picture of pure terror. "Is that... is that a train?"

"Sure as hell sounds like one."

Marcus backed up a few steps before sitting down on the floor. "No, no, no. No trains. Not this time."

Leonard sat down next to Marcus and put an arm around the man's shoulder. "I know. You need to get ahold of yourself, though. Whatever's driving that thing is a long way from us."

"Actually," Krylov said, speaking from the window, "it's a 'who,' not a 'what.'"

"What?"

Krylov turned and smiled at Marcus, then held out his binoculars. "Come, look for yourself."

Marcus stood up and took the binoculars in his shaking hands. Steadying himself against the window frame, he peered at the train in the distance. Moving along at a slow pace, the train was being chased quite closely by a veritable army of creatures—both human and animal alike. It took Marcus a moment, but realization slowly dawned on him, and the shaking in his hands and arms gradually stopped.

"There are people on that train."

"Yes." Krylov took back the binoculars and stared through them again. "And if I had to guess, I'd say that is Ms. Sims' diversion. Gunfire is coming from the engineer's compartment, and I don't think any of the survivors in this city would be taking something like that out for a midnight drive."

"How the hell did they get a train up and running?" Leonard shook his head in wonder.

"They probably didn't have to." Marcus watched as the small dots of light moved along the edge of the docks. "Not if the train was brought here by the swarms."

"Ah," said Leonard, "that makes sense." He frowned as a thought occurred to him. "It actually makes *too* much sense, now that I think about it."

In 2038, in the final days leading up to the destruction of the artificial intelligence at its Nexus along the Gulf Coast, Marcus—along with David Landry and Rachel Walsh—had used a train to transport Bertha to the Nexus. Bertha, a specially designed EMP weapon, was meant to be used to wipe out the AI once and for all. After discovering it had been damaged in a firefight, however, an alternate plan had to be developed—deploying the Arkhangelsk's nuclear missiles on the Nexus.

While the final moments of the battle had been harrowing, what had disturbed Marcus for months afterward had been something he'd never expected: the train. Climbing in, around, on top of and beneath one of many trains that had been repaired by the swarms and used to transport supplies to build the Nexus had left him with a savage fear of the vehicles. It hadn't helped that he, along with David, had barely escaped the Nexus on one after Marcus had been forced to leave Rachel behind as she worked to distract the AI long enough to allow the Arkhangelsk to open fire.

Lost in his musings, Leonard didn't notice the look of fear that had reappeared on Marcus's face. When he did, he walked over and embraced Marcus in a bear hug, holding the man tight for several seconds.

"Marcus." Leonard pulled back and looked him in the eyes. "It's okay. Every single one of us is scarred. What you and David went through on that damned thing was horrible. Hell, even I still have nightmares about this." Leonard tapped the barrel of the EMP cannon against his prosthetic, prompting a grim smile from Marcus.

"Thanks." Marcus squared his shoulders and sighed, then looked quizzically at Leonard. "What was it you meant by it making too much sense?"

Leonard was just about to reply when Krylov ran past them, hissing in a low voice. "Get into position, quick! Those things are coming our way!"

Roman and Mikhail hurried to follow their commander while Leonard and Marcus brought up the rear. Krylov knelt down near the door leading to the street outside and put a finger to his lips. The door had nearly been torn from its hinges, and it was mostly standing upright by leaning against its doorframe. Leonard crouched down on the other side of the door and watched the street through the crack, trying to make out what Krylov was talking about. He didn't have to wait for long.

An angry group of mutants charged down the street, seemingly coming from out of nowhere. The creatures ignored the factory completely, much to Leonard's relief, but the shock at seeing just how many of them there were made his stomach churn. The creatures numbered in the hundreds—perhaps more—with the majority of them being animals. There was no preference given by the creatures to each other as they ran side-by-side. They kicked, clawed, scratched and howled at one another from the smallest cat up to an obese man who managed to move quite quickly despite his physical appearance.

Marcus and the soldiers crouched on the floor a few feet away from the door, holding their guns at the ready, staring at Krylov and Leonard intently. It took several minutes for the creatures to pass, but once they did, Leonard slowly stood up and pointed to the door. Krylov nodded and gingerly set his rifle down on the floor. He then took the door in both hands, lifted it slightly above the ground and began turning it to one side. Once the door had been moved out of the way, Leonard poked his head outside the building and glanced around.

Aside from a plethora of footprints on the ground, there wasn't a trace of the creatures that had passed by only moments before. Glancing back for a second, Leonard motioned out the door with his head and then took off at a run across the street, keeping his body low to the ground. He reached the side entrance to the row of shops just as Krylov had predicted and sank down into the shadow of the building, keeping his EMP cannon shouldered.

Leonard waited for what felt like an eternity before motioning to the others to join him across the street. Krylov went over next, followed by Mikhail, Roman and Marcus. Once they were all safely on the other side, Leonard pressed his mouth up against Krylov's ear and whispered. "Get the door open. I'll cover us. Then, move inside."

Krylov nodded and began working on the door. To his surprise, the lock needed no force to break, as it was already dangling off of the door, held on by a few threads of a lone screw. Krylov tapped Leonard's shoulder and pointed at the lock, then stood up and to the side, ready to open the door.

Leonard nodded and turned to face the doorway. Krylov swung it open, and Leonard flinched as it squeaked gently. He stepped inside and switched on his weapon's light, then began to check the corners of the room. It was a small storage room—almost a closet—with cardboard boxes stacked high to the ceiling and broken bottles scattered about. Leonard pressed forward and glanced to his right at the main area of the shop as he passed, being careful not to shine the light directly out of the front of the store.

"Some kind of a liquor store, it looks like," he whispered as Krylov, Marcus and the soldiers stepped inside and closed the outer door.

"Keep moving. We have a lot more to pass through before we reach the end." Krylov readied his crowbar at the next door that divided the first shop from the second. As he began to try to pry it open, the door swung freely. Krylov frowned, puzzled by the fact that two locks had been removed, but he shrugged it off and opened the door for Leonard to push through.

Leonard, however, was not as sure of the situation as Krylov. His mind raced, trying to figure out why the locks would be broken but the doors still shut. *Can't be the explosions. Was it the survivors? No, makes no sense. Dammit, what's going on here?*

It wasn't until they reached the fifth door—after passing through two restaurants, a small engine parts shop and a general goods store—that Leonard had his answer. Krylov swung open the door, and Leonard stepped forward to perform his standard sweep of the floor, walls and ceilings with his weapon. But instead of being greeted by boxes of supplies and old stock, he saw the light of the weapon reflected back at him in the form of dozens of bits of silver scattered throughout the room.

Leonard froze at the sight and blinked a few times before he registered what it was. There, on the floor of the shop's stockroom, was a pile of creatures—some human, some animal—lying peacefully together. Lacking eyelids, it was impossible to tell if their eyes were "closed," but the fact that they didn't immediately attack Leonard when the door was opened seemed to indicate that they were sleeping. Leonard stepped back as Marcus gasped behind him, and he put his hand up to block Krylov's gun from being lowered toward the creatures.

"Back!" he hissed at Krylov, then swung the door closed and put his back up against it.

"What the hell was that?" Marcus pointed at the room beyond the closed door, panic lighting up his eyes.

Leonard shook his head several times. "I don't know. This is all far too strange. This whole city and the creatures in it are… different."

"Can we get around them?" Marcus asked, looking at Krylov expectantly.

"Not unless you want to go outside and travel in the open."

Leonard shook his head. "No, we're not doing that. Those things didn't attack, so we should be able to take them with just this." He patted the barrel of his EMP cannon, then looked at Marcus and the two soldiers. "When Krylov opens this door, I'm going to drop to a knee and open fire. I want you three behind me ready to shoot anything that gets too close, okay?"

Marcus nodded and flicked the safety off on his gun.

"And for God's sake, don't shoot me!" Leonard added.

Krylov looked at Leonard, waiting for the order to open the door. Leonard double-checked the battery level and charge on the device, then wiped a trickle of sweat from his brow. "Go."

This time, Krylov wasn't subtle about opening the door. It flew open with a bang, and several of the creatures flinched in their sleep. Leonard didn't wait to see if they would stay asleep or turn their flinching into an attack. He opened fire immediately, pulling the trigger as fast as he could. He aimed for the creatures closest first, sending them writhing against the others as they died. Next came the largest ones, which had been only partially affected by the cannon on the first shot.

The EMP cannon was deathly quiet, but the noises from the creatures were quite the opposite. As they screamed and howled, they also clawed at each other and the walls of the room, trying to escape the electrifying inferno and eliminate the source of their destruction. As each creature died, its body let off rivulets of smoke that soon coalesced and filled the room. The smell was rancid, and Leonard had to choke back the bile that began to fill his throat.

Less than a minute later, the sounds from the creatures stopped as the entire pile of them smoldered in death. Leonard still continued pulling the trigger on the weapon until Krylov stepped forward and pulled it out of his hands, breaking Leonard from his trance.

"Ease up there, Mr. McComb. They're dead."

Leonard coughed in the smoke and turned away from the pile of creatures to drink deeply from a bottle of water that Marcus held out to him.

"Come on." Krylov pushed through the pile of bodies, moving them out of the way with his feet as he walked. "We have to keep going. These things made a lot of noise."

Leonard rubbed his eyes. He was suddenly overwhelmed by a feeling of exhaustion and revulsion, and he wanted nothing more than to sit down. As Marcus guided him through the smoke-filled room, Leonard wondered why he felt like he did—until he looked down at his feet. The light from Roman and Mikhail's flashlights illuminated the creatures, revealing features that Leonard had only seen by the light of flickering flames and a shaking light.

"Holy hell. Are they—are those... did I just...?" Leonard trailed off as Marcus pushed him forward and whispered to him.

"They were mutants, Leonard. Whatever they were before, they're mutants now. They would have killed us if you hadn't killed them first."

Leonard said nothing as he walked forward, feeling—for the first time in a long while—numb throughout his entire body. He barely noticed as Krylov handed him the EMP cannon and remarked on the excellent job he had done. He didn't look as Marcus replaced the depleted battery with a new one and commented that they were beginning to run low on batteries for the weapon. He didn't respond as Krylov led them across another street into another row of buildings and noted that they appeared to be safe.

The way was clear and the team was nearing their destination. But Leonard didn't care. In his mind's eye, he replayed the seconds over and over again, watching every detail in slow motion. Every pull of the trigger. Every jolt of a small body. Every monstrous child's scream of pain. Every pup's whimper as it died. Every detail seared into Leonard's mind, threatening to overwhelm him in terror and shock over what he had just done.

And still, in the back of his mind, in the far recesses, he thought the same thing again:

This all makes too much sense.

Chapter Seven

Seven weeks have passed since the city turned from a thriving hub of trade into a nightmarish husk. Ash fills the air, carried by the winds across thousands of miles, blotting out the sun. On the edges of the city, away from the dangers within, three figures wrapped in tattered rags shield their eyes against a few faint rays of sunlight that manage to pierce the cloud cover. The air is cold, cutting through their ramshackle clothing and piercing down through to the bone. They are weak. Hungry. Exhausted. They have been scavenging for days for food, but each house they visit offers only the most meager of supplies.

"We must go into the city." The first to speak is the youngest, a girl of only sixteen. She walks beside her mother and brother, pleading with them. "We will die if we do not find food soon. The others—they will die, too!"

"Quiet, Maria," her mother whispers, looking around fearfully. "The city will kill us if we go there!"

"She's right, Mama," the son says next. "We cannot survive. Three have died from starvation already."

"Would you rather starve or be taken by one of them?" The mother's eyes are filled with tears as she speaks. Her children stare back at her, unblinking.

"Come." The mother pulls her shawl closer and takes her children's hands. "We will search this way. Perhaps we missed a house last week."

Trudging on, the trio winds their way along the edge of the city. Hours pass as they search, until finally there is a cause for celebration. A small collection of tins is discovered. Carrots are passed around and devoured, filling their starving bellies just enough to give them hope. The remaining tins are tucked away, saved for the rest of the group when they return.

"Come, it's getting dark." The mother looks to the sky, worry etched on her craggy features. "Let's get back."

The hope that has filled them is dashed as they exit the last house. The mother is the first to spot them: seven of the demons, lined up in a semi-circle around the fence. They are more terrifying in the light than they are in the dark. The mother screams, trying to push her children back into the house. The creatures stop her, pinning her to the ground. Two of them grab her children and force them down. The creatures inspect the three people carefully before making their selection.

The mother screams as her eldest child is lifted by one of the creatures and carried off. He shouts and kicks at the creature carrying him, but it is to no avail. The other six surround it, escorting it and its live cargo up to the north, to the factory that spews smoke and flame. Maria holds her mother tightly, fighting against the tears.

"Hurry, Mama," she whispers, "before they come back."

The pair make their way to an apartment building on the outskirts of town. The building is barricaded; all of the windows are blocked and the doors are sealed. A pair of men holding guns and shivering in the cold let them in. Inside, the mother tearfully recounts the tale to the other survivors. They offer her what small comfort they can while dividing the pitifully few tins of food amongst themselves.

"We cannot keep living like this." A tall man wearing a long overcoat and pants with military camouflage steps forward. "Those things have taken dozens of us. I heard last night that they've been going as far out as the farms. We have to stop this!"

The others in the room mumble words of agreement. Maria is the only one to stand. She speaks forcefully, her eyes still red from tears. "How can we stop them? They are too fast, too powerful—there are too many of them!"

"Then we take the fight to them."

"Where?" She is ferocious, advanced beyond her years. In the strange new world she has to be. "How can we fight devils that can see in the dark and steal us from our beds?" More murmurs. An elderly woman crosses herself.

"We kill them at the factory grounds." No more murmurs. The man's statement is met with an explosion of sound.

"Impossible!"

"We'd be killed!"

"The radiation would turn us into those things!"

The man raises his hands and waits for the noise to die down. When the room is quiet, he picks up a small device from the floor and turns it on. "This is a radiation detector. A Geiger counter. I spent the entire day in the city. There isn't a speck of radiation anywhere. Not even in the blast areas. None of us show any signs of radiation, either. Look for yourselves!"

The man tosses the device to Maria, who looks at it in shock. She is young, but not too young to understand the implication.

"As for the creatures," the man continues, "we are through with hiding." He pulls back a brown piece of cloth that covers a pile of objects in the corner. Brass, wood and steel stare out, glistening in the low light. "Boris and Alexei helped me gather these from the armory today. Starting tonight, every one of us will be armed. We will not cower here any longer, starving and dying." The man picks up a rifle from the pile and hands it to Maria.

"Each one of us, so long as they can hold a gun, shall fight. The rest will go into the city, to a secure location, to wait for our victory in safety."

Maria stares at the man, absorbing his every word. Her eyes are still red, but she carries more than just pain in them. For the first time in weeks she carries something else. Hope.

Chapter Eight

THE ARKHANGELSK

Nancy paced back and forth on the sub, twisting the long microphone cable as she spoke. She racked her brain, trying to think of what they should do next. "Should we just abort? I can have a team on shore to meet you within the hour."

In the background she heard the muffled sound of Krylov saying "no," then Leonard replied. "Is that transmission still going?"

Nancy glanced at the communications officer, who nodded. "Still alive, strong and not responding to anything we send back."

"Then we keep going." Leonard's voice sounded weary. "Do whatever you can to draw their attention. These things learn and adapt, so you may need to be creative."

"Will do. Stay safe, Leonard. Arkhangelsk out."

Nancy slammed the transmitter into its cradle and lowered her head for a few seconds, then slammed her hand against the table. "Dammit!" The three-dimensional map displayed on the table flickered in response to the abuse.

"Ma'am?" Nikolay stepped up beside her. "What can we do to help them?"

"I don't know, Nikolay. They're holed up in a church right now. The muties don't seem keen on falling for our tricks again."

"Then what do we do?"

Nancy sighed and sat down in her seat, putting her head in one hand and staring off into space.

"Ma'am?" he persisted.

"I don't know. Do you have any suggestions?"

"Well." He began pacing, mimicking Nancy's movements from only a few moments earlier. "The creatures won't respond to any more explosions, and it's likely—based on what you, Mr. McComb and Mr. Warden have said—that they won't fall for anything similar, either."

"No chance."

"So what we need to do is create a diversion somewhere else."

Nancy looked up at Nikolay and started shaking her head slowly. "Oh no. You're not going to suggest what I think you're going to suggest. Are you?"

Nikolay stopped pacing and straightened his back. "Although Commander Krylov gave us orders not to send anyone else ashore, I believe that our only course of action would be to go ashore and divert the attention of the creatures there."

"How can you possibly think that's a good idea?" Nancy's tone was incredulous, but in the back of her mind, she was cheering Nikolay on, hoping that he would give her something to justify taking action.

Nikolay shrugged. "You are the acting commander of this vessel, ma'am. Our rescue team is in grave danger. If we can do nothing else from this distance, then we must change tactics and adapt to our enemy."

Nancy stroked her chin as she squinted one eye at Nikolay. He was a wily one, she would give him that, but she wasn't about to endanger the Arkhangelsk and her remaining crew without taking every possible precaution.

She got up and walked to the sonar station and spoke in a quiet voice to the technician. "How accurately can you map the underwater features if we were to get closer to shore?"

The tech glanced at her with wide eyes, then blinked a few times and regained his composure. "We can get meter-wide resolution, if we move slowly enough."

"What about the cameras?"

"This water is just too murky for them to see anything, ma'am."

"Do you have maps of the underwater environment here?"

"Of course. But they are old and outdated. With the amount of debris we've seen even this far out, I would not trust them with my life."

"Hmm." Nancy stepped away and mused. "Nikolay, what depth can we sail through while running on the surface?"

"Twelve meters, ma'am. Just under forty feet."

"Hmm." Nancy hung her arms on the periscope handles and watched through the viewfinder. The port was clearly visible, as most of the smoke from the destroyed ship had cleared. The sun was setting behind the Arkhangelsk, offering an unobstructed view. Nancy flicked the magnification on the viewfinder to its maximum level and began to slowly scan the area.

On the far left of her view, near where the rescue team had landed, stood a variety of large tanks. Tracing the path of the pipes from the tanks to the right, toward the port, the number of buildings gradually increased until the first pier appeared where the smoldering wreck of the ship they'd destroyed was located. She continued scanning the port and city immediately beyond, looking for anything that could possibly be used as a distraction.

Nikolay stepped up next to her and spoke in a soft voice. "What are you looking for, ma'am?"

"I'm not entirely sure yet. It'll need to be something we can use as a tool to draw the attention of the muties, though."

"Ma'am?" He cocked an eyebrow and frowned. "We have no ordinance onboard that can hit a target on land. Why not launch another torpedo?"

Nancy kept her eyes glued to the viewfinder as she talked. "Muties are smart, Nikolay, you know that. They aren't going to fall for a second trick like that again. We already established that. Besides, even if we wanted to destroy another ship, there aren't any that are left that would do more than fizzle in the water.

"No, we need something on land. Something for them to chase. Something..." Nancy's eyes widened as she reached the far south end of the docks and port. "Something like that."

Nancy stepped back from the periscope and motioned for Nikolay to look. He peered through and scanned the area. A small train depot was located at the southern end of the docks, used for transporting goods throughout the region. Boxcars and pieces of locomotives were scattered about the yard, rusted and dilapidated, but there was one object still left on the track that looked like it had just rolled off the assembly line.

"A train?" Nikolay raised both eyebrows and stepped back to stare at Nancy. "You want to... destroy a train?"

"Not destroy it. Well, maybe. If we have to. But no, I want to do something far better." Nancy's grin was wider than she had intended, and she realized that she was finally enjoying herself on the Arkhangelsk for the first time since the mission had started.

"Should I make a call to the team?"

"No!" Nancy practically lunged toward the transmitter that Nikolay was reaching for. "No, no that... that wouldn't be the best idea."

He raised an eyebrow. "Ms. Sims? Is everything all right?"

"Oh yes. Everything's great. It's just... Marcus kind of has a thing about trains. After... well, you know the story."

"Ah. I see. And you think he would disagree with this decision?"

"Maybe? Look, I'm all ears if you have a better idea. But that thing looks brand new. Chances are that the swarms repaired it just like they repaired the ones back in the States. If they did, then it's going to start up and make a hell of a lot of noise. It should be more than enough to get the creatures pulled out of the city."

Nikolay nodded slowly. "It seems... foolish. But our options are limited and time is running short."

"Exactly." Nancy sighed and looked back through the viewfinder. "But you know what... let's do one more thing, just as a backup. In case this doesn't work."

"Ma'am?"

Nancy stood up straight and took on a formal tone. "Mr. Sokolov, take us in to the port. Be quick about it, but once we get in close enough for the depth to be a problem, cut the speed and start using the old maps along with sonar to get a picture of what's down there."

Nikolay's eyebrow shot up and Nancy glanced at him. "You heard me. We're getting in close. Pass the orders along, then have Andrey and Sergei meet us here to devise a plan. I'm done sitting on my ass on this boat. We're going to give our rescue team the distraction they need no matter what."

Nikolay gave the orders, then called out over the boat's intercom. Andrey and Sergei arrived at the con a few minutes later, both wiping their mouths and brushing crumbs from the front of their shirts.

"Ma'am?" Sergei, the older of the two cousins, nodded at Nancy. "You wanted to see us?"

"That I did. We have a bit of a situation going on. Commander Krylov's team is in trouble. Our little distraction wasn't enough, and we need to up the ante." A mischievous twinkle appeared in Nancy's eye. "How would you boys like to cause a little ruckus on shore?"

"But, I thought Commander Krylov said—"

"Commander Krylov left me in charge. You let me worry about what he said." Nancy motioned to the table, and the four of them stood around it. She brought up a map of the city and zeroed in on a point near the center.

"They're trapped in this church right now with muties roaming the streets searching for them. You know it's only a matter of time before they're found, and their only real shot is if we manage to get the attention of those things again."

Sergei glanced at his cousin Andrey and the two men nodded and spoke in unison. "How can we help?"

"There's nothing left on the water that's going to make enough noise to attract the muties again. They wouldn't even fall for something like that again if we had a target. The only way we're going to get them off the scent of the rescue team is if we give them a nice big target."

"Us?"

"Exactly." Nancy moved the map to display the port. "There's a train depot here at the south end of the port. Most of the locomotives and boxcars there have long since been destroyed. Except, apparently, for one. There's a shiny new train sitting right on the tracks that's ripe for the picking. Based on the behavior of the swarms back home, it's very likely that this thing is ready to go."

The two soldiers were staring at the map as Andrey spoke. "So you want us to go ashore, get the train and then what?"

"Run it straight out of town. The tracks look good on the latest satellite images we have of the area, so you should be able to get at least a mile or two out without any issue. You can then ditch the train, circle back around, get the inflatable and get back to us."

"And what if it doesn't work?"

"Then you blow it to high hell, along with the depot and anything else you can find there that might be flammable. If that doesn't work, strip down, grease yourselves up, start shooting into the air and try to find some air horns." The two men looked at her with confused expressions, and she rolled her eyes. "That last bit was a joke."

They relaxed and Sergei spoke. "Understood. We can handle this, ma'am. No problem."

"Good. You've got about—say, Nikolay, how long will it take us to get in close?"

"One and a half, maybe two hours, if we're being safe."

Nancy grinned. "Good. Have someone get the other inflatable ready to go. Once we're as close as comfortably possible, I want them deployed for the shore. We don't have much time."

Nikolay gave a quick salute. "On it!" He turned and began shouting orders.

Nancy spoke to Sergei and Andrey again. "You two make sure you have everything you need for a stay. My plan is to have you in and out in a short amount of time, but if something happens, you'll need to be able to survive out there for a while."

"No problem, ma'am. We'll handle it."

"Good." Nancy touched both men on the shoulder and lowered her voice. "I remember what you did back in Panama, along with all the other missions you were on. I wouldn't ask you to do this if I didn't have complete confidence in you both."

Andrey and Sergei nodded with appreciation and left the control deck, running for the armory. Nancy leaned against the wall and sighed, lost in her thoughts for a few precious seconds. *Has it really been over a year since we first stepped foot on this old thing?* Nancy and Leonard had been rescued by the Arkhangelsk in Alaska, and had managed to convince Commander Krylov to sail for the Gulf of Mexico to aid in the destruction of the AI.

Reaching the Gulf in a timely manner had meant passing through the newly constructed replacement to the Panama Canal. On their way through the canal, Andrey and Sergei had been tasked with planting explosives on multiple bridges that stretched over the canal to help stem the flow of mutants. The pair had nearly died multiple times during their attempt, but ultimately, they had come out on top, helping to stem the flow of mutants and ensuring that the Arkhangelsk could pass through the canal without incident.

Their actions had earned them accolades from the entire crew, and their bravery had been tested repeatedly, most notably during missions they took part in along the Eastern Seaboard of the United States and in several search and rescue missions in South America. Nancy could think of no better soldiers to carry out the mission she had in mind.

"Nikolay, I'm going to get something to eat. Call me when we're close?"

"Yes, ma'am."

Nancy left the con, heading for the galley. The menu featured creamed corn, some sort of bean casserole and a lump of grey matter that smelled like chicken. It wasn't the best, but she dug in, not realizing until she was halfway through that she hadn't eaten in the last day. A combination of non-stop stress and pacing the room without rest had taken its toll. After she finished, she sat back in her chair and stared into space, slowly drifting off to sleep.

"Ms. Sims, please come in." The ship-wide intercom blasted through Nancy's thoughts. She ran to a nearby box and answered.

"Nancy here. What is it?"

"Mr. Sokolov asked us to inform you of our progress at regular intervals. We're closing in on the port. At our current speed, we'll be a few hundred meters off shore within the next thirty minutes. That's our maximum estimated range before we'll have to stop and start scanning the bottom."

"Understood. I'll be on deck shortly; if you need me, I'll have a radio."

"Yes, ma'am."

Nancy stood up, stretched and headed to the armory, where Sergei and Andrey were busy gearing up for their mission. She grabbed a jacket and radio, tossed on the jacket and affixed the radio to the front with a clip before zipping the garment up.

"Are you two ready?"

The cousins glanced up at her as they stuffed small packs of plastic explosives and extra mags of ammunition into their packs. "Just a few more minutes, Ms. Sims."

"Excellent. Meet me on the deck when you're done. And remember
—see if you can get it moving. That's the priority here. Only destroy it
if absolutely necessary."

Sergei nodded, and Nancy bounded out of the armory and ran
down the corridor toward one of the main ladders to the upper deck.
The bitingly cold wind that blew down the corridor told her that
Nikolay was already up top, helping to get the inflatable ready to go.
Nancy couldn't help smiling as she climbed the ladder. She was, techni-
cally, disobeying what Krylov had told her. *On the other hand*, she
thought, *I'm finally getting off my ass and helping.*

On the deck of the Arkhangelsk, the wind and waves clawed at
Nancy's face. She pulled the jacket tighter as she walked down the
length of the deck to where the inflatable was being prepared.

"Is everything ready?" she shouted over the noise of the wind and
water.

"Just waiting on the team. Everything else is ready to go!"

Nancy looked back at the sail and saw two figures dressed in black
climb out of a hatch. The size of the Arkhangelsk made them look like
toys being battered about by a gust of wind. She raised a hand and
shouted at them as they approached, each carrying a weapon in one
hand and a large backpack in the other.

"Are you two ready to go?"

Andrey threw her a grin and raised his rifle. "Ready to save the day,
ma'am."

Nancy smiled. "Get going, then! You don't have long! Radio us
with updates on your progress as often as you can."

The two men tossed their packs into the inflatable, then secured
their rifles on their backs. Nancy watched as they loaded everything up,
then she jumped in surprise as the radio in her pocket flared to life.

"Ms. Sims? Control here. We have a transmission from shore."

Nancy glanced around. "Dammit! Fine, put them through."

Nancy waved at the two soldiers in the inflatable and then cupped
her hand around the radio, trying in vain to minimize the noise as she
spoke.

"Commander? Nancy here. I was just getting ready to call you. I
think we've found the answer to your distraction problem!" The inflat-

able's engine fired up, and Nancy broke into a run across the deck, trying to get away from the source of the sound.

"Ms. Sims? What do you mean?"

Oh damn, she thought, *he's going to be pissed.*

"Can't explain right now, Commander!" she shouted, trying to drown out the sound of the waves and wind as she ran. "I just need you to get your asses moving. Your distraction is going to be up in about fifteen minutes, and it's going to be loud as hell!" Nancy reached the hatch and stepped into it, then tripped and fell, dropping the radio down into the ship. She cursed loudly and hurried down the ladder, then picked up the cracked radio and gingerly turned it off before she could make out what Krylov was saying.

"Come on, boys," she mumbled, looking up the ladder into the sky beyond, "don't make me into a liar."

On the inflatable, Andrey sat low in the front, clutching his rifle to his chest. The flimsy clear goggles he wore barely protected his eyes against the spray of the water, and he struggled to see where they were going. Behind him, Sergei sat at the outboard, clutching the controls with both hands as he fought to keep the craft on a straight course.

"Hard right!" Andrey yelled out, and Sergei slammed the inflatable to the right, barely missing a jagged spire of rusted metal that loomed out of the water.

"Hard left!" The craft skidded left to avoid the half-sunken wreck of a small ship.

"Throttle it back; we're getting into the shallows."

Sergei eased off the throttle and the inflatable slowed to a crawl. The water shined in the light of the fading sun as it reflected off of the oil on the surface, leaking from some underwater wreckage. Bits of debris bobbed in the surf, caught in the currents and doomed to endlessly float in the bay.

"There!" Andrey pointed at a short patch of sand in between two of the largest piers. "We'll land there and tie up. It should only be a few minutes to the depot."

When the inflatable hit the beach, Andrey already had his pack on. He jumped out and held on to the craft while Sergei grabbed his pack and jumped out. Both men hauled the light craft across the sand and secured it to a piling above the tideline.

Sergei checked his watch. "Ten minutes left. Let's move."

Both men took off at a sprint across the sand, scrub and gravel. The depot was quite close to the port, and the rail line ran along the length of the port and followed the curve of the land to the west once out of the city. The train that Nancy had described to them was already on the tracks and appeared—from a distance, at least—like it was ready to roll at a moment's notice.

Three minutes later, the pair arrived at the depot. Sitting on the tracks, surrounded by piles of rusted parts, was the shining black form of an M62 diesel locomotive. A staple of the Eastern Bloc, the M62 was first manufactured in 1965, and quickly grew to be a reliable and common sight on freight lines. With a small control cab and simplistic controls, the M62 was easy to operate, even for those without experience in handling locomotives.

Andrey climbed up to the small step leading to the cab of the train and peeked inside while Sergei stayed on the ground, crouching next to the train and keeping his eyes open for any signs of danger. The interior of the cab was clear, and Andrey moved inside to examine the controls. The startup switches and knobs were all self-explanatory, and he quickly engaged all of them. Within seconds, the deep throb of the diesel engine started up, and he smiled.

Andrey peeked his head out of the cab and motioned at his cousin, who took the proffered hand to quickly climb up the side of the locomotive. Once inside, the two men glanced at each other.

"Ready?" Andrey said, his hand on the large circular throttle control. Sergei nodded and Andrey turned the wheel slowly through the first two positions. The engine's pitch changed and the locomotive started moving slowly down the track. From inside the cab the sound of the engine was loud, but from the outside it was even more so. The deep throaty roar carried for miles through the empty city, echoing off of the streets and buildings.

In the dark corners of the city, the engine's vibrations called out to the creatures. Their priorities immediately shifted from hunting down the new intruders in the city to finding the source of the new sound. They knew precisely what it was, of course. They had, after all, used the locomotive countless times. Upon hearing it, they reached out to the others and posed the same question to every creature and trace of nanobot left in the city: is this us? The answer came back the same each and every time: no.

"Can't we move any faster?" Sergei asked, looking out the windows of the cab toward the city. He held his rifle loosely, tapping one finger on the side of the trigger guard with impatience and nervousness. "If they show up now, we'll have no chance!"

"I'm trying." Andrey twisted the throttle again to push it to the next setting. The engine's pitch changed again, and the bulky vehicle lurched slightly, gaining more speed and momentum. When the locomotive emerged from the group of buildings where the track came to an end, Andrey reached for the pull cord for the horn on the right wall of the cabin and gave it a tug. The first blow wasn't impressive, but once the air pressure built up for the second tug, the shrill horn echoed out like a knife.

If the sound of the locomotive's engine had merely piqued the curiosity of the creatures, the horn turned that curiosity into a full-blown investigation. The hive mind of the creatures summoned each and every one of them to hunt down whatever was in the train, and they did so with great fervor and intensity.

Watching out the window while Andrey kept an eye on the controls, Sergei kept scanning the city, looking for any signs of movement. It took a few minutes for what he was looking for to appear, but when it did, it came all at once. Hundreds of creatures flowed down three streets and burst out onto the open areas that separated the train tracks from the city. The creatures moved like a wave, slamming into each other and obstacles that were in their way, but still inexorably heading for the locomotive.

"Get us out of here!" Sergei shouted. Andrey glanced over his shoulder, and his eyes widened in panic as he saw the creatures charging at them.

"Working on it!" Andrey twisted the throttle control to the maximum possible setting. The engine screamed in protest, and the train again surged forward, clacking along the tracks. With no boxcars hooked up, the locomotive was surprisingly speedy, and had already reached the other end of the port. The path ahead wound along the coast and through the mountainous terrain where the soldiers hoped to lose the creatures.

As he watched the mutants through the back window drawing steadily nearer, Sergei thought—for a moment—that they would outrun them. Ahead of them the road turned into a bridge that crossed over a river, at which point it began to divert inland. If they could get ahead of the creatures enough, he thought, they could bail out of the train and let the creatures chase it for miles.

It was at that precise moment that two separate events took place. First, Sergei suddenly wondered why all of the creatures were slowing down. The speed of the locomotive hadn't increased all that much in the last several seconds, but he could see that the creatures were running slowly while almost seeming to try to give the appearance of still being hotly in pursuit.

What are they doing? he wondered, then he began to turn to tell his cousin about the strange sight.

At the same time, Andrey happened to glance off to the right, up at a hill that was rising next to the train. At the top of the hill were some old microwave radio antennas along with a few buildings. What concerned him, though, were the two massive shapes lumbering down the hill, heading for the locomotive at a tremendous speed.

"What in the—" Andrey didn't get a chance to finish his sentence. The two shapes emerged from the shadows at the base of the hill and slammed into the side of the train just before it hit the bridge. The impact sent the train teetering over on its side, and the two soldiers struggled to hold onto anything to avoid being flung across the cab. As the train slammed back down on the track, the men thought that it would stabilize. The two massive creatures, however, were still on board. They clung to the outside of the locomotive, digging their massive silvered claws into the metal and growling with a ferocity that terrified the soldiers more than the movements of the locomotive ever could.

The weight of the creatures pulled the train over on its side, sending Sergei and Andrey tumbling head over heels inside the cab. If the locomotive had been on the ground instead of on a bridge, the movement would have stopped there, but it instead smashed through the concrete and metal rail of the bridge and toppled thirty feet below. The locomotive hit the river and bounced down the slope, its momentum causing it to roll several times before coming to a halt.

No longer gleaming like it had just rolled out of the factory, the locomotive was damaged beyond repair. The engine sputtered and coughed a few more times before it grew silent. The enormous vehicle lay lengthwise across the small river in a foot and a half of water, the last few rays of the fading sun glinting off of the steel as the evening turned to complete darkness. Above, in the shadows, crowded around the edge of the bridge, stood the army of creatures. They watched the locomotive carefully for a great length of time, each pair of silvered eyes studying it, waiting to see any signs of heat or movement, but there were none forthcoming.

Chapter Nine

"Leonard. Leonard? Hey Leonard, you awake?" Marcus shook Leonard's shoulder. Leonard glanced up at Marcus and nodded slowly.

"Yeah."

"You good?"

"No." Leonard shook his head this time. "Not at all."

Marcus stepped away from the window of the building they were resting in and sat down next to Leonard. After leaving the disturbing contents of the storefronts behind, the group had continued on through the city. Krylov, upon seeing that Leonard was in rough shape, had taken the lead. When they'd arrived at a location near to where Krylov thought the metro station should be, he'd left Leonard, Marcus and Mikhail to rest in a nearby building while he and Roman went out to scout the area. Leonard sat in a back corner of one of the front rooms and stared out the window whilst not saying a word.

"You want to talk about it?" Marcus probed gently.

"What's to talk about? They were kids, Marcus." Leonard looked him in the eyes. "Kids of all ages. All types. They weren't just creatures —they were children."

"No." Marcus put his hand on Leonard's arm to steady the sudden shaking. "No, they weren't. You've told me this countless times before;

they aren't people anymore. Whatever was in them that used to be human vanished the instant the swarms got to them."

"These were different, Marcus."

"How? We've seen this kind of thing before. It's disgusting and sickening, but this isn't the first time. I remember your stories about the first time you saw them, when they attacked you and Nancy."

"Have you ever seen them like that, though? All settled down?" Leonard's brow furrowed. "It was like… like they were sleeping. Like they were normal people, not muties."

"But they were."

"No, Marcus, that's not the point."

"What, then?"

Leonard sighed. "I don't know. It's just—something's wrong in this city. Everything is wrong. The bodies in the factory, the animals, the… the small ones. The swarms infected and moved on, or at least that's all we've ever seen them do. We've never seen something like this."

Marcus shifted position on the floor and glanced over at Mikhail, who had taken watch at the window. Mikhail looked back at Marcus and shrugged, then resumed his watch. *Damn*, Marcus thought, *where is Krylov? He wasn't supposed to be gone this long.*

"Okay, Leonard, I'll bite. What do you think is going on here? Take your best guess."

"The end result? I have no idea. But based on everything I've seen so far—and this is going to sound insane—it almost looks like they're building some kind of society here."

"A society?" Marcus had to stifle a laugh. "The AI? Forming a society? Are you serious?"

"Like I said, it sounds insane. We've never seen anything like this before. But look at it without all that prior knowledge. They're trying to improve themselves. They've infected animals and are using them as part of their hunting. They're caring for the young, both animal and human alike."

Marcus's half-laugh froze on his face and quietly melted away. "I must be going insane, because that almost makes sense."

Leonard nodded. "You see why this is bothering me so much? Who knows what those things were. I mean sure, the chances that they're anything but infected muties is miniscule. But what if they were the first generation of something different? Or what if they were only partially infected, and were hiding there?"

"That's…" Marcus coughed and tried to sound sure of himself. "That's crazy."

"I know. But everything in this city is crazy."

Marcus and Leonard sat in silence for several more minutes as they each processed the conversation. After a while, Marcus patted Leonard on the arm and spoke again. "I don't know if any of what you're thinking is true, but even if it is, you still did the right thing."

"I know. But it never gets any easier, does it?"

Marcus stood up and held out his hand. Leonard grabbed it and rose to his feet, then they stood together for a second looking eye to eye.

"No. But that's why we have each other's backs." Marcus embraced Leonard and patted his back, then turned to Mikhail. "Still no sign of Krylov?"

"None. I am beginning to think we should go to looking for him." Mikhail's English was good, but a few misplaced words still snuck in here and there.

Marcus nodded. "Right. Probably not a bad idea at this point. Leonard, you okay to go?"

Leonard held a thumb up as he tightened the straps on his backpack.

"Okay, Mikhail, let's head out."

"Head out where?"

The voice from the back of the room made the trio jump. They all raised their guns and pointed it at the source, which emerged from one of the doors.

"It's me, gentlemen. Relax."

"Krylov, where the hell have you been?" Marcus's adrenaline was still pumping as he lowered his gun and stormed forward to help the commander through the half-collapsed doorway.

Out of breath, Krylov sat down and took several deep breaths before replying. "We ran into trouble. Some of those things are still lurking about."

Marcus's frustration with being startled evaporated when he realized that Roman wasn't with Krylov. His feeling of dread was shared by Mikhail, who called out from across the room.

"Where's—"

"He's fine. He is continuing the scouting. I came back here to get you all. I believe we located an entrance that will get us into the section of the metro system where the survivors are, but we cannot linger here. I fear that the creatures will soon turn their attention away from whatever scheme Ms. Sims devised and back toward us."

Leonard and Marcus helped Krylov to his feet, and Marcus noticed him wincing. "Are you okay?"

Krylov pushed his jacket aside and pulled up his shirt to reveal several deep gashes across the front of his chest. "As I said, we ran into trouble. Nothing that we couldn't handle, of course." Krylov glanced at Leonard, eying him up and down. "How are you doing, Mr. McComb?"

Leonard clapped Krylov on the shoulder. "Better, thank you, my friend. I'll be much better once we find these survivors, though. Did you see any signs of them?"

Krylov shook his head. "No. Nothing. Has there been any response to short-range radio broadcasts?"

Marcus shrugged his shoulders. "I've been calling on every frequency. If they're listening to us, they either can't respond, or they don't want to. Their broadcast is still going, though, so something's still powering it."

"Then we may yet be in time. How they have survived for this long, I do not know."

Leonard raised an eyebrow. "I thought you said these people were tough."

"So they are, Mr. McComb. So they are. But in a place like this, toughness isn't always enough."

Krylov extended the EMP cannon to Leonard. "Are you good?"

Leonard nodded and took the rifle. "As good as I'll be. Let's get moving."

The commander nodded and peeked out the front window, scanning the street up and down. "I came in through the back of the building, because I noticed movement along the street out here. There's nothing out there now, but it would be wise to exit through the back entrance."

"After you." Leonard motioned for Krylov to lead, then followed him. Marcus and Mikhail trailed behind, each of them taking care when moving through the back doorway to avoid collapsing it further. The building they had sought refuge in was small, and though its original purpose had been lost, it was situated with a perfect view down the street where Krylov had indicated the metro entrance lay. After sneaking out the back, Krylov and Leonard walked side-by-side, with Marcus and Mikhail doubling up on the rear.

Leaving the older part of the city behind, the group passed into the parts that had been constructed in more recent history. The streets—cracked and showing signs of years of age—suddenly turned near-pristine, except for the damage and debris from the bombs. The buildings were different as well, constructed more of steel than of cinderblock and brick. The majority of the windows had been blown out, but there were still some that, like those in the cathedral, were shielded enough from the blasts to remain intact.

As the group proceeded down the street, the area opened up into a large intersection. This section of the city had been part of the new construction and had served as the bridge between the western and eastern portions. The intersection consisted of a large square with several government buildings in the middle that were surrounded by crisscrossing streets, pedestrian walkways and four metro entrances, one on each side of the square.

As the group approached the edge of the square, Krylov held up a hand to stop them. They crouched alongside a rising arch of concrete that served primarily as a decorative backdrop. A bright mural—barely visible in the dark—was painted on the side of the arch, depicting an archetypical soviet scene with workers and great fields of crops.

"Which of the entrances do we use?" Leonard asked. Two of the metro entrances in the square were visible from their location.

"Neither," Krylov replied, then swiveled around on his heels. "Come. This way." Built into the mural wall was a steel door—colored to blend in with the painting—with no knob. The only thing indicating that it was a door at all were the small slits in the metal at the top and bottom of the door and the thin outline of the frame.

Krylov knocked twice on the door and waited. From inside the arch came scuffling sounds, then a knock in reply. Krylov stood up and moved back from the door, as did the others. The door swung outwards a second later, and Roman appeared, his form partially illuminated by a light from somewhere past the door.

Roman looked out into the square nervously, then at Krylov. "Did they follow you?"

"No." Krylov shook his head. "But get inside quickly. Who knows what's watching us out here." Mikhail, Marcus and Leonard stepped inside as Roman moved out of the way. Krylov came in last, taking one long last look at the square and surrounding city. He glanced up to the cloudless sky, drinking in the richness of the stars and moon before retreating inside the arch and gently pulling the door closed.

Directly inside the door, the room was small and uncomfortable, with a low angled ceiling that followed the curve of the arch. A few meters along the arch, the room abruptly stopped and a long metal staircase began. It was on this staircase that the light source rested. Once everyone was inside, Roman grabbed his flashlight and stood in front of Krylov to give him a report.

"What else did you find?"

"Nothing, sir. The paths down there are long and winding. Some of the ones that the maps show leading one way seem to go another. Many are blocked. Some don't exist at all."

"Do you still think we can reach the location?"

"It's our best shot, Commander. The four main entrances have been completely sealed. It would take heavy equipment and weeks of work to clear them."

"Any sign of survivors?"

"Not a trace."

Krylov sighed. "Damn. Very well, then. Is everyone ready?"

Leonard leaned over the stairs and pointed the EMP cannon into the darkness, illuminating it with the rifle's flashlight. He raised an eyebrow and turned to Krylov. "I don't know about you, but I *hate* wandering around the underground. Are you sure none of the main entrances will work?"

"It's impossible, sir." Roman replied before Krylov could. "We checked each one thoroughly."

"Lovely." Leonard sighed and shook his head. "No sense in wasting time, then. Let's get to it. Who's leading us on this underground romp?"

Krylov nudged Roman. "You take the lead. Leonard will follow."

As the five men grouped together to prepare to descend the stairs, Krylov noticed movement out of the corner of his eye. He turned slowly toward the closed door and watched the ventilation slits at the bottom of it. In the dimmest light of the moon that came through the slits, he could see, with a rising horror, that there were shadows moving back and forth. As the other four checked their weapons and spoke quietly amongst themselves, Krylov shuffled closer to the door and raised his weapon.

The attack came with no further warning. Though the door swung outwards from inside the arch, it bowed inward under the force of the initial blow. Two large dents appeared in the middle of the steel as it sagged in on itself, nearly torn from its hinges by the force. An ear-splitting howl was followed by the door being wrenched and flung into the darkness of the square beyond.

Krylov hadn't had time to move, and the others barely had time to turn their heads, before the next assault arrived. Two of the creatures attempted to push their way into the room at the same time, only to be stymied by the narrowness of the entry. Instead of plowing into Krylov, as had been their intention, they merely fell to the floor, writhing and grasping for a handhold to pick themselves up. For all of his exhaustion, Leonard was the first to respond as he raised the EMP cannon and fired blindly at the creatures. The invisible waves turned the snarling creatures into balls of flames in an instant, and Krylov threw his hands up to shield his eyes as Mikhail pulled him away from the door.

"Move!" Marcus thundered, then pushed Roman, Mikhail and Krylov toward the stairs. Standing next to Leonard, Marcus fired several shots into the creatures to ensure their demise. The next assault was not as clumsy as the first, however, and another pair of creatures appeared in the door, one following directly behind the other. Like the first pair, these two were also human, a man and a woman, and both fell to Leonard and Marcus' combined fire.

"Get down here, you two! Hurry!" Krylov's voice bellowed from down the stairs. Marcus and Leonard both stepped backward cautiously for fear of falling, then Marcus reached back and grabbed the rail of the staircase with one hand and put his foot on the top step.

"Come on Leonard, get down some more; I'll cover you!"

Leonard turned and dashed down several steps until he was at eye level with the floor. Another creature dashed through the door, rolling and tumbling over the bodies of its comrades in an effort to dodge any shots. As Marcus turned to head down the stairs as well, Leonard fired on the creature, and it fell to the floor, its body writhing and smoking. Falling back in their staggered fashion, Marcus and Leonard soon reached the bottom of the staircase. Creatures continued advancing down the stairs, doing their best to avoid being killed, but the tight confines of the small room and the narrow stairs made it easy for Leonard and Marcus to eliminate them.

"Now what?" Leonard shouted at Krylov as Marcus fired a burst from his weapon.

"This!" Krylov held aloft a small black device with a button on the top and a rubber-covered piece of metal sticking out of the bottom. He squeezed the handle on the device and pressed the button. The explosives that Roman had planted in the room at the top of the stairs detonated, blowing a hole in the top of the arch and sending plumes of dust into the sky and down into the faces of the rescue team. Huge chunks of debris fell onto the stairs, and within a matter of seconds, the path was blocked.

Unprepared for the explosion, Marcus and Leonard coughed in the dust as their ears rang from the noise. After several seconds, the shaking flashlight beams in the darkness were replaced by a steadier, brighter source as Krylov pulled a small electric lantern from his pack and placed it on the floor.

"Krylov," Marcus said, choking out the words in between fits of coughing, "if you ever do that again without telling us first, I'm going to make sure the creatures don't find enough intact bits of you to experiment with!"

Krylov's white teeth shone bright in the light of the lantern as he smiled and slapped Marcus on the back. "I am sorry, my friend. I had Mr. Lebedev place explosives at the entrance in case we ran into trouble. I was about to tell you, but those bastards attacked us before I had a chance."

"Oh, don't get me wrong, it was fantastic." Marcus looked over at the pile of debris that covered all but the last few steps. "I'd just rather get some warning next time before the ceiling collapses in on me."

"Yeah," Leonard gasped, "me, too. Nice work, though, except now we don't have an exit."

"One thing at a time, my friends. For now, let's take some solace in the fact that we are safe."

"For now," Marcus mumbled under his breath as he pulled out a pair of water bottles, passing one to Leonard.

Leonard drained the water and tossed the empty bottle aside. The echo of the noise carried far into the distance, and Leonard suddenly realized that they were standing in an open area. "Krylov, where are we?"

Krylov picked up the lantern and directed their attention toward the chamber they stood in. "Gentlemen, welcome to the Magadan metro."

The bottom of the stairs emptied out into a small maintenance room that had double doors on the wall opposite the stairs. After retreating down the stairs, Marcus and Leonard had unknowingly passed through these open doors to where Krylov, Mikhail and Roman were waiting. While the contents of the maintenance room were impossible to see over the mounds of debris and dust that now covered them, the large chamber was clearly visible in the light of both their weapons' flashlights and Krylov's lantern, which he held aloft.

Russian metro stations were opulent more often than not, and the Magadan metro was no different. The station that the group stood in was enormous in width, depth and height. Light from Krylov's lantern sparkled on the ceiling as it refracted through several large chandeliers. All but one of these had fallen to the floor, scattering their glass and metal across the colorful tiles that lined the standing and seating areas. At least two dozen benches were arranged in rows in the station, facing the area where the metro trains arrived on a regular schedule.

Magadan was isolated in the country, but it had grown rapidly, and the local government coffers had been full enough to afford the installation of the metro with room to spare. As expansion into the surrounding countryside had grown over the years, the city had become a hub of commerce and trade. To say the metro had been unnecessary for the area was an understatement, but the local government had hoped that its installation would elevate the opinion of the city and future-proof it against the inevitable population boom.

The number of riders in the metro had been relatively low—a few thousand per day, at most—so the trains had only run heavily during the evening and morning hours. The bombs had fallen in the late morning when most people had been at work, and the number of riders had been at its lowest point. If any survivors had been in the tunnels when the two bombs had hit the city, it was unlikely that they would have survived the metro train crashes.

The government was no fool, though. The well-known secret of the first Russian metros was that they served the dual purpose of transportation and acting as a fallout shelter in the case of nuclear war. Magadan's metro, while not built to the same specifications as the one underneath Moscow, was nonetheless soundly constructed. Aside from the damage done by the trains as they had sped out of control and eventually crashed, the tunnels and stations had stood up remarkably well. It made sense, then, that the survivors of the city would eventually congregate in the stations, though how they had survived for so long was still a mystery to Leonard, a fact that he brought up again with Krylov.

"Look, I know at this point you're tired of hearing this question, but I have to ask it again. Are you certain that there are people still here?" Leonard aimed his light around the room, illuminating the cracks and crevices as he started to slowly walk down the length of the station.

"Again, Mr. McComb, I do not know. But I am certain there were."

Leonard sighed. "Whatever you say. Can we reach the Arkhangelsk from here to give them an update?"

Krylov pulled out his radio and frowned. "I doubt it." He switched it on and began transmitting.

"Arkhangelsk, Arkhangelsk, this is Krylov. Do you copy? Over."

Static was the only response. The commander tried three more times, but each one had the same result: nothing.

"Damn." Marcus groaned. "So much for that."

"Well it's not like they could do anything to help us out right now." Leonard looked around at their surroundings again. "How much exploring did you and Roman do down here anyway, Krylov?"

"After we found this entrance, I returned almost immediately. While I was gone, Mr. Lebedev explored further." Krylov turned to the soldier. "Perhaps you can describe to us where you went?"

Roman stepped past Leonard and Marcus and began gesturing around the station. "This is one of the main hubs, which is good, since that means we can get around to most of the city from here. Or we could, if the tunnels weren't partially collapsed."

Leonard walked over to one of the fallen chandeliers and kicked at it with his boot. "From the bombs?"

"I don't believe so." Krylov's eyebrow went up at this and Roman continued. "The cave-ins of the tunnels are too precise to be caused by the bombs, neither of which impacted this local area. These chandeliers and some of the masonry damage was caused by them, though that's due more to the shoddy craftsmanship."

Leonard wandered as he spoke, exploring the area with his flashlight. "Why would someone cave in the tunnels? Were they trying to hide from something?"

Krylov nodded. "That would make sense, yes."

"But from what? Muties?" Leonard stopped and leaned out over the rails to peer down the tunnel. His light didn't extend far enough to see how long it was, but the mere thought of the tunnel made his skin crawl.

"Undoubtedly." Krylov turned to Roman. "How far into the system did you get before returning to the entrance?"

Roman motioned for the group to follow him and led them back to the maintenance room. The soldier pulled out a scrap of paper from his pocket and pointed at a large map of the metro lines that was painted on the back of the door of the maintenance room. Several lines extended in the various compass directions under the city, with the major arteries extending in the North/South and East/West directions. The smaller lines were ones that only ran twice a day, or were used primarily to ferry goods under the city. These crisscrossed the city, extending from one coast to the other and even going to the north beyond the factory complex.

Roman pointed a light at the map and glanced at the notes he had scribbled down on the piece of paper. "The main lines to the north are blocked by some of the metro trains just a few hundred meters from here, though we could probably press through. The tunnels to the south are completely blocked from a cave-in. The lines to the east and west, however, appear to be open. I went up and down those a fair distance and saw no signs of survivors."

Leonard waggled the beam of his light over the thin squiggles on the wall. "What about the maintenance and freight tunnels?"

"Those I have not investigated."

"So where on this thing do you think the survivors are, Krylov?" Leonard turned to the commander.

Krylov flicked on the laser attached to his pistol and pointed at an area slightly south of where they were located. "The transmission tower is here. The closest station to this area would be the one here." Krylov steadied the laser on a purple circle with Cyrillic writing underneath it.

"That's where they are?"

"That is my best guess."

Leonard chuckled. "Well, I sure hope your guess is right." Leonard backed up from the map and took it in as a whole, studying the complex layout. He had spent years with maps that were a hundred times more intricate, and it took him only a moment to memorize the paths and decide on the route that would be quickest for them.

Leonard turned to look at Roman. "You said the main tunnel to the south is blocked?"

"Yes. Completely."

"Hm. Show me. I'd like to see it for myself."

Roman glanced at Krylov, who nodded. "Mr. McComb is in charge down here."

Roman nodded and set off down the tunnel. Mikhail ran to catch up with him while Krylov, Marcus and Leonard followed behind.

"Thanks for the vote of confidence, Krylov."

"Not at all, Mr. McComb. Your experience underground is most valuable here."

"Say, Krylov," Marcus said, "is the transmission from the survivors strong enough to pick up under here?"

Krylov tuned his radio to the frequency of the emergency transmission. The static was immediately replaced by the clear, steady recording they had heard before. A gruff man's voice spoke in Russian, then there was a pause, then the same voice spoke again in broken English.

"We are fifty survivors trapped underground. Our food and weapons are low. We need help immediately. Please, if you hear this, send aid. We are located in metro, in Magadan, Magadan Oblast. Please help."

Krylov let the transmission repeat twice before switching off the radio. "For it to be that strong this far underground, we must be right under the radio tower."

Leonard nodded. "Absolutely."

The five walked in silence for a few minutes along the tracks, scanning forward, back, up and down with their lights for any hint of movement. The air underground was cool and still, with the slightest hint of staleness, though at times Leonard could swear he felt a breeze on the back of his neck. When the two soldiers came to a halt several feet ahead, Marcus, Krylov and Leonard swung their lights forward to reveal what was in front of them.

The entire tunnel seemed to vanish several meters in front of the group, swallowed by a massive pile of dirt and debris. Leonard felt a chill on his back and gritted his teeth, trying to maintain his composure as he remembered his recurring dream. "So…" Leonard cleared his throat a few times, swallowed and continued. "So this is the blockage. Everybody, shine your lights across it; I need to see how the entire thing looks."

The tunnel wasn't very wide or tall, so it only took a moment for the lights to spread across the blockage. Leonard stepped back and squinted at it. "You're right, Roman. This isn't natural at all. There were explosives used here. Look at the ceiling above us." Leonard pointed to the cracks extending out above them for several meters back along the path they had taken. "We need to move back. This entire section could give way without warning."

The group hurried back, getting well beyond the damaged portion of the tunnel that Leonard had pointed out. When they stopped, Krylov questioned him. "So where do we go from here?"

Leonard closed his eyes and pictured the map of the underground. "There's a maintenance tunnel that overlaps with this one right around here. It'll either be directly above or below us. Look for a doorway in the wall that leads to a ladder. That's how we can cross into it."

Krylov raised his eyebrow, suddenly feeling hopeful about their chances of navigating the metro system. "Maintenance shafts?"

"Yeah." Leonard swallowed hard again. "Maintenance shafts. Come on now, everybody; spread out and start looking." Leonard was relieved when Krylov and the two soldiers walked off, talking amongst themselves as they swept the walls with their flashlights to locate the door.

Marcus stuck close to his friend and spoke quietly, so that the others wouldn't hear. "You doing okay, Leonard?"

"It's been a while since I've been underground."

"Still having the dreams?"

"Every night."

Marcus was quiet for several seconds. "Let me know how I can help."

Leonard nodded and sighed. He was about to reply when Mikhail came running back down the tunnel. "Mr. McComb, sir, we found it."

Leonard and Marcus jogged behind Mikhail until they passed a slight curve in the tunnel. There, on the right side, was a small set of steps leading up to a narrow concrete platform that ran along the rail line. At the top of the steps, set a couple of inches out from the wall, was a door. Krylov stood in the doorway, holding the door open as he smiled broadly.

"I believe you were looking for this, Mr. McComb?"

Leonard hopped up the stairs and peered into the room beyond the door. The room was small, but in the far corner—past large electrical boxes, scattered tools and a small workbench—was the exact ladder that Leonard was anticipating. "Beautiful, Krylov. Well done, all."

Leonard reached out to lightly brush the electrical boxes and the workbench as he led the team into the room, his eyes flicking over all of its contents. The room had the appearance of being used for working on small mechanical parts, most likely for equipment not directly connected to the metro rails or the trains themselves. The workbench was well-worn, and tools lay scattered across its surface. Leonard stopped at the bench and frowned at the tools. He brushed his fingers across them, then held them up to examine.

"Krylov?" Leonard turned his fingers to the commander. "What do you see here?"

Krylov shook his head, a puzzled expression on his face. "I have no idea."

"No dust." Leonard rubbed his fingers together, demonstrating the fact. "There's virtually no dust on these tools. Or on the bench." Leonard stood on his toes and craned his neck to see the tops of the electrical boxes. "There's plenty up there, but none on the bench."

Marcus raised an eyebrow. "Someone's been in here."

"Quite recently, too. Within the last month, at most." Leonard nodded at Krylov approvingly. "I think your case for survivors being down here just got a lot stronger."

Marcus laughed nervously as he spoke. "Unless the muties have taken to using hand tools."

"God, let's hope not. Though after seeing that factory...." Leonard gave the tools another once-over before heading to the ladder.

The group descended the ladder one at a time, exiting into another small maintenance room. Like the one above, this one also had several large electrical boxes on one wall, but there was no workbench in sight. Instead, the discarded and torn remnants of cardboard cartons were strewn across the floor, leaving an ankle-high mess to shuffle through. Leonard pulled the door to the room open as quietly as he could, wincing at the slight squeak it gave off. He peeked his head out into the darkness and shone his light up and down the tunnel, trying not to think about the fact that they were moving even deeper into the metro system.

"All clear," he whispered to the group, and they each exited the room and jumped down onto the tracks. As five lights illuminated a small section of the tunnel, they could see that it was shorter than the one above, but also a few feet wider, built to accommodate the special freight trains that ferried goods under the city.

Krylov looked up and down the tunnel, trying to determine its orientation in relation to the tunnel above. "Where do we go now, Mr. McComb?"

Leonard pictured the map in his mind again and squeezed his eyes tightly as he concentrated, orienting himself on the map based on the twists and turns they had taken. "This way." Leonard shone his light to the left, down the tunnel. "We follow this, and it'll branch off into a few directions. If we take the left-most path, that'll get us to another maintenance shaft. We follow that up, and we should be in the same tunnel as the station you think the survivors are in."

Roman clapped Leonard on the back and shook his head in wonder. "Mr. McComb, your sense of direction here is remarkable. When I scouted the tunnels above, I felt lost just traveling a straight path."

"Yeah, well, that's what happens when you're a shit-raker for half your life underneath Manhattan."

"Mr. Egorov, I want you with Leonard and Marcus at the front. Mr. Lebedev and I will stay a few meters back to guard our rear." Krylov's face grew serious. "We have no idea what's down here. Stay alert, and Leonard—don't hesitate to use the weapon."

Leonard nodded and gripped the EMP cannon tightly. They were down to a single battery, though he had reduced the power on the rifle, hoping that the less-powerful energy bursts would be enough to at least slow down any attackers so that conventional firearms could finish them off. The momentary joy brought about by Roman's praise of Leonard had evaporated with Krylov's words, and the group fell into an uncomfortable silence.

Walking along in the darkness with only their fragile lights to guide them was suddenly nerve-wracking. Every bump into a wall caused their hearts to beat faster, and every loose stone that was accidentally kicked into the steel rail made them jump. Although the path down the tunnel wasn't very far—a couple hundred meters at most—it felt like ages for the team. Finally, when they arrived at an open circular room, Leonard broke the silence.

"This is it," he whispered and then pointed to a passage that branched off to the left. "This should take us behind the blockage. We'll move up through the maintenance tunnel and approach the station from the unblocked side. At least, I hope it's unblocked. If those fools completely sealed themselves in, we'll never be able to get to them."

"Have faith, Mr. McComb." Krylov smiled at Leonard and gestured at the indicated passage. "Shall we continue?"

The team lapsed back into silence, exiting the circular chamber.

Their lights rapidly faded as they walked down the tunnel and finally vanish in the darkness. Behind them, in the large open room, silence persisted for several long moments—until it was replaced by the soft tapping of paws and feet against the dirt and gravel.

Chapter Ten

"For God's sake, run!"

Heat and flame tears through the air as the man shouts, sending him flying backward. He skids along the wet grass, feeling every bump of the ground as he rolls to a halt. His hat lays still next to him. He reaches for it with a shaking hand and places it back on his head as he stands.

It is dark, and the rain is strong, thundering across the mountains and sending streams of water flowing past his feet. The water sweeps along dirt and grass, turning the lower flatter areas into a mud-caked mess. He wipes water from his eyes and examines his hand—it's covered in blood.

Another explosion. The man shields his face this time, squinting against the light. Though the night is dark, the fires and flames around the factory complex illuminate the area as though it's midafternoon.

The man steps forward, gritting his teeth in pain. He looks down and sees a dark red stain on his thigh, a reminder of the last fifteen minutes of hell. 'This was going so well.' he thinks. 'Where did we go wrong? What happened?'

Two dark shapes tear through the complex ahead of him, chasing down a figure that runs from the buildings. She screams as the shapes gain on her. The man draws his weapon. The gun's sights shake and he blinks several times and breathes slowly, trying to force his heart rate to slow.

Two shots ring out. Two figures crash to the ground, sliding to a halt in the wet dirt. Maria embraces the man, sobbing in terror.

"Where is Boris?" the man shouts at her through the thunder and driving rain.

"He's gone! They're all gone!"

"All?" The man recoils in horror. "How? Where?"

Maria turns to point at the factory complex in front of them. The man squares his shoulders and moves in front of Maria. "Get back to the others. Tell them to pack. We are moving underground, to where it's safe. Go!" The man pushes Maria and she stumbles, then catches herself. She sobs as she runs, her clothing torn and the streaks of blood staining her face and arms slowly dissolving in the rain.

The man walks toward the factory complex. Another explosion comes from a nearby field, along with the howls of the devils and the screams of his men. Inside the twisted fence he stops at a body to pick up a rifle. The magazine is full. He shakes his head as the rage begins to build.

"To me! My brothers, come to me!" He fires the gun several times into the air, shouting at the top of his voice. There are replies to his call, though they are far fewer than he'd hoped. From the grounds outside the factory come pounding footsteps and scattered gunfire. Seven men with rifles assemble, each of them breathing heavily and nursing deep wounds.

"This is our last stand, brothers!" The man's speech is halted by movement at the corner of his vision. He takes to one knee, tracking the movement with the sights of his gun. Three shots later, the movement stops. "Our brothers inside the building are gone. Our only hope is to destroy the entire place—ourselves, too, if necessary."

There are murmurs of agreement among the men. One steps forward, holding out a small black pouch. "We bring down the building."

The man nods. "Yes. We must do it from the inside, though. It must be complete!" A deafening buzzing fills the air. It is accompanied by the tortured screams of too many voices to count.

"Quickly, brothers! Kill everything that moves! Do not hesitate! You—you and I will plant the explosives!"

The man who held out the satchel nods and falls in line. Together, the seven men march for the door to the building. Their goal is impossible, their victory improbable. But still they march.

Chapter Eleven

THE ARKHANGELSK

"**M**a'am?"

Nancy felt the soft tap of a hand on her shoulder, startling her from her thoughts. "Yes? Oh, yes, what is it?"

Nancy shook her head to clear her thoughts. Sitting slumped over in the commander's seat on the Arkhangelsk's control deck, she had become lost in her mind.

"Everything okay, ma'am?"

Nancy nodded. "Yes. Well, I guess so. Not really. But it's as good as it's going to get for now, I suppose."

The young seaman looked at her nervously. "Can I get you anything?"

Nancy smiled at him, and he relaxed. "Sure. A cup of tea would be great."

"Yes, ma'am. Right away."

He ran down the corridor, and Nancy sighed before pulling herself out of the seat. She arched her back and stretched her arms, popping every joint and tendon she could before relaxing again. She took a few minutes to walk across the con, inspecting each station and nodding quietly at the individuals manning them. Most were young—too young, she thought—men, though Krylov had taken on more than a few women during their travels and trained them in various duties and assignments. Nancy had tried to talk with more than a few of them, but the inevitable language barrier kept her from forming any strong attachments with most of the crew.

Aside from Krylov himself—and Leonard and Marcus, of course—the only other person she had managed to connect with was Nikolay, her acting second-in-command. He had been a virtual nobody when she and Leonard had first boarded the Arkhangelsk, but during the missions that the Arkhangelsk had undertaken over the last year, he had proven himself more than capable of handling the additional responsibilities. His strong knowledge of English made it easy for Nancy to talk with him, and they had spent many late evenings on the control deck conversing.

Tired of wandering about with nothing to do, Nancy was about to head to the galley when Nikolay stepped into the room. "Ms. Sims."

"Nikolay!" Nancy smiled. "What's the good news?"

He shrugged. "Nothing, I'm afraid. I've had spotters on deck all night searching, but we've yet to see any sign of anyone."

"Damn. Not even Andrey and Sergei?"

"Not since the locomotive vanished. The creatures that were chasing it seem to have dispersed. Some of them went back to the city while others have been wandering aimlessly, though their paths are taking them toward the city and port in a very roundabout fashion."

Nancy closed her eyes and pinched the bridge of her nose. "Damn."

"There is another matter I wish to discuss with you." Nikolay lowered his voice and glanced around.

"What is it?"

"I believe this is a conversation that should be held elsewhere."

"Lead on." Nancy motioned toward the door, and Nikolay stepped through, leading them to one of the several lounges on the ship. After checking that they were alone, Nikolay and Nancy sat down across from one another at a table, and Nikolay placed a thick brown envelope between them.

"I know we looked at these briefly, ma'am, but I think we need to take a closer look. Mr. Landry's had a chance to examine them, and he sent along some notes to review."

"David did some analysis?" Nancy's eyebrow went up. "Let's see it."

Nikolay opened the brown envelope and slid the contents out onto the table. A small black tablet came out first, followed by several sheets of paper with dense amounts of writing and a few charts. Nancy powered on the tablet, and a photo viewing application opened. She began flipping through the pictures, which had been taken by Krylov's team in the factory, and she cringed as she saw the carnage again.

"This is awful."

Nikolay nodded as he browsed through the papers. "Indeed. I believe you'll find Mr. Landry's report to be even more so."

Nancy put down the tablet and accepted the stack of papers from Nikolay, who began browsing through the photos himself. The report was thorough, beginning with an overview of the factory's location in relation to the city, speculation on what had been manufactured there in years past and an analysis on the remains of the heavy machinery that were scattered in the backgrounds of some of the photos.

The next few pages went into detail on the remains themselves, detailing the materials used for the modifications and giving a summary of all of the visible modifications. There was also an estimate on how many individuals had been killed and distributed across the factory floor, which made Nancy queasy to even look at. The last two pages of the report were where things got scary enough that Nancy felt the prickle of goosebumps on her skin as she read, particularly when she got to the last few paragraphs.

As to what the goal of this AI is, I cannot be certain. I've consulted with two fellow researchers here in the city, and we've so far been unable to come to a solid conclusion as to what the AI's end goal is regarding the experimentations with organic and inorganic hybrids. The lack of swarms in the area could be an indicator that the AI is running on a lower processing level and existing as a hive solely inside mutated organisms, and that said organisms are attempting to increase their processing power through this experimentation.

In conclusion, given the evidence shown in the photographs attached, it is my strong belief that your team is dealing with a forked version of the AI's hive mind. This version appears to be more primitive than the branch we dealt with in the States, and if this theory is proven true, could open the door to a frightening new reality. I recommend extreme caution in dealing with anything associated with this particular version of the AI. Any swarms, mutants and even survivors should be dealt with using extreme caution and, if necessary, lethal force without hesitation.

Nancy sat back and let the papers fall out of her hands to the table. She stared at them for a moment, then glanced up at Nikolay. "Did you read all that?"

"Yes."

"Even the last bit?"

"Yes."

Nancy paused for a few seconds. "We have to warn the teams."

Nikolay shook his head. "We've been trying repeatedly. I've had someone calling both teams every five minutes, and spotters are working in four-man groups. We can't locate or see any trace of them."

"This is really, *really* bad, Nikolay."

"I know."

Another short silence. "Can you get in touch with David?"

Nikolay looked at his watch and stood up from the table. "It's possible. Do you want to speak to him here or in the con?"

"Here."

He nodded. "I'll make the arrangements to have the shortwave piped through down to the phone here. Just pick up when it buzzes. If we can't raise anyone, I'll let you know."

"Thanks, Nikolay." Nancy gave him a grim smile, and he nodded before heading back to the con. Nancy stood up and stretched her neck as she wandered around the small lounge area. Built with luxury in mind, the Arkhangelsk had multiple lounges, a gym and even a small swimming pool on board. While the facilities were a few decades out of date, the crew had spent the last year slowly refitting them with equipment and supplies they'd found while out on missions.

The chairs, couches and bunks had all been upgraded, and fresh tiles, paint and all-weather carpeting had been laid down in the appropriate areas. The original plumbing had been left mostly intact, though, and the dark rust stains throughout the sub proved its age. The galley's equipment was all original, too, though anything that was small enough to be broken down and passed through the sub's largest hatches had been replaced at least once.

In the lounge where Nancy paced were two small tables, six chairs and a pair of couches. The couches were angled around a small television that had been bolted to the wall. A large pile of DVDs sat in a nearby basket, a testament to the crew's ongoing hunt for more entertainment from before the bombs had fallen. While the sub wasn't the best of homes, it had all the amenities anyone needed to keep morale up while at sea for months at a time.

Nancy's thoughts were interrupted by the soft buzzing of a grey phone in the lounge. "Hello?"

Static came through the earpiece, and she held it away from her head. A few seconds later, a familiar voice called out to her. "Hello? Nancy? It's David."

"David! It's good to hear your voice."

Static flowed under the entirety of the conversation, though if Nancy closed her eyes and focused, she could hear everything David said. "Nancy! Yes, good to talk to you, too. I'm glad we had someone monitoring the shortwave. Is everything going well?"

"Not really, David. Listen, I won't keep you long. I just called to discuss the photographs."

"Oh." Even with the static, Nancy could hear the shift in David's tone. "Yes. The photos. They're something else, aren't they? Have you seen them in person? Any more information you can get would be helpful."

"No, I'm afraid not. I'm on the sub, and we've lost touch with the rescue team. They may have reached the metro, but if they're underground, then we won't be able to contact them."

"Oh dear. Should I retask the satellite? It'll take some time, but it's yours if it'll help."

Nancy glanced up as there was a soft knock at the door to the lounge. A crewman bearing a steaming cup of tea hurried in and placed it on the table before backing out as quickly as he could.

Nancy paused for a long few seconds to consider David's offer as she contemplated the beverage. The sole satellite that David was able to connect to and control had been their lifeline for the last year. New satellites were being built at New Richmond to be launched in a few months with the hope of establishing a rudimentary communications network that wouldn't rely on bouncing radio signals off the Earth's atmosphere. Having David retask their single satellite would delay their work in Canada for months—maybe longer.

"No, we'll manage. But I may change my mind soon."

"You let me know if you do."

"David, just one other thing; it's about why I wanted to speak with you." Nancy picked up the tablet and thumbed through the photos as she talked. "You said in this report that the muties may be trying to increase their processing power. Is this like what happened with the Nexus?"

"I honestly have no idea. I wish I could tell you more, but I don't know. If I had to take a stab in the dark and guess, then… yes, that's what my gut tells me. To get more definitive would require a lot more data and analysis."

"How do we stop them? If that's what they're doing, I mean."

David's bemused snort cut through the static. "Pull out one of the sub's reactors and lob it at them? I have no idea. If they're running on a forked version of the AI program we encountered, then their goals may be different than the AI we destroyed at the Nexus. That could be better, but I suspect it's much worse, given what those photos show. I suppose that if they're not operating with the same level of intelligence and cunning, then conventional weapons might be able to defeat them. After all, there've been no signs of swarms from all the satellite passes we took of that area."

Nancy set the tablet down on the table and stared at the image on the screen while she digested David's insights. "Thanks, David. I have some thinking to do here. I'll be in touch again soon."

"Stay safe. Just call if you need any help—not that I can give you much from here—but we'll do all we can."

Nancy smiled. "Thanks, David." The line went dead, and Nancy placed the phone back on the receiver.

In the year that Nancy had partaken in dozens of rescue missions and supply runs on board the Arkhangelsk, they had never faced a threat like the one that was appearing before them now. None of the remnants of the creatures they had encountered had posed much of a threat, nor had they seen any signs of an artificial intelligence still operating. The evidence in Magadan was overwhelming, though, and try as she might, Nancy could think of nothing she could do to help.

Chapter Twelve

THE MAGADAN METRO

"Leonard, buddy, you know it's okay to admit you're lost." Marcus sat down on the ground next to his friend and patted him on the back. Leonard rolled his eyes and shrugged off the arm, returning to the crude map he was drawing in the dirt on the floor.

"Shut up, Marcus. My memory is as good as it's always been. There's something off with this map."

"Are you sure it's not something off with you?"

"Marcus…" Leonard's tone became one of warning, and Marcus stood up, grinning as he backed away with both hands in the air.

"Okay, okay, I get it. Take a hike while you un-lost yourself. Got it." Marcus laughed quietly as he walked away from Leonard and toward Krylov.

After wandering for a full hour in the metro tunnels and looping back on themselves twice, Leonard had called for a break while he recreated the map from memory so that he could study it carefully to determine where they were. Krylov had taken up position several meters down from Leonard while Roman and Mikhail took up a position several meters from Leonard in the opposite direction down the tunnel. While Leonard drew lines in the dirt, the others kept a careful watch for any signs of movement in the tunnels.

Marcus stopped next to Krylov and looked at him expectantly. "See anything?"

"Nothing. Though I have felt what I can only surmise is a breeze more than once. I'm not sure what that means, but given our luck so far, I don't like it."

"Well there, that's the spirit; way to keep morale alive."

Krylov turned his head to give Marcus a quizzical look. "And what has you acting this way, laughing and nervous?"

Marcus laughed and darted his eyes around. "Nervous? Why would you say that?"

Krylov pointed his flashlight at Marcus's face. "You're sweating profusely, you've been unable to stop moving since we stopped here and you can't leave Mr. McComb alone for more than thirty seconds."

Marcus' smile froze on his face, then slowly fell. "Yeah, I don't know, Krylov." Marcus sighed and leaned against the wall. "I think this place is getting to me. By now we should have found your survivors, gotten them back on the Arkhangelsk and be sailing away. Instead, though, we're wandering in circles underground just trying to find them without even knowing if they're still alive or not."

"I understand, Mr. Warden." Krylov looked back at Leonard. "Is Mr. McComb still holding things together?"

"For the most part. I don't know how he does it, what with the nightmares and all."

"I do it," Leonard called out as he stood up and brushed his pants off, "because I must. Also, just because I'm sitting over here doesn't mean I can't hear you. This place is a giant echo chamber."

Marcus shrugged apologetically. "Sorry."

"You have my apologies as well for questioning your state of mind, Mr. McComb."

"None needed, Krylov. We're all a little bit off in the head. I do have some good news, though." Leonard looked down the tunnel toward Roman and Mikhail. "We need to go this way to find your survivors."

"We've already been down there, though," Marcus replied. "Twice."

"Indeed, we have." Leonard set off walking. Krylov and Marcus looked at each other and then set off to follow him.

"Leonard, this might sound a tad rude, but what the hell are you talking about? We've already been down here. There's nothing."

"Oh, there's something all right. The problem is that we weren't expecting it to be hidden."

"What?"

"Come on, keep up!" Leonard's spirits were brightened by his sudden insight, and the others trotted along after him, each of them silently wondering what had gotten into the man.

A hundred meters down the tunnel, Leonard stopped and stood still in the center of the passage. "Here we are."

"Where's here, Mr. McComb?" Krylov asked.

"According to that map, this is a spot where this line and the line above us—the one we want to reach—intersect."

Marcus moved his flashlight around, illuminating the walls and ceiling. "Yeah, and we've already been here. There's no door. See?"

Leonard grinned. "That's where you're wrong. There *has* to be a door here to another maintenance passage. I realized it earlier when I was trying to figure out where we had gone wrong. The problem isn't that we're in the wrong passage or that the door isn't here—the problem is that we aren't looking hard enough."

"Mr. McComb, we're all weary. Could you please explain yourself?"

"These people have been down here for what, a year? Maybe less? At first I was skeptical that they could have survived down here for that long, but we've seen a small amount of evidence of their activity. They've been sneaky, using the tools and workbench in the one maintenance room and scavenging for supplies in another. They know that muties come down here, so they aren't taking any chances on being found. Well, they weren't, anyway. Who knows? Maybe that's what happened to them and why they're radioing for help.

"I'm getting off track here, but the point is that these people are being *very* careful to hide themselves. They blocked off one of the major ways into the station they're in, and they've used the maintenance passages to move around. It seems to me that they know these things have some measure of intelligence, and they're doing all they can to stay undetected."

As he spoke, Leonard walked along the right-hand side of the tunnel, running his hand along the wall. He suddenly stopped and turned his light to the wall, then rapped his knuckles on it. Instead of a dull thud, which would have been expected from knocking on tiled concrete, there was the hollow ring of metal.

"What the hell?" Marcus ran forward, followed closely by Krylov, Mikhail and Roman. Leonard stepped back as Krylov jumped up on the narrow walkway and felt the area around where Leonard had knocked. He pulled out his knife and rapped the handle around on the wall, gradually revealing the edge of the door. With a hasty look around to ensure that the noise wasn't going to immediately draw any attention, he plunged the knife into the wall around the metal door.

Dry chunks of plaster fell from the space, slowly revealing the cunningly hidden door. Like the previous ones, this door was also set out a few inches from the wall, but plaster had been applied to the wall around it so that the door itself wasn't clearly visible. A few layers of grey paint had been applied to match the color of the tile, and the door became virtually invisible in the darkness of the tunnel—even to the advanced eyesight of the mutants and especially in the dim light of the group's flashlights.

After peeling away the plaster and scratching off some of the paint, Krylov gingerly opened the door. Mikhail stood behind him, his rifle at the ready, but the room beyond was quiet. "So, what do you think now, Mr. McComb?"

"I think we're nearly there, Krylov. And I think we need to be damned careful."

"Agreed. Mr. Egorov, I want you on point with me. Mr. Lebedev, you take up the rear. Mr. McComb, Mr. Warden, stay close to the front. I want the EMP gun ready to fire at a second's notice."

The five men slowly climbed the ladder in the room one after the other and found themselves in yet another identical room. In this one, though, the electrical boxes had been removed, and the only trace of their existence were some severed wires that vanished into the floor. One wall had several large nails hammered into it, and from a few of them hung a series of makeshift weapons.

Leonard gently picked up one of the weapons and examined it. The blade from a limb-cutter had been affixed to an axe handle. The blade's serrations had been removed and sharpened to a single, continuous, razor-sharp edge. A baseball bat with nails hammered through it and a string looped around the handle hung from another nail. A sledgehammer with a railroad spike welded to one end sat on the floor, leaning up against the wall.

Marcus whistled quietly at the sight. "These are brutal. Who makes something like this?"

Leonard replaced the weapon he had taken and whispered softly. "People who have been desperate for a very long time. Come on, let's go."

Krylov grunted and pointed at the exit. Mikhail switched off his light and pulled open the door, checking the tunnel outside for signs of light and sound. He moved quickly into the tunnel and flipped his light back on, scanning the tunnel in both directions briefly before relaxing. "Clear, sir."

Krylov went out next, followed by the rest. Once out of the maintenance room, Krylov whispered to Leonard. "Which way now?"

"We've just bypassed the cave-in, which should be that way." Leonard pointed to their left down the tunnel before turning the other direction. "If we go this way then we should reach the station."

"Let's move. Everyone keep quiet; no talking unless necessary," Krylov whispered before patting Mikhail on the back and prompting him to start moving. The group returned to their quiet walking, staying on either side of the rails and cringing every time the dirt crunched and a pebble happened to bounce off the steel rail.

After several minutes of walking, Leonard felt the hairs on his neck start to stand on end. He looked at Marcus, who glanced back, wide-eyed. They both stopped, along with Roman, and Leonard whispered to Krylov and Mikhail to stop as well.

"What's wrong?" Krylov stepped back toward the group while Mikhail kept watch ahead of them.

"I don't know. Something doesn't feel right here," Leonard said.

Marcus nodded in agreement. "I've got the same feeling. We need —wait a minute, what's that?"

With all of their lights either temporarily switched off or pointed at the ground, Marcus caught sight of something in his peripheral vision. He angled his flashlight up at the roof of the tunnel. Instead of the sloping tile that he was expecting to see, a black hole a few meters long and wide extended up into the ceiling, directly over where Mikhail was standing.

"Leonard? Why is there a hole in the ceiling?"

Leonard took a few steps forward and shone his light at the hole, trying to see how far up it went. "I have no idea. Is it a ventilation shaft? Maybe the survivors used it for something? Or...."

Mikhail took a step back as he noticed what was going on, then looked up through the hole in the ceiling. He could see the sparkle of a dozen stars twinkling in the night sky. As he watched, the stars began to move, descending down through the sky, rotating around each other and making him feel as though he were falling up through the darkness. It took a moment too long to realize what the stars actually were.

"They're here!" Mikhail screamed and angled his gun up through the hole. He fired wildly several times, hitting nothing but the tiles and sides of the hole and raining down dirt and debris on his face. In the light of the muzzle flashes, he could see the creatures' silvered bodies and faces as they crawled faster toward him, clinging to the sides of the shaft with their claws.

Mikhail backpedaled down the tunnel toward the rest of the group as the first creature extended its arm to swipe at him. The sharp metal fingers cut through the front of his jacket and into his chest like hot knives through butter. Krylov moved forward with his gun out, firing at the limb of the creature as it swiped again, trying to find its prey. Mikhail crawled backward on the floor, clutching his wounded chest with one hand as he continued firing his rifle wildly with the other.

"Lebedev! Get him back!" Krylov's yell thundered down the tunnel, sending up a chorus of howls from the hole in the ceiling above. Roman ran forward and grabbed his comrade by the top of his backpack and pulled him backward several meters to where Marcus was standing. Leonard, meanwhile, had moved forward and taken up position next to Krylov. When Mikhail was pulled out of the way, the creature's arm vanished back up into the hole, though they could still hear the sounds of the creatures moving about and snarling at each other.

"Any suggestions?" Krylov whispered frantically to Leonard.

"We have to get past them to get to the station. We can't go backward because of the cave-in, and there's no way we can hold out in the maintenance room while we patch up Mikhail's wounds."

Krylov nodded. "Right. Get them ready to move." Leonard nodded and ran back to the others while Krylov fired several more shots into the ceiling around the hole to distract the creatures. He reached inside one of the several pockets on his front jacket and pulled out a small sphere with a pin sticking out of one side. Marcus and Roman appeared on his right, holding Mikhail between them as he groaned loudly.

Leonard stood on Krylov's left and spoke quietly. "Use whatever you've got to make them pull back a bit. I'll get the cannon lined up and fire off a few shots while the rest of them squeeze around. Then you and I follow up as a rearguard. Got it?"

Krylov nodded and then slung his rifle on his back and hefted the small object in his right hand. "No need for the cannon. You should cover your eyes. This might hurt."

Chapter Thirteen

"**G**ood God... what hit us?" Andrey was the first to wake up, having lost consciousness as the locomotive had tumbled over the bridge. He looked around and groaned as a wave of pain passed through his head. It was too dark to see anything inside the cab of the locomotive, but through one of the windows, he could barely make out the pale light of the moon and stars. As he started moving around and regaining his faculties, he realized that he was incredibly wet and cold.

"What the..." Andrey grumbled, trying to sit up, but sliding back down with each attempt. "What is this?"

It took another moment, but his mind finally caught up with him, and he realized where he was. His hand snapped to a light on the front of his jacket. He flipped the switch, but nothing happened. He cursed, then groped through his pockets until he landed on a thin plastic rod. He bent it with one hand, snapping the inner membrane and mixing the chemicals in the rod together. The glow stick flared to life, and Andrey dropped it to his feet, trying to make out what was going on.

The train had come to a halt on its left side in the small river. The left portion of the train was submerged, and there were a few inches of water on the "floor," which was the reason for Andrey's soggy clothes. The glow stick's light was bright enough even under the water that he could still make out the interior of the cab, including the slumped-over form of his cousin.

"Sergei?" Andrey knelt down next to his older companion and shook his shoulders. Sergei stirred slightly, groaned and coughed.

"What the hell happened?" His voice was groggy, and his teeth began to chatter in the cold.

"Come on, get up. You're sitting in water. We need to get out of here." The weather was abnormally cold, and spending who-knew-how-many hours in the water didn't help things. Sergei stood up slowly with his cousin's aid, and the two men leaned against the back wall of the cab for support while they got their bearings.

With one of the side windows of the locomotive lodged in the ground and the other one too high to reach, their options for escape were limited. Andrey reached for the door to the engine compartment of the locomotive, but it was jammed shut and wouldn't budge.

"Out there." Sergei pointed out the front window. "Shoot out the glass, and we can get out that way."

"And if those things are around?"

"If we don't get somewhere to get warmed and dry, then we might as well be one of them."

Andrey grunted. "Fine." He tugged on the charging handle and cycled the action, sending a cartridge flipping through the air. Satisfied that the weapon was still functional, he shielded his face with his arm and waited for his comrade to do the same. "Ready?"

"Do it."

Glass shattered as Andrey dumped five rounds into the windshield of the locomotive, starting at the bottom and letting the rifle's recoil carry it up. While the window didn't completely break apart, a swift kick from the soldiers' boots turned the small holes into larger ones, and the glass finally gave way.

Andrey was the first to exit, tossing his rifle out onto the ground and quickly following after it. He grabbed the gun and rolled onto his back, scanning in every direction around him for movement. After several seconds, when he was certain the area was clear, he motioned for Sergei to follow.

While Sergei crawled out, Andrey stood up and walked around to look at the locomotive from the side, glad to be able to stretch his legs.

When he had walked a short distance downstream, he stopped and blinked several times at what was pinned under the locomotive.

"Sergei, get down here and see this!" he hissed at his partner, who quickly finished getting out of the cab and ran to see the source of the commotion.

"What is—what the hell is that?"

Sergei grabbed for his flashlight and flicked it on, relieved to see that it still worked. He pointed it at the two enormous shapes that were trapped under the locomotive. Half of each of the bodies were out of sight under the vehicle, but the two halves that were visible painted a picture that made the soldiers' blood run even colder than it already was.

The creatures were a pair of massive East Siberian brown bears, each weighing nearly a full ton and measuring over eight feet in length. The brown fur on the animals had been nearly completely stripped away, leaving small mats of fur across a largely bare body. Like the other animals that had been infected by the nanobots, their flesh was intertwined with the same silvery metal. This metal was most prevalent in their enormous claws and teeth, a few of which had broken off and were resting at the bottom of the river.

Andrey stepped into the water, his already numb feet barely sensing the cold. He used the barrel of his rifle to prod the face of the creature whose head was sticking out from underneath the train, then he leaned down to pick up the silver teeth in the water.

"Hey," said Sergei, "fetch me one of those, too."

The younger cousin rolled his eyes and used the butt of his gun to smash at the creature's mouth until another large fang fell out. "There. Happy now?"

Sergei smiled as he caught the long tooth and placed it in his pocket. "I can't believe those things are what knocked the train off the bridge."

"Just be glad they weren't strong enough to survive this thing falling on top of them."

The pair stood at the bank of the river and stared at the bodies of the dead creatures for a few more minutes. Their condition was temporarily forgotten until Andrey coughed, then doubled over in pain. "My ribs! Dammit that hurts!"

Sergei was suddenly very aware of his injuries as well. Their adrenaline was wearing off, and the cold was continuing to set in. "Come on. Let's get away from these demons and get a fire going. We can radio the Arkhangelsk and tell them we'll be late."

Twenty minutes later, after walking back toward the city, both men sat huddled inside a small building on the edge of the port. A small stack of fuel disks sat in a metal pan, burning brightly while the pair warmed their extremities and swapped out their waterlogged socks for dry ones from their packs. They couldn't find any signs of permanent damage from the water and cold, which was a relief after their experience.

Andrey flipped over their gloves, which were hanging on the back of a rusty metal chair in front of the fire. "We should go soon. Ten more minutes at most."

His cousin nodded. "Agreed. I'll radio the sub and let them know we're on the way."

Sergei pulled out his radio and switched it on. "Arkhangelsk, Arkhangelsk, this is Usov. Come in, please. Over." When he released the microphone switch, there was silence instead of the static he expected to hear.

Andrey watched Sergei fiddle with the radio for several seconds. "Is it broken?"

"Damned thing must not be as waterproof as they claim. How's yours?"

Andrey pulled out what was left of his radio after it had been smashed to bits during the tumble in the locomotive. "I don't think we'll be using this one."

"Signal flare?"

"No. Not yet. The inflatable should still be at the pier. Fifteen, maybe twenty minutes of running will get us there."

Sergei stood up and collected the gloves from the back of the chair. "Still damp, but they'll do." He passed his cousin's pair over and then extinguished the fire. As they headed out of the building and began their run for the docks, Andrey reached into his pocket to feel the teeth they had collected from the beasts that had attacked the train. Even through his gloves he could feel the texture of the silver metal that had permeated the enamel to strengthen and increase the size of the tooth. *It will make a fine necklace*, he thought, *assuming we get home in one piece.*

The soldiers' run back to their inflatable went off without a hitch, much to their amazement. They didn't encounter a single creature on their way back to the pier, and their craft was exactly where they had left it. Sergei loaded their backpacks into the craft while Andrey loosened the rope that held it fast to the piling.

"Ready?" Andrey's eyes skimmed over the craft, and he went through his mental checklist. Everything was in order, and there was no objection from his comrade, so he gave the inflatable a push and jumped in. The engine fired to life and the craft sped backward for a few seconds, then did a quick turn and made for the bay. In spite of the darkness, the seas were calmer, making leaving significantly easier than their arrival had been. The few obstacles in their path were easily avoided, and they were soon clear of them all and heading out over open water.

"Any sign of her?" Sergei yelled over the roar of the outboard motor.

"Nothing!" Andrey crouched in the front of the craft, straining his eyes against the darkness to find some sign of the Arkhangelsk's black hull.

"Send up a flare! We should be nearly there by now!"

Andrey reached inside his pack and pulled out a three-shot flare pistol. Fitted with uniquely built charges that gave it a faster ascent, longer burn and slower descent than regular flares, it was purpose-built to light a large area for an extended period of time. With a soft *ka-chunk*, he launched the flare ahead of the inflatable, sending it arcing high into the air in front of and above the craft. Light blossomed in the dark sky, and the soldiers shielded their eyes from the intensity of the flare.

As the light slowly drifted toward the water, the two men searched for any sign of the Arkhangelsk. Finally, as the flare nearly touched the water, the sky lit up again, though this time the signal did not come from them. A bright light cut through the sky several hundred meters ahead of them as it illuminated the shape of the submarine.

Sergei gunned the inflatable's motors, pushing them to their maximum. As they closed in on the Arkhangelsk, they could see that she wasn't holding still in the water, but was heading out into the bay and traveling at a fast clip to boot.

"What's she doing?" Sergei yelled at his comrade.

"No idea! Someone's on the deck, though! Get ready to toss the line!"

Sergei looked ahead of them, and sure enough, there were three figures on deck. Each of them had a harness tied around their waist to keep them from falling overboard, and one of them held a spotlight while the other two crouched near the edge of the sub. They motioned with their hands as the inflatable grew closer and drew alongside the sub. The Arkhangelsk's wake was ferocious, and keeping the inflatable from jerking from side to side or flipping over was a challenge. Finally, as they got as close as they could, Andrey heaved the coiled rope toward the men waiting on deck.

"Hold on!" Andrey watched as the men caught the rope and affixed it to a bitt before beginning the arduous task of pulling the inflatable onto the deck. As the two men on deck pulled, the third kept the spotlight aimed at the water between the sub and the inflatable to help both them and Sergei keep the craft upright.

When the inflatable was just a few feet from the sub, Sergei gunned the motors one last time, and the front of the craft slammed into the side of the Arkhangelsk's deck. The two men who had been hauling it in pulled it back, and the inflatable finally came to rest. Sergei shut off the motors and leapt out, leaving Andrey to grab their weapons and packs.

"What the devil is going on?" Sergei yelled at the man holding the spotlight.

"Emergency, sir!" Nikolay's face was white, and Sergei could see the fear painted on it. "A pump on one of the reactors failed! We're estimating less than forty-eight hours until it goes critical."

"Where the hell are we going?" The cousins stood together on the deck, gripping the safety cable tightly. The two crewmen who had pulled them on board worked to let the air out of the inflatable's pontoons and get it down to a small enough size to stow.

"Rybachiy!" The sound of the wind and water were loud enough that they had to yell at each other to be heard. "Tech thinks there will be spare parts there to repair the reactor."

"Why not just shut it down?"

The man holding the spotlight shook his head. "Techs say we can't!"

Sergei was too dumbfounded to say anything else. A few moments later, after the inflatable was stowed away, all five of the soldiers made their way across the deck and through a hatch. As Andrey and Sergei began heading toward their quarters to change, the man with the spotlight shook his head.

"Sorry, but the commander wants you in the con right now. She said it's urgent."

Sergei fumed. "It can't wait five minutes? Dammit!"

"Sorry. I'll have some coffee for you there in just a moment." Nikolay smiled apologetically before dashing off.

As the two cousins made their way toward the control room, they quickly became aware of the red flashing lights and the occasional siren that echoed from corridors further down and to the aft on the boat. After barely making it back to the Arkhangelsk, all they wanted was a hot meal and a full night's sleep, but it was beginning to look like that wasn't going to happen anytime soon.

Chapter Fourteen

THE ARKHANGELSK

After Nancy had finished her conversation with David, she'd made her way back to the control room. Once there, she'd settled back in the center chair and resumed the undeniably boring task of overseeing the various systems. With the Arkhangelsk idling in the bay, there was nothing to do except sit, wait and try not to go insane from boredom.

That's what Nancy thought, at least, for approximately ten minutes after returning to the conn. When the eleventh minute rolled around, though, her game of "which sailor has the worst haircut" was interrupted by a seaman stumbling through the hatch into the control room. He tripped over himself twice coming in and gave Nancy a nervously hasty salute before approaching her chair.

"Ma'am." He tried to whisper, but his voice shook, and she could barely make out what he was saying.

"What's that?"

"Ma'am, we have a situation."

Nancy's eyebrows went up. "What kind of a situation?"

"A very bad one, ma'am. I need you to come with me right away."

Nancy stood up quickly, relieved at finally having something to do, while at the same time feeling incredibly nervous about what was going on. After Nancy stepped through the hatch and they had walked several meters down the hall, she stopped the young man with a hand on his shoulder.

"What's going on?"

The young seaman's nervousness doubled, and he audibly gulped before speaking. "There's a problem with one of the reactors, ma'am. Something one of the technicians just found. They just said they needed you right away and not to go shouting it across the boat."

Nancy's curiosity vanished, replaced entirely by seriousness mixed with a bit of fear. "What kind of a problem?"

"They didn't tell me. They just said to get y—"

Nancy was off in a flash, racing down the corridor to the aft of the ship. She called over her shoulder as she ran. "Radio the tech, and tell him I'm on my way!"

Nancy's footsteps thundered down the halls of the Arkhangelsk as she broke into a full-on run. She jumped over and through the hatches, slid down ladders and finally arrived at the hatch to enter the sub's reactor chamber. The guard posted outside the chamber saluted her as she approached and then opened the hatch. She slid through and was greeted on the other side by a group of three men dressed in white jumpsuits and wearing small radiation detector badges.

"Ma'am!" The head technician nervously saluted as she approached, and she waved off the formality.

"Save it for Krylov. What's going on down here?"

The lead tech nervously glanced at his companions before he spoke. "We started noticing some unusual readings in our second reactor a few hours ago. It wasn't much, just some temperature fluctuations. We kept an eye on it, though, and noticed that the pressure on the coolant lines was dropping."

"Which means... what, exactly?"

"The temperature in the reactor is going up because our coolant pump is failing. If we don't get a new pump installed immediately, the reactor won't be cooled anymore, the temperature will rise and we will lose containment."

"Christ. That doesn't sound good."

"No, ma'am."

"What can we do?"

The technicians shuffled their feet and glanced between each other.

"We… we don't know yet, ma'am. We're in the process of isolating the exact part that's at fault. If it is the pump, then it would be straightforward to replace… if we had another one."

"Can't we fabricate one? We've got enough equipment here to make pretty much everything we need."

"Most things, yes. The pump, however, uses a special anti-corrosion coating that we don't have."

"And we need that… why?"

"The pump takes seawater in and sends it to a desalinator before it's cycled through the system. The water first acts as a coolant for the system and is turned into steam to power the turbines. If we lose the pump completely, then we'll be… what's the phrase your people use? Up shit creek without a saddle?"

Nancy couldn't help but snicker at the attempted joke. "Paddle. And it sure as hell sounds like it. So, what do we do? We can't just sit here. Can't we shut the reactor down?"

"Easier said than done. Even if we did, the reactor would still generate an enormous amount of heat, and we need water circulating to take care of that. No, ma'am, we need to fix this. And fast."

"How fast are we talking?"

"Forty-eight hours, no more. Perhaps less if the damage inside the pump is worse than we think."

Nancy's mind raced. Despite having been in more than a few tight spots over the last year, this was a situation that was completely foreign to her. Having her life or the lives of her friends in danger was pretty standard as things went, but dealing with a crisis that would cripple the Arkhangelsk? Nothing had come close.

"Ma'am?" The three technicians stared at her, awaiting her instructions. In the muddiness of her thinking, a beacon suddenly appeared.

"We're in Russia, right?" Nancy started pacing back and forth in the small compartment as she thought out loud.

"Uh… ma'am?" The lead technician looked at her quizzically.

"We're in Russia and this bucket of bolts was built here. That means that there has to be somewhere nearby that has parts for subs, right?"

The technicians simply stared at her and she rolled her eyes in frustration. "You three are no good to me right now. Just get back to work.

Figure out the *exact* source of the problem. Every screw, seal and lick of paint that we need replaced. Got it?"

"Um. Are you—"

"That wasn't a request!"

Nancy's eyes blazed with fury and fire, and the three technicians automatically snapped to attention. "Yes, sir! Ma'am!"

"Get moving!"

Nancy turned without another word and slid through the hatch. She raced for the nearest communication console and picked up the microphone. "Nikolay, I need you in the con right this second!" Nancy replaced the microphone without waiting for a reply and ran back down the corridor, making a beeline for the control deck.

Forty-eight hours. Forty-eight hours. Damn. That's not much time at all. What's this thing do, fifty klicks an hour underwater? Maybe sixty, if we push her? Doubt the reactors can put out that much power anymore, though. Maybe. Dammit!

Nancy arrived in the control room a few minutes later, where Nikolay was waiting for her. His face changed to one of concern as he watched her barrel into the room and start mashing controls on the center display table.

"Ms. Sims? Is everything all right?"

"One of the reactors has forty-eight hours left until it starts to over-heat. So, no, Nikolay, I don't think so."

Nikolay's eyes widened, and he glanced around at the crew. None of them appeared to have overheard Nancy's pronouncement, so he leaned in close and whispered intently. "Are you certain?"

Nancy stopped manipulating the table's controls for a moment and glanced at him. "I just came back from the reactor room. There's a pump that's dying, and the reactor's going to overheat. If you want the technical details, go talk to them. Not right now, though; I need you here with me."

Nancy focused on the controls again, trying desperately to remember the more technical Russian words and phrases she had learned over the last several months. "We have to find a place that has something we can use to fix this bitch before she explodes." Nancy's habit of referring to the Arkhangelsk in less-than-pleasant terms during situations of high stress was always a source of great amusement to

Krylov, and she desperately wished that he was in her place at that very moment.

"Still nothing from Krylov's team?" she asked offhand, though she didn't expect to get an answer that would make her happy.

Nikolay shook his head. "Nothing. We did catch sight of some movement on the far shore, though. I believe it's Usov and Lipov. Our spotters lost sight of them after a moment, but they looked to be alive from what we could tell."

"Good. Let's hope they get back here soon. Ha! Here we go." The map zoomed out from their current location, and several dots appeared on the screen with Russian names next to them.

Nikolay stepped up to the table and studied the map for a few seconds. "You're looking for military bases?"

"Anything that might have parts that we can jury-rig to fix this sub. Come on, Nikolay; help me out here. Which one of these is close enough for us to reach before we all start glowing green?"

Nikolay nodded as he realized what Nancy was attempting to find. "What you want are Russian submarine bases." He smiled. "I believe I can help with that." He tapped a few keys. The dots on the screen vanished, and a new set appeared.

"Hey, what's this one down here?" Nancy jabbed her finger at a dot several hundred kilometers to their south.

"Rybachiy Nuclear Submarine Base."

"No way." Nancy's jaw dropped open. "A nuclear submarine base so close?"

Nikolay nodded. "It is fortuitous that it is so near. Truth be told, I do not know if we will find anything there to help us, but…." Nikolay zoomed out on the map and nodded grimly. "This is the only place that we could possibly reach in the time you described that also has a high likelihood of having the parts that we will require."

"That settles it." Nancy straightened her back. "I want you to get down to the reactor chamber and talk to the techs. See what progress they've made—if any—and light a fire under their asses. Find out if anyone on this boat knows anything more about this Rybachiy place and what we could expect to find there. You've got thirty minutes to tell me if this place is going to save this rusting piece of crap or not. After that, I want us underway—either to Rybachiy or someplace else that you think is going to have what we need."

"Yes, ma'am. What about Commander Krylov and the others?"

Nancy paused and sighed. "We'll have to rig a beacon to send out a repeating message telling them what we're doing. The techs made it sound like this would be a simple swap job, so we should only be gone for a few days if we hustle. If Sergei and Andrey don't make it back here before we leave... well... I don't know, Nikolay. They'll survive. They'll have to. Every second we sit around here is another second closer we come to being stranded here for who knows how long."

"I understand." Nikolay took a step toward the exit, then paused briefly. "Just so you know, Ms. Sims, I agree with your assessment. It is still a difficult choice, but I believe it's the right one."

Nancy felt a portion of the tension in her body relax at Nikolay's words. She nodded in silent thanks, and he dashed out of the control room to take care of his tasks. Nancy leaned back over the table and stared at the small point on the map marking the nuclear submarine base, wondering what would be in store for them there.

Twenty minutes later, Nikolay returned to the control room with a clipboard in hand. "Ma'am. I have something here for you."

"Yes?"

"I was able to glean more information from the techs, who—I might add—you terrified." Nancy couldn't suppress a slight smile as Nikolay continued. "They say the problem is in the pump itself. There aren't any leaks. It's just the pumping mechanism that's failing. The replacement time for said mechanism is approximately six hours once we have a new one secured."

"What about Rybachiy?"

"One of the technicians was familiar with the base. He actually worked there for a few months as part of his training. He said that—so long as the base itself wasn't too badly damaged—we should be able to source the parts we need from the warehouses. The pump that the coolant system uses is somewhat unique, but we can substitute a pump meant for a different class of vessel and it should work."

"So, we go to Rybachiy?"

"That would appear to be the best choice."

"Do we have any satellite data of the area?"

Nikolay pulled out a photograph from his clipboard and handed it to her. "I took the liberty of radioing New Richmond. Mr. Landry was unavailable, but one of his assistants was able to pull up the relevant data. It's two months old, but that's good enough for our purposes, I think."

Nancy examined the photograph closely. "This doesn't look all that bad. I'm not seeing any signs of a nuke hitting the area."

"Mr. Landry's assistant also came to the same conclusion. We can wait for his assessment if you'd like, but I believe this is our only shot at repairing the reactor before the problem becomes too bad to contain."

Nancy nodded. "Okay. Let's make it happen. Spread the word, and sound a general alarm. Do whatever you can to get us there as fast as possible without putting any additional stress on the reactor."

"Shall I keep some crew on deck to search for Lipov and Usov?"

Nancy hesitated, then nodded. "Yes. We'll run on the surface at half throttle until we get out of the bay, then we'll submerge and turn things up to eleven."

Nikolay had a puzzled look on his face, but nodded nonetheless. "Very good. I'll take care of it."

Nancy stepped back as Nikolay took over and began bellowing orders to the crew. Within a few moments, red lights began to flash on the control deck as the general alarm sounded out across the boat. She felt a rumble far beneath her feet begin to grow as the turbines spun up and directed their power into the Arkhangelsk's twin screws.

Come on, you two. Nancy paced on the con, hoping to hear some good news about one of the two teams on shore.

"Ma'am?" Nikolay walked up behind her. "We have the beacon ready."

"Still no sign of anyone?"

"Nothing. I'm sorry, ma'am."

Nancy sighed. "Fine. Deploy the beacon."

Nikolay was turning to give the order to deploy the radio beacon when the crewman who was stationed on the periscope gave a shout. "Sir! Ma'am! We have a signal! Someone fired a flare off our aft!"

Nikolay jumped over a chair and railing and pushed the crewman out of the way. He peered into the periscope and adjusted the zoom and angle. A flare was, indeed, arcing through the sky from somewhere far behind them. Nancy stepped beside him, and he stepped out of the way so that she could see it as well. After glancing at it for a few seconds, Nancy called out her orders.

"That must be Andrey and Sergei! Get someone up on deck now! I want a team ready to pull the inflatable in as they get here. Get our own flare up so they can see where we are, and have someone up there with a spotlight. Move!"

Nikolay repeated the orders, directing them through the ship's communications system to the crew working on other decks. After receiving confirmation that his orders had been received, he addressed Nancy.

"I'd like to be on deck with them for when they arrive, if you don't mind."

Nancy nodded. "Go. Make sure they get aboard—whoever "they" are. And make sure they come here as soon as they do. I want to get a full briefing."

Nikolay nodded. "I'll make it happen."

As Nikolay left the control room, Nancy slowly sat down in the central chair and steepled her fingers together. With a twenty-four-hour voyage ahead of them, they were going to be crunched on time once they arrived at the Rybachiy Nuclear Submarine Base. Six hours were required to repair the reactor, leaving them with—assuming everything went well, which it never did—a scant eighteen hours to search for and secure a replacement pump.

"Plenty of time," she mumbled, trying in vain to convince herself that what she said was true.

Behind all of the sudden worry over the Arkhangelsk was the concern over Krylov's team and the survivors they were tasked to find. Whether or not the distraction that Andrey and Sergei had been sent ashore to accomplish was successful no longer mattered. The rescue team would be on their own for at least a few days. Their fate was now in their own hands.

Chapter Fifteen

I nside the factory, there is nothing but chaos. In the building that was half-collapsed and then whole again within a day, there is naught but pandemo-nium. Blood soaks the floors as rivers of rainwater mingle with standing pools of red, combining into a frothy mix that churns the man's stomach. He fights against the nausea and raises his weapon once again. A crack issues forth, and another devil falls to the ground. The faces of the creatures are nightmares unto themselves—the flesh is broken and bleeding as silvery threads wind their way across the bodies that move with strength and speed that they had never seen before in life.

Seven men pass through the factory doors. Their goal is clear and their intent true, but like waves crashing against the rocks, so their hopes are dashed. The first wave of devils falls easily enough, until the men see the faces. Neighbors. Acquaintances. Friends. Family. Their numbers are untold, issuing forth from some unknown place like so many locusts descending upon a field.

The man struggles to reload his weapon. His hands are slick with blood. A voice beckons to him—the first he has heard since the man with the explosives died before his eyes.

"Alexander."

The voice is familiar, but changed—it cracks and elongates the sounds as the mouth struggles to form them.

"Alexander."

The man turns to the voice. His friend stands before him and does not stand *before him all at once. The figure is soaked in red, its clothes torn and barely clinging to its gaunt form.*

"Brother. Alexander."

Inside the figure's mind, the spark of original thought and life fights to be heard and seen and freed once again. The fight is short-lived. The spark is extinguished.

"Boris?" Alexander's tears flow freely now. His spirit is broken, and he falls to his knees. The figure steps forward, no longer speaking. It raises an arm—cruelly and crudely grafted to an industrial tool—in the air and prepares a blow to cripple Alexander.

Another shot rings out, and Boris' stance wavers. He staggers back and falls away from Alexander, the overburdened limb crashing to the ground. Another man runs to Alexander's aid, sliding on the slick floor.

"Come on! We have to go!"

Alexander barely moves. His gaze is trapped upon the body of the shell of his friend. The shell that was occupied by something else, something that tore out his friend's mind, soul and spirit and replaced it with something entirely different.

"Alexander!" The man turns Alexander around and slaps him in the face. "Come on! We must go! There are hundreds more of them coming! There are only four of us left now; we must retreat and find shelter with the others before these demons come for them, too!"

Alexander looks around slowly. More of the devils have appeared. Their movements are becoming more coordinated. They close in on the men, who are joined by the two other survivors of the assault party. He nods slowly, grinding his teeth until the pain lances through his jaw and skull.

"Go!" He moves again. There is newfound strength in his muscles—newfound determination in his heart. One last look at his friend seals his decision. They cannot fight the devils. So they must run. They must run and hide and outlast the devils, no matter the cost. Someone will come for them one day. Until that day, they must survive.

Chapter Sixteen

THE MAGADAN METRO

U tter chaos. That was the best phrase that Leonard could think of to describe the situation that their team found themselves in. While Leonard had initially thought that the round device Krylov held in his hand was a grenade, it had turned out to be far more potent. Using an underhanded throw, Krylov tossed the device upward into the shaft, where they heard a metallic *thunk* as the device attached itself to one of the creatures. Krylov knelt on the ground and shielded his eyes, and Leonard—following Krylov's lead—did the same.

Two seconds after the device magnetically attached to one of the creatures, it detonated. The interior of the device was packed with a hybrid of explosives and what was essentially highly energetic napalm. The initial blast sent a torrent of flame both up and down the shaft, leaving a burning circle of fire on the ground. Small bits of the creatures fell from the shaft as the flames—impossible to extinguish even though they tried—melted through the metal and burned away at the flesh.

Leonard turned away from the intense heat of the inferno and shouted at Marcus and the two soldiers. "Get going! Move around the flames! Hurry!"

Krylov watched as the three shuffled slowly around the edge of the circle of fire before he and Leonard followed up. As they passed by, Krylov glanced up into the shaft, noting with some disappointment that there was still movement inside as the flames were beginning to die down. While the "super grenade" was extremely lethal, the small amount of fuel inside combined with the fast burn time meant that the aftereffects only lasted for a couple of minutes at most.

By the time the group was a few meters away from the shaft and down the tunnel, the flames had died down enough that the creatures began to emerge from the shaft. The first out were effectively dead—pushed out by other creatures to fall on the ground and twitch about helplessly. The next group that emerged bore scorch marks on their faces and upper torsos, but were otherwise unharmed. As Marcus and Roman helped Mikhail continue down the tunnel, Leonard and Krylov turned back to face the creatures.

Though the shaft in the ceiling was small, the creatures continued to pour out of it at an alarming rate. Groups emerged two and three at a time, pushing, clawing and biting at each other in their efforts to be first on the ground. All of them were formerly human, a fact that Leonard was silently grateful for. While the animals had been smaller and arguably easier to deal with, their unnerving appearance was something Leonard still wasn't used to.

"Mr. McComb!" Krylov shouted at Leonard over the noise of the creatures. "Now would be a good time to start firing!"

Leonard gripped the EMP rifle tightly—still anticipating a recoil, even though there was none—and pulled the trigger. Seconds later, the first row of creatures crumpled to the floor, their bodies sparking into flame as they twitched from an overload of energy. The creatures behind them descended upon their comrades while the rest simply climbed around and over, continuing in their slow pursuit of the group.

"Why aren't they charging us?" Leonard glanced over at Krylov, who had his finger on the trigger of his rifle, ready to fire.

"I don't know. Let's take advantage of it while we can, though. Marcus! Roman! Get your asses moving! We need to get to this station and get secured right now!"

"Uh, Krylov?" Marcus called out from down the tunnel. "You'd better get up here right now!"

Krylov looked over at Leonard, who nodded at him. "I've got this. Go!"

Krylov turned and ran toward Marcus and the pair of soldiers who had stopped several meters away. "What's going on?"

Marcus pointed ahead of them at what had appeared around a turn in the tunnel. A massive barrier had been constructed from scrap wood, large pieces of concrete, barbed wire, rebar sharpened into spears and the shell of part of a metro car that was wedged sideways. The barrier was clearly man-made and blocked the entire width and height of the tunnel. Even the side doors and windows of the metro train were blocked, with no clear path through.

"I guess we found your survivors!" Marcus yelled over the howls of the creatures behind them as he and Roman helped Mikhail down onto the ground and propped him up against the wall near the barrier.

"You," Krylov barked at Roman, "get back there and help Mr. McComb. Mr. Warden, assist me here!"

Krylov used the butt of his rifle to break apart a few of the boards that were nailed across one of the windows of the train. He then strained over the lengths of barbed wire to see inside. The interior of the train car was dark, and there were more boards nailed up on the opposite side of the car, making it impossible to see into the station beyond.

"Hello!" he yelled out in Russian, hoping he could be heard over the other noise in the tunnel. "We are a rescue team responding to your transmission! Hello!" Krylov strained to hear any response for several seconds. When he heard nothing, he turned back to Marcus.

"Any replies?" Marcus asked hopefully as he worked to apply basic bandages and antiseptic to Mikhail's wounds.

Krylov shook his head grimly. "Stay here and listen." He jogged back to rejoin Leonard and Roman, who were braced against the wall at the bend in the tunnel, taking turns peeking out at the creatures and firing at them.

"Mr. McComb! What's the situation?"

"These bastards haven't given us anything yet. They're just testing us so far, seeing how we respond. They're probing for weaknesses. They're probably none too eager to charge in here after that explosive you used."

Krylov nodded. "Keep it up! I'm going to try and break through this barrier and see if we can get to the other side."

"No response from the survivors?"

"Nothing."

"Damn!" Leonard glanced at the battery level on the EMP rifle. "I'm down to a few bursts before I'm back to a conventional weapon. We're not hurting for bullets, but when these things decide to rush us as a group, it won't matter. Whatever you're going to do, you'd better hurry."

Krylov ran back to the barrier and called for Marcus to help him. "Come on, Mr. Warden. We must clear a way through this barrier before we're overrun."

Digging into his pack, Krylov pulled out a large multi-tool and opened the wire cutting attachment. After snipping away a section of the barbed wire, he once again began hammering at the boards that were covering the door to the train car with the butt of his rifle. Where other weapons would have had their internal mechanisms knocked out of alignment by the intensity of the blows, the AK-47's design meant it could go through hell and back and still function properly.

"One, two, three!" After the boards were gone, Krylov and Marcus used their feet to batter open the door, breaking what looked like a wooden broom handle off of the inside. With the path to the interior of the car clear, Marcus ran back for Mikhail and helped him to his feet. Mikhail hobbled into the train car and sat down in one of the seats, grunting with pain. As Marcus moved to go back outside and retrieve their packs, the young man pulled at Marcus' jacket.

"Give me a gun." He croaked the words out through pale lips.

"No." Marcus shook his head. "Stay still. Try to rest. I'll be right back."

"Mr. Warden!" Krylov shouted at Marcus as he left the train car. "Tell those two to get up here! I'll be through the other side of this door in just a moment!" After Marcus departed, Krylov turned to Mikhail and handed him a pistol. The young man nodded gratefully at Krylov and gripped the weapon tightly in his shaking hand.

A moment later, Leonard, Roman and Marcus came back to the train car, walking backward as they watched warily down the tunnel. Krylov peeked his head out of the train car door and watched, waiting for the creatures to come around the bend. He could still hear their noises, but they hadn't stepped into view of the blockade yet.

"What did you do to them?" Krylov directed his question at Roman, who looked back at Krylov and shrugged.

"No idea, sir. We killed a bunch of them, but they didn't move any closer to us. It was like they wanted to, but they were afraid."

"It makes no sense," Leonard said. "Why would they stop chasing us here, when we're trapped up against this... wait a minute." Leonard turned to look at the blockade, then back down the tunnel. "You're right. They're afraid."

"Afraid?" Krylov snorted at the suggestion. "Those things? Afraid of what?"

Leonard gestured to the blockade. "Of this. Of the people who built it, or what it represents. They won't come within sight of it."

Krylov's dismissive look vanished as he realized what Leonard meant. "They must have lost so many that they decided to stop coming here at all. They know it's a killing field."

"But now they've seen us down here. We're not dead yet, so they might decide that it's worth the risk to take a peek around the corner."

Without another word, Krylov turned back into the train car and started smashing against the boards on the opposite side. With no direct way to access them, he was forced to break the glass on the small windows and attack the wood through those with less force than he could otherwise bring to muster. As Leonard, Roman and Marcus spread out in the car, Marcus took over giving directions.

"Leonard, let's see if we can't get some of these scraps here and barricade the door again. Jam them in wherever you can." Leonard nodded, and they closed the doors before jamming the edges with pieces of broken wood and miscellaneous debris.

"Roman," Marcus looked over his shoulder as he spoke, "I want you watching out that window for the muties. If one of them so much as pokes his head around the corner, I want you to blow it off. Understand me?"

The soldier nodded and took his pack off. He slid the barrel of the sniper rifle through a gap between the boards that were nailed across a window and adjusted his scope to account for the extreme close range he would be working with. There wasn't a lot of light to go off of, but a small thermal imager on his scope revealed the cold contours of the tunnel, along with some splotches of heat where they had been sitting and standing for an extended period of time.

"Gah!" Krylov shouted as he broke through one of the boards and fell forward, smashing his face against the door of the train car. With one of the key supports broken, the door fell open, and Krylov went tumbling forward to land on the ground. He quickly scrambled to his feet, grabbed his weapon and scanned the area.

"We're clear! Get through now!" Krylov called back to the rest of the team in the train car. Marcus helped Mikhail get down onto the ground, where he knelt next to Krylov, putting his arm around his commander for support. Marcus carried both his and Mikhail's packs out of the train, then went back to check on Leonard's progress.

"Good enough?" Leonard stood back and ran his eyes over his handiwork. After wrenching a piece of metal tubing from the ceiling of the car, Leonard had forced it through the windows and bent it twice, forming a makeshift lock. The edges of the door had been filled with debris, and several longer boards were wedged between the door and the interior of the train car.

"It'll have to do." Marcus glanced over at Roman, who was still glued to his scope. "Come on. We're leaving."

After they had exited the train car, Leonard started working to seal the other set of doors before Krylov called to him. "Leave it! Let's get moving. We need to find a secure location to dress Mikhail's wounds!"

Krylov and Marcus took Mikhail's arms around their shoulders and began hurrying down the tunnel. Leonard stayed ahead of them with a light, while Roman followed up in the rear, alternating between watching behind them with his flashlight and looking through the thermal scope on his rifle.

After encountering the blockade in the tunnel, Krylov had hoped that they would be greeted by the friendly faces of desperate survivors on the other side, not another length of seemingly endless tunnels. "Where the hell is the station?" he shouted at no one in particular.

"Hey Krylov?"

Krylov and Marcus were both looking at the ground, watching their footsteps, when Leonard called out. When they looked up, they saw the silhouette of Leonard standing in the middle of the tunnel with both of his hands raised in the air. His gun and flashlight were on the ground next to him, but he was illuminated by a bright beam of light a few meters in front of him. Before Krylov could ask what was going on, the dark tunnel became awash in light, temporarily blinding the group and sending Krylov and Marcus grabbing for their weapons as Mikhail tried to hold up his pistol and Roman swung around with his rifle. Before they could locate targets to aim at, a booming male voice echoed down the tunnel. The Slavic accent was thick, and the voice spoke in Russian, shouting a short phrase a few times in a row.

"Krylov! What the hell is he saying?"

Krylov looked at Marcus and then back at Roman before slowly lowering his weapon to the ground. He translated the man's commands quietly as he knelt on the ground, helping Mikhail to do the same. "He says to drop your weapons and fall to your knees. If you are human, you will live. If you are machine, you will die."

As the team's eyes adjusted to the light, they could make out the shadows of over a dozen figures, all standing in front of them in the tunnel and wielding various weapons. Details were hard to make out, but the figures were thin and covered in filth, and they seemed more than eager to coat their weapons with a fresh layer of blood and gore.

While Mikhail, Roman, Marcus and Krylov all immediately complied with the voice's command, Leonard remained standing in defiance. "Krylov, you tell these sons of bitches that we're here to help them. Dammit, we're here to help you, assholes!"

As Leonard spoke, a tall figure stepped forward. He crossed the gap between the rescue team and the other figures in a few quick strides. With a swift movement, he grabbed Leonard by the front of his jacket and kicked him in the groin. Leonard shouted in pain and his legs went limp, but the man still held on, dangling Leonard in the air.

The man's breath was warm and came in ragged gasps, the result of a lung infection that had never fully healed. He eyed Leonard from top to bottom in the space of a few seconds. A pistol appeared in the man's other hand, and he tapped it against Leonard's artificial leg before turning it to point squarely at Leonard's head.

The man spoke again, though this time it was in heavily accented English.

"So, which are you? Man? Or machine?"

Book 2 - Archangel Falling

Chapter Seventeen

THE ARKHANGELSK

"Can't we go any faster?"

"Ma'am, you gave us the order yourself. If we increase speed while we're this close to shore we'll risk hitting debris in the bay."

Nancy paced the con nervously, watching the low-resolution feed coming through on several monitors at various stations. Hooked up to small cameras embedded in the Arkhangelsk's hull, the monitors displayed a real-time view of virtually every direction around the sub. Unfortunately, the water in the bay was murky, and the view only extended a few meters out in any direction.

While night was quickly approaching, the view from the sub's upper cameras showed an entirely different picture, albeit one that wasn't as useful to navigating the potential hazards of the bay. Located on a small peninsula called Poluostrov Krasheninnikova that jutted out inside of a large bay called Avachinskaya Guba, the small bay that held the nuclear submarine base of Rybachiy was called Bukhta Tar'ya.

The entire area was located on the massive Kamchatka Peninsula, and the capital of the area, Petropavlovsk-Kamchatsky, was located directly across Avachinskaya Guba. Several smaller cities dotted the area around the submarine base, which was lush with vegetation. Farms had once been located along the river on the northwestern side of the bay, though they had all but vanished as nature continued to reclaim the land.

The small peninsula where Rybachiy was located was no different than the rest of the area, containing rolling hills and large swaths of grass and trees. Several docks jutted out into the Bukhta Tar'ya Bay from the peninsula, and the view from the periscope confirmed the wreckage of a few vessels alongside them. A number of warehouses, barracks and administrative buildings stood at regular intervals up the side of the mountain facing the bay, and they too were being consumed by the surrounding vegetation.

Shipping containers lay half-submerged in the water just off the shore, and a dozen or so vehicles were parked along the road and in front of the warehouses. The entire area had an eerie feel to it, particularly in the fading light of the sun as it set behind the Arkhangelsk. The military appearance of half the buildings, the sunken ships and the overgrown buildings made Nancy wary of the whole area, a feeling that she could sense in the rest of the crew manning the con as well.

"Fine." Nancy sighed and addressed the sonar operator. "Do the best you can." While the bay was more than wide enough for the Arkhangelsk to traverse with ease, Nancy had wanted them to sail as close to the shore as possible for scouting purposes, so the going was painfully slow.

The man nodded and went back to his work while Nancy went back to her pacing.

"Ms. Sims?" Nikolay—her second in command—stepped up behind her and whispered. "You really should get some rest. It will be a couple more hours before we arrive and—"

"No thanks."

"Something to drink or eat, then?"

Nancy stopped and considered it for a moment. "Yeah, I suppose so."

"In the galley. I insist. Nothing will happen here that can't be immediately relayed to you."

Nancy started to protest, then another wave of exhaustion slammed into her and knocked the argument away. "Lead on." Nancy and Nikolay stepped through the hatch and off the con, but not before

Nancy gave a quick glance back, as though her mere look could spur the Arkhangelsk to a faster speed.

Thanks to the hard work of the boat's three technicians, the journey to the Rybachiy Nuclear Submarine Base had taken less time than Nancy had originally estimated. Only two of them were formally trained, but when the Arkhangelsk had lost a large portion of its crew to the swarms, they had recruited a technically-minded crewman and taught him how to maintain and repair the Arkhangelsk's machinery.

Now, with the sub and crew at risk, Nancy felt especially responsible for everyone on board. *Damn it, Krylov,* she thought for the hundredth time that day. *Why the hell didn't you let me go ashore and you stay with your damned boat?*

As if sensing what she was thinking, Nikolay broke the silence as they walked into the galley. "Commander Krylov would be proud of you, I think."

Nancy snorted. "Proud of what? Wearing out the floor in the con from pacing so much?"

"For responding so well under pressure."

Nancy took a plate and walked down the line and scooped spoonfuls of oddly-colored mush onto it. "I don't know, Nikolay. If this doesn't work... if we don't get the reactor repaired in time, I don't know what we'll do."

"It will get repaired in time, ma'am. There's no other choice in my mind."

"I sure as hell hope you're right."

The meal was eaten in silence—partially due to the mood in the air and partially due to the fact that it required an excessive amount of concentration to eat the food on board without gagging. It had been some time since they had taken any fresh supplies on board, and all that was left was a nutrient paste that provided plenty of nutrition but very little taste. Some canned vegetables and stale crackers were the high point of the meal, and everyone—including Nancy—generally took two or three times the normal serving size of those.

"Do you know what I would like to find on this base?" Nikolay asked the question while poking at a suspicious lump in the paste.

"What's that?"

"The first is a pump for the reactor."

"Well obviously."

"The second is one of those American-style buffets you've told me about."

Nancy groaned and pushed her plate away. "Oh, come on now, don't start talking about those again."

"Roasted meat, breads with butter, salads and pastries. It would be heaven!"

"I'm telling you, Nikolay, they were never as good as they sound." Nancy paused to wipe her mouth. "But I'll admit that even the worst of them would be better than this. We've got to find something fresh to eat. If we have to wait until we get back to New Richmond to eat something with actual flavor that didn't come out of a can, I'm going to pick out the plumpest person on board and roast them myself."

"I will be your alibi, Ms. Sims, so long as you save a piece for me."

Nancy laughed and stretched her back and shoulders before standing up. "Come on, Nikolay, let's go see how much longer this is going to take."

As the pair walked back to the control deck, Nancy couldn't help but feel slightly better after the diversion. The past twenty-four hours had been pure hell, and she hadn't slept a wink. There had been nothing to do, but she had stayed on the con the entire time, getting updates on their position and pleading with the technicians to eke every spare bit of speed out of the engines.

Upon arriving at the tip of the peninsula, the submarine had slowed to perform sonar scans of the docks and other underwater features near the coastline with two goals in mind. The first was to enable the Arkhangelsk to safely make its way to a dock where the crew could go ashore and start searching for parts to repair the reactor's pump. The second was to search for any sunken vessels that could—if the search for parts ashore failed—be scavenged. With a deadline of just over twenty-four hours left before the technicians estimated the pump would fail completely, time was not on their side.

"Report!" Nikolay had been a few paces ahead of her and entered the con first. He barked the order, causing every slumping back to suddenly stand straight to attention.

"Sir!" The crewman at the sonar station replied. "We're making good progress. It shouldn't be more than another hour before we've scanned the bottom along the entire coast."

"Any good news to report?" Nancy stepped up beside Nikolay and scanned the monitors. The ones showing an underwater view were still murky even though the Arkhangelsk's underwater lights were on. The cameras above water were now black, but one crewmember was standing at the periscope, watching through what Nancy assumed was the night vision camera affixed to it.

"Nothing, ma'am." The crewman standing at the periscope backed up and looked at her. "No bad news either. No movement on the shore, and no signs of radiation. We've also not found any major obstructions preventing us from getting to at least two of the docks."

"Keep it up, gentlemen." Nancy turned to Nikolay and motioned toward the central table. "Get Sergei and Andrey up here. I want to solidify a plan of attack so we can start searching immediately."

Nikolay nodded and spoke into the ship's intercom, summoning the two soldiers to the con. After they had barely made it back on board while the Arkhangelsk was departing Magadan, Nancy had thoroughly debriefed them on the events of their mission. Once all of the details had been rendered, Nancy dismissed them to get some much-needed rest, though she cautioned that they would be called upon again once they reached Rybachiy. True to her word, the plan she was formulating required that they again play a potentially pivotal role in the future of all on the sub.

"Andrey. Sergei." Nancy nodded at the two men as they walked onto the control deck.

"Ma'am." The pair stepped up to the center table and looked at the map on its surface. "Is this where we're headed?"

"We're already here, gentlemen. The Rybachiy Nuclear Submarine Base. We've been in the bay for a while now, but we're taking it slow while sonar scans the bottom for any obstructions. As soon as we can locate a safe place to dock, we're going to deploy teams to start scouring this entire base for a replacement pump for the reactor."

"Where do we fit in, ma'am?" Andrey glanced at his cousin. "We're soldiers, not physicists."

A sly smile passed Nancy's lips. "No, but you're about to get a crash course in becoming one." She waved for a man standing in a corner of the room wearing a white jumpsuit to step forward. "I believe you're familiar with Mr. Luka Delov, one of our three reactor engineers and all-around techies on board."

The men greeted each other and Nancy continued. "Luka, I'd like you to explain to Andrey and Sergei here exactly what we're going to need. They'll take that information in turn and pass it off to the teams they'll be leading through the base."

Luka nodded at Nancy and tapped a control on the side of the table. The three-dimensional display changed from a map of the region to a schematic of a series of pipes with a cylindrical object attached. "This housing you see here is the assembly that covers the salt water pump for the Arkhangelsk's reactors. Each reactor has one of these pumps, and they bring in seawater that is desalinated before cycling around a closed water system that flows through the reactor.

"By bringing this water in and exposing it to the high heat environment of the closed system, it rapidly heats and generates steam, which we then use to drive the turbines and power the vessel and everything inside."

Sergei rubbed his chin thoughtfully. "Seems simple enough."

"On the contrary. It's far more complicated, but those are the basics that you need to know for this exercise."

"So this is the pump that's failed?" Andrey pointed at the cylindrical object and Luka nodded.

"Indeed. Or, rather, the pump that is in the process of failing. Based on our experience, we estimate it won't last more than another twenty-four hours or so. Once it fails and the supply of cool water is no longer available, the reactor will begin to overheat."

"That's a bad thing, gentlemen," Nancy interjected. "A very bad thing."

"That is an understatement, ma'am." Luka glanced at her. "In any event, here's what we are looking for." Luka adjusted the controls on the table again, and it changed from a three-dimensional schematic to a series of black and white photos, along with engineering drawings. "These images are what the pump looks like outside of its housing. These are pictures of the housing itself. And these are some drawings to give you an idea of the rough shape and size."

Andrey looked up from the display at Luka. "Can't we just go look at the thing down in the reactor room?"

"That would be inadvisable. Things are…" Luka hesitated for a few seconds. "Tense."

"All you need to know is in these photographs here, gentlemen." Nancy tapped on the controls, and the display began automatically cycling through the images in series. "Memorize them. As soon as we dock, I'm going to have each of you lead a search party. I'll be taking a third party with Luka, and we'll coordinate to make sure we're close enough to both of you. Then, if you find something, he can confirm it as quickly as possible."

"Any idea where we'll find something like this?" Sergei stopped the flow of images, pausing the display on a photograph of the housing unit.

"Rybachiy is a repair and maintenance base for nuclear submarines. Before I was assigned to the Arkhangelsk, I worked with an engineer whose love for vodka and telling stories about his deployment to Rybachiy hounded every moment that I wanted to be asleep." Luka shook his head at the memory. "The man thought that everyone was dying to hear the intricacies of reactor repair and how many boxes he had to move from one side of a warehouse to another."

"This helps us how?" Andrey interrupted, growing impatient with the wandering story.

"Forgive me." Luka cleared his throat and continued. "According to his ramblings, parts for reactor systems were held in two separate warehouses. I don't know their exact locations, but I've marked what I believe are their general locations on the map for Ms. Sims."

"Thanks, Luka." Nancy pulled up an aerial view of the peninsula again. "It's a shot in the dark that things are still organized as they were years ago, but it's the best we've got to work with right now. Our other option is scavenging parts from any ships or subs that may be at the base, but that's a second priority. The swarms did a number on pretty much every single vessel above and under the water, so even if there's a compatible pump out there, it's probably going to be at the bottom of the bay."

"Make no mistake, gentlemen." Nancy began to circle the table while the three men watched the display. "We will find what we need here come hell or high water. Commander Krylov didn't leave me in charge just to lose this dilapidated piece of history to something as trivial as a water pump. We will succeed."

Nancy paused for a moment and looked over at Nikolay, who had been watching from the opposite side of the con. He smiled and nodded at her as she continued. "Sergei. Andrey. I want you two some-place quiet with Luka for the next hour. Ask him every single question you can think of. Memorize what these components look like, and then print out these photos to use as backups. Familiarize yourself with every aspect of this system. Once we deploy, I want a new part found and on board within six hours. Got it?"

The three men saluted smartly. "Yes, ma'am!"

"Good. Now get out of here and get to work!" Nancy watched the three men hustle off the control deck with a smile.

After they left, Nikolay walked up beside her and spoke softly. "Good speech, ma'am."

"Not too much?" Nancy sat down in the center chair and whispered back.

"Not at all. You're growing into the role quite well, I think."

Nancy smiled and patted Nikolay on the arm. While she was still feeling unsure about her command of the Arkhangelsk, Nikolay's encouragement and the positive responses of the crew were helping her to overcome those fears. As she watched the swirling waters glide by on the monitors, Nancy felt her eyes drooping and her head tilting to the side as she was lulled to sleep by the distant throb of the Arkhangelsk's engines. After what felt like only a few seconds, she was started awake by the voice of the sonar operator calling to her.

"Ma'am! Ms. Sims!"

Nancy stood up quickly, feeling the blood rushing from her head, and stepped toward the sonar station. "What is it?"

"There's something odd here on the scan, ma'am." He pointed at his screen, a green circle with a line lazily going around in a clockwise direction.

Nikolay approached the station and leaned in to get a better look. "What's being scanned right now?"

"We're looking at the area beyond the docks at the moment, where the rocks protrude into the water. There are a few vessels at the bottom along with some unidentified debris. I decided to scan the side of the rock wall itself, though, and I'm seeing a cavity."

"A cavity?" Nancy's eyes darted over the screen as she tried to interpret what it meant.

"Yes, ma'am. There's some type of opening in the rock wall. It's regular and circular—and there are two of them side by side."

"How big are they?" Nikolay asked.

"Still trying to get the exact dimensions, sir, but they're far larger around than our boat."

Nikolay stood back and nodded thoughtfully. "It's a submarine pen."

"A whatsit?" Nancy looked at him, confused.

"A submarine pen. A dock of sorts for subs. Used to keep them away from prying eyes in the sky. Many of them have underwater entrances so that a submarine may move in and out without being spotted."

Nancy caught the attention of a passing crewman and summoned him over. "Go find Mr. Delov. Tell him he's needed on the con immediately."

Nancy turned back to Nikolay. "I want to know what he knows about this. Continue, though, please."

Nikolay shrugged. "Unless Mr. Delov knows anything else, I'm afraid the only way we'll find out more information is by infiltrating the pen ourselves."

Nancy addressed the sonar operator. "This underwater entrance – you're sure it's wide enough for the Arkhangelsk to pass through?"

"Without a doubt, ma'am. Two of us could pass side by side if we were careful."

Nancy mused for a long moment in silence, then called out in a loud voice. "All stop!" After a brief flurry of activity, the pitch of the boat's engines changed. Luka appeared a moment later, out of breath as he stepped onto the control deck.

"Ma'am! You wanted to see me?"

Nancy waved him over and motioned toward the screen at the station. "Sonar's detecting a hole in the side of the rock face, circular and big enough for the Arkhangelsk to fit through even if she were pregnant. Apparently it's some kind of a sub pen, or that's what Mr. Sokolov thinks. What do you know about this?"

Luka shook his head slowly. "This… is the first I've heard of such a thing. But now that you've found it, it doesn't surprise me at all. If I had to guess, I would say that sensitive repairs and refits would have taken place in there."

Nancy looked at Luka incredulously. "Underwater?"

"No, ma'am. The entrance to the pen is underwater, but after a short distance, there would be a large chamber hollowed out. If the entrance is wide enough for us to pass through, it's likely big enough in there for us to surface."

"What about alternate means of entry? Is there a way down from the surface?"

Luka glanced at Nikolay and then back to Nancy. "I don't know. I'm sorry, ma'am."

Nancy sighed. "It's no trouble. Thanks anyway. Return to your work."

"Yes, ma'am." Luka gave a quick salute and then dashed out of the con. Nikolay examined the green display again before speaking next.

"If I might make a suggestion, Ms. Sims."

"By all means, Nikolay. I'm at a loss here."

"This presents an opportunity for us. A hidden submarine pen could—if protected from the swarms and the elements in general—potentially house not only parts to repair our reactor, but other supplies and spare parts we will need in the months and years to come."

"So you think we should give up on the surface plan and take the Arkhangelsk into this unknown place?"

Nikolay shook his head. "Not at all. I believe we should deploy a small team on the surface to sweep the warehouses while we explore this pen. We'll rendezvous with them back in the bay after a designated period of time, at which point one or both of our plans will hopefully have resulted in the procurement of the required part."

Nancy didn't hesitate in her answer. "Let's make it happen. Take care of the details here of getting us through that hole without scratching her paint. I'll take care of briefing Sergei and Andrey."

"They will be the surface team?"

Nancy nodded. "They did a damned fine job last time. I'm not leaving a job this critical to anyone else."

"Very good. I'll have us prepared to enter the pen in…" Nikolay glanced at his watch. "Twenty minutes?"

"Sounds good. Let's make this happen."

With that, Nancy left the control deck as Nikolay began shouting orders to the various stations. His voice echoed down the hall as Nancy ran to find the two soldiers and inform them that the plan they had been briefed on just a short time earlier was getting a few adjustments.

It took just a few minutes to find the pair and less than five more to explain to them the new plan. Both of them rushed to the armory to hastily put together their supplies, weapons and ammunition while Nancy arranged for the remaining inflatable to be prepared on the deck.

Twenty-five minutes after leaving the con, Nancy stood on the deck with Sergei, Andrey and three other crewmembers. Two of the crew held the inflatable steady as Sergei and Andrey boarded it, and the other held a light. Night was fully upon them, and after spending so much time cooped up inside the Arkhangelsk, Nancy felt strangely vulnerable crouched out on the deck.

"Remember – we'll be back out in six hours, no matter what. The radios probably won't work through all the rock, but we'll try anyway. Our transmitter's a lot stronger than yours, so we might be able to punch through. If you find the parts, secure them on the shore, and once you see our signal flare, fire yours and get back on board."

"Yes, ma'am!" Both men nodded at her and Nancy looked them both squarely in the eyes.

"I'm sorry to send you two out so soon after your last mission, but there's nobody else I trust enough with the fate of the Arkhangelsk. Take care of yourselves, and find that pump."

The two men nodded again, and Nancy patted the back of one of the crewmen who was holding the inflatable in place. In what seemed like a matter of seconds, the inflatable slipped off the deck, the twin motors started and the small craft vanished into the night, racing across the still waters toward the shore. Nancy stayed still, watching as the inflatable disappeared and silently praying that the two men would once again be successful.

"Ms. Sims?" Nancy's radio crackled, and she grabbed it.

"What is it, Nikolay?"

"We're ready, ma'am."

Nancy took a deep breath. "Understood. We're coming back down now. As soon as the hatch is sealed, take us under."

Chapter Eighteen

THE MAGADAN METRO

"WHICH ARE YOU?"

The man's pistol dug into Leonard's cheek, and he gritted his teeth in pain. Unable to speak with the weapon in his face, Leonard turned his head to the side to try and see what the others were doing. More of the strange people in the tunnel had appeared, and several of them were behind Krylov, Leonard, Mikhail and Roman. The people tied the rescue teams' hands behind their backs as Leonard tried to shout.

"Krylov! Tell this bastard who we are!"

The momentary surprise that had fastened Krylov's tongue was loosed as he was pulled to his feet. He shouted in Russian, his voice booming through the tunnel and making the captors behind him pause in their efforts.

"My name is Pavel Krylov, commander of the Russian nuclear submarine Arkhangelsk. We are here on a rescue mission!"

The man holding Leonard furrowed his brow at Krylov's pronouncement. "And which are you? Man or machine?"

"We are all men here, brother!" Krylov took a step forward, twisting out of the loosely tied bonds around his wrists as he pointed to Leonard. "Even him!"

The man narrowed his eyes at Krylov, then turned his attention back to Leonard. He spoke in Russian, directing his question at Krylov. "This one's hiding a metal leg. How do I know you're not some new trick by those monsters?"

Thinking quickly, Krylov tore the bandages off Mikhail's chest, causing the young man to yelp in pain. Blood oozed from the wounds over his shredded shirt and down over his pants. "See? No silver! No metal! We are all men!"

A light from one of the survivors flashed over Mikhail's chest, and the leader's eyes grew wide. He dropped Leonard to the ground and stepped back, waving his pistol at the group. "Why are there Americans with you? What's going on?"

Krylov took another step forward and held up his hands in a nonthreatening gesture. "Relax, please."

As Alexander passed the gun over Leonard's head again, Leonard seized his opportunity. He sprung up and wrapped both of his arms around the man's arm, twisting his body and wrenching the arm around. The man's arm went limp from the force of the blow, and his pistol dropped into Leonard's waiting hand. Following through on the motion, Leonard slammed him into the ground and put his right knee on the man's chest, holding the pistol a few inches from the man's right eye.

"Krylov, you tell this sorry sack of shit that we are here to help them!" Without waiting for Krylov to translate his words, Leonard stepped off of the man's chest, tossed the pistol to the side and stood back, his hands in the air level with his chest. The soft sounds of wood and metal bounced around the tunnel walls as every weapon in the room suddenly redirected to point at him.

The man stared at Leonard for several long seconds, eying him up and down before slowly standing to his feet. Krylov began to repeat Leonard's sentence when the man held up his hand to stop him.

"It is not necessary. I can understand." He spoke in accented English as he rubbed his sore arm and grimaced at Leonard. "You are not machine?"

Leonard pulled up his pant leg to reveal his prosthetic limb. "No monsters here."

The man nodded, then turned to Krylov. "You. Krylov. Why do you travel with these Americans? What's going on?"

"We're on a rescue mission. We are all part of the crew of the Arkhangelsk, a nuclear submarine in the bay outside the city."

"A submarine?" The man's eyes widened in shock, and there were murmurs from the surrounding survivors. "How—how has a submarine survived?"

Krylov smiled wryly and extended his hand. "I would love to tell you about it. But we have a man who's been wounded. Is there any place we can take him to get treated? We have supplies, but he needs to lie still for stitches and rest."

The man's gaze snapped between the five men and his fellow survivors for a moment before he nodded slowly, accepting Krylov's handshake. "Yes. Yes, of course." He then pointed at a pair of survivors who were still aiming their rifles at the group. "You two, help this man to the refuge." When the pair glanced at each other questioningly instead of moving, the man barked at them. "Now!"

The two survivors took Mikhail on their shoulders and helped Roman drag him down the tunnel, in the opposite direction of the barricade. "My men will make sure he is treated."

Leonard stepped forward and held out his hand after Krylov. "Thank you, Mr….?"

"Kozlov. Alexander Kozlov."

"Alexander." Leonard shook his hand firmly and forced a smile. "Thanks for not shooting me."

"You are welcome…" Alexander trailed off.

"Leonard McComb. Just call me Leonard. This is Marcus Warden, our wounded man is Mikhail Egorov and with him is Roman Lebedev."

Marcus, who had been loosed by the survivor standing behind him while Krylov and Alexander were talking, took Alexander's hand with some hesitation. "Quite a greeting you gave us there."

Alexander looked at Marcus and lowered his head. "It is regrettable. We did not expect anyone to answer our calls for aid, nor did we expect them to bring Americans." Alexander turned to Krylov and looked at him questioningly.

"How is it you have come here with Americans in tow?"

"These Americans are the ones that stopped the end of the world, Alexander. You would do well to show some respect."

Alexander scoffed. "Stopped the end of the world? For you, perhaps. For us?" He shook his head. "The end is still here."

"What's going on here?" Leonard asked.

Alexander started to answer, then a howl from down the tunnel in the direction of the barricade cut him short. "Quickly—we must get to the refuge. We can talk there. We mustn't stay here longer or they'll come after us."

Alexander turned abruptly and waved at the other survivors. "Move!" They started running down the tunnel in the direction Roman and Mikhail had gone, and Leonard, Krylov and Marcus picked up their backpacks and weapons and hurried to catch up. As they ran along at a breakneck speed, they had no time to converse further either amongst themselves or with Alexander. After a few minutes, though, Alexander slowed down as a yellow glow appeared in the tunnel ahead of them.

As the group turned a corner in the tunnel, they could see the source of the glow shining through two holes that had been cut into pieces of sheet metal. The sheet metal covered the tunnel completely, forming another barricade. This one, though, was far from abandoned. Three guards stood visible behind the slots, their weapons trained on the group as they approached.

"Hold your weapons, and open the gate!" Alexander shouted at the guards, and one of them disappeared from view. He reappeared a moment later as a door in the sheet metal swung open, allowing the survivors and rescue team access to the area beyond. Alexander and the survivors went in first, followed by Krylov, Leonard and Marcus. As soon as the last of them was through the gate, the guard slammed it, threw a large piece of rebar into a latch to lock it and then hurried back to his post.

Just inside the gate, the area was well-lit from small lights hanging on the walls. Another hundred meters down the tunnel, they could see an identical gate, though the second one appeared to be more heavily armored. The section of the tunnel between the gates was a chamber all to its own, acting as an airlock of sorts between the tunnel outside and—presumably—the station inside. Alexander's comrades had already passed through to the noisy and well-lit area beyond the second gate, but Alexander stayed inside the chamber with Krylov, Marcus and Leonard, standing in the middle of the tracks to block their path forward.

"Before we enter the refuge, I want more information."

Krylov leaned his rifle against the wall, unbuckled his pack and swung it onto the ground next to his weapon. "What do you want to know?"

Alexander eyed the three men carefully. Above him, the three guards stole occasional glances at the new arrivals as they stood watch. "You said these Americans stopped the end of the world. How?"

"That would be a very long story, but—"

"Just the basics, if you please, Commander."

Krylov spent the next several minutes giving Alexander an overview of Leonard, Rachel, Nancy and Marcus's general stories, ending with the Arkhangelsk expending her missiles on the AI's nexus. Alexander remained quiet throughout the story, watching Krylov intently as he soaked in every detail. Leonard watched Alexander closely as Krylov spoke, able for the first time to take in the details of the man.

Standing a few inches taller than Krylov, Alexander's build was surprisingly broad, though like the other survivors Leonard had seen, he was also extremely thin. He was dressed in a thick jacket that could have started off as green in color, but had taken on a dirt-brown appearance. His hands, though cracked and filthy, were rock-steady as he held his rifle. His pants and boots, like his jacket, were brown in color, and every exposed piece of skin on Alexander's body was caked in dirt, blood or some mixture of both.

Ragged breaths were drawn through cracked and dry lips, and Alexander's face was covered in half-healed wounds and jagged scars that cut dull white lines through his black beard. His hair was long and ragged with a stringy appearance, and he had the aroma of a man who hadn't taken a bath in a very, very long time. Alexander's eyes, though, were his most striking feature. A mixture of blue and green, they very nearly burned in the low light of the chamber. Though they appeared sunken on his ragged face, they had a natural fire to them that pierced the darkness.

When Krylov had finished his story, Alexander immediately continued with the questions. "So these nano-robots...you say they were responsible for what happened?"

"Yes."

"What do they look like?"

"In a swarm, they have the appearance of a silver cloud. If they infect a living host, though, they radically alter its appearance."

"Yes, we know this effect well."

"Mr. Kozlov," Krylov said, pivoting the conversation to ask his own questions, "how long have these creatures been attacking you and your people?"

Alexander took a deep breath and stared at the floor for a moment before looking back up at Krylov. "Since the beginning."

"You mean the last year?"

"A year. Ten years. A thousand. It doesn't matter any longer. While you've been rebuilding your cities, we've been clinging to the edge of life and trying not to fall off."

"Why didn't you radio for help sooner? Your transmissions only started recently."

Alexander leaned against the wall and sighed. "We tried. Many times we tried. We had the power to operate the transmitter for months before we could access it."

Leonard interjected himself into the conversation. "Wait, before you could access it?" He looked at Krylov with a puzzled expression. "Based on the location of the transmitter, we assumed you were able to tap into the controls from underground, in the metro. Isn't it right above us?"

Alexander snorted. "If only that were true. It is nearby, yes, but it took us many weeks to dig out the rubble. Then we spent weeks more repairing it from parts scavenged from the tunnels." He shook his head grimly. "No, if we could have called for help sooner, we would have done it."

"Alexander," Leonard continued, "why are the mutants—the creatures—so desperate to get in here?"

"They've been digging here for a long time. Two, maybe three months."

"But why?" Leonard persisted.

Alexander grew quiet at the repeated question and flicked his gaze between the members of the team. He pushed off the wall and stood up as he adjusted his grip on his rifle. "Follow me. You'll want to see your comrades. It will be easier to answer your questions inside the refuge."

Alexander waved to the three guards at the gate, and they nodded at him in response. He began walking toward the second gate without waiting for Krylov, Leonard and Marcus. As Krylov picked up his rifle and pack, Leonard whispered to his friend.

"Marcus, right now I'd give anything to be back up top running from those damned things."

Marcus nodded. "It sure as hell beats being surrounded by pissed-off Russians."

"Gentlemen." Krylov stepped close to them and glanced back and forth. "We three—and Mr. Egorov and Mr. Lebedev—are a team. No matter what happens here soon, you would do well to remember that."

Marcus felt his face flush. "Sorry, Krylov. I didn't mean—"

Krylov held up his hand. "It is water beneath a bridge, Mr. Warden."

Marcus smiled. "Water *under* the bridge, you thick-headed Ruskie."

Chapter Nineteen

RYBACHIY NUCLEAR SUBMARINE BASE

Andrey reached into his pocket and gently rubbed the large bear's tooth—his new good luck charm. "It's too quiet."

"You watch too many American movies, Andrey."

"Bah." Andrey waved his hand dismissingly at his cousin, jostling his night-vision goggles in the process and nearly sending them flying off his face. Sergei stifled a snicker, then grew quiet and serious again as they approached yet another warehouse.

After landing on the beach, Sergei and Andrey had quickly made their way to the marked buildings. It had taken nearly two hours over rough terrain and through thick vegetation, but after scouring both buildings thoroughly, they had discovered an abundance of rusted-out old submarine parts, but nothing that resembled what they were looking for.

With another four hours to go before the Arkhangelsk was due back on the surface, the pair continued to explore the small peninsula. The rest of the warehouses near the two they checked were quickly searched and then abandoned as they contained nothing of use. As the pair wound their way up into the dense tree-covered slopes of the base, the buildings' appearances became more and more dilapidated. Vines wound their way through roofs and walls of barracks, outbuildings were completely buried under moss and leaves, and every so often they would come across a building that looked intact from the outside but whose roof and floors had completely caved in many months prior.

The base was, in a word, a disaster zone. Fortunately, however, there were no signs of blast damage from any bombs, confirming the story told by the outdated satellite imagery of the area and the brief pre-dusk reconnaissance performed by the Arkhangelsk as she'd sailed into the bay. Radiation was a constant worry in the thick vegetation, but despite frequent checks of their Geiger counters, there was no sign of anything greater than normal background levels.

Andrey stopped to rest for a moment as he scanned the tree line ahead. "Do you really think they'll have stored parts this far up?"

"No. But it doesn't matter. Anything we find could be useful."

Andrey started trudging up the steep slope behind his cousin. "How old is this place anyway?"

"I have no idea. Some of these buildings have been overgrown for a lot longer than a year, though." After another few minutes of walking, Sergei stopped and looked back down at the coast. His vision was tinted green by his goggles, but he could still make out every detail in the trees, brush and buildings. Andrey's comment from earlier was beginning to nag at him, and he started wondering the same thing.

"Why the hell is it so quiet?" Sergei mumbled to himself, and Andrey patted him on the back.

"After our last experience, I'm glad for it." Andrey pointed at a squat building with remnants of white and blue paint on it near the top of the hill. "Come on. That's got to be the main building. Maybe we can find some information there."

The sound of nighttime insects grew louder the further the pair hiked into the dense undergrowth. They cut and slashed at overhanging branches as they went, creating a makeshift path straight up the hill to the next paved road. Once there, they picked up their speed, jogging for the main building in the distance.

It, unlike most of the other structures they had seen on the peninsula, was largely intact. Andrey lifted his goggles and saw in the moonlight the faint faded blue and white colors that mottled the surface in between splotches of the building's natural grey coloration. It sat half on a large piece of exposed stone and half on poured concrete, and the vegetation had been cleared from around it enough that there were only slight hints of growth creeping along its base.

There were still no signs of movement anywhere on the peninsula, though as they approached the building, both men felt their heartbeats quicken. The possibility of encountering any number of mutated creatures inside the closed quarters of the structure had them tense and ready to fire at the slightest provocation.

"We'll clear the building to the top, then work our way back down," Sergei whispered to his younger cousin as they neared the main door.

Andrey shook his head. "That'll take far too long. This place is massive. Manifests and repair logs should be on the second floor. We'll clear the first floor, then the second. Once we're done, I'll start searching their records while you keep lookout."

"Fine. If there's even a hint of something in there, though…"

"Yes, we'll do a full sweep."

Both men double-checked their rifles and the straps on their night vision goggles and backpacks. Once everything was secured and verified, Sergei quietly stepped through what used to be a large glass door that had long ago been shattered. The main hall through the building stretched directly from the front door to the back, with the far back wall visible even from the front. Doors branched off from the main hall at regular intervals, their signs long since faded and worn away, and halfway down the main hall, a smaller one crossed over to the left and right.

The cousins moved quickly as they went through the building. Sergei moved along the left side of the hall while Andrey stuck to the right. Each time they passed by a door, they would quietly open it, quickly scan the room and then move on to the next door. With a larger team, the sweep would have been more thorough and involved checking every nook and cranny in the rooms. Given their time constraints and the fact that they were only two men, though, they opted for a more balanced approach.

By the time the pair had reached the midpoint of the first floor, they were already beginning to relax. Each room they checked was free of movement and signs of mutants. In fact, the building's interior and contents were surprisingly intact. When the pair finally reached the double staircase at the back wall of the first floor, Andrey tapped his cousin on the shoulder as they started to ascend the stairs.

"This place is remarkably well-preserved. How is it no one was here to be mutated? You'd think we would have seen signs of them if they were."

Sergei shrugged and then motioned at the floor above them. "Come on. Let's get this place cleared and start searching for those parts."

Starting at the back of the second floor and working their way to the front of the building, the pair encountered more of the same. More dusty rooms, well-preserved furniture and a lack of anything resembling mutants. Andrey had the desire to pull off his goggles, turn on his flashlight and start shouting in the hall to see if there was anything in the floors above them, but he restrained himself for fear of waking something that might be lurking in the shadows.

"We're clear here," Sergei whispered to Andrey as they checked in the final set of rooms. Outside, off the front of the building, they could see the road through a large hole in the building that looked as though it, like the front door, had once held a large piece of glass. A slight breeze sent the trees outside the building shaking and swept away a few drops of perspiration from Andrey's neck.

"Come on, then. Let's get to searching."

"Where to first?"

"I saw filing cabinets a few rooms back. I'll start there."

Sergei followed his cousin as Andrey retraced his steps and walked into a large room with several desks spread out in the middle. Filing cabinets lined every spare inch of wall space, and Andrey motioned for Sergei to close the door behind him.

"I can't do this in the dark with these damned things." Andrey yanked off his goggles and rubbed his eyes, then pulled off his backpack and took out a flashlight. "Keep watch at the door while I search."

Sergei cracked the door open and leaned against the doorframe, keeping himself pointed away from the light and training his eyes on the hallway. Flashes of bright green crossed the edges of his vision as Andrey began rummaging through the cabinets, swinging his flashlight around as he went.

"Come on…" Andrey muttered to himself as he rifled through the cabinets, pulling out folders at random in an attempt to figure out what the cabinets contained. Some folders were full of photographs of soldiers, along with their medical records. Others contained records of vessel deployments in the area. Still others were full of nothing but repair and maintenance logs for each and every building on the peninsula.

After fifteen minutes and two dozen filing cabinets, Sergei whispered across the room. "Anything?"

Frustrated, Andrey threw a folder of papers into the air over his head. "Not a damn thing!"

With no hint of anything else being in the building with them, Sergei quietly closed the door, pulled off his goggles and switched on his own flashlight. "Come on. I'll help."

The pair worked together in silence for another half hour until, finally, just as Andrey was beginning to feel another surge of rage, he hit the jackpot. "Hey, look here," he whispered to his cousin.

Sergei dropped a stack of papers back into the drawer he had open and walked over to Andrey. "What is it?"

"Submarine arrival, departure and repair logs. It says here that there was a P949 that came in for repairs and maintenance two weeks before the bombs."

"So what? We need spare parts, not another boat."

Andrey sighed and jabbed his finger at the sheet of paper. "Don't you remember anything the tech told us? The Arkhangelsk uses OK-650 reactors. Two of them. This says the P949's used the same reactors."

Sergei's eyebrows went up as he realized what Andrey was saying. "So… they should be interchangeable? The parts for the pump, I mean."

"If it wasn't torn apart by the swarms, then yes, I think so." Andrey flipped through the other papers near the one he had picked out and scooped them up and into his pack. "None of the warehouses had anything close to what we need, and we're not going to get anywhere trying to sort through the rest of this. Let's just get out of here."

Sergei nodded. "Agreed. But I don't want to give up on the warehouses just yet. We can search them again while we wait for the

Arkhangelsk." He checked his watch. "There's more than enough time."

Andrey sighed. "Fine. Can we go already? This building is starting to feel strange."

The two men turned off their lights, gathered their gear and donned their goggles. The shadows of the room changed into shades of green as they stole quietly through the door, making their way down the hall at a fast pace toward the stairs. Upon reaching the first floor, Sergei put his arm out in front of Andrey to stop him, and they both stood still for a moment before Andrey whispered.

"What is it?"

Sergei shook his head and put his finger to his lips, then closed his eyes and tilted his head. From somewhere, far off, he could swear that he had heard something.

Tap. Tap. Tap.

The sound of metal was louder this time, though still faint enough that it couldn't be heard unless you were straining. In the back of the dark building, with its wide hall and distant doorway, the sound was faint, but distinct enough that Andrey felt his skin crawl. He slowly raised his rifle and took a step forward before Sergei put a hand on his shoulder.

"Wait." The whisper was quiet, and Andrey stopped. Sergei tilted his head in every direction, trying to identify the source of the noise as it continued.

Tap tap. Tap. Tap. Tap tap tap tap.

There was no pattern to the noise, and the more he listened, the more he could make out the rise and fall in its volume. It sounded, he finally thought, like someone was banging on a wall or a door, trying to get through.

"This way," Sergei whispered to Andrey, and he began moving down the hall, trying to find the source of the noise. He took a left at the side corridor through the building, both pleased and increasingly nervous to hear the sound getting louder.

"It's somewhere in there." Andrey pointed at the end of the hall. As the two men approached, Sergei could see that a narrow staircase sat off to the right, leading down into some kind of sub-basement. The sounds were growing increasingly louder as the pair approached the stairs, and as they began to descend, Andrey was overcome with a wave of fear.

"Shouldn't we just go?" he whispered to his cousin, who was just a step or two below him.

"Not until we see what this is." Sergei wasn't about to admit it, but he was itching to put a bullet or twelve into a mutant. There was something off about the tapping, too, and he wasn't entirely sure whether it was being made by a mutant, or by something—or someone—else entirely. *Only one way to find out,* he thought.

After making a few turns, the stairs ended abruptly, dumping out into a small room. The room was barren and, unlike the rest of the building, comprised entirely of steel. The metallic tapping was nearly painfully loud inside, and the two men finally saw the source. At the back of the room, held in place by a heavy iron bar, a riveted steel door stood. It was being struck by something stuck on the other side.

As Sergei advanced on the door, Andrey tried to pull on his arm to stop him, but Sergei broke his cousin's hold. "Sergei!" Andrey hissed. "What the hell are you doing? Are you insane?" Andrey's eyes were wide with panic.

"Cousin." Sergei turned to look at Andrey. "If this is a threat, you're going to put it down. Besides, who knows what's under this building. It might have exactly what we're searching for, eh?"

"Mother of God…" Andrey's gave the bear tooth a quick pat for good luck, then tightened his grip on his weapon and widened his stance, bracing himself for whatever might appear through the door.

"On the count of three, be ready to fire!" Sergei positioned himself on the side of the door and placed his hands on the bar, ready to throw it off of its hooks and allow the door to swing freely.

Tap tap tap tap. Tap.

"One!" Sergei whispered.

Tap. Tap. Tap tap.

"Two!" Andrey mouthed the word along with Sergei's whisper.

Without warning, the tapping stopped, just as Sergei whispered the final number.

"Three!"

Chapter Twenty

THE MAGADAN METRO

W hile he had been distracted by the drama that had ensued with Alexander and the other survivors, Leonard was starting to feel a mild sense of panic set in. The enclosed portion of the tunnel in between the two gates somehow felt even more restrictive than the rest of the metro, for reasons he couldn't fathom.

It was at that point, when he was glancing between the lights that were strung up on the walls on either side, that one of the three guards that had been stationed at the first gate came rushing fast. His feet pounded on the gravel and his rifle bounced from the strap around his neck as he ran full tilt to catch up with Alexander, who had just stopped at the entrance to the second gate. A hurried conversation ensued, with the guard pointing back at Leonard and the others. Even from a distance, Leonard could see the scowl on Alexander's face as the survivor turned to glare at the trio before starting to walk back toward them.

"Hold up," Leonard whispered to Marcus and Krylov. "Something's wrong here. He looks really pissed off."

The trio stopped in their tracks, standing shoulder to shoulder and gripping their weapons tightly, but still keeping them pointed at the ground.

"What game is this that you play?" Alexander thundered at them. He stopped a few feet away, his grip tightening on his pistol.

"Mr. Kozlov, what's wrong?"

"You know damned well what's wrong!" Alexander motioned behind the rescue team with his pistol, and Leonard flinched as he readied himself for what felt like an inevitable gunfight.

"Alexander, we don't—" Marcus tried to speak, but Alexander cut him off, pointing the gun at his face and shouting.

"You will shut your mouth!" He waved his pistol at Krylov. "These monsters have moved past the blockade! Our guards on the outer gate spotted them down the tunnel, moving closer. This is the first time they've broken past the blockade in months!"

"You think *we're* responsible for that?" Marcus stared at Alexander in shock.

"Of course you are! You brought the monsters down upon us once again!"

Krylov stepped forward, and for the first time that he could remember, Leonard watched the commander of the Arkhangelsk very nearly explode with rage.

"Alexander Kozlov! You will stop this nonsense at once!" Alexander took a half step back as Krylov advanced on him. "We are here on a rescue mission, to save you and your people and bring you to safety. These men are part of *my* crew, so you will cease this hostility *now*." Krylov pulled the radio from his jacket pocket and held it up. "Otherwise, all it will take is one word and my vessel will ensure none of us leave this place ever again."

Leonard and Marcus both looked at Krylov in shock. He was bluffing, of course, but the threat felt very real. It, combined with the looks on Marcus and Leonard's faces, was enough to send Alexander back another half step. His features softened, and he lowered his pistol. Krylov, in response, tucked his radio away and stepped back, his voice calm and level once again.

"Mr. Kozlov. We are here to help you. If those creatures followed us in, then I am truly sorry, but what else were we to do? We're answering *your* call for help. Please give us a chance to help you and your people before you decide that we're some new evil you have to dispatch."

Alexander nodded slowly, then looked up at Krylov. "I am sorry,

Commander. And to you two as well. Forgive me. These monsters have been growing bolder every day. They would have broken through the barrier soon, even if you hadn't shown up. They're growing desperate."

"Desperate for what?" Leonard asked.

Alexander sighed and slid his pistol back into its holster. "Come with me."

Marcus, Leonard and Krylov walked behind Alexander to the second gate. When Alexander waved at the guards, the door slid open and the four men walked through. "Welcome to the refuge," Alexander said. "Our home."

Passing through the gate, the rescue team shielded their eyes from the brightness within. It took their eyes a moment to adjust, but when they did, all three of them stopped in their tracks to take in the sight. The massive underground station had been converted from a waiting area for metro trains into a full-fledged city.

Wooden stairs led up from the tracks to a platform that had been built over the metro line for the entire length of the station to extend the available floor space. Lights hung haphazardly from long wires that had been nailed into the walls and ceiling. Decorations in the form of children's drawings, elaborately crafted blankets and even a few paintings hung in various places on the walls. The crystal chandeliers were all intact, unlike in the first station the team had visited, and while they provided no light themselves, they acted as a place to hang even more LEDs along with miniature Russian flags.

The refuge consisted of two sides divided evenly down the middle by a narrow passage. On the left side, as the team entered the station, were makeshift beds stacked three high and laid out behind shoddily-constructed wooden privacy barriers with sheets and clothing draped over them to help keep the noise level down. Beyond the sleeping area were a few handcrafted tables made from scrap lumber. Behind the tables were three large cookpots atop electric burners.

On the right side of the room, atop the wooden platform, was a mishmash of crates and boxes, tools, weapons and other equipment. A series of thick blankets hung from the station's support columns down the center of the room in an attempt to keep the noise on the right side from reaching the relative calm of the left, but it was obvious that it was a futile attempt.

While the unexpected brightness and complexity of the refuge assaulted the rescue team's eyes, their ears were also filled with the sound of dozens of people talking, crying and even singing. A few of the survivors who had been in the tunnel with Alexander were there, and their wretched appearance was matched quite evenly with every other person in the refuge.

Children clung to their parents as the camouflage-clad rescue team walked through the door, and Leonard could feel eyes from every corner room roving over his person, taking in his clothes, gear, weapon and generally healthy, well-fed appearance. On the right side of the room stood and sat several men and a few women, all covered in grease smudges and wielding various tools as they worked on repairing weapons, reloading ammunition or constructing new equipment for use in the refuge. Through a gap in the divider, Leonard could see a few people tending to the cookpots and a few children running in and out of the sleeping area as their mothers sat on the floor, talking quietly together.

As Leonard took in the whole of the station, he at once felt relieved to be out of the confines and darkness of the tunnels, but also incredibly saddened at the state of those who had spent months living underground. As a small child no older than six ran by on the left side of the refuge, she paused for a moment and clung to the divider, staring through the opening at Leonard with wide eyes. Leonard smiled and raised his hand to wave, but she was gone in a flash.

"Holy hell." Marcus whistled quietly. "It's like a whole city in here."

Alexander turned back and nodded grimly. "It is, yes. This has been our home for…" He paused and thought for a moment. "Longer than I care to recall."

"How have you managed to survive down here for so long?" Leonard walked forward, craning his neck to take in the entirety of the setup. "Where are you getting power for your lights? And food? And anything else?"

"This will take time to tell." Alexander motioned at the trio. "Please, take off your packs. You may keep your weapons, if you wish."

Krylov eyed Alexander carefully. "A show of good faith?"

"Of trust."

Krylov nodded with approval. Alexander started to speak, but he stopped when a young woman ran up to him. "Alexander! They're pushing against the barriers in the north end, and one of the patrols heard digging in a side passage!"

Alexander sighed and closed his eyes. "Damn. They're growing bolder. You three may need your weapons sooner than you thought."

Leonard glanced at the young woman as he addressed Alexander. "What's going on?"

"Thank you, Maria." Alexander patted the woman on the back. "Get some food and beds prepared for our guests, will you?"

"Alexander?" Leonard asked again. "What's going on?"

Alexander sighed deeply again before speaking. "They're testing us now. Finding our new limits. We drove them off once, months ago. Killed hundreds of them in front of the barrier you three broke through. Now that they've seen that there is a way through, they're starting to push us again, from all directions. It's only a matter of time before they break through and overwhelm us."

"You killed... hundreds of them? At the barrier?" Marcus shook his head. "How could that be? There were no bodies."

"This was months ago. Every time we gunned one down, two more would leap in, grab the corpse and take it away. Sometimes we'd see the same devil fighting again a day later, though with a few more holes in its body. Sometimes we never saw them again."

Leonard looked at Krylov and Marcus as he began to piece together the connection. "You saw the same creatures multiple times? Even after killing them?"

"Yes."

"Did you recognize any of them?"

Alexander swallowed hard. "Yes. Many friends. A few family."

Leonard's voice dropped, and he spoke slowly. "Alexander. This is very important. I need to know *everything* about these creatures. Where you've seen them on the surface, where they started coming from; everything."

"Of course. There will be time for that. Our defenses will hold for now. But come, get some food and rest first. We can talk later."

Krylov shook his head. "Alexander, we've not come to rest. We're here to get you and your people out."

Alexander laughed at the statement, then began coughing. When the coughing died down, he gave another chuckle and smiled grimly. "Don't you understand? There is no rescue from this place now. The devils are at our every doorstep, and it's only a matter of time before they break in. There's nothing that you and your friends can do to stop that."

Chapter Twenty-One

Submarine Pen

When the Arkhangelsk was running underwater, it was an entirely different experience than when it ran on the surface. The physical effects were minor—but present nonetheless—and mostly consisted of not being subjected to the wind and waves of the surface. The mental effects, however, were entirely different, especially for those not born and bred into the service. As the submarine descended into the depths, the hull creaked and groaned under the increasing pressure, and Nancy once again had the distinct feeling of being trapped in a soda can that at any moment could be trod upon and burst.

Although the entrance to the submarine pen was not far below the surface of the water, the feeling returned to Nancy when she heard water rushing around the sub as it slowly sank into the depths. "I hate this stupid boat," she muttered to herself as she walked down the corridor, winding her way back to the control deck.

A few minutes later she stepped onto the con, and Nikolay stood to greet her. "We're about to enter the passage, ma'am. Sonar's guiding us in, and we're watching the cameras carefully. The water's clear enough to see out to the passage walls with the spotlights on."

Nancy circled around the control deck to peer at the bank of monitors showing the sub's external camera views. Smooth walls of rock punctuated by the odd discoloration, crack or group of sea creatures passed slowly by as the crew regularly called out the distances between the Arkhangelsk and the passage. While pushing a tube through a cylindrical hole twice its diameter might have sounded like child's play, the massive sail jutting from the top of the sub made the operation all the more delicate. Keeping her speed slow and constantly monitoring their position both visually and through their instrumentation was the only way to make it through without tearing apart the hull.

A full half hour after the nerve-wracking journey had begun, the sonar operator called out with delight. "We're near the end of the passage; it's opening up!"

The smooth rock walls began to vanish into darkness as the tunnel widened, and it was only a few minutes later when a crewman called out. "We're clear!"

"All stop!" Nikolay thundered, and the pitch of the engines changed once again. "How do we look up top?"

One of the crew answered immediately. "Showing all clear, sir. We can surface any time."

Nikolay turned to Nancy. "Ma'am. Whenever you're ready."

"Do it." Nancy clenched her fists. "Take us up."

A flurry of orders raced across the con, and Nancy could hear the ballast tanks emptying as the Arkhangelsk slowly rose to the surface. The view on the cameras was still dark, showing only stray motes of debris swirling by in the spotlights under the water. When the upward movement finally came to a halt, Nancy turned her attention to the monitors showing the upper cameras.

They, too, were dark, as the lights positioned on the hull were not powerful enough to pierce whatever cavern the Arkhangelsk was in. "Get me a team ready to go out there. I want Luka Delov and three soldiers to run guard duty with me. And get some lights going that'll let us see more than our hands in front of our faces. I'll be in the armory. Sound a general alert when we're clear to go out."

"Ma'am?" Nikolay looked concerned. "You're going out?"

Nancy leaned close to Nikolay and whispered harshly—more so than she intended. "There is no way in *hell* I'm staying on this boat this time. I'm taking a group with me, and we're going to explore the area and see if we can locate that pump. Keep several men on deck ready to shoot at anything that moves that isn't us. Got it?"

Nikolay nodded. "Yes, ma'am."

Nancy's features relaxed, and she nodded sheepishly back at him. "Thanks." She turned and left the con, heading for the armory as she heard Nikolay making calls over the intercom to the crew that would be joining her. It had been a few months since she had picked up a rifle beyond using it for target practice, but if the last year had taught her anything, it was how to adjust on the fly.

An alarm on the boat's intercom preceded Nikolay's voice calling out a general alarm. "Exploratory team to their designated exit, guards to their posts. All hands, we are now at a general alert status."

Nancy felt the tension wash over her, as it no doubt was doing for the rest of the crew as they all prepared to potentially face hostiles at any moment. The placement of several guards on the top deck and sail of the Arkhangelsk was designed to prevent any mutants from gaining access to the interior of the vessel, but it was difficult to be over-prepared to face the creatures.

Nancy triple-checked her rifle before grabbing several extra magazines and a spare radio and tossing them into a small shoulder bag. She slung a pair of night vision goggles around her neck and jogged out of the armory and toward the hatch where her team was waiting.

"Everyone ready?"

One of the Arkhangelsk's engineers, Luka Delov, and three soldiers stood before her, all nodding in unison. "Yes, ma'am!"

"Good. I want this to be a quick and quiet run. We have absolutely no idea what's going to be out there once we step off the boat. We'll have more than enough light around the Arkhangelsk, but once you get beyond its reach, switch to your active infrared night vision. Our goal is to locate and secure something that looks like this."

Nancy passed out copies of a few of the pictures of the reactor pump to the three soldiers. "This is our top priority, a replacement pump for our reactor. If you have any questions about something you locate, ask Luka for confirmation. Make sure you prioritize his protection as well. We can't afford to lose one of our technicians on this run." Nancy checked her watch. "We only have a few hours, so time is of the essence here. Got it?"

"Yes, ma'am!"

"Let's go." Nancy started ascending the ladder as the rest of the group fell in behind her.

When Nancy emerged from the hatch onto the deck of the Arkhangelsk, she took a deep breath of the cool, musty air. It felt old and moist, with a hint of metal, rotting wood and plenty of salt mixed in. On the long, flat deck of the sub, half a dozen soldiers holding rifles were spread out, each manning a portable spotlight that had been set up on a tripod. More powerful than handheld spotlights, these cast a wide beam over vast distances, and the soldiers moved them slowly as they scanned the interior of the submarine pen.

Nancy wasn't sure what she had been expecting to see inside the mysterious underground cavern, but it certainly wasn't anything close to reality. The pen was huge—so large, in fact, that not even the spotlights were powerful enough to reach the far end of the cavern off the port side of the Arkhangelsk. The top of the cavern was at least several stories high, and half a dozen cranes loomed overhead, their cables dangling over the water from some long-forgotten task. Heavy coats of paint hadn't kept the rust away in the last year, and corrosion covered every metal surface in sight.

The sides of the cavern that were visible were dark and slick, with only the faintest hints of some light-abhorring plant life clinging to them. Built up against the walls was a massive U-shaped set of pilings and planks, with additional metal and concrete supports. This dock structure surrounded the port, starboard and fore of the Arkhangelsk, though the area of open water was much longer and wider than the boat itself.

Nancy guessed that there was room inside the pen for at least five submarines of the Arkhangelsk's class to sit side by side, and the length of the pen allowed for at least three of them end to end. To top it all off, the pen was subdivided by short docks that jutted out from the back of the cavern, where the top's inverted "U" shape wrapped around, to allow crew and workers to easily board and disembark from the craft they worked on.

As Nancy looked to the back of the cavern, she saw that there were structures that had been built, partially out of wood and partially carved into the living rock. While she couldn't quite tell what they were from a distance, she was certain that if a spare pump was to be found, it would most likely be inside one of the structures.

Nancy walked across the deck, followed by Luka and the four soldiers, then stopped midway and motioned for them to join her. The Arkhangelsk had surfaced with a dock close to the starboard side, and as Nancy stood on deck, she could feel the vessel slowly moving closer to the dock so that they could disembark with ease.

"All right, listen up. As soon as we're close enough, I want everyone off. We're going to clear this place from the right side all the way to the back, where those buildings are." Nancy pointed off across the fore of the Arkhangelsk at the structures she had noticed before. "Luka, you stay with me in the back. I want a fast sweep done here. I want you gentlemen to clear us a path and do it correctly, but don't waste any time. Got it?"

The three soldiers nodded. "Yes, ma'am."

Nancy turned to watch the dock slowly approaching. After another few minutes, the Arkhangelsk gently bumped up against it, causing both the vessel and the dock to groan from the light impact. "Go!" Nancy watched as the three soldiers charged across the deck and leapt onto the dock. She and Luka followed, and she spoke to him as they ran.

"You've done your mandatory firearms training, right?"

Luka clutched his rifle nervously, holding it as though he hadn't touched one before in his life. "Oh yes. Well. The mandatory minimums."

Nancy rolled her eyes. "Just stay behind me and keep your finger off the trigger. Try not to shoot yourself or me, okay?" Luka tried to smile, but Nancy had already made the jump from the Arkhangelsk and was running after the trio of soldiers. Luka followed her, nearly slipping as he landed on the damp wood of the dock.

Ahead of Luka and Nancy, the three soldiers were spread out a few meters apart as they moved quickly down the length of the dock, checking underneath rotting tarps and inside large boxes for any of the mutants. Every time one of them kicked open a shipping container, broke the lock on a box or lifted the edge of a covering, Nancy was certain that a creature would come charging out. After she had lost count of how many checks the soldiers had done without incident, she began to relax, glad for some small measure of peace.

Once Luka caught up with her, Nancy began having him check some of the larger crates and boxes on the dock with her, on the off chance that one of them might have traces of a manifest or other information that could lead them to a replacement pump. Instead, what they found were miscellaneous pieces of machinery—half of which excited Luka for reasons Nancy didn't want to know about—and half of which contained scrap that had been pulled off of vessels and would have usually been hauled away to be disposed of.

It took nearly a full half hour for the soldiers, Nancy and Luka to clear the right side of the dock. After meeting back up with the soldiers at the right back edge of the cavern, Nancy took a moment to sit down and plan their approach for searching and clearing the buildings.

"You've seen nothing, right?"

The soldiers shook their heads and one answered. "No."

"Good. Let's start from this side. You three start clearing the buildings. Go slower now, more methodically. Once you reach the end, come back to meet us. I'll want one on patrol out front while two help us search."

The soldiers nodded and rose to their feet. They approached the first structure and opened the door carefully, using their goggles to pierce the blackness. A moment later, one of them popped back through the door and called out softly to Nancy and Luka. "Clear!"

Nancy nudged the technician, and they both headed for the building, flashlights in hand. "Wait till we get inside to turn them on," she whispered to Luka, not wanting them to give away their position to any enemies unless absolutely necessary.

The building's façade was aluminum and wood, thin enough that it wouldn't have held up under the slightest of breezes. For its intended purpose of organizing supplies, though, it did the trick. Built partially into the side of the cavern, the small structure was filled with short, wide shelving units full of cardboard boxes. The boxes were in surprisingly good shape given the fact that they had been sitting in the damp environment for the last year. The lack of sunlight had helped to halt the spread of most plants and insects that would have consumed them.

Nancy and Luka entered the building, and Nancy waved at the

soldiers to move on to the next structure. Once they were gone, she and
Luka pulled off their headgear and switched on their flashlights. The
light was blinding at first, but as their eyes adjusted, they began to rifle
through the boxes for some trace of the pump they were after. Disappointment soon followed as they discovered nothing that they needed
or wanted for the Arkhangelsk.

Over the next hour, the results were more or less the same with
every building they checked. Each contained plenty of equipment, but
nothing resembling the necessary pump, and very few with anything
worth saving to load onto the Arkhangelsk. The last building along the
back wall, however, was different. Unlike the others, it was constructed
of thick steel, and the soldiers spent several minutes working to break
the dual locks on the door. By the time they finally got the door free,
Nancy and Luka were waiting behind them and followed them in, no
longer concerned about the potential for danger.

Inside, their flashlights revealed a room far larger than any of those
the other buildings possessed. The building extended for a dozen
meters back into the cavern wall, and the ceiling was high, with a wide
staircase leading up through the darkness at the back. Like the other
buildings, this one was also lined with shelving units, though instead of
holding broken-down machinery and old cardboard boxes, the shelves
were filled with polished metal and shining plastic.

Freshly machined or imported parts were stacked and organized
neatly, with small handwritten labels beneath each separate section to
denote what they were. Most of the equipment was foreign to Nancy,
but based on their condition and the look on Luka's face, she knew that
they had finally hit upon pay dirt—or something close to it.

"What've we got here, Luka?"

Luka's eyes were wide as he walked around the front of the room
and ran his hand along the parts and equipment. "We need all of this
back on the Arkhangelsk."

"You found a pump?"

Luka scanned the front of the room and shook his head. "I don't
see one here, no. But it's very possible there's one in a crate somewhere
else in here. We need to start checking everything thoroughly. But even
if not… this is incredible. We can upgrade several of the Arkhangelsk's
systems with this equipment.

"The navigation systems, sonar, half a dozen of our broken hydraulics and compressors… most of what they have here is compatible with our systems." Luka turned to look at Nancy. "We need all of this on board, ma'am. Right now."

Nancy furrowed her brow. "Quality of life improvements are all well and good, but that's not our primary concern. I'll have Nikolay send some people with dollies to get whatever you want from here, but we need to keep looking for a pump."

"Of course." Luka's expression sagged as his excitement was dampened. "Otherwise, we will have nothing to upgrade. I understand." He paused for a few seconds and smiled again. "But still—if we find a pump, the things we'll be able to repair… this is amazing, ma'am."

Nancy forced a half-smile. "I'm glad to hear it. And that's 'when' we find a pump. Not 'if.' Just remember that."

"Of course. When we find a pump."

Nancy turned to one of the soldiers standing near the entrance to the room. "Get back to the Arkhangelsk and report to Sokolov directly. Tell him we need four more men here to start emptying out this room, and have them bring some lights with them. I saw hand carts in one of the other buildings; they can use those for the time being." Nancy looked at the other two soldiers. "Start setting up a post outside this building. Keep an eye on the left side of the docks, and make sure nothing approaches. We'll check and clear that area shortly, after Luka and I finish searching this room for the pump."

The soldiers nodded and went about their tasks while Nancy tugged on Luka's sleeve to pull him away from the miscellaneous piece of equipment he was engrossed in. "Come on. Let's go see what else we can find here."

As the pair made their way through the voluminous storage room, Nancy stopped after a moment. "Hey Luka, are these diving suits?"

Luka crossed the room to join Nancy, took a large piece of material she had been holding and held it up. "Yes!" His voice grew giddy with excitement. "This looks like an experimental one. I think—wait a minute…" Luka rifled through a pile of the rubbery material on the shelf and pulled out a clear helmet with hoses coming out of the back. "Yes, this is it! I remember reading about these. They provide complete temperature control, pressurization and some level of impact resistance. As I recall, our government was creating them for—"

Nancy held up her hands. "Whoa there, save it for later. We're on a timer. Just make sure those get on board; we could use them for something down the road, I'm sure."

"Absolutely!" Luka wasn't deterred by her interruption, and together they continued their search of the room.

When they finally reached the back, Nancy glanced across at Luka. "No pump?"

He shook his head. "None. But there has to be one here somewhere! It's not that unique of a component. Maybe we can find one of similar design and modify it…" Luka trailed off as he continued wandering.

Nancy, meanwhile, cocked her head to the side as she shone her flashlight at the stairs at the back of the room. Taking up a full half of the width of the chamber, the stairs continued out of sight of her light, and as she squinted into the blackness above, she began to feel vaguely uneasy at what might be at the top.

"Luka?" Nancy called, and the technician ran over to her. She spoke to him without taking her gaze off the stairs. "Go get the soldiers; tell them I need them in here immediately." Luka glanced up the stairs and nodded, then dashed off. A moment later, the two men who had been standing guard outside the chamber ran up to her.

"Ma'am?"

Nancy nodded her head at the staircase. "This seems a bit odd, don't you think?" Neither of the soldiers responded, and Nancy continued. "I want to see where it goes. Come on. Lights off, goggles down and weapons out."

The soldiers did as she asked, and Nancy followed suit. The pair began creeping up the stairs, keeping their weapons pointed ahead of them while Nancy followed a few steps behind, keeping her rifle angled downward. After a short climb, the staircase took a turn, doubling back on itself on a landing and then continuing upward.

Nancy had lost count of how many stairs they had ascended before, finally, the end came into sight. After one final turn, the last flight of stairs was short, and dumped out at a landing that had a doorway built into the far back. The staircase had been completely devoid of any signs of life or movement, and Nancy relaxed. The two soldiers lowered their weapons as she walked around them to the door.

"Let's see where this goes," she mumbled to herself as she pulled on the handle. Nothing happened. She gave it another tug, but there was still nothing. She turned back to the soldiers and held out her hand. "Who's got something that can get through this thing?"

A short, three-foot-long pry bar was a standard piece of equipment each soldier carried, and both men fished theirs out of their packs and held them out to Nancy. She, in turn, stepped back and waved her arms at the door with a flourish. "Have at it!"

The two soldiers wordlessly advanced and jammed the ends of their crowbars into the gap between the door and the frame. They strained against the door, trying to break whatever lock was keeping it secure, but through all of their exertions, nothing budged. After a few minutes of working at the door from various angles and locations, they stopped and looked back at Nancy with sweat pouring down their faces. "It's no good, ma—"

At three inches thick, the steel door wouldn't have moved even if a dozen men had been going at it. When the bar holding the door in place on the other side was removed, though, it swung open on greased hinges with ease. Nancy was the first to react, bringing her rifle up to aim at the bright light that suddenly appeared in the doorway. The light was blinding in her night vision goggles, and they went dark an instant later to try and protect their user's eyes.

Nancy ripped the goggles off and ducked low to the side, fully expecting to take a frontal assault from a creature. The two soldiers with her, meanwhile, spun around as they fumbled with their weapons, completely surprised by the now open door. Nancy's finger wrapped around the trigger and began to squeeze, but then a voice behind the light boomed through the small room.

"Ms. Sims?"

Chapter Twenty-Two

THE MAGADAN METRO

"Magadan was a fast-growing city. There were nearly two hundred thousand people living here a year ago, before it happened. I was working in the metro when the bombs hit—as were many of those you see here. Between the bombs falling on the places where the most people were working and the radiation that came after, I'd say we had perhaps ten thousand alive by the time those things arrived. What did you call them? Swarms?"

Leonard nodded and referred to one of the effects created by the swarms when the bombs first fell. "I imagine the loss of consciousness didn't help matters either, did it?"

Sitting across the table from Leonard, Alexander snorted. "I had forgotten that. It's funny how the mind works, covering up the bad."

Krylov lifted a mug and sniffed the contents before taking a sip. His meager supply of instant coffee had been thoroughly expended on the survivors, as most of those in the refuge had happily accepted his offer without hesitation. "What happened when you awoke?"

"The metro was filled with smoke. Most of it vented out, but a few died from inhalation. Fires were widespread from the trains losing control and crashing. It took a while to figure out what had happened, but then the swarms came. We lost hundreds to them—they chewed through them like they were made of paper. Anyone who survived that hid in the center of the city, in the apartments.

"At first there was nothing to hide from except the weather and our fear of what the swarms might do to us. We had no idea why they ignored us."

"DNA filtering," Leonard interrupted. "It was something that a person I knew installed in the AI's low-level code. They're equipped with remote DNA scanners, and anyone with certain markers is ignored. It's like they don't exist to the swarms."

Alexander nodded slowly. "So that is why some of us survived. Because of random chance?"

Leonard shrugged. "I wouldn't call it random."

"What would you call it, then, for some of us to watch others be turned inside out?" Alexander's eyes narrowed and anger seeped into his voice as he started to stand up.

"Easy there." Marcus gave Leonard a quick shake of his head before turning a sympathetic gaze toward Alexander. "Please, continue."

Alexander sat back down and took a deep breath. "Those... *things* appeared not long after the swarms disappeared."

"The mutants?" Krylov asked.

"Yes. At first they appeared from seemingly nowhere: grotesque amalgamations of metal and man. That went on for two, maybe three months. They were aggressive, but we barricaded the doors and windows of the apartments so they couldn't get in. Then, people started to vanish, only to reappear later as one of the creatures."

"What did you all do for food and water during this time?" Leonard interrupted again.

"We lived off of canned goods; the apartments are large, and there weren't many of us there. Once those supplies ran low, those of us in the city began to spread out, searching the markets and other buildings for anything to eat or drink. There were some—those who lived on the outskirts of the city—that made do by scrounging from the homes out there, or taking what little food was growing on the farms. Those were the ones who were scared of radiation in the city, and of the creatures."

Leonard nodded and leaned back in his chair. "What did the mutants do, exactly, when they came back?"

Alexander finished his drink and sighed deeply. "When people started to disappear, it happened when they were outside of the apartment buildings—sometimes alone or sometimes in pairs. It was never when we were in a large group—not at first. After they vanished, though, they would appear again a few days later. At first, they weren't aggressive, not like the other creatures. We could still recognize their faces, but their bodies..." Alexander trailed off and stared into space.

"Their bodies what?" Krylov asked gently.

"They were mutilated. Completely mutilated. Torn apart, with strange things grafted on. It was like if a child took a person apart, then tried to put them back together."

"But they weren't aggressive?" Leonard was leaning in, listening intently to Alexander's every word.

"No, not at first. We tried to get them to come inside, to help them, but we soon realized that only their bodies were returning to us. Their minds had long since been destroyed. After a few weeks of that, the aggression started, and they became just like the others." Alexander clenched his jaw. "Shooting your friends and family members after they disappear and reappear as monstrosities isn't something I'd wish on my worst enemies.

"At that point, we were trapped. We couldn't go out and search for supplies, tend to the meager crops we were growing in the fields or anything else. Every time we stepped outside—even in large groups—they attacked us."

Marcus shook his head in amazement. "How on earth did you all manage to survive for so long?"

Alexander glanced around at the survivors in the refuge, most of whom were still crowded around as they quietly listened to him speak. "We were out of food and drink and had to move out of the apartments. Those of us still alive picked up one night and headed for the outskirts. We clung to life there for a little while more before we— before I—foolishly decided that counterattacking the devils was a wise idea."

Alexander closed his eyes as he remembered every detail from that night. "We had found some weapons—rifles and plenty of ammunition—and decided to attack the factory."

The hair on the back of Leonard's neck prickled. "The factory? What factory? Where?"

"Forgive me; I forgot that part." Alexander cleared his throat. "It didn't take long for us to realize where those who vanished were taken to. There are factory buildings at the edge of the city—"

"We've seen them," Leonard said quietly, and Alexander looked at him, confused.

"You've… seen them? How?"

"That's how we entered the city," Krylov replied. "We came in at the far edge of the port and circled around. We spent a few hours on the factory grounds resting, and we happened to look inside one of the buildings the next morning."

Alexander's body went stiff, and a few of the other survivors began muttering amongst themselves. "You went inside the building? How are you still alive?"

"What do you mean?"

Alexander leaned his head back. "We attacked the factory with all we had. It wasn't much, but the fires we had started in the nearby oil tanks had already killed a large number of the creatures. We thought we could pierce into their heart and destroy the factory. I was one of the only ones who made it out alive that night. The creatures were relentless, and their numbers were far greater than I could have imagined. How they were able to hide so many of them inside the building is something I still ponder."

Leonard was still watching Alexander with an intense gaze. "How many were there?"

"It had to have been several hundred, all in all. We killed many of them outside the factory, and even more inside. No matter how many we slaughtered, they kept coming."

"Where did they come from exactly? Inside the factory somewhere?"

Alexander shrugged at Leonard. "I can't say. But I believe so."

Leonard sat back in his chair and stared down at the table as his eyes flicked back and forth. His mind raced with the new information, and he tried to fit it into what he had already learned so far. Leonard's thoughts—and the conversation—were derailed when Roman walked up and coughed quietly. Krylov saw him and stood up to shake his hand, smiling as he did.

"Mr. Lebedev! We were told you and Mr. Egorov were resting. How is he doing?"

"He's resting, sir." Roman gestured at a woman standing behind him. "We were able to clean the wound and sew the worst of it up. I used all of our antibiotics and painkillers on him, so he'll be out for a few hours."

Krylov nodded with approval. "Good. Go on. Get some sleep. We'll join you shortly."

Leonard cast a questioning look at Krylov at the statement, but said nothing. Marcus glanced at Leonard, and the pair shrugged at each other as Krylov sat back down. "Please," he said, "what happened after the factory?"

Alexander shook his head slowly. "There isn't much to tell. I fled the factory and found a few others outside who had survived. We ran back and gathered the rest and made for the metro."

"Why did you come here, though? Why not return to the apartments?"

"Return to what? An enclosed area with no supplies? No, that was a tomb."

"It strikes me," Krylov said as he looked around the refuge, "that this isn't much better."

Alexander nodded and smiled. "I concede your point. But it was not always this way. When we first arrived, we were chased by the creatures. Hounded by them as they nipped at our heels, nearly wiping us all out. We made a stand here, at this station, and drove them off. It was then that it became clear to me that we could survive down here."

"What prompted you to choose the metro instead of fleeing for somewhere outside the city?"

Alexander looked at Marcus for a few seconds before responding. "Experience, mostly. I left the special military forces before I came here."

Krylov raised an eyebrow. "You were Spetsnaz?"

"Something like that. After I arrived in Magadan, I worked on the shipping lines moving freight from the docks into the city. That's why I was underground when it happened. We had scrounged in the metro a few times while we stayed in the apartment buildings, but we never took very much. It was easier—and felt safer—to search above ground."

Leonard shifted in his uncomfortable seat. "What kind of supplies did you have?"

"Everything." Alexander looked up at the lights. "Everything you see here is thanks to Magadan's supply lines being mostly underground. Electronics were shielded—for the most part. Industrial batteries and two weeks' worth of discreetly placing solar panels above ground allowed us to have lights."

"I thought the creatures would attack you if you went above ground," Krylov said. "How did you avoid them?"

Alexander shrugged. "After we beat them back, they left us alone for the most part. We had to be careful on the surface, but as long as we paid attention, we were able to travel back and forth safely in small numbers. I suppose their priorities shifted."

"Alexander," Leonard said, "I'm amazed by all that you set up here. But how did you grow food? Or were you able to get that from the supply lines, too?"

"Some of it, yes. We also kept farms outside of town from before we moved here. We were able to tend to those and grow fresh food to supplement our diet."

"I have to say," Leonard continued, "what you're describing— being able to come and go almost as you pleased—sounds a far cry from what's going on now. What changed?"

"You tell me. I lost two friends one day, three months ago. That was the start. We were seventy strong when we came here, and our numbers swelled to just over two hundred at the peak, after we found others clinging to life across the city and surrounding regions. From that day three months ago, though, we've been on a steady decline." Alexander spread his arms. "These you see here are all that are left."

Krylov, Marcus and Leonard looked at the thin, filthy faces around them. There couldn't have been more than a few dozen people at most. "How did you lose so many?" Marcus asked quietly.

"Once we realized that they were on the attack again, we tried to gather as much food as we could, thinking we could simply hole up here, fight them off and wait for them to lose interest again. We lost a few here and there to the same type of vanishing that had happened at the apartments—except this time, we saw it happen. The creatures would spend days testing our defenses, and once they learned about a weakness, they would break in, take one or two people and flee before we could react. Every time we went out to the metro trains to search for supplies, we lost one or two to ambushes in the tunnels."

"How did you get the transmitter working?" Leonard asked. "It hasn't been operating for long."

"That was a difficult one to pull off." Alexander smiled grimly. "We didn't think it *was* operating. Once it became clear that the creatures were continuing to push in on us, we knew we would have to fall back to this station, and from here we would either starve or die to the creatures. So we decided that someone should try and get the transmitter operational."

"How was it difficult to pull off? Isn't it easy to access the transmitter from near this station?" Leonard looked around as though he could spot an access point.

"Unfortunately not. Power lines run through an access shaft nearby, which we were able to access to provide electricity. But the transmitter's electronics were destroyed by the bombs. It took us a good week to rig together a replacement unit that we were confident would survive the weather and be small enough for a three-man team to carry with them through the tunnels. Once they were ready, the rest of us pushed against the bulk of the creatures in one tunnel as a diversion. We were able to help them get out, but they never returned."

"You didn't have a radio to use to try and pick up the transmission?"

"I'm afraid that radio signals will not penetrate into this refuge, Commander Krylov. And we dared not send anyone out to try and find out for themselves. They never would have made it back."

"Well," Marcus said, shifting in his seat, "that explains why you were so surprised to see us."

Alexander nodded. "We assumed you were simply the first wave of the creatures, coming down on us."

"So," Leonard said, "that's why you've run out of supplies. They have you pinned down with nowhere to go."

"Indeed. The attacks on our refuge early on grew so frequent that we had to erect the gates. When those were nearly broken through, we collapsed the main tunnels, thinking that would stem their flow." Alexander shook his head. "It did nothing. They simply burrowed through other areas. We used the maintenance access rooms to try and gather what supplies we could, but we were but mice surrounded by starving cats."

"What about the blockade? Why were they so afraid to come near it?"

Alexander smiled. "That was one of the last barriers we erected. The battle at that barricade kept them from coming near it ever again. This is the first time they've been bold enough to come close since then."

Leonard whistled appreciatively. "You mentioned that before. It must have been a damned good beating."

"The likes of which we've been unable to give them again, I'm sorry to say."

Krylov took a deep breath and put both hands on the table. "So, what do we do now?"

"Now?" Alexander coughed as he laughed. "Commander Krylov, in this entire story, did you fail to see the point? There is nothing to do now. Nothing except to take as many of them with us as we go. They are pressing in from all sides, and we do not have enough bullets to kill them all. I sincerely doubt that you carry enough to make any significant difference."

Krylov stood and looked around, addressing the crowd as he shook his head. "I don't accept that. We didn't travel across the ocean and risk our lives to come to your aid only to be told that we have to sit down and wait to be killed. We have traveled beyond the gates of hell and back countless times, and we will not roll over and die in this place!"

Contrary to Krylov's expectation, his short speech did nothing to stir the hearts of the survivors assembled around the tables of the dining area. In fact, after he finished, they began to turn and wander back to what they had been doing previously, realizing that Alexander's story was done.

Alexander watched the survivors go, then crossed his arms and looked at Krylov. "You see? They understand the truth. I am sorry,

Commander. Truly I am. You have come here on a fool's errand. And now it is not only us that will die—but you five as well."

The leader of the survivors pushed his chair back from the table and stood up slowly. "Your beds should be prepared. Please, sleep. We will have a meal in a few hours. If you can contribute anything, it would be appreciated." With that, Alexander walked off, leaving Marcus and Leonard sitting beside Krylov, who was still standing as he stared at Alexander's back.

"Well then." Leonard cleared his throat. "That was anti-climactic."

Krylov sat down slowly, shaking his head. "These are... my countrymen."

"These are a bunch of fools," Marcus said.

Leonard chimed in. "I'll second that. How can this guy be their leader anyway? He's a defeatist."

"They've lost hope." Krylov closed his eyes and sighed. "You heard him. They've been under constant siege for the last year. At some point, that would break anyone."

Leonard and Marcus grew quiet, and for a moment, no one said anything. Then, from nearby, a soft voice spoke. "Even Alexander can hope. He just needs something to believe in."

The trio turned and saw a young woman no older than eighteen leaning on a narrow wooden stave in front of them. She was dressed in rags and covered with dirt like the rest of the survivors. Unlike most of the others, however, her eyes sparkled, and the expression on her face was one of determination, not resignation.

"I'm sorry, you are?" Leonard stretched out his hand. The girl accepted it and shook it firmly.

"Maria."

"Nice to meet you, Maria. I'm Leonard, this is Marcus, and this is Krylov—Pavel, really, but we all call him by his last name."

Maria nodded to each of them, then Krylov spoke. "What was it you were saying about Alexander?"

Maria stepped softly up to the table, making nary a sound as she sat down in Alexander's empty seat. Her stave leaned up against the edge of the table, and she looked between the three men, eying them carefully. "Everyone here has lost hope. You were right about that. But they still possess the ability to feel it. They will follow Alexander wherever he goes; he saved us, after all. So if you want to give them hope, you have to make Alexander feel hope."

"And what about you?" Marcus asked. "Do you think we can make it out of this alive?"

Maria smiled coyly. "I think that anything's possible, especially for someone who traveled the world to come and save us."

An older woman passed by and called to Maria, who stood and nodded at Marcus, Leonard and Krylov. "Remember what I said. Find a way to give Alexander hope. Do that, and you have a chance to save every one of us."

Chapter Twenty-Three

Submarine Pen

The sound of her name made Nancy pause for an extra second before firing. In that second, the lights in her face dropped, and she could see—barely—that the figures standing in front of her were clad in camouflage and were decidedly not mutants.

"You bastards!" Nancy shouted at Andrey and Sergei as she stood up, though the verbal assault was tempered by a smile at the sight of the two men. The soldiers behind her relaxed and lowered their weapons, grateful that they didn't have to face an onslaught of hostiles.

"Ma'am! We heard some sort of tapping behind the door and—"

Nancy wrapped her arms around Sergei and squeezed. "I nearly took your heads off!" She stepped back and shook her head. "What are you two doing here anyway?"

Sergei motioned behind him with a thumb. "We were exploring this building and heard noises downstairs. It's the main base facility, full of offices and records for the base here."

"Did you find anything in the warehouses?"

Sergei shook his head grimly. "Nothing, ma'am."

"Shit." Nancy leaned against the wall and groaned. "As good as it is to see you two—and good that we have a way to reach the surface without leaving the sub pen—this is very bad all around."

Sergei leaned around Nancy to look past her down the stairs. "You've found nothing?"

"Not a thing. We've searched almost the whole area and found plenty of equipment for the rest of the sub, but nothing we could use to replace the pump."

Andrey stepped around Sergei and pulled out a few pieces of wrinkled paper from inside his pocket. "We did find this, though, ma'am."

Nancy accepted the papers and tried to read them before pulling off her goggles in frustration and turning on her light. "What's this?"

Sergei, who had forgotten about the records in the confusion, spoke up. "We searched every warehouse and several other buildings that looked like they might contain something like what we're looking for. After nothing turned up, we found a record-keeping room on the second floor of the building above. That's where we found these. They show that a P949 nuclear submarine came in for repairs and maintenance."

Nancy rifled through the papers and shook her head. "I don't see what that—"

"A P949?" Luka spoke up from behind her. He snatched the papers from her hand, and she stepped back, bemused by the excitement that had taken over his entire body, causing his voice to quiver. "The P949 series used the same reactor type as the Arkhangelsk—right down to the pump." Luka looked at Nancy and waved the papers triumphantly. "This is it! We need to get the pump off of this boat!"

"There's one little problem with that," Nancy said. "We don't have a clue where this sub is. It's certainly not in the pen, and we didn't see anything at the docks outside either."

Luka shook the papers in his hand. "Ma'am, if there's one thing I know, it's that this paperwork is accurate. It says that a P949 was brought into the pen for repairs and maintenance. There's nothing here about it being released. That means it's here somewhere."

Nancy crinkled her nose and eyebrows. "Where on earth would it be, then?"

Andrey spoke again. "How deep is the water in the submarine pen?"

Nancy and Luka turned and stared at Andrey, who suddenly appeared quite nervous in the face of the attention. "What?"

Nancy whirled around and addressed the soldiers standing behind her. "Get back to the Arkhangelsk. I need a detailed sonar map of the floor of the submarine pen *right now*. Tell them they're looking for a sub that's sitting at the bottom of the water. It might be intact or it might be in pieces; we don't know yet."

The two soldiers nodded and ran back down the stairs to carry out Nancy's order. Nancy motioned for Andrey and Sergei to follow her and Luka, and together they all walked back down into the submarine pen. "So you found nothing else of value on the surface?" Nancy asked.

"Nothing, ma'am," Sergei answered. "The warehouses held virtually nothing related to submersibles. They must have been used for storing equipment and parts for surface vessels."

"Hm." Nancy sighed. "Let's hope to high heaven we can find this mystery boat of yours, then. Otherwise, we'll have to start considering plan B."

"What's that, ma'am?"

"I don't even want to think about it."

There was, Nancy thought as they descended the stairs in silence, no "plan B." Without a functioning pump, the reactor of the Arkhangelsk would go critical, and the crew would be forced to evacuate, leaving them stranded on the shore of a place they knew next to nothing about. They would eventually be able to make their way back to Krylov, Leonard, Marcus and their team—along with the survivors —but it was anyone's guess if they would still be alive.

Nancy pushed such thoughts from her mind and sealed them away with a clenched jaw, balled fist and an iron will. *No. Not now. Not on my watch.* The salvation of the Arkhangelsk dangled by a thread of hope, but that was enough. *It has to be.*

At the bottom of the stairs, in the large storage room, several portable lights had been set up, and crewmembers from the Arkhangelsk were busy searching through and moving boxes out of the room and down toward the sub. Nancy was surprised to see that Nikolay was directing the operation with a clipboard in hand.

When she walked up, Nikolay shouted at a young woman who was busy sorting through crates. "No! Not that crate, the one next to it!"

"Nikolay?" Nancy said with surprise. "What the hell are you doing off the boat?"

Nikolay turned and smiled at her. "Ma'am! I got word that there was a large cache of potentially valuable parts for the Arkhangelsk, so I took it upon myself to personally supervise their cataloging and loading."

A thin smile crossed Nancy's lips, and she lowered her voice conspiratorially. "Couldn't keep yourself cooped up anymore, eh?"

Nikolay cleared his throat and looked around before whispering back. "I have no idea what you mean, ma'am. I'm merely here to supervise this delicate operation."

Nancy sighed and shook her head as her grin widened. "Just make sure the sub stays in one piece, okay?"

Nikolay nodded, and Nancy patted him on the back as she walked by. She stopped a few steps later and pointed to half a dozen rubber blocks sitting on the floor, along with several small outboard motors. "Nikolay. Are those what I think they are?"

Nikolay turned to see what Nancy was referring to. "If you think they are inflatables along with last year's top of the line electric outboard motors, then yes, they are what you think they are."

Nancy nearly shrieked for joy at the sight of the small blocks of plastic and rubber, but managed to restrain herself to a short hop and a giant smile. "Make sure these get on board and tested immediately, Nikolay."

"Will do, ma'am."

"Good. Now I need your help with something else." The smile faded, and her tone grew serious. "Sergei and Luka will fill you in on the details, but the basics are that we likely have a P949 submarine sitting at the bottom of the water down in the pen. It apparently has the same reactor type as the Arkhangelsk and will likely have a pump that will not only fit our reactor, but be a perfect match."

Nikolay's eyebrows shot up. "Really?"

Sergei, Andrey and Luka stood next to Nancy, and Sergei spoke while Nancy passed over the papers. "Here, take a look at these."

"These are maintenance records." Nikolay held the papers close to a nearby light and studied them. "It never checked out of maintenance, so it must have been on the surface when the swarms swept across the world."

"They would have had no problem getting in here and into the sub," Nancy said. "Luka, would they have had any reason to go after anything except the reactor?"

Luka shook his head. "The cooling system that the pump is attached to is completely separate from the reactor chamber itself. The swarms would have bored into the reactor, depleted it and then exited."

"I sure as hell hope you're right." Nancy looked at Nikolay. "Sonar should already be searching for the sub. I need you on the Arkhangelsk spearheading the search."

Nikolay's features slumped, but he nodded dutifully. "Yes, ma'am. Once we find it, I'll let you know."

"Thank you." Nancy watched Nikolay head back to the Arkhangelsk along with another crewmember pushing a dolly. She turned to Andrey and Sergei. "Gentlemen. Get your gear on the boat, and then get back here. If that sub really is down there, I want you two and Luka to be the ones to board it."

"Ma'am?" Andrey's eyes widened.

"You heard me. I'll brief you when you get back."

Andrey and Sergei looked at each other and then took off at a jog for the Arkhangelsk. Nancy felt a slight tapping on her shoulder after they left and turned around to find the pale white face of Luka staring at her. The technician visibly gulped and stammered as he tried to address her. "Y-you want me to g-go down there? Under the water?"

Nancy motioned with her head for Luka to follow her, and she walked several paces down the room before stopping in front of the underwater diving gear that she and Luka had found earlier. "The Arkhangelsk has facilities for refilling these air tanks, right?"

Luka nodded, gulping again. "Y-yes, ma'am."

"Good." Nancy waved over one of the nearby crewmen and pointed at the air tanks. "Get these on the Arkhangelsk immediately. Inform Mr. Sokolov that I want them checked and filled and ready to go by the time they find that sub."

"Ma'am?" The crewman looked at her in confusion at the mention of the sub.

Nancy shooed him away with a wave of her hands. "Just tell Nikolay. And hurry!"

As the crewman struggled to load the air tanks into a crate at the top of a stack perched precariously on a dolly, Nancy headed out of the structure. Luka tagged along behind her, his eyes still wide with nervousness.

"Ma'am… Ms. Sims. Please. Reconsider. I-I really don't need to be down there, under the water. I can just tell them what to look for and how to remove it."

Nancy held up her hand to cut Luka off, and she stopped in her tracks, spinning around to face him head-on. "Mr. Delov." Her tone grew dark. "I've told you what you'll be doing. My decision is final. If you have any further questions, I'd advise you to keep them to yourself."

Luka's back straightened, and he nodded. "Yes, ma'am."

"Good." Nancy glanced around and waited for a few nearby crew to walk out of earshot. She lowered her voice and relaxed her tone. "I know you're nervous, Luka. I need you on this, though. If something goes wrong down there—if there's an emergency—you're the expert. We can't afford to let this slip away from us. If we don't get that pump…" Nancy trailed off.

"We lose the Arkhangelsk." Luka nodded and gulped. His heart and breath were racing, and he couldn't get his body to calm down.

"Deep breaths, Luka." Nancy put her hands on his shoulders. He swayed slightly as he tried to fight off a wave of nausea. "Come on, now. Deep breaths. In and out."

It took a few minutes, but Luka finally calmed down enough to stand on his own. His heart was still racing, but his breathing had slowed enough to talk again. "Thank you, Ms. Sims." He barely managed to croak the words out.

Nancy clapped him on the back. "Come on. Let's get you back to the Arkhangelsk so you can help get those tanks filled."

As Nancy walked Luka to the Arkhangelsk, she watched the sub's crew running back and forth around her in a whirlwind of organized chaos. Her original order had been for a fraction of the crew to be out working, but Nikolay's addendum had turned out to be the right decision. Spare parts, equipment and much-needed supplies were being loaded onto the Arkhangelsk at a rapid pace, and it wouldn't be long before everything usable in the submarine pen was on board. Nancy's only hope was that all the extra work would be worth the trouble.

Chapter Twenty-Four

THE MAGADAN METRO

K rylov, Leonard and Marcus found their beds, and Leonard volunteered to be the first to stand watch while the others slept. While everyone in the refuge was treating them well enough, neither of the trio liked the idea of leaving their possessions— not to mention themselves—unguarded in the current environment. Before settling down for a few hours of sleep, Krylov spoke with Roman for a few minutes to catch him up on the story told by Alexander, along with the subsequent conversation. Marcus, meanwhile, checked on Mikhail to make sure his wounds didn't show any signs of infection.

The gashes to the front of Mikhail's chest had looked quite dirty when Krylov had ripped off his shirt in front of Alexander in the tunnel. Fortunately, though, Marcus could see no signs of them worsening, and he hoped that within a week or two, they would be mostly healed. The thought was immediately replaced with a lump in the pit of his stomach as he remembered their current predicament.

After Roman, Krylov and Marcus had laid down, Leonard dragged a chair from the dining area and planted himself in front of the sleeping quarters. Keeping his spare rifle close at hand, he disassembled his primary weapon and began to work on cleaning the mechanisms, using some spare rags and a bit of gun oil from his pack. After cleaning and checking both his primary and secondary rifles, Leonard turned his attention to his EMP cannon.

The strange-looking rifle had somehow managed to make it through all of the drama without taking any significant damage. *The only problem,* he thought, *is how I'm going to manage to use it when I've got one drained battery and one with only a few shots left.* While Leonard was certain he had put more than one spare battery in his bag before they'd left the Arkhangelsk, he hadn't been able to find one, even after searching everyone else's bags, too. *Damned things must have fallen out somewhere.*

After checking and re-checking his weapons, Leonard tipped his chair back against one of the metro station's support columns and swung his artificial leg idly as he watched the survivors go about their routines. The hours passed by slowly with little of interest for Leonard to see, until he noticed a couple of men wearing thick gloves and carrying insulated tools. He sat forward in his chair and arched his neck as he watched them walk through the station, trying to see where they were going. As they vanished through the cloth barrier running down the center of the station, Leonard leapt to his feet and dashed inside the sleeping quarters.

"Marcus. Marcus!" Leonard whispered in Marcus' ear and shook him awake.

"Wha—what's going on? Leonard? What's wrong?" Panic started to creep into Marcus' voice, and Leonard shook his head.

"Nothing. I just need to talk to some people. Can you take over for me?"

Marcus sat up and swung his feet over the edge of the cot, rubbing his eyes. "Yeah. Yeah, sure." Marcus yawned and waved at Leonard to leave. "Go do your thing. I'm good."

Leonard nodded and ran out of the sleeping quarters, then dashed off toward where he had seen the two men go. He found them a moment later, as they were crouched over a piece of paneling that had several thick bundles of wiring running into it. He waved at them as he approached, and they stood up to greet him.

"Hello! Do you speak English?" Alexander and Maria both spoke English fairly well, but as Leonard had yet to talk to anyone else in the refuge, he didn't know if he would be able to hold a conversation with the men. The alternative was to be reduced to falling back on the dozen or so Russian words he had learned, which wouldn't be the most ideal situation.

One of the men shrugged, but the other nodded and took off his right glove to shake Leonard's hand. "Hello! Yes, I speak small English, yes."

Leonard smiled. *This I can work with,* he thought. "I saw your electrical tools and gloves." He pointed at the tools that the men had scattered around the insulated panel. "May I use them?" Leonard presented the dead battery from the EMP rifle and pointed at it. "I need to charge this battery. I need some tools and parts to use."

The man had at first nodded slowly and furrowed his brow, trying to understand what Leonard was saying. But when he heard the words "charge this battery," his eyes had lit up. He pointed at the tools and a large plastic crate that was sitting nearby. "Please, yes! Use!"

Leonard grinned and nodded his thanks, then dug into the box. Until he had seen the men walking around with their gloves and tools on, he had somehow completely forgotten that the refuge had a source of power. *If they have the right materials,* he thought, *then I can probably make a charger for this thing.* Leonard worked feverishly, putting his rudimentary knowledge of electronics to the test.

As Leonard worked, the two men slowly shifted their attention from their own task to his, and they began assisting him by pointing at various components, handing him parts and even taking over at points. Two hours passed by before, finally, Leonard had something that he thought might work. One of the men handed him a cable that had been stripped, then pointed at a connector on the charger. Leonard gingerly touched the cable to the charger, and a small LED soldered on one side lit up.

Using the blade of his knife, Leonard popped off the cap from the battery pack to expose the wiring, then attached it to the charger. Leonard winced as a few sparks flew at his face, but when nothing else happened, he set the battery down on the ground and watched the series of lights on the side of the battery intently. Several minutes passed, and Leonard was about to smash the entire contraption to pieces, but then one light on the battery pack lit up. Leonard couldn't suppress a cheer at the sight, and he grabbed the two men who had helped him in a hug. "Thank you!" Leonard's smile was infectious, and the two men smiled and cheered with him, even though they weren't entirely sure what he was excited about.

After managing to communicate to one of the men that the battery needed to charge until the last light turned green, Leonard left the charger and battery and headed back to the sleeping quarters. He was intercepted along the way by Marcus, who had come to see what the cheering was about.

"Leonard? Everything okay?"

Leonard grinned and couldn't resist hugging Marcus as well. "The EMP cannon! I rigged—well, me and those two over there rigged up a charger for the battery, and it's working! So far anyway. I'll admit that the battery might explode at any minute, but for now, I think it's charging!"

A smile spread across Marcus's face. "You mean we've got ammo for that thing again?"

"Yes! Well, soon. As long as the battery doesn't explode, like I said." Leonard's smile suddenly dropped. "Aren't you supposed to be on guard?"

"Oh, yeah. Krylov and Roman are up. They're changing Mikhail's bandages. Apparently, some sort of meal is happening soon, and I came to let you know in case you wanted to eat." Marcus looked around and whispered. "Frankly, I don't recommend it, though. Something about it smells off, and this is the last place I want to start having… distress."

Leonard chuckled. "Noted. I'll grab something from my bag."

"Good plan. You should check with Krylov, too. I think he wants to try to talk to Alexander again. I'll be back in a few minutes, once I check out the fabulous facilities that I'm sure this place has to offer."

Leonard shook his head and laughed as he headed back to the sleeping quarters. Inside, after pushing back the blanket covering the entrance, he heard a sharp yelp followed by Roman's bark. "Dammit, Mikhail!"

Krylov also chimed in. "Mr. Egorov, I must insist you hold still."

"Respectfully, sir, it *fucking* hurts!"

Roman patted his friend's shoulder in sympathy. "They used all the painkillers to help knock you out earlier. You'll have to tough it out now."

Krylov stepped back and nodded with approval. "There. Those bandages will do for the next few hours, at least. I've applied some topical antiseptics. Those, plus the dose of antibiotics you had earlier, should keep you on the mend."

"I feel fine, sir, except for the pain and itching."

"Good," Krylov said.

Roman helped Mikhail to his feet, and they walked slowly out of the sleeping quarters together. "Come on. Let's get some food in you."

Leonard watched them go before whispering to Krylov. "Are you sure they can handle the food here? Marcus said it looked suspicious."

Krylov snorted in amusement. "Those two have cast-iron stomachs. They will be just fine."

"I hope so. They're sure as hell not borrowing any of *my* toilet paper." Leonard and Krylov chuckled, then Leonard grew serious. "Marcus also said you wanted to talk to me. Something about speaking with Alexander?"

Krylov nodded. "Yes. I believe my previous approach to stir up the emotions of these people was unsuccessful due to what that young girl, Maria, said. I am going to speak with Mr. Kozlov now, and I would appreciate your assistance."

"Sure. What's the plan?"

"I am uncertain at this time. I trust you to help sway his opinion in any way that you can. I do not believe we are in a hopeless situation here. But if we cannot convince him—and the others—to see things the same way, then we will all die."

"Makes sense to me. I'm with you."

"Good. Let us go find him."

As the survivors gathered at the dining area to accept small bowls of a thin, brown-colored and oddly smelling soup, Krylov and Leonard looked for Alexander, who was sitting by himself at a small table. The two men sat down next to Krylov, who looked up at them and grunted. "There's food—if you can call it that—if you want it."

Leonard shook his head, and Krylov responded. "No, but thank you, Mr. Kozlov. My soldiers are partaking, and they appreciate the gesture."

Alexander glanced over at the two soldiers who were talking to and laughing with each other through mouthfuls of the hot liquid. "I see your injured man is doing better. Are you always so lax in discipline with your men, letting them sit alone and eat and laugh while you do not?"

Krylov shrugged. "We've adapted, Mr. Kozlov. We aren't a military any longer, and the Arkhangelsk's crew isn't simply made up of Russian soldiers. We've taken in survivors from all walks of life and will continue to do so."

Alexander finished his soup and wiped his mouth with the back of his sleeve. "Yes, your mighty Arkhangelsk. What kind of a ship is this?"

"She's a submarine. Typhoon class."

Alexander sat up as straight as a board in his chair, and his eyes widened to the size of saucers. "Typhoon? An Akula?"

Krylov nodded. "Yes."

Alexander shook his head in disbelief. "Your boat is a Typhoon. What type of armaments do you have on board?"

"Not all that many anymore. We have half of our original torpedoes. Our missiles were expended a year ago on the swarms. We have numerous small arms, though, and we've taken on enough equipment that we can manufacture just about anything we need on board. We also have plenty of supplies—enough to feed everyone here."

Leonard watched Alexander's eyes grow even wider. Krylov's description of the Arkhangelsk was having the desired effect on the survivors' leader as he contemplated what the Arkhangelsk could mean for the survivors.

"You...I—I didn't realize you had a Typhoon. You could sail around the world and back a thousand times in a boat that size."

Krylov smiled. "She is our home. And you are all welcome to join us on her once we get out of here. The city I told you about—New Richmond—we have brought survivors there from many places, and we will bring many more. Humanity is not dead yet, Mr. Kozlov. There are those of us who are still fighting—and winning."

Alexander's expression darkened, and he shook his head as he slumped back into his seat. "I hope you left someone competent in charge. You won't win here. We won't be leaving this place. It is a tomb."

"Actually," Leonard said, "it doesn't have to be." Krylov glanced at Leonard and nodded slightly, prompting Leonard to continue. "It would only take a few of us to create enough noise to distract the muties—the creatures—long enough to allow everyone here to escape. Do you think we could make it to the docks underground?"

Alexander nodded. "It would be possible. But the creatures would catch up with us and kill everyone."

"Not necessarily. Not if we have your help." Krylov made his statement with such conviction that Alexander didn't immediately dismiss him as before.

Alexander gave him a long look before replying. "How?"

And with that simple question, hope was rekindled within the leader of the survivors. The thought of the people he had watched over being freed from their prison raised his spirits enough to finally give some consideration to what Krylov was saying.

Leonard jumped in with a plan he had been mulling over for hours. Krylov listened eagerly, grateful for his friend's assistance. "I watched some of your people earlier doing an ammo and weapons count. You don't have much, but it's enough to arm at least five, maybe six survivors for a heavy fight. We'll want to allocate a few weapons to the bulk of the survivors who escape during the diversion, so let's say you can provide three heavily armed individuals to aid in the diversion. Marcus, Krylov, Roman and myself have more than enough weaponry amongst ourselves to put up a fight. Mikhail will need to go with the bulk of the survivors due to his injuries."

Alexander nodded slowly. "A plausible division of forces, but the number of creatures is too large. How are we to pull the bulk of their forces away from the western tunnel? The survivors would have to escape through there and use maintenance passages to bypass the collapsed section."

Leonard fished through his pockets until he came across a short black marker. He pushed Alexander's bowl and cup to the side and drew a rough diagram of the main tunnel system from memory onto the surface of the table. A large rectangle in the center designated the station, while a circle off to one side represented the docks.

"When we came in through this route, we were nearly trapped by the creatures just outside the barrier you erected, thanks to the creatures coming through a hole in the top of the tunnel. It seemed to me that they either dug it or used an existing ventilation or some other shaft to get down."

"Yes, they've done that in many places."

"Good." Leonard smiled. "That means they have extreme freedom of movement. We need to spend some time fortifying the main barricades—your gates—so that the muties have more incentive to go up and over to get to the distraction."

"I'm not understanding."

Leonard circled a few sections of the tunnels on the map and pointed at them. "We'll secure the western approach so that those things couldn't get in even if they had dynamite. We'll then take a small team to the eastern section of the tunnel and use bait to draw the muties in. We'll let them advance and think they're getting the upper hand, so that the ones who are to the west will be drawn to where the fighting is taking place. The survivors will then push through whatever stragglers are left to the west and move straight down to the docks."

Leonard stepped back and gestured at the map as a whole. "As long as everyone moves quickly and there really is a clear path around the collapsed sections, it will work."

Alexander tapped the circled section of the tunnel to the east of the refuge. "And what about those involved in the distraction? How do they escape?"

Leonard glanced at Krylov, who replied. "We're carrying explosives. Enough to bring the station down. Once the survivors are away, we'll retreat through the station and detonate the explosives as soon as the bulk of the creatures are inside. We can then act as a rearguard to the survivors and guard them at the docks until we can get them onto the Arkhangelsk."

"And how will that take place? Do you have boats at the dock?"

Krylov shifted his feet uncomfortably. "That… will be a challenge. We have a single inflatable, but it is on the northern side of the city, to the west of the edge of the docks. It won't be large enough to hold more than six or seven at a time, and it's not close enough for us to get to quickly."

Alexander stared at the crudely drawn map on the table in silence for a moment, then crossed his arms and began stroking his chin with one hand. "Months ago, I ventured to the docks in search of fuel and generators to help supplement our solar panels. The ships that I saw in the bay were destroyed, but there is an enclosed dock to the southeast that at one time held a few powerboats. *If* they are still there, their engines will not function."

"So we row," Leonard said. "These things aren't exactly the best swimmers. We learned that in Cuba. We just need to get out on the water far enough that they can't wade to us, and the Arkhangelsk can send someone out on the spare inflatable to tow us in."

"And if the boats aren't there?" Alexander asked.

"Then everyone grabs a board and paddles out." Leonard threw up his arms. "We will figure something out when the time comes. Something will get screwed up between now and then, I promise you. And we'll figure that out, too. Let's just solve the problems we have right now, then worry about the other ones later."

Krylov thought—for a moment when Alexander closed his eyes and sighed—that Leonard's over-enthusiasm had caused Alexander to go back on his more hopeful outlook. The survivors' leader was quiet as he contemplated the hastily assembled plan. He slowly rose to his feet and nodded at Leonard and Krylov. "It is... better than dying here."

Leonard and Krylov both grinned, causing Alexander to crack a thin smile. "Come on," said Leonard. "We have a lot of work to do and not much time in which to do it."

"Where would you like to begin?"

"I'll leave the military planning to Krylov. I, though, would like to get some details on the maintenance passages, as well as any and all other tunnels that are connected to the station."

Alexander looked around, then whistled at someone across the station. "Maria!" He waved at the young woman, and she ran over and smiled.

"What can I do, Alexander?"

Alexander pointed at Leonard. "Leonard McComb wants a tour of any and all tunnels connected to the station that we use to get around."

Leonard interjected. "Or that the creatures might use."

"Yes, exactly. Please show him around, and give him all the information he requires. Commander Krylov and I have much to discuss."

Leonard nodded. "I'll see you later, Krylov. I'll tell Roman and Marcus to sit in on this with you two."

"Thank you, Mr. McComb."

Leonard and Krylov waved at each other before Leonard and Maria walked off, leaving Krylov and Alexander to begin making their plans. Leonard spotted Marcus wandering by, brushing his hands against his pant legs and mumbling to himself as he shook his head. Leonard got his attention and gave him a summary of what had happened.

"Sounds great." Marcus continued wiping his hands on his pant legs. "Maybe I'll suggest that they just get the creatures to go through that excuse for a latrine. They'd all die within seconds."

Leonard laughed. "Get Roman—and Mikhail, if he's feeling up to it—to go with you to sit in on the planning. Once I'm done looking around this place, I'll be able to give my recommendations for which places are the most fortifiable and which to use for the escape."

"Sounds good. Stay safe."

Marcus wandered off, continuing his muttering as he went, and Leonard turned to Maria and rubbed his hands together. "So. Where should we start?"

Chapter Twenty-Five

THE MAGADAN METRO

L eonard spent the next few hours walking in the refuge with Maria in relative silence, both because he was starting to feel fatigued, and because his mind was racing from all of the new information Maria was providing about the metro system. Each seemingly simple question spawned lengthy sets of answers, all of which gave Leonard more insight into the Russian metro than he had ever imagined possible.

Having lived in the tunnels for months—and not being one of the few 'scroungers' who used to go out in search of supplies—Maria knew them like the back of her hand. In addition to the main and side tracks used for transporting cargo and passengers, and the maintenance passages that the rescue team had encountered, Leonard soon learned of another, deeper system.

This deeper system was a short series of tunnels that had been carved by advanced machinery as a secret experiment—likely military, Alexander had wagered—that were far below the main metro lines. Upon hearing about this system, Leonard's interest was piqued, and he asked Maria if she would be able to take him to see it.

"That would be… difficult."

"How come?"

"We haven't been there since we first established the refuge. It could be dangerous, with the monsters."

Leonard looked at the battery that was charging for the EMP cannon. The display read out a ninety-five percent charge, so he disconnected the battery and swapped it for the nearly depleted one in the device. With the EMP cannon ready and his weapons freshly cleaned, Leonard was starting to feel eager for a firefight.

"You see this?" Leonard pointed to the rifle, and Maria nodded. "This fires an electromagnetic pulse. It's like a really powerful microwave oven. It will kill any of those creatures that we come across."

Maria gulped hesitantly. "I—I'm still not sure."

"Maria, if we're going to be successful in getting out of this place, I need to know everything about it so that I can bring that information back to Alexander and Krylov. I promise you, we won't get hurt. Besides, if these tunnels go nowhere and have no purpose, I can't imagine the creatures would have any interest in going there."

Maria sighed and nodded, finally relenting to Leonard's argument. "Follow me."

On their way out of the eastern entrance to the station, Maria picked up a rifle and two magazines. In addition to his EMP cannon, Leonard was carrying his primary rifle and several spare magazines, though he had opted to leave his backpack with the rest of his supplies behind in order to travel faster and more discreetly.

As Maria and Leonard approached the first of the two eastern gates, Leonard thought that they would have to pass through it to reach the area Maria had mentioned. She, however, diverted into a mainte-nance room like the ones the rescue team had used to traverse the metro system. "We go down from here."

Leonard peered down the ladder, feeling a slight bit of discomfort about the fact that he couldn't see anything below. "How far down to the next room?"

Maria smiled as she climbed onto the ladder and started downward. "Far."

It took a few minutes to reach the bottom, proving Maria's words correct. Leonard's arms and shoulders were burning when he stepped off the ladder, and he leaned against a nearby wall and slid down into a sitting position. Maria stood opposite of him, breathing heavily as she watched him with a grin.

"You don't get much exercise?"

Leonard chortled. "I've done more climbing, crawling and running in the last day than I expected to do on this entire mission. I just wasn't entirely expecting to have to climb down a small skyscraper; otherwise, I would have traveled even lighter. How far down are we anyway?"

Maria shrugged. "I don't know. This is the deepest part of the metro that I know of. There used to be one of those large elevators on the surface, but Alexander had it blocked off to keep the monsters from getting through."

Leonard slowly eased himself up. "Makes sense. So, where do we go now? Is this the super-secret experimental system?"

"Now," Maria said, moving toward the maintenance room doorway, "we walk."

Twenty minutes of cautious walking later, Leonard was beginning to regret not asking Maria for more details about the under-underground tunnels before they'd started. The tunnel they were in seemed almost exactly the same as the one farther up—aside from there being no set of tracks for a train to run on—and Leonard began to wonder whether they were in the right location or not.

"Maria, how much longer till we're there?"

"Not far now."

"How far into these tunnels did you all explore?"

Maria wrinkled her nose as she thought. "Not far. There were no signs of any creatures when a group came down. We haven't heard or seen anything from this area since we arrived, so it's been forgotten, I guess. There are a few patrols that peek down, but no one ever goes far."

"So, no one's ever explored the entire area?"

Maria shook her head. "I don't think so, no. Why?"

Leonard grimaced and adjusted the grip on his rifle. "It seems to me that you can't be absolutely sure there's nothing down here unless you take the time to check. How would you know that the place isn't very big?"

"Someone found building plans back in that room we came through. They show how far the tunnels go."

"Whoa, whoa, wait a second." Leonard stopped and groaned. "There were plans back there? Maria, you've got to start telling me this sort of thing ahead of time."

Maria stopped walking as well. "I'm sorry. I didn't think it was important."

"These days, *everything's* important. Especially taking a breather once in a while." Leonard sat down on the ground and laid his flashlight beside him.

There was silence for a few minutes until Maria spoke again. "Tell me about your leg."

Leonard suddenly became acutely aware of the lightness of his prosthetic limb. "What about it?"

"Where did you get it?"

Leonard rolled up his pant leg and shone his flashlight on the piece of metal. "This baby's one-hundred percent made in America."

"No, I mean, how did you get it? What happened to your leg?"

"Oh." Leonard cringed slightly at the memory of the pain. "There was a guy who was chasing my friend and me. He tried to kill us, but only managed to take my leg off instead. The only reason I survived was because of Commander Krylov and the Arkhangelsk. They rescued us just in time."

"How does it work, though? Alexander said that if metal things weren't kept far underground when…" Maria grew quiet for a second, "…when *it* happened, then anything electronic was destroyed."

Leonard shrugged. "I don't know where this came from. A doctor in New Richmond hooked it up for me. It's not perfect by any stretch of the imagination, but it's better than crutches. Plus, it means I can do fun activities, like wandering around underground in the dark waiting for monsters to jump out at me."

Maria laughed, and Leonard smiled, glad to have broken the somber mood. "We'll get out of this, Maria. Krylov and Marcus and all the rest of the crew—they're good people."

Maria's smile faded, and she shook her head. "I don't know. These monsters are strong. They've taken so much from us."

Leonard seized upon the opportunity to learn more about the creatures. "Tell me about them, Maria. Alexander told us the story, but I need to hear specifics about the swarms and the creatures."

"What do you want to know?"

"Everything. Tell me everything that you saw the swarms and creatures do."

Maria furrowed her brow. "I'm not sure what to tell."

Leonard shifted his legs. "When we encountered the swarms after the bombs fell, they were silver in color and very fast. The first ones I saw were tearing apart a set of generators for some reason. They seemed very intelligent, with their own agenda to fulfill. What about the swarms you saw?"

"We didn't see much of them, actually. They were around at first, for a while, but after some people started turning, they sort of disappeared. We mostly saw them around the factories in the north after the first few days."

"How long did you end up seeing them around the factories?"

"I don't think they ever left."

Leonard frowned. "That's curious. The bulk of the swarms I saw traveled to the Nexus to centralize their processing power. The swarms here should have died off a long time ago. What about the creatures? What was their behavior like?"

"The creatures have changed a lot. They've been aggressive sometimes, and other times, they've just left us alone."

"Yeah, Alexander was describing something about that. Like when you all first went below ground and had a battle with them, they just left you alone for a while."

Maria nodded. "Yes. And there were other times, too."

"Tell me about them."

Maria's face darkened, and she clenched her jaw, trying to fight back tears. "My mother and brother and I were on the edge of the city, searching for food. She never liked going into the city, because she was scared of radiation. She thought the creatures would leave us alone on the edge." Maria paused and wiped her eyes.

"What happened?" Leonard asked softly.

"Several of them appeared. They must have been following us. They cornered us and took my brother to the factory."

"Wait, what?" Leonard shook his head in confusion. "You're telling me that these things followed you, waited until they had you trapped...

and then took *one* of you with them—alive, no less? And they didn't even touch you or your mother?"

Maria shook her head. "No."

"That makes no sense." Leonard stood up and began pacing in the tunnel as he talked. "The mutants we've always encountered—no matter the location—have been smart, cunning and resourceful, but they've also been violent. Extremely so. They've never taken anyone alive, let alone left people unharmed."

The same uneasy feeling that Leonard had felt near the start of their rescue mission was back and feeling twice as strong. "There's something seriously wrong here, Maria. I feel like I'm on the verge of figuring out what it is, but I don't know... all of these pieces have to fit together somehow. The bodies in the factory, the behavior of the swarms and all the mystery surrounding the mutants. What the hell is going on here?"

Maria stood up. "I don't know what else I can tell you that you haven't heard from Alexander. This is what we have lived with for the last year."

"All right." Leonard pointed his flashlight down the tunnel. "Let's keep going. We need to finish this up and get back to the others."

The pair walked in silence for a few minutes until the tunnel suddenly changed. The tiled and concrete walls were abruptly replaced by smooth stone and dirt, the likes of which Leonard had never seen before. As he reached out to touch the side of the passage, Maria spoke.

"This is the start of the system. You see how the walls and floor are different?" She pointed ahead. "There is a machine farther down the tunnel that I think dug all of this."

Leonard stroked the wall gently. "I've never felt anything like this before. The rock and dirt have some sort of coating on them, and they're incredibly smooth. It's like someone coated them in plastic."

"There's more up ahead. Come on."

Leonard and Maria continued down the tunnel, and Leonard began to see more evidence that it wasn't the same type of construction as had been used in the metro lines. The temperature in the tunnel began to increase as the tunnel took on a slightly downward slope, making it more difficult to keep traction on the smooth floor. After a few hundred feet, the slope leveled out, and Leonard could see something shining in the distance. He readied his rifle and motioned for Maria to stay quiet, but she merely looked at him with a confused expression.

"What is it?" she asked.

"There's something ahead."

"Yes. The machine I told you about."

"Oh." Leonard relaxed, feeling slightly foolish. As they drew closer to the machine, he could see that it appeared to be the size of a small tractor, with a single enclosed seat. Attached to the front of the machine was a tube that had several holes in it on all sides, from which small clear tubes emerged. The contraption on the front of the machine was flimsy looking, but as Leonard inspected it, he began to suspect what it was.

"I think you're right about this being a digging machine. The back of it has some ports for connecting what was probably extremely high capacity batteries, or maybe even power cells. My guess is that this array in the front is some sort of energy emitter your government was experimenting with to be able to create tunnels much faster than normal." Leonard reached out and touched the wall again. "Whatever this coating is, it seems to give some structural support to the tunnel, given that there's bare rock and dirt behind it."

Maria walked around the machine and pointed at the short length of tunnel left in front of them. "This is as far as anyone has been, but there are more tunnels ahead."

Leonard gave the machine an admiring pat before continuing on with Maria. As they approached the end of the main tunnel, Leonard could see that it branched off in several directions. Leonard stood, staring at the various passages and wondering where to go next, when Maria sniffed a few times.

"Do you smell that?" she asked, turning her head.

Leonard inhaled deeply, catching the faintest whiff of fresh air. He licked his finger, held it up and felt a slight breeze coming from the right. He walked to the right-most passage and peered down into it. It went on for ten or twenty feet, like the main tunnel did, before narrowing and becoming much less uniform.

"Come on," he said. "Let's see what's down door number one."

Unlike the main tunnel, the narrow passage appeared hand-hewn, with copious amounts of wooden supports put into place to help keep it from collapsing. Leonard looked down the tunnel with his light, unable to see very far due to the meandering direction it took.

"I'll lead the way." Leonard kept a tight grip on his rifle as they entered the smaller shaft. The air was still growing warmer, and he could feel sweat beginning to drip down his back and chest despite the faint breeze. "Any idea why it's so hot down here?"

Maria shook her head. "I don't know. No one has ever talked about it being this hot."

"When was the last patrol down here?"

Maria shrugged. "I don't know. I'm sorry."

As Leonard walked, he noticed greater quantities of dust being kicked up into the air. He stopped and knelt down to examine the ground, running his fingers through the dirt to examine it. He then turned his attention to the wooden supports in the shaft. At first glance, they had appeared haphazardly put together, but as he slowly scanned over them with his light, he realized that they were following an odd— but cunningly devised—pattern designed to use the least amount of wood possible.

Leonard backed up several paces and looked at the wooden supports and the way in which the walls, floor and ceiling had been dug, then went forward again. He frowned.

"Nobody comes down here, right, Maria?"

She shook her head again. "No. Patrols will come down the ladder and check for the creatures sometimes, but no one comes into these tunnels."

Leonard stood up slowly and put the rifle to his shoulder. "Then we have a problem."

Maria looked around nervously. "What problem? Did you see something?"

Leonard continued advancing slowly down the tunnel, keeping his finger pressed up against the side of his rifle's trigger. "Yes. This part of the tunnel isn't like the last bit. Plus, this dirt is fresh. Someone—or something—has been down here recently doing some excavating."

"Wh-what do you mean?" Maria's voice shook.

Leonard stopped and turned to look at her. "It means one of two things. Either you or Alexander are lying to me for some reason, or those creatures have been digging to lengthen this side passage. I don't see the logic in you people lying about this, so I'm going with my second theory for now. Which, by no coincidence, is the worst of the two."

"I'm sorry, Leonard, I don't underst—"

"It's simple." Leonard continued moving slowly through the passage, whispering to Maria as he went. "The creatures got down here somehow. Maybe through that elevator shaft you told me about. Maybe through some other way. They found this side passage and began to expand on it."

"How do you know?"

Leonard motioned at the ceiling with his rifle, and Maria pointed her light up. "Look at the pattern in the boards. Completely different than what we saw earlier. Plus, this is a different type of wood. It looks newer, too. And this soil and rock has been freshly excavated."

"Shouldn't we turn back?"

Leonard paused for a second. "Yes, but not until we see where this leads. They may be trying to use this as some sort of a way to get at the station without being seen." He shook his head. "Hell if I know, but I'm going to find something out, one way or another."

The temperature in the passage increased with each step forward the pair took. Finally, after Leonard felt as though he were about to spontaneously combust, the passage abruptly widened into a small chamber. Instead of being enclosed, however, the back side of the chamber was open, revealing a vast, dark expanse beyond. As Leonard searched through the chamber with his light, he suddenly realized that they were standing at the upper edge of an underground cavern.

A steady warm breeze flowed through the chamber from the cavern, offering no relief from the heat, but providing the hint of fresh air nonetheless. Leonard ventured to the edge of the chamber and looked down to see a steep incline that emptied out into nothingness that his light wasn't strong enough to pierce. While the angle of the incline wouldn't be fatal to traverse, it would be nigh-on impossible to climb back out once a person began sliding down.

Leonard slowly backed up from the edge of the chamber and wiped the sweat from his brow. Behind him, Maria looked past him into the abyss, waving her flashlight to and fro in an effort to see what was beyond the chamber. Leonard pushed her light down and shook his head. "No sense in attracting attention. Come on. Let's get out of here."

As Maria left, Leonard paused for a moment and cocked his head to the side. He wasn't entirely certain what he was hearing—a year's worth of firefights without adequate hearing protection had given him more than his fair share of tinnitus. As he strained to listen in the darkness, though, he could swear that he was hearing—and feeling—a low frequency vibration coming from somewhere in the cavern. The more he listened to and felt, the more uneasy he grew. When Maria's hand touched his arm, he jumped, making some incomprehensible sound. "Dammit!" he hissed. "Don't *do* that!"

Maria tugged at his arm again. "Come on. This place doesn't feel right."

As Leonard's heartbeat began to slow, he noticed that the buzzing in his head and chest was gone. *Maybe I was just imagining it. But I swear, it almost felt like—*

"Leonard?" Maria whispered to him again, and he lost his train of thought. He nodded and followed her back through the winding tunnel, wondering how he was going to explain the strange situation to Krylov, Marcus and—most especially—Alexander.

Chapter Twenty-Six

Submarine Pen

"How's the pressure look?" Sergei asked, checking the seals on his suit for the third time.

Andrey tapped the gauge on the top of the tank on Sergei's back. "Good."

"How can I tell?" Luka spun around in a circle as he tried to see the tank on his own back.

"It's the—here, let me look." Andrey sighed and grabbed Luka, stopping the spinning before the technician toppled over. Andrey tapped Luka's gauge and gave him a thumbs up.

"You're fine."

"Are you sure?"

"Luka." Sergei spoke gruffly. "You're fine. Stop worrying about this and calm down, or you'll burn through your tank before we even get in the water."

Andrey fiddled with the straps on his gloves again, then pulled out the tooth from his pocket and gave it a kiss. Sergei rolled his eyes at the superstitious action.

"Do you need a moment alone with that thing?"

Andrey tucked the tooth back in his pocket and finished adjusting his gloves. "If you don't want the good fortune, then I'll keep it all for myself."

Sergei snorted with amusement. "You idiot."

It had taken just over an hour of precious time, but the Arkhangelsk had finally located the submarine they were looking for. It sat on the bottom of the submarine pen, right in the middle underneath a pair of large cranes. There had been no obvious signs of damage to the sub, but it would be impossible to discern any details until the dive team made their way to the vessel.

The dive suits in the storage facility had been in excellent condition, and there were no tears or cracks in the rubber or in the seals of the air tanks. Refilling the air tanks had taken more time than Nancy had wanted, and the bulk of the delay was attributable to that issue.

After the three men had thoroughly checked each other's suits, Nancy helped pass out the limited supply of weapons they would be carrying with them. "We've seen a few creatures that have survived in the water for long periods of time, as you know, so you'll want these."

Nancy handed each of them a compact spear gun with ten bolts each, a pistol and a submachine gun. Each also carried a small pouch containing a lifting bag that could be filled with air from their tanks and used to help bring the pump—along with any other essential parts —to the surface.

"You may have limited room once you're inside the sub, so I don't want to burden you with anything extra. We don't know anything about that wreck, so use extreme caution. If—by some miracle—the sub has a few air pockets left, be careful if you have to use the firearms.

"Remember, I don't care what else you find down there—the pump is your only priority. Get that thing back to the surface as soon as you find it so we can get it aboard and start the installation."

The three men nodded in acknowledgment as Sergei spoke for them all. "We'll be back with it soon, ma'am."

Nancy smiled. "See that you are."

She turned and walked back down the length of the Arkhangelsk's deck as the three were helped into the water by several of the crew who had been milling about. Sergei and Andrey slipped smoothly into the water, having been trained in basic underwater operations in years past. Luka, on the other hand, slipped as he neared the edge of the deck and fell into the water with a splash whose sound echoed throughout the cavern. Sergei took a deep breath from his regulator and clenched his jaw. He was doing his best not to lose patience with the young technician, but it seemed that every time Luka took a step, he had his foot in the wrong place.

Taking the lead, Andrey pushed off from the side of the Arkhangelsk. He descended at a shallow pace, turning his upper body frequently to look back and check on the others. Sergei positioned himself at the back so he could be certain that there was no chance of Luka wandering off. Each man carried an underwater flashlight attached to their left arm, along with a spare attached to their chest in case of an emergency. Without a way to communicate vocally, the trio was left to hand signals and—if a particularly complex message needed to be conveyed—small erasable magnetic boards and pens.

A set of tools was distributed amongst the three men, with a few of the most critical ones duplicated twice or three times over between them. While Luka would likely be the only one among them to utilize the tools to disconnect the reactor pump, they wanted to take no chances in case something happened to go wrong.

Compared to the frantic hustle and bustle above, descending through the waters' layers was both peaceful and relaxing. The threat of imminent danger was a constant presence in the back of all of their minds—Luka's most of all—but the water had the near-mystical power of reducing the worry significantly.

While the trio pushed downward, the water grew darker as the Arkhangelsk's powerful lights were no longer able to penetrate the depths. All three kept their lights on and moving constantly as they searched for the enormous metal tube that was hiding in the shadows. After a full fifteen minutes of easy swimming, Andrey began to slow his kicks. He came to a stop in the water at an upright angle, held a hand above his head and then pointed his arm down and to the right. Luka and Sergei stopped next to Andrey and looked at where he was pointing. Though it was hard to make out at a distance, there was no mistaking the instantly-recognizable shape of a submarine.

Swimming together in a cluster, the three pushed forward at a rapid pace. Luka could feel his heart pounding in his chest as he struggled to keep up with the two soldiers. As they approached the submarine from the stern, Sergei and Andrey slowed and separated, with Sergei swimming to the port side and Andrey taking Luka with him to the starboard side. The two soldiers scanned the submarine carefully, looking for signs of cracks in the hull as well as an easy entry point to the interior. By the time they got to the bow of the vessel and joined back up, both men signaled to each other that they had seen nothing wrong with the ship's hull.

With the swarms and creatures that no doubt had been aboard, this was an oddity—particularly since the vessel would have had to have sunk to the bottom of the water for some reason. If that reason wasn't because it had been damaged and taken on water, then it was possible that the interior was still dry. A brief written conversation took place between Andrey and Sergei as the pair discussed what to do. They finally settled on looking for the lock-out chamber—an airlock-like entrance into the submarine that would allow them passage without potentially flooding the vessel.

Designed as both a way to exit and enter a sub while underwater, the lock-out chamber's exterior often had specially designed connectors so that small submersibles could dock with the main submarine. The controls for nearly all aspects of the chamber had manual backups and overrides—aside from the pumps that could clear water out of the chamber since they lacked the required electricity to operate—so the idea was sound, at least in theory.

It took another twenty minutes of slow swimming around the large vessel before the men found the entrance they were looking for. The sub sat at a slight angle on the bottom, tilted toward the port, while the hatch was located on the starboard side near the base of the main sail. The trio gathered around the hatch before Sergei approached it and began the process of opening a small compartment containing the manual override controls.

After a few minutes of frustration, Sergei was able to unblock the handle attached to the hatch release. He glanced at Andrey and Luka to make sure they were clear, then maneuvered to the side of the entrance and pulled the handle. A veritable explosion of air erupted from the hatch, and the door blew open to the side. Once the bubbles cleared, Sergei peered inside.

The chamber was large enough to fit a dozen men in full diving or battle gear. A thin layer of air still rested at the top of the lock-out chamber, having been blocked from its exit by the upper lip of the outer door. A set of benches lined the base of each wall of the chamber, and there were various valves and apparatuses lining the walls and ceiling. Sergei swam inside first, followed by Luka—who had to be prodded more than once to keep moving—who was followed by Andrey. As Andrey entered the chamber, he braced his legs against the frame of the room and began to pull the outer hatch shut. Sergei motioned for Luka to stay in a corner of the room before swimming over to help Andrey close and seal the hatch.

When Sergei was satisfied that the outer hatch was sealed properly, he pointed at the two benches and scribbled on his board.

Hold on!

Luka and Andrey sat next to each other and linked arms before grabbing hold of the underside of the seat with their free hands. After his experience dealing with the outer hatch, it took Sergei less than a minute to release the seals on the inner door. While most doors on the submarine-side of a lock-out chamber would have opened inward into the chamber itself, the P949—for some unknown reason—had an inner door that opened the opposite way. This meant that instead of the door remaining in place and Sergei having to find a way to pry it open against the pressure of the water inside the chamber, it opened instantly and forcefully.

The handle for the inner hatch was torn from Sergei's fingers as water exploded from the lock-out chamber into the submarine's interior. Sergei struggled to find a grip as he was carried along with it, careening head over heels down the corridor as the water drained into other compartments in the vessel. Andrey and Luka could do nothing but watch as Sergei's light disappeared into the darkness. It took only a few seconds for the water level to drop enough for the two men to be able to remove their regulators.

"Sergei!" Andrey shouted, the first to tear the regulator from his mouth. He drew in a breath and coughed, surprised by the stale, metallic taste of the air. He then remembered that the submarine had been sealed for the last year.

Luka removed his regulator with more caution. He sniffed a few times before taking in a deep breath and grimacing. "It should be safe to breathe this, but we need to be careful. There's no telling how much oxygen is left."

Andrey nodded and stood up as the water level dropped to below his knees. "Come on. We need to find Sergei."

A clatter from outside the room and down the corridor drew their attention. Andrey assumed it was his cousin and shouted again. "Sergei! Are you all right?"

A cough came next, followed by a groan. "My head feels like it's going to split in two." Sergei appeared in the doorway, leaning against the wall and holding his head. "But yes, I'm fine."

Andrey grinned and motioned for Sergei to lower his head. "You've got a big gash, but nothing serious." Andrey opened a small watertight pouch and pulled out a bandage. "Keep pressure on it, and you'll be fine."

Sergei nodded and then winced as he regretted the movement. "Thanks."

Andrey's grin grew wider. "Next time, hold on better, will you?"

Luka chuckled behind Andrey, and Sergei rolled his eyes. "Come on. We need to get moving to the reactor compartment."

Andrey unstrapped his light from his arm and held it out, looking down the length of both sides of the corridor outside the lock-out chamber. "Which way is it?"

Luka pushed past him, holding his own flashlight. "Here. Follow me."

The interior of the submarine was pitch black and deathly silent. Water trickled by in the corridor and dripped into some unseen crevice. Emergency lights were placed at regular intervals on the walls, but their batteries had long since failed. The atmosphere was far different from that of the Arkhangelsk, even compared to night cycles when the lights and noise were at their minimum.

The knowledge that there were other people present on the Arkhangelsk made the cold metal tube seem less hostile and sterile, unlike the environment on the P949. While Luka was focused on his goal of reaching the reactor room as quickly as possible, Andrey and Sergei were concerned with scanning their environment as they went along. They both doubted that there was even the possibility of running into any creatures in the long-abandoned sub, but they weren't willing to take any chances.

After a few minutes of hurried travel, Luka slowed down and stopped outside a particularly thick door that was marked with various warning signs. "Here." Luka handed his flashlight to Sergei and pulled out a small Geiger counter from his tool bag. "Wait here while I check the radiation levels." Luka switched on the lamp on his chest, illuminating the path before him as he prepared to venture inside.

The outer of the two doors leading to the reactor compartment was already ajar. Luka eased it open and held the Geiger counter out in front of him. The device remained silent as he advanced, no matter which direction he pointed it or how close he held it to various objects in the room. Like the outer door, the inner door was also open, but there was still no sign of any radiation inside.

Luka nervously proceeded through the second doorway. His hands shook as he flitted the detector of the device back and forth. Constructed of lead and steel, the reactor chamber itself took up the bulk of the room. A small porthole with several inches of thick glass in it was mounted on one side of the chamber, though it was from that location that a large crack in both the glass and metal was visible. Luka froze at the sight of the crack and looked down at the counter again. Still nothing.

He crept along the side of the reactor slowly as paranoia got the better of him, and he began treating the potential radiation hazard as though it were a living beast waiting to spring upon him from a corner. After verifying—yet again—that there was no sign of radiation in the room, Luka summoned up the nerve to peer into the reactor chamber itself.

Andrey and Sergei stood up against opposite walls of the corridor outside the entrance to the reactor compartment. They waited in silence as Luka's slow footsteps passed through the rooms until, finally, they heard his voice call to them. "It's safe!"

Sergei took the lead as they entered the rooms, followed closely by Andrey. The pair reached Luka in a few seconds, and they were surprised to find that the man who had been a pile of nerves a few moments earlier looked relaxed and jovial.

Andrey looked around the room as he spoke. "Is everything all right, Luka?"

"Absolutely!" Luka showed them the Geiger counter. "See? Absolutely nothing. And if that doesn't convince you, look over here."

Luka gestured to the porthole in the side of the reactor chamber. Andrey and Sergei stepped closer and angled their flashlights to see inside. Instead of a mass of metal and liquid that they would have seen had the reactor been active, all they saw was an empty chamber that looked as though it had been eaten away. It had been completely stripped of the fuel and control rods, coolant and other equipment, as well as an inch or so of the inside of the chamber itself.

Sergei let out a long whistle. "Those little bastards are thorough."

"Aren't they though?" Luka laughed nervously.

Andrey turned to Luka. "So, where's the pump?"

"Right. The pump." Luka maneuvered around the chamber to the back of the room. He began removing a panel on the wall, revealing a nest of wires and thick metal tubing that extended behind it. A narrow crawlspace offered access to the tubing, though it was a tight fit. Luka stared down the crawlspace, bobbing his head back and forth as he examined the area behind the panel with his flashlight.

"The pump's back here, about halfway down. It looks intact, so as long as it didn't get damaged when this thing sank, it should be fine."

"Good." Sergei helped Luka remove his air tank and tools. "How long will it take you to remove it?"

"No more than an hour, I think. Maybe less."

Sergei looked at his watch and shook his head. "Try to make it a lot less if you can. I don't want to be stuck in this coffin for that long."

"I'll do my best."

Sergei nodded and looked back at Andrey. "Let's split up and search this boat room by room. We should have enough time."

Andrey checked his watch as well. "Sounds good." He glanced up at Luka, whose face was beginning to turn white again. "Relax. There's nothing on this thing, or it would have been after us already. Close the hatches if it makes you feel better."

Luka tried to argue, but Sergei shook his head against the technician's protest. "We can't just sit around in here while you work. Get moving, and we'll be back in half an hour." The two soldiers shuffled out of the reactor chamber, leaving Luka to stand and stare at their disappearing lights for a moment before he cleared his head and began his task.

In the corridor outside the reactor compartments, Andrey and Sergei paused to decide where they would each go. After a brief discussion, Sergei headed in the direction of the armory while Andrey took off on a general search of the sub. Although the Arkhangelsk was well-stocked with ammunition and weapons, Sergei was of the firm belief that you could never have too many of either. Andrey, meanwhile, wanted to take a general stock of the sub in case there was anything on board they hadn't thought about that could be transferred to the Arkhangelsk.

As each of the cousins began their winding course through the dark corridors of the submarine, they carried with them the thoughts of the mission and its potential success—or failure. With nothing else they could do to help Luka, all they could do was wait and hope for the best.

Chapter Twenty-Seven

P949 Submarine

PWhile Sergei knew the layout of the Arkhangelsk like the back of his hand, the interior of the P949 was different in both subtle and dramatic ways. The lock-out chamber's hatch reversals were merely the first on a list of oddities about the sub, and Sergei began to wonder what other surprises might lurk in the boat's belly.

After a few minutes of wandering, Sergei found himself standing in front of a closed door marked with a sign indicating that it was the armory. He cracked the door cautiously, then swung it open wide to reveal a veritable treasure trove of weaponry. While the room was smaller than the Arkhangelsk's armory by at least half, it bristled with enough armaments that Sergei began to wonder what task the submarine had been assigned to before it had put in for maintenance.

An entire wall of the submarine was filled with explosives, grenades and shoulder-fired rockets, while another was dedicated entirely to various calibers of ammunition. The ammo was stored in watertight boxes, a fact that pleased Sergei to no end as he thought about how he could best get it out of the sub. The other two walls in the room held dozens upon dozens of rifles, including several large-caliber snipers. A small table in the center of the room was dotted on all four sides with drawers that contained an abundance of firearm maintenance and repair kits, enough to keep a small army's worth of weapons clean and functional for years.

The sight of the myriad of weapons brought a smile to Sergei's face, and he immediately began scanning the rows of supplies to prioritize how he wanted to begin moving them to the lock-out chamber. The weapons, he thought, would have to suffer through a brief exposure to the corrosive salt water, but could be cleaned easily enough after they were brought onto the Arkhangelsk. The ammunition, however, would be fine, since it was all inside waterproof containers, and he decided to tackle those first.

By removing a row of ammo bricks from each box, Sergei found he could begin stuffing cleaning supplies into the empty spaces so that those could be brought off the sub along with the ammo. He did this to a few dozen boxes before beginning the arduous process of moving them from the armory to the lock-out chamber on the other side of the sub. With no hand cart available, it was a slow process, and as he moved the boxes, he began to wonder how his cousin was faring with his search.

AT THE OTHER end of the submarine, Andrey quietly padded down the hall. He kept his weapon out and pointed in front of him as he searched each room, staying alert for any sign of danger. The appearance of the mutated animals at Magadan had frightened him more than he wanted to admit, and the thought of encountering one on board was scarier than that of encountering a mutated human.

As Andrey peeked into one of the rooms, he started to move away, but returned as he noticed that the room contained only a single bed. Further inspection revealed several leather-bound books on a shelf above the bed, a notebook resting at a desk and a variety of knick-knacks scattered about on the floor. *It's the Captain's quarters*, he thought. Andrey moved toward the desk and pulled out the chair to sit down. His air tank hit the back of the chair as he maneuvered into place and opened the notebook to flip through it.

The Captain's log was mundane for the most part, describing journeys the submarine had taken on various missions, as well as small incidents among the crew. As the dates advanced, though, the entries became more detailed, describing strange orders from the Russian government and odd whisperings among the crew about passengers they had taken aboard.

The Captain had apparently been under orders to head for the United States coastline, where they were to wait for further orders. Andrey frowned as he read the entry, remembering that it was similar to the odd order the Arkhangelsk had been given. He continued to read as the log changed to the personal speculations from the Captain, describing how some close friends in the government had warned him that the Americans were on the cusp of developing a terrible new weapon. No details about the weapon were described to the Captain, but Andrey understood precisely what it was: the artificial intelligence.

The last entry in the logbook contained a mixture of details about the maintenance work the P949 required (work done to one of the turbines), as well as describing more odd transmissions from the Russian mainland about the need for the submarine to get to the American coastline as fast as possible. Andrey closed the book slowly as he remembered the Arkhangelsk's own encounter with the swarms and their subsequent journeys. He stood up and exited the Captain's quarters quietly as he said a silent prayer of thanks that he hadn't shared the fate of the P949's crew.

Andrey continued to progress through the submarine, eventually reaching the hatch to the area containing the P949's missiles. The hatch was open, and Andrey stepped through to find a level of destruction that was unmatched by any other on the vessel. Large pieces of metal lay scattered about on the floor: the remnants of the missiles and missile tubes that had once filled the area. The swarms had attacked the nuclear-tipped weapons with gusto, and as they'd destroyed key components of the room to get at their meal, key fittings in the structures that had supported the missile bodies had been destroyed. The domino effect this had had on the weapons was devastating, and Andrey was shocked that the hull hadn't been ruptured from the inside due to the forces involved.

As he slowly picked his way across the wreckage, Andrey's light reflected harshly off the twisted metal, giving the impression that every piece of debris was actually one of the creatures. When Andrey reached the midway point in the room, he realized that he could go no farther and that access to anywhere fore of the missile room had been blocked off. He began to work his way back through the room and then out, making a beeline for the final area of the submarine he wanted to check: the control deck.

Located a level above the armory, the control deck was the nerve center of the P949. Though smaller in size than the one on the Arkhangelsk, all of the same basic stations were still present. As Andrey opened the hatch and stepped through onto the deck, he expected to find it in a condition similar to the other portions of the ship—relatively intact, but in a state of mild disrepair. What he saw, though, was anything but.

The scent of death exploded over Andrey, and he scrambled for his regulator just to stop the coughing. Bodies littered the floor—at least two dozen of them in various stages of dismemberment. The cool temperatures of the submarine and the control deck being sealed off had preserved the bodies remarkably well, leading to several of them looking like they were nearly alive.

Andrey stepped over the bodies carefully as he made his way around the room, scanning each one of them with his light as he went. The first time that he saw a glint of silver reflected, he froze, then realized with a relieved sigh that it was merely a dog tag hanging from around the person's neck. The second time he saw the reflection of silver metal, though, he froze as he realized the metal intertwined the person's face, wrapping around their neck and piercing through their body.

Andrey held perfectly still as he watched the corpse, not daring to so much as take a breath as he quickly contemplated his next move. The mutated face on the creature showed no signs of the decomposition that appeared on the other bodies in the room, making Andrey wonder if it was going to suddenly spring to life.

A full minute passed before Andrey dared to take a shallow breath, but still the creature did not stir. He moved his light slightly, shuffled his feet and adjusted his gun, but the creature remained still. After Andrey gently kicked the creature's body in the side with no response, he finally began to relax, realizing the creature must have died and been preserved by either the metal, the nanobots or some other process.

As his attention shifted from the creature in front of him back to the room at large, the macabre atmosphere intruded upon his senses once again, and he wanted nothing more than to leave. He retraced his steps toward the door, trying to avoid stepping on any of the bodies, and then stepped through the hatch. He ran down the corridor, descended a ladder to the deck below and traveled almost the entire way back to the lock-out chamber before removing his regulator.

The smell of death still clung to his suit, though that wasn't the worst of it. He began to feel a sense of panic and claustrophobia as he thought about the creature he had seen on the con, and wondered where else on the ship the mutants might be, and if all of them were as dead as the one he had seen. A noise from behind Andrey made him jump, and he whirled around to be confronted by a light in his face accompanied by a harsh voice.

"Put the damned gun down, cousin! Are you trying to get us all killed?"

Andrey's shoulders slumped, and he breathed a sigh of relief. "Sergei!" Andrey's relief turned to confusion as he noticed the stacks of boxes in the corridor. "What's all this?"

"Ammunition. Come on. Help me get the rest of the boxes out here."

Andrey shook his head. "We need to check on Luka."

"Andrey?" Sergei's tone changed from annoyance to concern. "What's going on?"

"I was on the con—there were bodies everywhere. Half of them had been torn apart and spread all over the place."

"Christ," Sergei whispered. "I guess we know where the crew was when the swarms got on board."

"That's not all," Andrey continued. "I saw one of the mutants up there, too."

"A mutant?" Sergei dropped the box he was holding and reached for his rifle. "Did you kill it?"

Andrey shook his head. "It was already dead."

"How can you be sure?"

"I was standing right on top of it when I saw it. It didn't move a muscle."

Sergei began speaking faster. "You didn't put a blade across its neck or anything?"

"No… I saw no need."

"Were there others?"

Andrey hesitated. "I—I'm not sure. After I saw the creature, I left the con and came here."

Sergei ground his teeth together in frustration. "Please tell me that you at least sealed the hatch to the con."

Andrey shook his head, and Sergei let out a string of curses before opening one of the boxes at his feet. "Grab as much as you can hold. We're going back to the con and putting a few bullets into the head of each and every one of—"

Sergei's ranting was cut short by the sound of metal scraping on metal from somewhere above. Andrey and Sergei looked at each other as the scraping turned into the sound of growling, following by a primal scream. "You fool!" Sergei hissed at his cousin. "Forget everything else; get to the reactor chamber now!"

The pair grabbed a few spare magazines for their weapons from one of the ammo boxes before setting off at a run for the back of the sub. The sounds of scraping metal and howling grew faint behind them, though they didn't dare to slow down until they reached the outer reactor chamber door. Sergei pushed it open and whispered as they moved inside. "Luka!"

There was no response. "Luka!" Sergei whispered louder and raised his weapon in preparation for what he might find. After passing through the second door, he began inching around the reactor chamber as he continued to say the technician's name without answer. At the back of the room, in the crawlspace in the wall, he saw a faint light illuminating Luka's still form.

"Luka?" Sergei tapped the man's foot and swiftly received a kick in the chest followed by a yelp.

"Get off me you—oh! Shit! It's you!" Luka raised his head and peered back at the two soldiers from inside the crawlspace. "What are you trying to do, make me piss myself?"

"Why didn't you respond when I called?" Sergei whispered as he motioned for Luka to lower his voice.

"I was concentrating! What's going on? Why are you whispering?"

Sergei ignored Luka's question. "How much longer will it take to get the pump out?"

"Thirty minutes or so. There's more corrosion than I thought, and I have to be careful to—"

"You have ten minutes."

Luka stopped working and looked back at Sergei again. "Ten minutes? Why?"

"We're not alone here."

Sergei's words froze the blood in Luka's veins, and it took him a few seconds to respond. "Not alone? What are you talking about? Are those *things* here?"

"Don't worry about it," said Sergei. "We'll handle whatever comes our way. Just work quickly. We need to get out of here as soon as possible."

Sergei left Luka to mumble incoherently as he went back to work on the pump. Andrey was crouched inside the next chamber with his light off, staring wordlessly into the darkness of the corridor beyond. "Anything?" Sergei asked as he knelt down next to Andrey.

Andrey shook his head. "A few echoes. Nothing else. Damn it, though; I should have checked the bodies more thoroughly. It's my fault it—or they—woke up. But how could those things survive for over a year down here?"

"Some sort of hibernation, I guess."

Andrey shook his head again. "I screwed us, Sergei. I'm sorry."

Sergei patted his younger cousin on the back. "We'll make it out of here. I have a plan."

Andrey raised an eyebrow and looked at Sergei. "Oh?"

"You won't like it. Neither will Luka."

Andrey snorted. "Great. So, what is it? We blow a hole in the hull and swim out that way?"

Sergei shrugged. "Why waste explosives when we have a perfectly good hatch we can open?"

Andrey shifted position to look at Sergei. "You're joking, aren't you? A pressure change like that across the sub could crack the hull! We'd be killed!"

"We'll make it."

"Christ…" Andrey ran a hand through his hair, then took a deep breath from his regulator. His heart was still racing from when they had first heard the creatures a few minutes prior, and his chest ached and felt like it could explode. "How do you know that'll even do anything to slow them down? Just because they can't swim very well doesn't mean they can't swim at all."

"We'll make it." Sergei stood up and went into the back room. "How's it going, Luka?"

"Don't start asking me that!" Luka yelled out from the crawlspace. Despite the cold temperature of the sub, sweat was pouring down his face, both from nervousness and from being in the confined area for so long.

"Sergei!" Andrey yelled, and the older cousin ran back to the entrance of the chamber.

"What is it?"

Andrey had switched his light on briefly to look down the corridor while Sergei was gone. The light revealed several pinpoints of silver bobbing up and down in the distance and then quickly dispersing to the left and right as the creatures ducked into rooms to hide.

Andrey didn't bother to try to stay quiet. "They're advancing on us!"

"Damn!" Sergei pulled the outer door shut and spun the locking mechanism. "They can't get through this door, and we'll be able to spot them if they're anywhere immediately outside."

"Sounds great. What do we do when Luka's ready to go? Ask the creatures to move aside?"

Sergei drummed his fingers against his gun, racking his brain to think of a solution. "How far down were they?"

Andrey shrugged. "Half the corridor, at least."

"So, they're sitting just beyond the lock-out chamber?"

"I think so, yes. Why does that matter?"

Sergei unlocked the door and opened it again, then turned both of his lights on. A few points of silver appeared briefly before vanishing as the creatures hid once more. "Come on. Help me!" Sergei bounded through the hatch and ran for the nearest room. He pulled the hatch to the room closed and sealed it, then moved to the next one down the corridor. Andrey ran after him and did the same on the other side of the hall until they had nearly reached the point where they had last seen the creatures.

Sergei held up a fist and motioned for Andrey to move back. They crept backward down the corridor toward the reactor compartment, keeping their lights and weapons pointed at where the creatures had last been seen. "Now they've got nowhere to hide," Sergei whispered.

By preventing the creatures from accessing any more hiding spots between themselves and the reactor compartment, Sergei had forced their hand. If they wanted to make a move, they would have to expose themselves down a long stretch of hallway, where they would be easy to pick off.

"What if they wait us out?" Andrey whispered back.

Sergei patted a small pouch on his leg. "Then we get to find out how well they can swim... the hard way."

Andrey felt his stomach drop as he realized what his cousin meant. Blowing a hole in the side of the submarine was risky—to say the least. Though they weren't too far underwater, the P949 was already in rough shape, and any breach of the hull could destabilize the entire structure and flatten it like a soda can. But Andrey did have to concede that it was a slightly better option than suffering at the hands of one of the creatures.

The minutes ticked past as the two soldiers crouched quietly in the open hatch, watching and waiting for the creatures to show themselves. There had been no sight or sound from them, though, and Andrey was starting to wonder what they were doing when a loud crash from behind grabbed his attention.

"Shit!" Luka's voice accompanied the crash, and he followed with quiet muttering that carried through the compartments.

"Go see what happened," Sergei said. "I'll keep watch."

Andrey stood up and headed into the reactor room, where Luka was standing up in front of the crawlspace, holding his foot with one hand and his forehead with the other.

"Damn it all!" Luka mumbled to himself as he looked at his palm. His forehead was bleeding from a short gash he had sustained while dragging the pump out. Immediately after exiting the crawlspace, he had scraped his head against the edge, dropping the pump onto his foot in the process. The short flippers he still wore over his boots weren't protective at all, and he was fairly certain he'd broken a toe or three in the process.

"Is that it?" Andrey pointed at the hunk of metal and plastic on the floor. "That's the pump we need?"

Luka wiped his forehead again and winced. "Yes, that should be all we need."

"Should be?"

"Yes, it's all we need! Don't you have a bandage?" Luka's voice was full of frustration.

Andrey grabbed the technician's head and pulled it down to examine his wound. "No time. You'll be fine. Can you walk?"

Luka put weight on his injured foot and winced. "I think so."

"Good." Andrey slung his weapon over his shoulder and leaned down to pick up the pump. Weighing close to seventy-five pounds, the object's bulkiness made it more difficult to carry than its mass. "Come on; we need to get moving."

Luka followed Andrey out and into the next room, where Sergei was still crouched near the hatch. "How many of the creatures are there?" Luka whispered to Andrey as the soldier eased the pump down onto the ground.

"More than we'd like. Sergei—we have the pump. What's our exit plan?"

"Is he injured?" Sergei said, referring to Luka.

"I'm right here, you know. And I'm fine. Broke a few toes is all."

Sergei glanced down at the pump and nudged it to get a feel for its weight. "I'll take care of getting this to the lock-out chamber. Luka, once it's inside, I want you to get in with it, attach lifting bags and open the outer hatch. We'll seal the inner hatch so you can get that thing to the surface. Just make sure you close the outer hatch on your way out, okay?"

Luka nodded slowly as Andrey replied. "What about flooding the sub? I thought that was the plan."

Sergei motioned at the pump with his head. "It's going to be hell to get that thing out of here if we do it like that. If we get Luka and the pump inside the lock-out chamber, he can trigger the manual release inside to fill the room with water. Then, he just has to get it to the surface."

"Why can't you come with me?" Luka looked between the two men with panic in his eyes. "I don't want to do this on my own!"

Sergei stood up and patted Luka on the shoulder. "If we can, we'll be in there with you. Neither of us want to stay on this deathtrap any longer than necessary. You can't wait for us, though. The pump must be installed in the Arkhangelsk as soon as possible. You have everything you need, right? All of your equipment is secure? You have the lifting bags?"

Luka nodded. "I-I think so."

Sergei looked over Luka's gear, then spoke to Andrey. "Ready when you are."

Andrey moved from the reactor compartment out into the corridor. There was still no sign of the creatures, and the deathly silence was unnerving. Andrey moved forward quickly, followed by Luka. Sergei grunted as he picked up the pump and followed after the pair. Luka briefly took his gun off of its shoulder sling, but Andrey motioned for him to put it away. The last thing any of them needed was an untrained gunman firing wildly as they were trying to escape.

As Andrey approached the lock-out chamber door, he noticed that while they had left it open after entering the submarine, it was now closed, presumably by the creatures. "How the hell did they manage to do that?" Andrey whispered back at Sergei, who had caught up with him and Luka.

"Must have hit it when we weren't looking, maybe before we saw them. Just get it open fast. I'll cover you." Sergei set the pump down on the ground, pushed Luka back and pointed at him to stay. Sergei braced himself against the right wall in the corridor and pushed his weapon against his left shoulder before nodding at his cousin.

Andrey moved forward on the left side of the corridor until he reached the hatch to the lock-out chamber. He stood in front of the door and strained against the locking mechanism until he felt it give way. As the handle spun freely, the door suddenly flew open, throwing Andrey against the wall, where he fell to his knees. Behind the door, inside the lock-out chamber, a figure emerged, stretching its wizened metallic arms toward Andrey.

Before the creature could finish stepping out of the chamber, a hail of bullets streamed down the corridor, tearing one of the creature's arms off and sending it toppling over as it howled in pain. Sergei charged forward toward Andrey as he yelled at Luka. "Get the pump inside *now!*"

Ignoring his pain as a surge of adrenaline flowed through his body, Luka picked up the reactor pump and shuffled toward the lock-out chamber. Sergei was already in front of it when he arrived, helping Andrey to his feet. The creature snarled and grabbed at Luka with its good arm as the technician stumbled into the chamber and threw the pump to the floor. A series of howls echoed from outside the chamber as the creatures hiding in the compartments nearby began to emerge, intent on finishing the job that their comrade had attempted to start.

Before Luka could turn around, Andrey had slammed the hatch closed and was turning the locking mechanism. "Pull the manual release!" Andrey shouted over the sound of the automatic gunfire next to him. He jabbed his finger at the glass of the hatch's window, pointing Luka toward a large red lever near the outer door. Luka hurried to the lever and tugged at it a few times before it gave way. Water began rushing into the chamber, and Luka scrambled to put his regulator into his mouth.

Unable to devote any more attention to the technician, Andrey silently hoped that the man would be able to manage getting the outer hatch open and floating the pump to the surface without any more help. Turning away from the hatch, Andrey dropped low to the ground and ran back to Sergei, who was still firing down the corridor at any creatures that dared to show their faces.

"Is he inside?" Sergei shouted over the gunfire.

"The chamber's flooding. As long as he figures out how to open it and use those lifting bags, he'll be away within minutes."

"Good!"

"How are we going to deal with these things?" Andrey took a potshot at one of the creatures that was peeking out of a room and heard a satisfying shriek as his bullet tore off an ear.

"I'm open to suggestions!"

The pair retreated slowly, conserving their ammunition as they backed up to the reactor compartment. The creatures didn't venture any farther than the open compartments near the lock-out chamber, where they retreated to hide. Sergei kept a close eye on the lock-out chamber, silently daring any of the creatures to try and open it, but they left it alone. A soft *thunk* indicated that the outer hatch had been opened, and the two soldiers imagined Luka heading back to the surface with the pump.

After a few moments went by without any other sounds, Sergei suddenly became concerned. He had clearly heard the outer hatch open, but had yet to hear it close. Without power in the sub, there would be no way for the pair to close the hatch, which meant they would be forced to exit by explosively decompressing the sub. It had been his original plan for escaping the creatures, but it felt less appealing by the second.

"Sergei?" Andrey whispered to his cousin. "Did Luka forget to close the outer hatch?"

Sergei checked his watch. "Give him some more time. It might take him a while."

As Sergei spoke, a strange noise that was a cross between the sound of a zipper and a hiss of air echoed down the metal structure of the sub. The sound was accompanied a few seconds later by the sound of metal scraping against metal, then the noise stopped. Minutes ticked by as the pair strained their ears, but they heard nothing except silence.

"That must have been the lifting bag inflating," Andrey whispered. "But was that the hatch closing, too?"

Sergei shook his head. "No. Probably the pump knocking against the side of the chamber as he tried to push it out."

The two sat in silence for another few minutes. While Andrey knew full well that there was more than enough air in the sub for them to last for at least a day or two, he couldn't help but feel short of breath at the prospect of being trapped.

Andrey finally spoke again. "We can't stay here forever."

"I know."

"Should we try to leave now?" Andrey leaned over to look down the corridor to where Sergei had been staring. "They don't seem interested in trying to rush us."

"All it's going to take is for them to get one lucky swipe in while we're fighting the water and it'll be all over."

"That sounds better than suffocating."

Sergei grunted in affirmation, unable to argue with Andrey's point. "Fair enough. You want to do this now?"

"If we keep waiting, those bastards might come up with some new scheme to stop us."

Sergei sighed and pulled his regulator hose back over his head. He checked the straps on his goggles and the pressure gauge on Andrey's air tank. Andrey did the same for Sergei, and they both swapped out the partially depleted magazines in their guns for fresh ones.

"Ready?"

Andrey nodded. Sergei pushed open the door and advanced slowly and steadily down the right side of the corridor, staying a few paces ahead of Andrey, who stuck to the left. Though the hall was narrow, it still offered Andrey the opportunity to shoot past Sergei if necessary, and it kept them far enough apart that they couldn't be taken down at the same time quite as easily as if they were side by side.

As they reached the hatch for the lock-out chamber, Sergei heard a creature emerge from the next compartment before he saw it. He began firing as soon as its body appeared, allowing the recoil of the weapon to carry the burst from the creature's chest up through its head. Its body slumped to the floor with a muffled thump, and a few seconds later, the remaining creatures began to howl in rage.

"Get it open!" Sergei yelled behind him at Andrey, who was frantically turning the locking mechanism. He hesitated and winced with each turn, wondering which would be the one that caused the hatch to explode open and begin flooding the sub. When the moment finally arrived, it was exactly as he had anticipated. The hatch flung him against the wall, and the water began pushing him back down the corridor toward the reactor compartment.

Sergei reached out and grabbed Andrey's hand, having thrown the strap of his gun around the inside handle of the hatch as it had flown open. The pair's regulators were torn from their mouths by the force of the water, and their goggles were ripped off and lost to some far recess of the sub nearly instantly. As they strained to hold on against the force of the water rushing in, the creatures' howls of rage turned into cries of panic.

Although the creatures could apparently hibernate for long periods of time in the right environment without suffering ill effects, they were nearly helpless in the water. Designed for speed and strength on land, the mutations performed to the bodies by the nanobots rendered the creatures extremely off-balance while underwater. On top of being unable to swim, the corrosive nature of the salt water wreaked havoc on the small groups of nanobots still infesting the bodies. Unable to self-replicate due to being in a low-power state and not being joined to a larger group, the nanobots were limited to basic repair functions. Exposure to the salt water rendered these limited capabilities completely and utterly moot.

While the destructive effect of the salt would take some time, the effect of the rapidly rising water was immediate. The two creatures close enough to the hall to be caught in the initial wave were carried down the corridor, howling and screaming as they thrashed in the wave. Some of the boxes of ammunition crashed against Sergei and Andrey's legs as they were carried down the length of the corridor in both directions, and some of them smashed into the creatures. The other mutants were slammed against the walls of the compartments they were hiding in as they struggled—and failed—to remain upright.

As the water level rose above Sergei and Andrey's heads and the flow of water began to abate, the pair let go of each other and fumbled with their regulators before fitting them into their mouths. The flow of air was an enormous relief in their turbulent environment, and they began to pull themselves into the lock-out chamber. Once inside, Sergei braced himself against one of the walls and signaled for Andrey to do the same. They stayed there for the next several minutes as the submarine continued to fill, listening to the metal pop and vibrate as the internal structure flexed from the varying forces placed upon it.

When the water finally equalized and there was no more air rushing out and no more water coming in, Sergei pushed himself off the wall and through the outer hatch, followed by Andrey. Sergei paused to swing the outer hatch back into place, then sealed it with a few slow turns of the wheel. Once he was done, the pair began their ascent to the surface, the reality of having survived by the skin of their teeth—again—beginning to sink in.

Upon surfacing, Andrey and Sergei looked around as they rubbed their eyes to try and clear their vision. Andrey's eyes burned from the water, but he could swear he saw a light approaching. "Sergei, look!"

Andrey tapped Sergei's shoulder, and they watched the light coalesce into the shape of an inflatable boat. The motor—one of the new ones pulled from the warehouse—was virtually silent, though the person standing in the front of the boat holding a light wasn't.

"Andrey! Sergei!" Nancy wore a broad grin on her face as she swept her spotlight over the pair. "We thought you two didn't make it!"

"What about the pump?" Sergei asked as a crewman on the inflatable reached over the side to help them in.

"It's on board. The installation process is going to take a few hours, since they have to reroute the piping to minimize downtime, but it's going to work." Nancy smiled at the pair again and gave them each a hug. "The Arkhangelsk is saved, thanks to you!"

Chapter Twenty-Eight

THE MAGADAN METRO

"**F**orgive me, but can you tell this tale once again? You two found some sort of tunnel beneath us that leads to a cavern in which you think something bad is going to happen?"

Leonard sighed and rubbed his eyes. He had already told Alexander what had happened once, and Maria had told it a second time. Alexander—for whatever reason—was not understanding. Whether he was choosing to not understand on purpose, though, was Leonard's next question.

He looked Alexander square in the eyes. "Do you not believe us, Alexander? Is that the problem here?"

"Mr. McComb—Leonard." Alexander flashed a smile. "I believe that you found *something* down there. But I can promise you that whatever it was, it poses no danger to us. We've been here for months. If there was digging going on underground or any sort of danger, we would have heard it, or our patrols would have seen it."

As Alexander talked, Leonard started to tune him out. He stared into space as he thought about the immense amount of heat flowing through the tunnels and the strange vibration he had heard just as he and Maria had left to return to the refuge. Once they had arrived back at the digging machine, Leonard had paused for a moment to try and figure out where the airflow was going. It turned out that one of the other passages was the culprit, which explained why none of the patrols had noticed either the heat or the flow of air at the bottom of the ladder.

Krylov said something in response to Alexander, but Leonard still wasn't paying any attention. In his mind's eye, he assembled the various puzzle pieces he had accumulated since arriving at the Magadan shoreline. *First, there's the factory. Clear signs of experimentation by the creatures. But for what? Then, the oddity of the canal being completely dried up. The shifting weather patterns wouldn't have caused that. Then, the behavior of the muties and the new infections—there's some sort of programming shift in the ones around here. Then, the heat and the vibrations underground...*

"Leonard?" Krylov touched Leonard's shoulder.

"Hm?" Leonard blinked a few times and looked at Krylov.

"Are you all right?"

"No." Leonard stood up from the table. "I think I know what's going on."

Alexander, Marcus, Roman, Mikhail, Krylov and Maria all looked at each other before turning back to Leonard. "Well?" said Krylov. "What is it?"

"The AI's building a Nexus. Underground."

Marcus burst out laughing, though there was a hint of nervousness in the laughter. "A Nexus? Are you out of your mind?"

"No, I'm quite serious." Marcus's face fell as Leonard continued. "We know for a fact that there's something different about this AI. Maybe it was a split from the main group, used as an experiment. Who knows. But they're very different, and not as advanced as the AI we dealt with in the States. That explains the mutilations of the bodies in the factory."

Leonard turned to Alexander. "That's why they've been taking your people. They're continuing to experiment on them."

"We knew that already. Why would they do it, though?"

Leonard shrugged. "I don't know, and I doubt we'll ever know for certain. All that matters is that they *are* doing it. Now, Krylov, remember the canal through the city, the one that was completely drained of water?"

Krylov nodded, and Leonard addressed Alexander again. "How long ago did that canal have water?"

"You mean the river?" Alexander rubbed his chin. "It started to drop after the first few months. We started relying on desalinators and rainwater after it vanished completely."

"Wouldn't the weather changes have had something to do with it drying up?" Marcus asked.

"No way in hell." Leonard was vehement. "No, I think it was drained to be used as part of a cooling system."

"A cooling system... for their Nexus?" Krylov raised an eyebrow.

"Yes. If they built it underground—which they'd have to in order for it to be around here and not show up on satellite imagery—they would need a lot of cooling. Which explains the canal drying up, and which also explains the airflow in those tunnels below us. They probably dug dozens of ventilation shafts to try and bleed off the excess heat. I'd bet you anything they're building their structure in the cavern."

Everyone at the table was quiet for a minute as they digested what Leonard had said, then Alexander spoke. "Maria, tell the guards I want four men at the top and four men at the bottom of that maintenance ladder. Have them check in every ten minutes."

Maria nodded and dashed away. Leonard glanced at Alexander questioningly. "So, you believe me now?"

Alexander nodded slowly. "While you and Maria were away, your commander here shared a great many things about you with me. I realize now that I should have listened without questioning you at the start, and for that I am sorry."

"Thank you." Leonard sat back down and sighed. "The problem is that I don't know what to do with this information. If we had any missiles left on the Arkhangelsk, I'd say we should just escape and have them nuke the entire area, but that's not an option this time."

Krylov straightened in his chair. "Our first priority is still to rescue everyone here. Once we've accomplished that task, we'll begin the process of figuring out how to destroy whatever the AI is building."

"Good. And thank you." Leonard felt a small sense of relief at Krylov's words, though his fears were still gnawing at him.

"Speaking of an escape plan," Krylov continued, "we've been working on that, and I think we have the details sorted."

Leonard forced the thoughts of the cavern and the Nexus from his mind. "Let's hear it."

Krylov gestured to the map Leonard had drawn on the table. Several alternations had been made to it in the form of scribbled writing, arrows and additional tunnels branching off from the main lines around the station.

"Alexander knows of a supply line that runs parallel directly beneath the western line starting just inside the second gate. It only runs parallel for a couple hundred meters before taking off to the south, where it joins up with the main supply line that exits at the docks."

"The creatures," Alexander jumped into the conversation, "have never shown much interest in the supply lines. I believe that is because we mostly use the main lines and they are more interested in us than anything else."

"So how do we get down into the supply line?" Leonard looked at the map. "I'm not seeing a service passage or anything."

Krylov grinned. "We blast our way down."

"You... want to blow a hole in the floor to get down into the supply line?" Leonard smiled. "It sounds incredibly dangerous and foolhardy. I love it. Can all of the survivors handle it, though? That's going to be a fairly high drop."

"We will dismantle the outer gate and use the wood and metal to build a makeshift ramp," Alexander said. "It will be a twenty-foot drop, and we can easily deal with that."

"What comes next?"

"We'll do as you suggested before. A few of us will remain here, in the station, and we'll rig it up with our explosives. As we retreat, we'll allow the creatures into the refuge and then destroy it as we follow the survivors through the tunnels." Alexander looked at Krylov. "From there, it's up to you and your submarine.

Krylov nodded. "As soon as we're clear from the tunnels, I'll radio the Arkhangelsk and have them send an inflatable ashore packed with as many guns and men as possible. We'll set up a defensive perimeter and start ferrying survivors to the Arkhangelsk. If we can find some other means of transportation, then we'll take it, but I see that as our worst-case scenario."

Leonard looked at the map again. "It's not a perfect plan by any stretch of the imagination, but I think it's the best we've got. As soon as the survivors are on board the Arkhangelsk, though, I want to get a team back in here with some heavy firepower to figure out what the creatures are up to."

Krylov very nearly snarled as he spoke. "We will destroy every trace of them."

Leonard turned to leave and patted Krylov on the shoulder. "Good. Now we all need to get some rest for a few hours. After that, I want to go over the final preparations and start nailing down exact times for this escape plan. Sound good?"

Everyone at the table nodded and echoed their approval. As they went their separate ways, Marcus trailed behind Leonard to the sleeping area while Krylov, Roman, Mikhail and Alexander spent a few more minutes talking. Once they were alone, Marcus whispered to Leonard. "Tell it to me straight. Do you really think whatever swarms were around here are trying to build a Nexus?"

Leonard looked Marcus dead in the eyes, and Marcus felt his blood run cold as Leonard spoke. "Do you remember when you first saw a swarm? How you could feel it buzzing and vibrating in your bones? I felt that down there—except it was so deep and pervasive that it felt like the entire planet was softly buzzing and vibrating. They're doing something underground, Marcus. And we're going to stop them."

Too dumbstruck to say anything, Marcus merely nodded, climbed into a cot and closed his eyes. Leonard sat down on his own cot and rolled up his pant leg, then unlatched and twisted his artificial leg off. He groaned from the relief of being free of the leg, then swung himself into the bed and pulled a blanket over himself, clutching the leg to his chest as he closed his eyes. A lack of sleep and running on fumes for so long meant that Leonard was asleep within seconds. The peace of sleep didn't last, though, as he soon found himself in that familiar, unholy place. He pulled himself through the dirt and debris, gasping for air as his mind once again returned him to the realm of nightmares.

Chapter Twenty-Nine

RYBACHIY NUCLEAR SUBMARINE BASE

The Arkhangelsk

"What the hell?" Luka looked up at Andrey from the floor as he rubbed his jaw. "What was that for?"

Sergei put a hand on his cousin's shoulder to pull him back from another blow. "Andrey! That's enough!"

Andrey balled his fists, but held back and shouted at Luka instead. "He told you to close the damned hatch! You could have killed us both!"

"I'm sorry!" Luka took Sergei's outstretched hand warily and slowly stood up. "I was trying to get those stupid bags attached to the pump, but it wouldn't work. When I finally got them on, I didn't know they would break before it got to the surface, so I followed it up to make sure it got there." Luka wiped a few drops of blood off his split bottom lip. "I swear it was an accident."

"What's with all the shouting?" Nancy walked into the lounge and stared at the three men, trying to figure out what was going on. After Andrey and Sergei had been brought back to the Arkhangelsk, Nancy had given them half an hour to get some food and get cleaned up before they and Luka were to give her a full update on what had happened. The soldiers had arrived in the lounge first, with Luka coming in shortly after. Andrey—still incensed by Luka's mistake with the hatch—had taken out his anger on the technician by decking him without saying a word.

Nancy crossed her arms. "I can't remember the last time someone in this crew was thrown in that excuse for a brig, but I'll be happy to make an exception in your cases if someone doesn't tell me what's going on."

Andrey stared at Luka as he responded. "Nothing, ma'am. We were just discussing what happened on the sub."

"And the shouting was?"

"Reliving some of the more exciting moments, ma'am." Sergei gave Nancy a half-hearted smile, and she rolled her eyes.

"Whatever. The techs are getting the pump installed, so I don't really care what your disagreement's about as long as it's over. Now, sit your asses down, and give me a summary of what happened. Luka was babbling about creatures being down there, but I haven't gotten the full story yet."

As the three talked, Andrey gradually realized that Luka had been sincere when he'd said that he hadn't intended to leave the outer hatch open. The fact that he had forgotten was still a sore point for the soldier, but his anger at his and Sergei's near-death experience lessened slightly once he heard Luka's shaking voice recount the mission. Andrey's softening of emotions came also when he had to recount the missteps he had taken on the P949's con, where he had seen one of the creatures but retreated instead of investigating further. Although no one said it out loud, Andrey knew that Nancy and Sergei both thought that it was one of the reasons the trio had nearly died on the sub.

When the three finished summarizing what had happened, Nancy nodded approvingly. "It sounds like you went through hell and came out unscathed. Nice work."

"Thank you, ma'am," Sergei said. Nancy started to stand up, but Sergei spoke again. "If I could—just one last thing."

"Yes?"

"I mentioned the extensive armory on the P949. I believe we should try and retrieve the contents. It could prove invaluable for us long term."

Nancy shook her head firmly. "No way. We're not sending anyone back down there, especially not if there are creatures all over the place."

Andrey joined in to support his cousin. "We killed some of them, and the others will die very quickly from the water. I think if Sergei and I were to take—"

"Gentlemen," Nancy said as she stood up again, "while I appreciate what you want to do for us all, what you're describing to me is far too risky. I don't need my best men risking their lives for a few guns and bullets. Our supplies on the Arkhangelsk are more than adequate for the foreseeable future."

"But ma'am—"

"My answer is no, Mr. Lipov."

Andrey's shoulders slumped at the rebuke. "Yes, ma'am."

"Good." Nancy glanced over the clipboard in her hand. "You two are off any assigned duties for the next twelve hours. Get more food, get some sleep and try to relax. Luka, I wish I could say the same for you, but I need you in the reactor room to help monitor the installation."

Luka nodded. "Understood."

"Excellent." Nancy looked at the three and smiled at them. "Excellent work again, to all of you. It's because of your work that we've got a chance at survival again." Nancy walked out of the lounge, heading for the control deck.

Luka stood up next and tried to force a slight, weak smile at the soldiers. "I'm sorry again." He, too, hurried out, making a beeline for the reactors at the aft of the ship.

With Luka and Nancy gone and the lounge deserted, Andrey and Sergei found themselves alone again. Andrey stood and began pacing the room as he rubbed the bear tooth in his pocket. "You know those weapons are going to be unusable soon."

Sergei leaned his head back and closed his eyes. "Not the ammo. It'll be good until the seals on the containers go. The weapons will last a day, maybe two before we'll have to strip them down and scrub rust from every last ping and spring." Sergei opened one eye to follow Andrey's increasingly frantic pacing. "What does this matter anyway? You heard what she said."

"Yes," Andrey said. "Yes, I did."

Thirty minutes later, after forcing a few bites of unappetizing food-like substance down their throats, Andrey and Sergei went to their compartments to rest. Andrey laid down in bed and stared at the ceiling, unable—and unwilling—to go to sleep. Luka's failure to close the hatch was no longer in his thoughts after being reminded of his own failure on the P949's control deck.

The minutes ticked by at an agonizingly slow speed as Andrey recalled every detail of his short walk on the con. Every body, every stain and every potential creature was burned into his memory. The pain of failure over not recognizing the potential threat churned his stomach, sending bile crawling up his throat. Andrey sat up in his cot and looked over in the corner of the room. His diving gear was still there, as he hadn't taken the time to clean and store it away after returning to the Arkhangelsk.

With a fresh tank of air and some lifting bags... and what if I'm caught? No, she's too busy with the reactor. The rigors of the command structure were still drilled into Andrey from his years in the Russian military, but the last year had taught him that improvisation was often more important in the new and ever-changing world. After arguing with himself and rationalizing for a few more minutes, Andrey finally stood up and quickly changed back into his dive gear.

Exiting his compartment, he took a roundabout way down into the machine rooms in the belly of the Arkhangelsk, desperate to avoid being seen by anyone who might mention his attire. After some searching, Andrey found the diving supplies and the recently-filled spare air tanks he was looking for. He quickly changed out his old tank for a new one, grabbed a new pair of goggles and as many lifting bags as he could fit into the pouches on his chest and legs. While the diving suits had webbed feet built into them that offered a good compromise between walking on land and providing extra propulsion in the water, Andrey grabbed a pair of longer flippers as well. He wanted to be in and out of the P949 as fast as possible, and speed in the water was essential to his goal.

With his gear in hand, Andrey slipped down the corridors of the Arkhangelsk, listening breathlessly to make sure there was no one coming his way. As he rounded the final corner and jogged toward the ladder leading out onto the deck of the sub, a figure stepped out from a compartment in front of him. Andrey stopped short in his tracks and jumped in surprise before he recognized who it was.

"Ms. Sims?"

"Going somewhere, Andrey?"

"I-I... no ma'am?" As soon as the words squeaked past his lips, Andrey knew that they were worthless.

"Uh huh." Nancy looked him up and down. "If you're wanting to take a swim, the pool's back the way you came from." Andrey tried to stutter out a reply, but Nancy held up her hand to stop him. "Did you really think that breaking an order was the best way to make up for a screw-up? Christ, Andrey, I told you to stay on board for a reason. We don't *need* those supplies. We *need* you, though."

Nancy ran her hands through her hair in frustration. "You and your cousin are the two best soldiers on this pile of crap we call home, and I've been throwing you at every little problem that comes up like you're magic." Nancy leaned close to Andrey. "You have nothing to try and make up for. Do you understand that?"

Andrey nodded.

"Everybody screws up. I've done it plenty of times. So has Krylov. So has your cousin. Everybody does it. You'll do it again, believe me. Don't go breaking orders and getting yourself killed just because you—"

Nancy was interrupted mid-sentence by alarms and red flashing lights. She looked up at the lights, then back at Andrey. "What the hell?"

A booming voice echoed over the Arkhangelsk's internal speaker system. "This is a priority alert! Evacuate! All hands evacuate!"

Nancy ran for the nearest intercom and yelled over the sound of the alarms. "What's going on? Report!"

"Ma'am! Something's gone wrong with the reactor. The temperature is spiking, and there's radiation flooding the chamber. We have to get off the boat before it goes critical!"

Nancy dropped the intercom and raced toward the reactor compartment. Andrey ran after her, shedding his air tank and other diving equipment. On their way to the reactor, they nearly collided with several of the crew who were racing to escape the sub. Without knowing how serious the problem with the reactor actually was, she didn't want to stop them. Internally, though, she was screaming at herself for leaving the technicians alone long enough for them to do whatever they had done to cause the problem.

Outside the reactor compartment, Nancy skidded to a halt with Andrey close behind. Luka and the other technicians were working frantically on the controls outside the room, but the hatch to the compartment was sealed tight. Nancy yelled at them as she saw them. "What's going on?!"

"Ma'am!" Luka looked up at her. Sweat covered his face and permeated the white jumpsuit he wore. His face bore a look of sheer panic stronger than when he had seen the creatures in the sunken submarine. "There was a delay in installing the pump, and the temperatures started to rise. We attempted to insert the control rods to slow the reactions and buy us time to finish connecting the pump, but the reactor's burning too hot."

"Why are you out here? Why isn't the pump working?"

"One of the emergency ports on the reactor chamber opened; it was some kind of system malfunction." Luka glanced at Nancy briefly as he continued to work the controls with the other technicians.

"Meaning?"

"There are lethal amounts of radiation in there, ma'am, not to mention the heat! The compartment is a giant oven filled with radiation!"

Nancy turned from the door and closed her eyes as she pinched the bridge of her nose. "How do we fix this? If someone goes in there, I mean. How would they fix this?"

"Ma'am, they'd be dead in a matter of—"

"Answer the damned question!" Nancy snapped at Luka.

Luka thought quickly. "The pump's ready to go, but it has to be primed manually. There's a handle inside the crawlspace for that. Once the pump is primed, it'll turn on automatically and start cooling the core."

"What about the radiation and heat? How do you close the—the emergency port or whatever?"

Luka began to respond, but the *clank* of a closing hatch distracted him. He, Nancy and the other technicians turned to see a figure in the next compartment, moving toward the reactor chamber. As Nancy realized who had stepped through the hatch, she ran to the door and pounded on it and screamed as she tried to open the door herself. Andrey, however, had sealed the emergency lock, preventing access to the chamber and forcing her to stand by helplessly as she watched him on the small row of monitors outside the compartment. He stood still for a few seconds as he tucked his hand into his pocket and lowered his head before moving toward the next hatch.

"Can I talk to him?" Nancy yelled at Luka as she watched Andrey slowly turn the handle for the inner hatch.

Luka shook his head. "No. There's nothing to facilitate that."

Nancy felt panic grab her mind and shake her, threatening to tear her apart with every step Andrey took. Down the corridor to her left, Nancy heard the pounding of footsteps and saw Sergei arrive with concern written on his face. "Why are we having an evacuation, ma'am?"

Nancy pointed at the monitor. "The reactor's dangerously close to going critical, and your damned fool of a cousin decided to try and fix it himself."

"What?" Sergei's face froze in an expression of fear and disbelief. "He's doing what?"

Nancy turned and pounded on the hatch again in frustration. "Dammit! Come on, Luka; tell me there's something you can do!"

"Ma'am…" Luka shook his head and threw up his hands in sympathy. "I wish there were."

Nancy, Sergei and the three technicians turned to the monitor and stared as Andrey opened the door to the inner reactor compartment. As he entered hell, they could do nothing but watch and hope beyond any chance of hope that his sacrifice wouldn't be for naught.

Chapter Thirty

THE MAGADAN METRO

When Leonard woke up thrashing at nonexistent creatures, his first reaction was to wonder why one of them was poking him in the shoulder and calling his name.

"Leonard! Hey, wake up, peg-leg!" Marcus continued to poke Leonard until a hand swatted at him from under the blanket. Marcus jumped back and laughed. "Good. You're awake. Krylov wants to see us. Apparently, Alexander's going to tell the survivors about the plan, and they want us to be there to field questions."

"Right now?" Leonard mumbled.

"Yeah. Come on. Get both legs on, and let's go."

Leonard slowly sat up and yawned. "Two leg jokes in less than a minute? Maybe I need to calibrate the EMP cannon on your ass."

Marcus laughed again and backed out of the sleeping area. "I'll tell Krylov you're on the way."

Leonard popped his leg back on and eased out of the cot, testing the weight on the limb gingerly. The gyro once again felt out of alignment, but he knew the feeling would soon disappear, as it always did. As he pushed aside the curtain in front of the cots, he saw a crowd gathered outside the dining area. Inside, standing on a chair, was Alexander, who waved his arms in an attempt to calm the increasingly loud murmurs coming from the crowd. Leonard pushed through the survivors and stood in between Krylov and Marcus.

"Please!" Alexander shouted. "Calm down! I know you all have questions, but we must stay calm!"

Leonard nudged Marcus and whispered. "What's going on here?"

Marcus pointed at a few men and women standing in the front of the crowd. "See those particularly riled up ones? As soon as they caught wind of Alexander's plan, they decided to tell everyone that Alexander had defected to join the Americans in carrying out a plan that would get everyone killed."

"What the hell?"

Krylov, who had been listening in, joined the whispered conversation as he kept a close eye on the state of the crowd. "We're asking these people to put their faith in a group of strangers who came out of nowhere. They've been relatively stable here for months. The prospect of stepping out into the darkness at the bequest of a couple of Americans—and three Russians who might as well be Americans—isn't going over so well."

"You promised us a rescue!" One of the men in the front screamed at Alexander. "Not death!"

A woman in the front clutched a young child to her as she cried. "I already lost two children; I won't lose a third!"

"Please, just listen!" Alexander raised his hands again and tried to calm the crowd, but he was entirely unsuccessful.

As Krylov's eyes swept over the crowd, he noticed that it wasn't just the ones in the front who were looking particularly restless. The feeling was sweeping over all of the survivors, and if someone didn't turn the situation around quickly, the rescue mission would turn into a riot.

As Krylov prepared to step up on a chair to try to calm the crowd along with Alexander, the sound of a shout from the other side of the station drew his attention. Krylov was straining to see and hear over the throng of survivors when the person shouting started barging through the crowd as he yelled.

"They're here! They're here!"

The murmurs in the crowd exploded into full-blown panic. Alexander jumped down from his chair and ran toward the man who was yelling. A streak of blood crossed down his face and the front of his shirt, and his eyes were wide with terror.

"They're here! The creatures are here! They're pushing against the eastern gate! A few of them already broke through!"

Leonard glanced at Marcus. "Take Roman, and get the explosives and the spare battery for the EMP cannon. I'm going with Krylov to the eastern gate." Leonard turned to Alexander. "We'll hold them off for as long as we can. Get your people armed and ready for a fight."

Alexander nodded and began shouting orders at the survivors. Though the crowd was raucous, they slowly began obeying as they split into groups and gathered their weapons. Roman and Marcus ran off to grab the required explosives and the spare battery, and Krylov and Leonard retrieved their weapons and made a mad dash for the eastern gate.

Upon their arrival a moment later, they were greeted by the yells of the two remaining guards. Both of them bore extensive wounds to their arms and heads, but they were still alive and kicking. The bodies of several creatures littered the floor inside the second gate, and one of the two windows in the gate had been torn open as the creatures had forced themselves inside. The two guards were both standing in front of the intact window, firing their weapons in quick bursts as they tried to drive back the wave of creatures.

Krylov was first to reach the scene and yelled at the guards. "Where do you need us?"

The guard in charge turned back to look at Krylov before pointing at the opposite platform in front of the damaged window. "There!"

Krylov and Leonard raced up the platform and deposited their bags to the side. Leonard readied the EMP cannon and took a quick glance out the window at what was going on while Krylov began using the butt of his rifle to beat the damaged sheet metal back into place. In the tunnel beyond the outer eastern gate, the creatures were stacked a dozen deep, pressed up against the sides of the tunnel like they were sardines in a can. They were not rushing the gate, but instead they were passing chunks of concrete and metal from the back of their lines to the front, where two or more creatures were lobbing the debris at the gate. Each time a piece hit the gate it—along with the platforms behind it—shuddered from the impact.

Leonard peeked up through the window and lined up the EMP rifle with a cluster of mutants on the left side of the tunnel. He pulled the trigger, and a few seconds later, the rifle discharged, sending an invisible wave of energy exploding down the tunnel. The initial result—burning flesh and arcing electricity across the exposed metal on the bodies— was the same, though the creature's reaction was demonstrably not.

Instead of staying clustered together, the creatures separated themselves from their damaged comrades, keeping a few paces away from them on all sides. Thus, instead of the flames from the pile of dying creatures spreading to the other mutants, they simply died out.

"Krylov! They've adapted!" Leonard shouted over the roars of the creatures and the shouting of the guards.

"Hit them again! Try to force them back!" Krylov continued his makeshift repair work on the window as Leonard fired again and again, turning the first row of the creatures into a charred, smelly mess of remains. The creatures, however, did not pull back from their attack. Working around the bodies of their comrades, the creatures continued their assault in spite of incurring heavy losses from both the guards and Leonard.

After a few minutes of firing and dodging thrown debris, Leonard sat down next to Krylov and shook his head. "They're not stopping at all. Something's going on here, Krylov! We need to get these people ready to go now, before it's too late!"

Krylov looked up over the repaired window and grimaced at the sight and smell of the dead creatures still smoldering in the tunnel. The lights set up on the outer gate gave the illusion of liquidity to the smoke as it swirled from the constant barrage of bullets and debris flying back and forth. "Agreed. It looks like they're trying to distract us. Stay here; I'll get some more people to help shore up this defense so we can go try and find out what's really going on."

Krylov ran off, and a few seconds later, Marcus, Roman and Mikhail appeared. Roman and Mikhail jumped up on the platform next to the guards and immediately began opening fire, and Marcus knelt down on the platform next to Leonard and began taking potshots at the creatures while holding a shouted conversation.

"I saw Krylov running off; what's going on?"

"Getting more men to hold this gate. The muties are trying to distract us here while they work to get in somewhere else, we think."

"Shit!" Marcus ducked as a large mesh of rebar and concrete smashed against the gate. "If this is just a distraction, then they're doing a damned good job of it!"

"No kidding!" Leonard picked up the spare battery for the EMP rifle that Marcus had dropped at his feet a moment earlier and swapped it with the drained battery. As he started to get to his feet to resume his attack, he saw Krylov running back with three armed men behind him.

"You four!" Krylov shouted at Leonard, Marcus, Roman and Mikhail. "Get down; we're moving to a new position."

The four men jumped down and crowded around Krylov as he gave them an update. "Apparently, Alexander sent out a scouting party to make sure the supply line tunnels were clear."

"What the hell?" Leonard exploded. "What was he thinking?"

Krylov shook his head. "I don't know. They haven't come back yet, and I think we have to assume that the mutants overwhelmed them. It was a three-man team, and they were heavily armed, so if they were overwhelmed, then it means we can expect an attack from the western entrance very soon."

"Okay, so let's get some guards up there with guns and prepare for it." Marcus looked at the others and sighed. "Dammit. Don't tell me. There's something else."

Krylov shrugged. "I'm sorry, but there is something else."

"Son of a…" Marcus trailed off, and Krylov continued.

"If the attack on the eastern side is a diversion, then we must assume that the attack from the west will be in full force. They will no doubt assault the outer gate and attempt to tear it down. If that happens, we'll be unable to retreat. We cannot make it to the docks via the eastern tunnel."

Leonard nodded slowly as he realized what Krylov was getting at. "So, we need to evacuate now, right? As in right this second?"

Krylov nodded. "Precisely."

"What about wiring up the station for the retreat?" Marcus asked.

Krylov shook his head. "There's no time for that. The attack could happen at any moment. Alexander's already at work leading a group to dismantle the inner gate on the western side while Maria works to get the survivors ready to go."

"So." Leonard snorted. "They decided to come around, huh?"

"Gunfire and the threat of imminent death does tend to light a fire under one's ass, yes, Mr. McComb."

"Okay, so what happens once the inner gate's dismantled?"

"Mr. Lebedev and myself will plant shaped charges to carve a hole in the floor leading down into the supply line tunnel. Once that is done, Alexander and several of his men will construct the ramp leading down into the tunnel. You, myself and Mr. Warden will remain behind with three of Alexander's men to hold the line for as long as possible.

"Mr. Lebedev and Mr. Egorov will assist in directing the survivors to the docks and contacting the Arkhangelsk for assistance. The six of us here will continue with the plan as before, but instead of destroying the station, we will have to think of something more creative to halt the creatures in their tracks. I am open to suggestions."

"No time right now," Leonard replied. "We'll figure it out as we go along."

An abrupt lull in gunfire drew Krylov's attention, and he turned to look at the eastern gate. The five men there had stopped firing and were staring through the windows as they whispered to each other. Krylov cupped his hands to call out to them, but Leonard stopped him and spoke instead. "You and Roman get going with those charges. Marcus and I'll go see what the hell is going on down there. Mikhail, see what you can do to help the survivors get ready to move."

Leonard took off back toward the eastern gate with Marcus trailing behind. He shouted up at the guards when they arrived. "What's happening?"

The guards looked down at him, and one of them spoke as he pointed down the tunnel through the window. "They're gone!"

Leonard felt the blood drain from his face and a cold chill run up his back. "You three, come with me! You two, stay here, and come get help if they come back!"

Leonard ran back down the tunnel toward the station, cursing repeatedly as he went. Marcus trailed behind him and shouted at him, confused. "What's going on, Leonard? Where are they?"

"They're massing for an assault! Probably in the western tunnel!"

The abrupt arrival of the creatures' diversion and imminent attack meant that there was no time to put their counter-diversion strategy into play. Leonard sensed that it was only a matter of minutes before the creatures threw themselves at the station en masse, and with the only viable way out being through the supply line under the western tunnel, speed was critical.

"Where are we going?" Marcus shouted behind Leonard as the two continued running through the station, dodging passersby and leaping over obstacles in their path. Marcus veered sharply to the left and twisted his body to slip through a gap between several people who were milling around. Leonard was more forceful, pushing people aside as he ran and doing his best not to knock anyone over.

"To help Krylov and Roman get those charges planted!"

"Right. Of course. Let's blow up the floor while we've got the enemy literally at the gates." Marcus caught up with Leonard, and they ran side by side through the inner western gate and down toward Alexander, Krylov and Roman. "I really need to talk to you about my benefits package for this kind of work!"

Leonard laughed as he slowed down. "You'll have to talk to human resources about that."

Krylov glanced up at the pair as they arrived, then refocused on his work. "Mr. McComb, Mr. Warden. We're just about ready here."

"You need to speed it up." Leonard knelt down next to Krylov and Alexander to watch as they finished wiring the explosive.

Krylov didn't look up from his work as he responded. "What is happening?"

"They've pulled back from the eastern tunnel."

Alexander looked up at Leonard. "The creatures pulled back? All of them?"

Leonard nodded and relayed what the guards had told him. Alexander's face grew dark with worry, and he stood up. "Then we have no time to waste."

Leonard gestured toward the station. "Mikhail is helping with the rest of your people. There are two guards left on the eastern gate just as a precaution, plus you have a few guards left in the deeper tunnels. We need to pull them back as soon as the charges go off."

"I'll assist with preparing everyone. Can you all handle things here?"

Leonard nodded and patted Alexander's shoulder. "Go on. Make sure they're ready to go. Krylov, Marcus and I'll get things ready here."

As Alexander jogged back to the refuge, Krylov put the finishing touches on the explosives before standing up to admire his handiwork. A series of three charges laid out in a circular pattern on the tunnel ground were connected by thin strands of wire that led back to a small box. Krylov pulled a small spool of wire from his pack and attached one end to the box before handing the other end to Roman. "Unroll this from here to behind the inside gate. I will be there momentarily to finish the wiring."

Leonard looked at the charges on the ground and nodded in approval. "You think this'll work?"

Krylov nodded. "So long as there is actually a tunnel beneath us that is stable enough to handle this detonation."

Leonard rolled his eyes. "So, in other words, you have no idea. Lovely."

"No need to worry, Mr. McComb." Krylov flashed a grin. "If there's a pocket of natural gas beneath us instead of the metro line we're expecting, then we need not worry about the mutants."

Leonard snorted and rolled his eyes again. "Smartass."

"So, we're good here?" Marcus asked nervously as he rubbed his hands together.

Krylov took one final look at his handiwork before replying. "Yes. Everything is ready."

Leonard, Roman, Marcus and Krylov began heading back toward the inner gate. When they had gotten about halfway there, Leonard paused and yelled at the guards manning the outer gate. "Get back here! We're about to detonate!"

The guards, however, neither turned nor gave any indication that they were listening. Instead, the three of them stared through the narrow slots in the wall, looking at something beyond them in the tunnel.

"Hey!" Leonard yelled again. "Let's go!"

One of the guards turned around, and Leonard felt his stomach drop as a ripple of fear washed through his entire body. Adrenaline surged through him, causing his heart to race faster as the hairs on his arms and neck prickled. The figure standing on the platform of the outer gate wore the jacket and pants of one of the guards who had been there earlier. The figure's face and hands, however, were covered in dirt, dried blood, tattered flesh and the telltale silver metals that were the hallmarks of the creatures.

"Shit!" Leonard fumbled with his rifle as he tried to raise it to fire at the mutant. It snarled in response, and the other two figures turned, revealing that they, too, were not the guards, but more of the beasts.

Krylov turned to see the three figures leap from the platforms, crossing half the gap between the explosives and the outer gate with ease. Leonard raised the EMP rifle, but he didn't realize until he'd pulled the trigger that it was not the smartest thing in the world to do.

Powerful electromagnetic pulses destroy electronics by generating high current and voltage surges. This effect can be relatively harmless to organic tissue (if the intensity is low enough), but Leonard's experimental EMP rifle was on the high end of the intensity scale. As the invisible electromagnetic wave passed through the tunnel and impacted the creatures, it also traveled along the length of the wire connected to the detonators and explosives. With the sudden current passing through them, the detonators instantly triggered.

The effect was surreal. Krylov had intended for everyone to take cover behind the inner gate before the explosives went off, but with only empty space in front of them, the four men were blown back by the intensity of the explosion. Leonard tried to cover his ears as the shockwave passed over them, but it did little good, and he felt his left eardrum pop from the blast. Ahead of him, closer to the inner gate, Krylov, Marcus and Roman had been knocked down as well. There was very little in the way of fire and flames to deal with due to the explosives used, which Leonard was exceedingly grateful for, but as he covered his head with his arms to shield himself from the shower of debris, he silently hoped that the entire tunnel wouldn't collapse in on him.

The creatures, being nearly on top of the explosives when they went off, were obliterated, with virtually no trace of them left except for small bits of cloth, metal and a few red stains on the ceiling and walls. The lights in the tunnel blinked out, plunging the area between the two gates into darkness except for the spotlights hung on the inner gate.

Leonard coughed through the smoke and dust that clogged the room and pulled his shirt up over his mouth and nose. He blinked and waved his hand in the air as he stood up, trying to see what had happened to the floor of the tunnel using the light on the end of his rifle. While Krylov's "shaped" charges left something to be desired, the result was far better than Leonard had initially thought. There was no visible damage—aside from an enormous black scorch mark—to the walls or ceiling. The floor, however, had been completely blown apart, leaving only the small concrete walkways at the base of each wall intact.

The hole in the floor was a good ten feet deep, making it nigh-on impossible to get to the outer gate. Inside, as Leonard shuffled closer, he could see the remains of the tracks, gravel and concrete from the ceiling of the line below. These had fallen and scattered across several large boxes in the line below, which were stacked and piled along one side of the tunnel. In spite of the unexpected appearance of the creatures, Leonard's spirits were lifted by the sight of the supply line, and he grinned.

In the space of the minute or so it had taken for the creatures to turn from the outer gate for their surprise attack and for Leonard to stand over the hole in the floor, there had been no opportunity to see or hear any sign of other creatures in the area. As the ringing in Leonard's left ear began to slowly fade, the sound of howls, snarls and shouting from both directions made him look up and glance around.

Ahead of him, beyond the hole in the floor, the outer gate shook violently. Hundreds of creatures surged against it from the other side, battering it with their bodies in an attempt to bring the entire structure down. Behind him, Krylov shouted at him again, and Leonard, unable to fully hear, squinted to try and read his lips.

"Leonard! Are you okay?" Krylov ran up to Leonard and grabbed him by the shoulders. Leonard's entire body was covered in smoke, and blood trickled from his left ear. He nodded slowly and pointed behind him. "The supply line's down there. We need to get people moving. They're attacking the outer gate."

Marcus and Roman arrived a few seconds later, and Krylov took

Leonard's rifle from him and shouted over the noise of the creatures. "Marcus! Get Leonard back inside and check him over! We're going to dig in here and hold the line. Tell Alexander and Mikhail to get more men to aid us, and have Alexander start working on that ramp. We need to get these people out *now!*"

All formality was dropped as Krylov bellowed out the orders. He and Roman dropped to their knees and readied their weapons, preparing to fire on whatever came through the gate. Leonard hobbled back behind the inner gate with Marcus, who sat him down and checked him over, looking for any signs of external injuries. When he was confident that Leonard wasn't in danger of falling over, he looked around for Alexander, who was running back toward the western gate.

"What happened?" Alexander yelled over the sound of both the creatures down the tunnel and the survivors' shouting and screaming.

"The guards are gone, and we're about to be overrun! We need more guns in that tunnel, and we have to get everyone out immediately!"

When Marcus, Leonard and several of Alexander's men appeared bearing weapons, Krylov felt a small sense of relief. Alexander appeared a moment later, dragging long lengths of rope with him.

"Alexander," Leonard glanced at the ropes. "What about the ramps?"

Alexander leaned over the hole and looked at the boxes and debris scattered below. "No time. I'm going down there with anyone who's capable. We'll shift the crates and boxes around down there by hand and see if we can make it easier for the rest to climb down."

As Alexander and the other survivors worked, Leonard felt burdened by the feeling that all of the effort they were expending was arriving too late in the game to make a difference. Lined up behind the hole in the ground, the dozen fighters knelt on either side of the tunnel, making room for the survivors to descend into the tunnel below. Ahead of them, the outer gate was weakening as the creatures continued to ram it, threatening to tear it apart.

In the back of Leonard's mind, beneath the chaos and the din, the nagging feeling that had been overtaking him since they'd first arrived began to swell once again.

Something's not right.

Book 3 - Archangel Triumphant

Chapter Thirty-One

MAGADAN METRO

"They're pushing again!" Krylov shouted from the opposite side of the corridor from Leonard.

"Same as last time, then!" Leonard shouted back, then stood up, brandishing his weapon.

The humans the original AI had mutated, the ones Leonard had helped face down, were cunning creatures. They were masters of strategy, distraction, and combat tactics. They pushed and pulled their intended victims as though they were puppet masters playing with strings. The creatures in Magadan were, as Leonard was continuing to discover, not cut from the same cloth.

The EMP cannon was quickly becoming a sight that the creatures feared, and the wave that was pushing through over the bodies of their dead comrades instantly flinched at its sight. Leonard gave no quarter as he fired upon them, sending waves of electric arcs and flames over the creatures.

"Now!" Leonard ducked back down and yelled. Four men behind Leonard stood up, as did Krylov. Two of the men stood near Krylov's side of the tunnel while the other two flanked Leonard from behind. They all opened fire with their rifles, sending lead flying through the air and into the panicking herd of creatures that were fighting to retreat from the onslaught, but slowed by the veritable army of creatures behind them.

Leonard glanced over the small barrier he crouched behind and nodded approvingly at Krylov, who returned the nod with a smile. Three waves had thrown themselves forward to try and gain access to either the hole in the tunnel through which the survivors were escaping or to reach Leonard, Krylov, Marcus and the others who were located on the opposite side of the hole. Without the EMP rifle to slow down the advancement of the creatures, they would have broken through on the first wave. It was this fact that worried Leonard, as he was down to only a few shots before the current battery was depleted. After that, he'd have only a partially charged battery left.

"We have a window!" The shout came from behind Leonard. He looked back at Alexander, who stepped forward at the head of another group of survivors. "Move!"

The survivors surged forward toward the hole in the ground, grabbing hold of the ropes that trailed down into the supply line tunnel below. To save them from falling off, children were lashed to their parents with belts and short pieces of rope. Alexander helped the few elderly survivors over the edge after the rest of the survivors had gotten through, using pieces of cloth wrapped around their fragile hands as a protection against the thick rope.

While Leonard couldn't see down into the hole from his position, he assumed the evacuation process was going well due to a lack of screaming or cursing coming from Alexander and the survivors. "How many more left?" Leonard yelled to Alexander, who turned and looked back before answering.

"One more group! Do we wait, or go now?"

Leonard looked forward past Alexander to where the creatures were roiling down the tunnel, just out of reach of the torches and flashlights brandished by the survivors and rescue team. "If you move now, maybe! But I don't know if we can hold off another wave, so you'd better go now regardless!"

Alexander called out to the last group of survivors waiting in the refuge. Upon hearing that they were going down, the handful of Alexander's men who were hunkered down behind Krylov and Leonard started glancing between each other as they grew more nervous. The survivors dashed forward and Alexander helped them onto the ropes. As they were descending, Krylov peeked over the pile of debris he was hiding behind and shouted at the top of his lungs.

"Incoming!"

Another wave of creatures surged down the tunnel and Leonard once again stood and took aim with his rifle. In the few seconds it took for him to train the EMP cannon on the dead center of the pack, the movement of the creatures shifted. The large mass split into two smaller groups, creating a gap down the center, and the lead creatures began crisscrossing the gap, distracting Leonard and causing him to hesitate for a precious split second.

That momentary hesitation was the opening the creatures needed, as several of them leapt forward, covering the final open area with a single bound. Leonard fired the EMP cannon, sending sparks flying across the metallic structures of the creatures, and catching the main group on fire. Krylov and the others opened fire again, joined this time by Marcus and Roman, who had been helping to ensure none of the survivors were left behind.

Together, the combined firepower killed four of the five creatures that were jumping across the gap. The last one hit the edge of the hole closest to the survivors and clung to it for a moment before letting go and dropping down into the tunnel below. Krylov ran forward and shouted as decorum was thrown by the wayside. "Alexander!"

The warning was unnecessary as the sound of a pistol firing repeatedly cut through Krylov's words and echoed out of the hole and into the tunnel above. As Leonard watched the creatures retreating again, he ejected the now-depleted battery from the rifle and took the other partially charged battery from Marcus, who knelt down beside him.

"What's the situation?" Marcus peered over the pile of debris at the horde of creatures down the tunnel.

"They don't want us anymore," said Leonard, "they want the survivors!" Leonard stood up and ran up to join Krylov, who was looking down into the hole, watching Alexander trying to hurry the survivors down the tunnel.

"Alexander!" Leonard cupped his hands and shouted. "Get them as far as you can, as fast as you can!"

Alexander looked back and raised his hand in the air to give

Leonard a thumbs up sign. Krylov looked at Leonard. "What's wrong?"

Leonard motioned at the group of creatures across the gap in the floor. "They don't want us. They want the survivors, down there."

Krylov's eyes narrowed. "Of course they do. Any suggestions?"

"Yeah. But you won't like them." The pair walked away from the hole as Leonard continued to talk. "If we don't give the muties something else to chase, the survivors—and whoever's with them down there, including us—are going to be sitting ducks. We need the bastards to follow *us* instead. Or, at the very least, split up and try to go after both of us."

"What's the plan, Mr. McComb? I'm not aware of any other ways out of this system that aren't blocked off or filled with those things." Krylov gestured toward the creatures.

"Well…" Leonard shifted uncomfortably on his feet. "Not exactly."

Krylov's eyebrow went up. "What is it, Mr. McComb?"

Leonard shot a look at the creatures. "That pack of muties isn't our biggest concern. Not for the long-term, I mean. We still have a nexus somewhere around here to deal with, and I'm pretty sure it's located in that cavern downstairs."

Krylov glanced at the creatures as well, growing concerned over the uptick in the frequency of their howls and screams. "Fast, Mr. McComb."

"We can escape through that cavern I found. I'm sure of it. There has to be another surface exit. And besides, we don't have a choice. We have to find whatever they're building down there and destroy it before these things figure out how to take their AI and bring it to the next level."

Krylov shook his head. "You know what you're asking me, do you not? You want us to leave the survivors, descend into an unknown cavern in search of a structure you don't even know for sure exists, and then escape through a route that doesn't exist as well?"

Leonard shrugged. "More or less. Plus we need to make sure the supply line tunnel gets blown and then act as bait for the creatures to pull as many off of the trail of the survivors as possible."

Krylov closed his eyes and leaned back against the wall as he tried to think amid the cacophony of noise from the creatures. "Are you even sure that there's a nexus down there?"

Leonard took a deep breath. "I don't know, Krylov. All I have is a hunch. But it's a damned good one. There's something very wrong with this place. These creatures are all kinds of crazy and I think it has to do with whatever programming they've got going on. If we let them continue doing whatever it is they're doing down there, then we might as well throw down our weapons and let those bastards tear us limb from limb. Because if they do have a nexus, that's what they'll be doing soon enough anyway."

"Dammit!" Krylov hissed and pushed himself off of the wall. "Roman!" Krylov shouted for the soldier, forgoing his usual formalities once again.

"Yes, sir?" Roman looked as weary as Leonard felt, but his eyes were still full of fire, a trait Leonard admired in him.

"Get down the ropes. Set off the explosives the instant everyone's clear. We'll push back one last wave, then we're retreating."

"Sir?"

"You heard me. Now get down there. Now!"

Roman dutifully obeyed despite being perplexed by Krylov's commands. In less than thirty seconds he was down the rope, while the other soldiers that Alexander had left up top to support Leonard, Krylov and Marcus began to nervously talk to each other as they tried to figure out what was going on.

"Incoming!" Leonard was the first to call out the next wave of creatures, though he didn't hesitate to open fire as he had before. The EMP cannon annihilated dozens of creatures with each blast, though Leonard didn't bother to stop shooting even as the first several rows of creatures erupted into flames and arcing electricity.

"Move back!" Leonard shouted, and Krylov, Marcus and the others began shuffling backward. Leonard expected it to be another few minutes before Roman was able to set off the explosive charges in the supply line tunnel below, but it turned out to be much sooner than he had anticipated.

KABOOM!

A plume of dust and debris shot out of the hole in the tunnel like a volcano, covering both human and creature alike in a thick coating of cement dust and small pieces of shredded wooden crates. Leonard turned and ran back into the refuge, urging the others to keep up. "Let's go! Come on!"

With a renewed sense of purpose, Leonard took the lead as they raced through the refuge to the door leading to the ladder on the other side. When they arrived, Leonard's jaw dropped as the door opened to reveal Maria standing inside carrying a rifle and wearing a large backpack slung over her shoulder.

"Maria?" Leonard's brow contorted in confusion. "What are you doing here? Why didn't you evacuate?"

Maria tapped her left ear. "I have good hearing, Leonard. I heard you talking to Marcus, and I put three and three together."

"It's... never mind." Leonard glanced behind him at Krylov. "What are we going to do now?"

Krylov gave Maria a quick glance. "She goes with us, of course. Unless you want to tie her up for bait."

Leonard was about to reply when the sound of the creatures came from behind them. Leonard turned to see a large group of creatures quickly working their way through the refuge, tearing apart everything in their path. Every piece of furniture, cloth and makeshift structure was ripped apart as the creatures, deprived of their intended victims, sought anyone who might be left.

"Dammit!" It was Leonard's turn to hiss in frustration. "Get your ass moving, Maria. Get down there now! You two, go next. Krylov, you after them. I'll follow you." Leonard motioned at the last three of Alexander's men who he hadn't given instructions to.

"You three follow up behind us. Close this door, but don't lock it. They'll sniff us out soon enough and start following us down." The three men's faces turned white, but they nodded nervously.

"Come on!" Leonard whispered again as the group slowly began descending the ladder. "We need to go!"

Every step that Leonard took down the ladder was an exercise in sheer, unadulterated frustration. With so many people packed together, they could only go but so fast, and their slow pace meant an ever-increasing chance for one or more of them to be caught by the creatures above. As the last soldier climbed onto the ladder, Leonard could hear the sound of a door slamming open above him, followed by the sounds of the soldier screaming as he was pulled of the ladder by the creatures.

Thinking quickly, Leonard wrapped his left arm around the ladder and pulled out his EMP rifle with his right hand, and waved it in the general direction of the creatures that were starting to peer down the ladder. The mere sight of the weapon had an immediate effect on the creatures, and the pulled back from the hole in the floor, shrieking in panic.

"Hurry up!" Leonard hissed at the people on the rungs below him, though the pace did not pick up.

The creatures, startled and terrified by the sight of the EMP cannon, stayed to the edges of the ladder as they chattered their teeth at each other and exchanged furious growls. Leonard couldn't help but shake his head in amazement as he listened to the cacophony above, even as he continued climbing downward.

Finally, after a few harrowing moments more, the group made it safely to the bottom of the ladder. Leonard raised his flashlight upward and squinted as he tried to see into the darkness, only to open his eyes wide in shock.

"Get out, quick!" Leonard pushed at the group, trying to move them out of the maintenance room and into the tunnel. "Now! They're coming!"

Leonard was the last out of the room and he closed the door, then pointed down the tunnel. "All of you get moving! Krylov, help me with this door!"

Krylov took off his pack and pulled out the small box that he had last used when they were at the church. He quickly applied the torch to the hinges of the door and to several spots along the frame, welding the metal together crudely to seal the door in place. When Krylov finished, Leonard gave the door several hard pulls before nodding in approval.

"It'll have to do. Let's go."

"Where to now? Krylov asked as he stuffed the box back inside his bag.

Leonard pointed down the tunnel at the rapidly vanishing backs of the rest of the group. "Into the abyss."

Chapter Thirty-Two

THE ARKHANGELSK

S ergei screamed as he pounded on the door leading to the outer compartment. "Andrey! Andrey, you bastard! Get back out here!"

There was no response, though Sergei hardly expected one. With the outer door to the reactor compartment locked from the inside, it would be impossible to get in without cutting through the door. That process would take hours—time that none of them had. The reactor's temperature was still rising, and was nearly at the point where it would begin damaging the equipment inside the reactor chamber, leading to a further loss of containment.

"Sergei!" Nancy shouted at the man and grabbed his shoulder to pull him away from the hatch. "You can't do anything for him now!"

Sergei leaned up against the hatch and pressed his face against the glass of the small round window. He could barely make out movement through the window of the next hatch, inside the reactor compartment itself. The monitors in the hall outside the outer hatch, however, showed the movement inside the reactor compartment quite clearly.

Andrey was moving slowly, stripping off his dive suit as he tried to survive through the intense heat radiating through the compartment. With the emergency valve tripped, the reactor was dumping enormous amounts of heat and radiation into the compartment, and Andrey could feel his pores dumping sweat out in an effort to compensate and cool him down. Relief was not to be had, though, and he continued pressing forward, squeezing around the reactor chamber to a small crawlspace at the back of the room.

Andrey had watched Luka make his initial entry into the crawlspace on the sunken P949 submarine and thus knew precisely where to go to find the now-repaired pump that had to be manually primed. The interior of the crawlspace felt slightly cooler than the compartment itself, though Andrey felt in the back of his mind that the relief was merely an illusion. As he crawled along, fallen droplets of sweat hissed and spit as they dripped from his body, hitting swelteringly hot pieces of exposed pipe and metal.

"Come on, Andrey..." Nancy muttered to herself as she watched the monitor.

"He's in the crawlspace now; only a few feet more to go until he reaches the pump." Luka shook his head. "I don't see how he's going to make it, ma'am. The temperature in there is closing in on ninety degrees."

"Freedom units, please, Luka..." Nancy kept her eyes glued to the monitor.

"Almost two hundred Fahrenheit, ma'am."

"How can he even survive in that?"

Luka shook his head. "He won't survive for long, ma'am."

Nancy cursed again, silently, as she watched Andrey's torso, legs and feet disappear into the crawlspace. The seconds ticked by in agony as she waited, holding her breath and hoping beyond hope that he would be successful. Luka's sudden excited yelp made her jump.

"What is it, Luka?"

Luka jabbed a finger at a readout on one of the monitors. "We have flow through the pump! He did it! It's primed and running!"

Nancy exhaled sharply. "What else has to happen before we can get in there?"

"He has to unlock the door. The temperature will start to go down, but there are still massive amounts of radiation flooding the compartment."

Nancy nodded and continued watching in silence. Sergei stood behind her, not watching the monitors, but looking at the hatch instead, as though he could force it open by sheer willpower alone.

Nancy glanced back at Sergei and stepped back to stand next to him. She took his arm and spoke softly. "I'm sorry, Sergei. Your cousin is a hero. You know that, right?"

Sergei nodded and clenched his jaw, fighting against the tears that he could feel welling up. Nancy patted him on the back and stepped back up next to Luka, sensing that the soldier wanted to be left alone. On the screen, Nancy saw the faintest bit of movement and shouted in surprise. "There! In the crawlspace! Is that him?"

Luka nodded. "He's coming back out! I just hope he remembers to close the emergency valve. Delirium has undoubtedly set in and—"

Nancy jabbed Luka sharply in the ribs and gave him a dirty look as she bobbed her head back in the direction of Sergei. Luka's eyes grew wide and he nodded in understanding and grew quiet. The trio watched the monitor carefully as Andrey slowly crawled backwards out of the crawlspace. His legs shook as his feet hit the floor, and his entire body quaked as he struggled to stand upright. Andrey's entire body glistened, and his garments were drenched in sweat. Blood oozed from his eyes, nose and ears, and his expression was one of confusion as he looked around the room.

Standing in the heat, Andrey wasn't sure what to do next. After pushing the lever on the side of the pump several times, he had heard the flow of water rushing through it, but he couldn't remember what else he needed to do. His head felt as though it was enveloped in a thick blanket and his breaths were shallow and ragged as they drew in the hot air, singeing his lungs with every inhalation.

He stumbled forward, stretching out his hands for support, no longer caring that they hissed and crackled against the scorching metal of the reactor chamber or the walls of the room. As he passed by the reactor chamber, he saw the open hole on the side. A memory flashed through his mind as he saw it, and he realized what he had to do next.

Designed to be operated in conjunction with a venting mechanism in the top of the room, the emergency valve was never supposed to open when anyone was in the reactor compartment. The malfunction that had triggered its opening, however, had also rendered the motor controlling its movements inoperable, and the valve was easy to twist back into place. The relief from the closing of the valve was immediate as the air temperature dropped several degrees in response.

Still unable to feel anything in his legs and arms, Andrey continued pressing forward as he slowly rotated the locking mechanism for the inner compartment door. As the door opened, the emergency triggers were released, and the ventilation fans in the room kicked on, venting the contaminated air out while fresh air was pumped in.

Sergei stood at the outer door and watched, motionless, as the shell of a man who was his cousin shuffled forward, trying desperately to reach the outer door. His foot caught on the corner of a small table and Andrey fell forward, smashing his head against the metal floor. Sergei's ground his teeth and stifled a scream before pounding on the door again. "Dammit, Andrey!" Sergei's voice was deep as he pleaded with his cousin to stand up.

Andrey did not move. Nancy watched the monitor for several minutes before quietly speaking to Luka. "Get to work on the door. We need to get it open."

Luka nodded. "It will take a few hours to cut through the mechanisms."

"Can we set sail before that?"

"Yes, ma'am. We're ready anytime you are."

Nancy continued whispering. "I'll get word to Nikolay. We're leaving in twenty minutes. I want this piece of shit to get us back in record time, understand me? We've got no idea what Krylov and the others are doing or what kind of trouble they might be in."

"Yes, ma'am. Understood."

Nancy took a deep breath and turned around. "Sergei?" She took a few steps forward and put her hand on the soldier's shoulder. His face was still pressed against the glass in the hatch, his eyes glued to the still form of his cousin.

"Sergei?"

Sergei blinked a few times and turned to her. "Ma'am?" He said the word robotically, and Nancy could tell he was trying to clear his head of what had just happened.

"You're off duty indefinitely. Take as much time as you need. If you want to help break through the door and collect his body, do it. Or not.

As far as I'm concerned you have free reign to do what you want right now. Understand me?"

"Yes, ma'am." Nikolay's voice cracked slightly. "Thank you, ma'am."

Nancy wrapped her arms around the grizzled shoulder. Her eyes squeezed shut and she felt a tear run down her cheek. Losing one of the most valued crewmembers was a shock. Losing someone who she had been disciplining shortly beforehand was worse. But she couldn't imagine what Sergei felt like losing a family member, especially in a world where family was in such short supply.

⊏⊐

TWENTY MINUTES LATER, the evacuation order had been cancelled, the crew was back on the Arkhangelsk and Nancy was on the con, helping Nikolay coordinate for an emergency dive. Nancy's schedule was aggressive, and didn't leave any room for things like system checks and slow, coordinated maneuvers. As soon as the outer hatches were confirmed as sealed, she ordered the Arkhangelsk to descend into the waters of the submarine pen beneath the Rybachiy Nuclear Submarine Base.

The enormous craft slowly reversed through the tunnel bored into the mountain and out into the bay beyond. Once the Arkhangelsk was clear of the bay and out in the open water, Nancy turned to Nikolay. "Do whatever you have to do to get us back to Magadan. I want this sorry excuse for a bath toy back there in sixteen hours or less." Nancy's habit of referring to the Arkhangelsk in less than glowing terms when she was stressed had reared its head again.

Nikolay stared at her. "I don't know if that's possible, ma'am."

Nancy advanced on Nikolay and lowered her voice to a level that she thought was quiet but was still loud enough for everyone on the con to hear. "Make it happen. Pull power from every other part of the boat if you have to. Get the crew out on deck and have them paddle if you must. Just get us there *now!*"

Nancy turned and stormed off the bridge, feeling the rage burning inside of her as she went. Behind her, the crew on the control deck all turned to watch her storm down the corridor for several seconds before Nikolay recovered and clapped his hands.

"You heard Ms. Sims. Get the techs on the line and figure out how to make this happen! Both reactors are at full power again, so this should be a walk in the park! Move!"

Nancy could hear Nikolay shouting at the crew as she walked down the hall, though she swept away any thought of it as she turned her attention back to the matter of Sergei and Andrey. When she arrived back in the corridor outside the reactor compartment, Sergei stood several feet from the door while a few of the crew worked in front of him. Two were standing next to each other, wearing white "bunny" suits for protection against the radiation they would face once they went inside.

Three more crewmen crouched in front of the door, working with a torch to finish cutting through the last bit of steel to gain access to the locking mechanism. Nancy put her hand on Sergei's shoulder. "I'm sorry, Sergei. You know you don't have to be here for this; you can return to your compartment if you'd like."

"I'd prefer to be here, actually, if you don't mind."

Nancy nodded and turned back to watch the men work. "Do you know how they'll secure his body?"

"They're already figured that out." Sergei motioned to the two men in white suits standing in front of him. "Every nuclear submarine in the Russian fleet kept a small quantity of lead-lined body bags on hand in case something like this happened."

Nancy's eyebrow shot up. "Really?"

Sergei nodded grimly. "Yes. I was not aware that they were standard issue. They say that he can be stored in one of the rooms in the back. He'll be far enough away to not affect anyone."

Nancy sighed again and shook her head. "I'm sorry, Sergei."

"As am I, Ms. Sims. As am I."

Nancy and Sergei watched in silence as the crew worked on the door for several more minutes. Finally, there was the sound of strained metal being cleaved in two, and a loud bang from inside the door.

"Got it!" The man holding the torch stood up and smiled, then his face sunk as he glanced behind and saw Nancy and Sergei standing there. The men working on the door quickly cleared out of the way and Nancy spoke to the white-suited men in front of her.

"Show him some dignity, and make sure you stick a radiation tag on the bag. Just in case something happens. Understand?"

"Yes, ma'am." The men spoke in unison, then advanced on the door, carrying the heavy lead-lined bag between them.

As Sergei watched the leave, he turned to Nancy. "I'll be going now, if you don't mind."

"Of course." Nancy gave Sergei a sympathetic nod as he walked down the corridor. Nancy waited in the hall for a few more minutes, listening to the rustling and grunting as the crewmen inside the compartment worked to ease Andrey's body inside the bag. When it sounded like they were finishing up, she too turned and left to head back to her room.

An hour later, as Nancy was writing in the Arkhangelsk's logbook, there was a soft knocking at the door. She looked over to see the face of one of the younger crew looking at her with wide eyes.

"Ma'am?"

Nancy pushed back in her chair and swiveled around to face the young woman.

"Yes? What is it?"

The woman took a step inside Nancy's compartment and spoke, her eyes darting around as she did. "You wanted to know when the… when, uh… when the—"

"When Andrey's body was stored away?"

The young woman nodded. "Yes, ma'am."

Nancy sighed and stood up. "Very good. Thank you. You can go."

The young woman didn't hesitate to leave, and Nancy smirked as she heard the woman's running steps echo down the corridor. "Time to go find Sergei, I suppose."

It didn't take long to locate the soldier. Nancy's first stop was the galley, which was empty, though the lights were turned on and a radio was playing a scratchy rendition of some classical music she wasn't familiar with. As she walked through the room, she spotted Sergei sitting at a corner table, facing the wall, with two bottles of vodka and a small cassette player sitting on the table next to him.

Nancy approached the table and sat down across from Sergei, then motioned at the cassette player. "I haven't seen one of those in years. I'm amazed it still works."

Sergei snorted as he threw back what was in his glass and poured himself another drink in one smooth motion. "Is Stravinsky. Was Andrey's favorite."

Nancy picked up one of the bottles and let out a whistle as she saw the label. "Mind if I have a drop?"

Sergei shrugged his shoulders. "You are captain."

Nancy kept her eye on Sergei as she put the bottle to her lips and took a long drink. Sergei had obviously been drinking for a while, based on how much of the other bottle was gone, and by how much his English had deteriorated. Liquid fire drew circles in her mouth and ran down her throat, and she slammed the bottle back on the table and cringed.

Sergei chuckled at the sight of Nancy squirming over the vodka, then poured himself another drink. "So, captain. What is plan?"

"Plan?" Nancy coughed a few times as she spoke, trying to catch her breath and clear the burning out of her throat and mouth. "We're getting back to Magadan as fast as we can. Then we're going to find out what happened to Krylov and the rest of them."

Sergei nodded slowly and Nancy raised the bottle again. "To Andrey."

Sergei looked up at her and raised his glass. "To cousin Andrey."

They both took another drink. When Nancy finished coughing again, she spoke, her voice noticeably raspier. "You know, I wanted to apologize to Andrey. For what I said to him when I caught him trying to sneak off the boat. He was a good man, and I know he was just trying to do the right thing and make up for what he felt like was his fault on that sub."

There was a lengthy silence as Sergei slowly filled his glass again before speaking. "He respected you. He looked up at you. You... he was proud to have you lead us." Sergei waved his glass through the air as he spoke. "You are not Russian. But Andrey? He did not care. You were good leader. He knew that."

Nancy fought back the lump that was forming in her throat and nodded slowly. "Thank you, Sergei. I—"

Nancy was interrupted by the speakers in the galley blasting Nikolay's voice. "Ms. Sims, you're needed on the con."

Nancy sighed and patted Sergei's hand as she stood up. "I'm sorry. We'll talk more later, okay?"

Sergei grunted as Nancy walked off, then turned up the volume on his cassette player. The sound of The Firebird playing over a tinny speaker reverberated through the empty room as Sergei closed his eyes and threw back yet another drink.

Chapter Thirty-Three

THE CAVERN

Leonard could hear his heart pounding in his ears as he ran down the corridor behind the rest of the group. Behind him, the sounds of the creatures throwing themselves against the jammed door echoed, spurring him on to greater speeds. By the time he reached the experimental digging machine near the intersection of tunnels, the rest of the group had already grouped up behind Maria, who was waiting on Leonard to lead them into the cavern.

Leonard raised a finger as he gasped for air. "One second." He felt his heart rate calming, and Marcus passed him a canteen of water. Leonard nodded in appreciation and took several gulps before returning it.

"Okay," Leonard said, looking around at the group, "the muties are going to break through that door any minute. When they do, they're going to be really *really* pissed off. We need to haul ass through this tunnel and get down into the cavern."

"What?" One of Alexander's men, a guard who hadn't made it down into the supply line tunnel in time to join the rest of the survivors, spoke up. "What do you mean, a cavern?"

Leonard glanced at Krylov, who answered. "We must continue luring the creatures away from Alexander and the rest of the survivors. We are buying them time to get to the docks and the safety beyond."

One of the other guards spoke next. "Why do we have to go into a cavern?"

"Because these men say we do." Maria jumped into the conversation, lashing out at the guards with a stern voice. "They have traveled across the depths of hell to reach us. And now they have a plan to make sure what's left of us have a fighting chance to survive. If you want to go back and try to reason with the monsters, please go. Otherwise listen to them!"

The guards murmured to each other and shuffled their feet, but none of them would look Maria in the eye or respond to what she said. Her eyes glittered with fire as she glanced between them before finally looking back at Leonard.

Leonard nodded gratefully and began heading for the tunnel entrance. "Come on. Let's go. Marcus, I'd like you and Maria to take the rear. Krylov, you're with me up front."

As the group wound their way through the twisting passage, Leonard and Krylov sped up until they were several paces ahead of the group, so that they could hold a brief whispered conversation.

"She's a damned firecracker."

Krylov nodded. "She has a natural fire, that is certain."

"What's your take on the others? You think they'll try to run?"

"If given the chance, yes. They have fear in their eyes—I've seen it before.

"Any suggestions on what to do about it?"

Krylov glanced behind him. "We watch them carefully. If they run, that is their choice. But we must make certain that they do not endanger us—or our mission—if they do."

Leonard mulled over Krylov's words as they continued walking. He wiped his sleeve against his head, noticing for the first time the heat in the tunnel. The air felt several degrees warmer than when he and Maria had traversed it previously, and he began wondering why it was so hot.

As if on cue, Krylov spoke again. "Is it supposed to be this hot?"

"It was before, but not like this. It feels like the air is moving more, too. Maybe they've added additional processing power."

"If it's a nexus."

Leonard glanced at Krylov. "What do you mean, *if* it's a nexus?"

Krylov shrugged. "I'm not doubting your theory, Mr. McComb. I merely meant—"

A shout from behind cut Krylov short. Marcus pushed through the guards until he reached the pair, panic written on his face. "They're coming. We can hear them, running through the corridors back there."

"Damn!" Leonard looked at Krylov. "Help form a rearguard. Send Maria up front. We're almost at the cavern. I have no idea what's down there, but we're just going to have to make a run for it and try to hide from these things."

Krylov nodded. "We'll follow your lead, Mr. McComb." With that, Krylov and Marcus pushed back through the group. Leonard ran ahead, calling for the others to follow him.

"Pick up the pace! We're almost there!"

The lights bouncing off of the walls were soon absorbed by the seemingly infinite blackness that stretched forth in front of them as the group finally arrived at the edge of the cavern. The whole group barely fit onto the small ledge, and Marcus leaned over, shining his light down the steep slope that fell off into darkness.

"Uhh…" Marcus looked over at Leonard. "I hate to say this, but you're crazy, Leonard. I think you finally, really snapped."

A howl from the tunnel behind the group made them all look back. "Want to stay here instead?" Leonard quipped.

Marcus gritted his teeth and looked down the slope again. "Dammit, Leonard. If we die…"

Maria pushed through Leonard and Marcus, then stepped out onto the slope without saying a word. She leaned back, taking the occasional step to steady herself, but let gravity do most of the work as she slid down, swaying side to side to stay on her feet. Marcus and Leonard went next, their lights growing smaller and fainter as they slid down the slope after Maria.

Krylov stood at the edge of the slope, looking at the guards behind him. There were five in total, and they stood in a huddle, clutching their weapons as they stared into the darkness of the cavern, afraid to move even a muscle. Another howl came from the tunnel, closer than the last one, and they jumped in unison.

Krylov motioned to the slope as he spoke. "You are welcome to come with us, if you wish. Or you may stay. The choice is yours. With that, Krylov stepped off onto the slope and crouched, using his arms, back and legs to remain steady and control his speed. The guards' eyes grew wide as they realized that they were alone—but wouldn't remain so for longer. The creatures in the tunnel were close enough that the guards could hear them snarling and gnashing their teeth, and they realized that there was no time left.

While Leonard, Marcus, Krylov and Maria had all been able to slide down the slope in a controlled, reasonable fashion, the guards—spooked by the approach of the creatures—had no such luxury. They tumbled down the slope head over heels, with all but one losing their grip on their weapons on the way down. By the time they reached the bottom they were covered in dirt and bruises and had lost all sense of direction. Krylov stood back shaking his head slowly as the men slowly stood up, helped by Marcus and Maria. Leonard, meanwhile, gathered their weapons and handed them back, each accompanied by a look of extreme displeasure.

"Are you quite done jerking around?" Leonard nearly growled as he spoke to the men, and they all nodded slowly, unsure of the meaning of "jerking around" but understanding him perfectly by his tone.

"Good. Now get your asses ready to move." Leonard walked back next to Krylov with Marcus while Maria checked the men over.

"What's our next step, Mr. McComb?"

Leonard looked around the cavern, waving his flashlight in every direction. "If the muties were going to follow us down here they'd be on top of us already. Given that they haven't… I don't know what that means. But I think we need to move away from where we are, in case they decide to jump down and join in the party."

Krylov sniffed the air and wrinkled his nose in displeasure. "The air at this level is much cooler than that in the tunnel, but the smell is… unpleasant."

Leonard took in a deep breath and nodded. "That smells like… farts?"

Marcus burst out laughing, quickly followed by raspy coughing as he choked on his spittle trying to keep quiet. "What the hell, Leonard?" He finally managed to squeak out the question after several seconds of coughing and laughing.

Leonard snorted in amusement, and for a second he thought he saw the edge of Krylov's mouth twitch. "Sorry. It just sort of came out."

Marcus began laughing again and Leonard groaned. "Really? Dammit, Marcus, this isn't the time." Despite his words, Leonard wore a grin, and was pleased to see Krylov finally crack a slight smile. "What I meant to say was that it smells like natural gas." Leonard took another deep breath and nodded in confirmation. "Definitely methane."

"From a natural source?" Krylov asked. "Or do you think the creatures are manufacturing it?"

"I sort of doubt that muties have a need to manufacture methane, or that they have a process that would produce it as a byproduct. No, if I had to guess, they're tapping into a supply of natural gas from the city and using it as a power source. That's the only reason it would smell like this, if it came from a processed source. Methane's the primary ingredient in natural gas and it's odorless, but this stuff has the classic rotten egg smell. Definitely not natural."

"A power source?" Marcus frowned. "For what?"

Maria came up to the trio and interrupted the conversation. "I'm glad to see that you all are able to find some humor in our situation, but the others are not so easily amused. They are ready to move out, though."

"Well, Marcus my friend," Leonard slapped Marcus on the back and began walking deeper into the cavern, "I guess there's only one way to find out."

The group of nine walked along in silence. None of the creatures had been heard since the guards tumbled down into the cavern, and there had been no sight of anything hostile as the group moved forward. After spreading out and searching around for a few moments, they began to gain an idea of the sheer size and scale of the cavern, and how large it could potentially be.

Their lights didn't reach the ceiling, nor did the stretch from one side of the cavern to the other. Measured off of how long it took to walk from the base of the slope until hitting a wall on the opposite side of the space, Leonard estimated that it was at least five hundred meters wide, and a natural formation. The ground was smooth and riddled with sediment clusters that had formed over thousands of years as water dripped down from the ceiling to the floor.

The rock shone under the lights, and natural channels were carved into it through which small rivulets of water ran, sometimes vanishing into the stone and then reappearing a few meters away. The air was warmer than any of them would have expected for a cave so far underground, but based on how hot it had been in the tunnel, Leonard was surprised at the temperature near the floor, and remarked to Krylov that the ventilation for the cavern was extraordinarily good.

After a good hour of slowly walking along and picking their way through obstacles along the cavern floor, the natural appearance suddenly came to a halt. The smooth, rolling and glistening floor became perfectly flat and rough, with the telltale signs of having been cut with a tool at some point in the recent past. When Leonard first noticed the change, the group was spread out with several meters in between each person, and Leonard called for everyone to come to him.

Maria was the first to speak. "What's wrong?"

Leonard motioned at the ground and swept over it with his light. The others followed his cue and they soon had a large area of the ground around them illuminated.

"Look." Leonard stepped forward and aimed his light at a break in the flat, featureless rock. In it, a channel around two feet wide had been cut, and it extended off into the distance in a straight line. In the channel flowed a fast-moving stream of some sort of oddly-colored liquid that gave off a foul odor.

Krylov knelt down near the channel and sniffed a few times before standing up and waving his hand in front of his face. "That's not the source of whatever we smelled earlier, but it's terrible. Any ideas what it is, Mr. McComb?" Krylov looked over to his side, where Leonard had last been, but he was already gone, walking along the channel to see where it went.

Krylov motioned for the group to follow, and they quickly caught up with Leonard. "Mr. McComb?" Leonard didn't respond and Krylov tapped him on the shoulder. "Mr. McComb, what is it?"

Leonard glanced at Krylov, his concentration broken. He looked down at the channel where Krylov was pointing and began to speak as the rest of the group followed close behind.

"This looks like a cooling channel to me, Krylov. A way to draw heat away from a structure and radiate it through this cavern. Not a very good design, but I bet it's used in conjunction with other, more active cooling designs."

"A cooling system?" Krylov frowned. "Does that mean…"

"Oh yes. It does indeed." Leonard picked up his pace. "If we follow this channel, we should find exactly—yes."

Leonard stopped abruptly and pointed out into the distance in front of them. No longer pitch black, the cavern now glowed with a dull, unearthly red light that radiated from something none of them had ever laid eyes on before.

The structure was enormous, standing a full twenty or thirty stories in height. Its twisted, demented shape appeared almost alien in nature, with aspects equally sterile and rigid as they were organic and flowing. The building wrapped over on itself as it rose from the floor of the cavern up to its very heights, revealing the true immensity of the cavern they stood in.

The red glow from the structure was hypnotic, and Leonard found himself drawn in by its pulsating warmth. It was impossible to say whether the red glow was designed as a lighting mechanism or if it was simply a byproduct of whatever processes went on inside the structure. Though the glow from the structure did not extend far enough for the group to see where they were going without their lights, it did act as a beacon of sorts, showing them where the were going in the enormous cavern.

Upon seeing the enormous structure, Leonard's first reaction was one of awe, followed swiftly by a twisting in his gut as he realized the implications of his suspicions being confirmed. Krylov and Marcus both gasped, while Maria merely stood still, mouth agape as she struggled to comprehend what she was seeing. The guards, however, were less subtle in their reaction, as they began to shout and wail in their native tongue. While Leonard was familiar with the basics of the Russian language, he couldn't make out anything they were saying. Krylov, however, understood perfectly, and turned on them in an instant, silencing them with a harsh glare.

"What were they going on about?" Leonard whispered to Krylov as the commander turned back to gaze upon the structure.

"They said we brought them down into hell, where our souls will be torn from our flesh and we'll be tormented forever."

"Oh. Pleasant."

"They are superstitious, Mr. McComb. But can you truly blame them, after all they've experienced this last year?"

"I'm not superstitious." Maria whispered at Leonard and Krylov, and they both looked at her.

"And why not?" Asked Marcus.

Maria looked at Leonard. "Because they're just us. They're changed versions of us, all messed up and twisted and turned into monsters, but they're still people under everything. They're not devils. And this isn't hell."

Leonard nodded with approval. "Very true."

"So," said Krylov, "what are we looking at, then, Mr. McComb?"

Leonard turned back to look at the structure and shook his head again in amazement. "This, my friends, is what I've dreaded since we first encountered these creatures. This… this is a nexus."

Chapter Thirty-Four

THE CAVERN

"Why the hell would these things build a nexus underground?" Marcus crossed his arms. "The last one was—"

"Completely vulnerable?" Leonard interrupted.

"Hm. Good point."

"Mr. McComb, I thought your suspicion was that the artificial intelligence that controls the creatures in Magadan was completely separate from the main intelligence that was attempting to evolve itself in the United States."

"Correct."

Krylov gestured at the glowing structure. "So then why would this version of the AI want to build their nexus underground?"

Leonard sighed and looked around, then sat his pack down on the ground. "You'd better have the guards take a rest. It might be a while before we can stop again."

Krylov's looked at Leonard questionably but he turned and barked at the guards, who looked both relieved and even more nervous to get a chance to sit down for a few moments. When they were finally situated and had started whispering quietly amongst themselves, Leonard sat down nearby with Marcus, Krylov and Maria.

"Understand, first of all," Leonard said, "that this is still just a theory. We might never know the full truth, or we might find it out in the next hour." He stopped for a few seconds to see if there were any questions forthcoming, then proceeded when there was naught but silence from the others.

"I think that we can definitively say that the whatever swarms came to Magadan after the bombs dropped were not the same as the others we've encountered. Supporting this belief are the behavioral differences in the creatures and the types of creatures that have been infected.

"Working off of this assumption we can then start to question why the AI would be split apart into two distinct types, with one being arguably less aggressive and possessing more creative elements."

"Less aggressive?" Maria shook her head. "Have you seen what they've done?"

"Believe me when I tell you that the behavior of these creatures is nothing when compared to the behavior of the ones that we've encountered numerous times in the past. These are, in fact, nearly docile." Maria shook her head again in disbelief, but said nothing as Leonard continued.

"So why split into two distinct 'personalities' so to speak? I've had a number of ideas, but I think there are two that make more sense than any others. The first thought is that the AI we've encountered—the one that we ultimately destroyed—created this offshoot as a way of experimenting with other evolutionary branches. It was obsessed with improving itself and it could have thought that creating another—less complex—version of itself was the key to ensuring its success."

Krylov swallowed some water. "And the second theory?"

"That the person responsible for the original AI also developed this one, and they both escaped and developed separately. The intelligence and swarms in the States could have been a more advanced version of the type here, which is why they were able to accomplish so much in such a short amount of time, or perhaps there are other differences between the two that we've yet to see."

"So, uh," Marcus interrupted, "these are great ideas, really, but I'm not seeing where you're going with this."

Leonard smiled. "I'm getting there. Anyway, so regardless of how or why this AI exists, we know that it's different and unique and shows a remarkable trait for adaptation and spontaneity and creativity. Perhaps that's why this exists at all." Leonard turned to look at the nexus. "If this AI had discovered what happened a year ago—and that wouldn't be hard for the swarms to find out—they may have constructed their nexus underground to avoid a similar fate."

"But why construct one at all? And why has it taken so long to build?" Marcus pointed at sections of the nexus on the sides, where the building was clearly unfinished. "The damned things are still building it, from the looks of it."

"If I had to guess," Leonard glanced at Maria in sympathy, "I'd say it's a lack of resources."

"A lack of resources in a city of over two hundred thousand?" Krylov sounded incredulous.

"If we were talking about the same AI that built the nexus in the States, I would agree with you. This AI had a tendency to use time and resources on things like what we saw in the factory. They were never too keen on pushing through the defenses erected by the survivors and taking them all down at once, either. "

"But that's because of our defenses." Maria argued with Leonard, but he merely shook his head.

"I'm sorry, but that's just not the case."

Maria stood up and clenched her fists. "What are you talking about? The creatures threw themselves at us and we defended against them each time."

"Easy," Krylov pleaded, "just sit down and list to Mr. McComb."

Leonard nodded at Krylov in appreciation as Maria slowly sat back down, her fingers still balled and her eyes lit with fire. "I'm sorry, Maria, but it's true. I had my suspicions when I first saw the gates that you all erected, but nothing was concrete until I saw the creatures as they were throwing themselves at us while the survivors were moving down into the supply line tunnel. They were clearly holding back, and that was obvious once the bulk of the survivors went down into the supply line. Then, instead of continuing to just surge forward to let a few of their number be killed as part of their charade, they actually went on the offensive."

Krylov rubbed his chin as he considered Leonard's analysis. "I do believe that Mr. McComb is correct. The normal level of aggression and determination that we've seen from the creatures in the past has not yet been exhibited here." Krylov looked behind him at the direction they had come from. "If these creatures were truly pursuing us, they would have followed us down the slope and slaughtered us."

Leonard nodded, pleased to see that someone else had caught on to what was happening. "Exactly. I don't think it's a coincidence that they were pushing us down here. They've got some kind of purpose for us here."

"Then shouldn't we just... leave?" Marcus asked. "Wouldn't we want to do the opposite of whatever these things want us to do?"

"Under any other circumstances I wouldn't hesitate to get as far away from whatever the AI wants us to do. Unfortunately..." Leonard trailed off and lifted his arms to gesture at the cavern they were in. "We didn't have many options left to us. However, I will say that we're in better shape now than the creatures are expecting."

Maria shook her head in confusion. "How is that? They have us trapped down here right where they want us!"

A sly grin broke across Krylov's face as he replied before Leonard could. "Because now we have the element of surprise. We know they're herding us somewhere, so we just need to find the opportune moment to break away and we'll be able to eliminate any advantages they have."

Marcus frowned. "Guys, it's great that you've figured all of this out and we're going to be just fine and dandy. Really just great. What about Roman, Mikhail, Alexander and the survivors? If we're being herded down here, then wouldn't the creatures try to do the same thing to them?"

Krylov's smile dropped and he looked at Leonard who nodded grimly and answered. "You're probably right, Marcus. That's why we have to get to that structure and bring it down. If we do that, there's a decent chance that we'll disrupt the network that the creatures communicate on, given how basic they seem to be in comparison to the ones in the States."

"What's our next step, Mr. McComb?"

Leonard turned back to look at the alien structure. They were still quite a distance away, but he could swear that he could see small points of shadow moving about on the exterior of the structure. On the left side of the cavern, as they faced the structure, Leonard could see from the glow of the structure that the ground began to rise, offering a perfect vantage point of the nexus without having to get too close.

"There." Leonard pointed. "We'll make for that spot. It should be secluded enough to offer protection while we decide the next move.

Chapter Thirty-Five

THE MAGADAN METRO

Though the hole in the floor of the metro tunnel looked relatively clean from above, from down in the supply line it was anything but. Twisted pieces of metal, chunks of wood and pieces of concrete lay scattered on the floor, embedded in the walls and dangling precariously from the tunnel above as though they were daring someone to walk beneath them.

The utter mess in the supply line tunnel made Alexander's job of helping the survivors move through the tunnel even harder, as they were working in near-darkness with a number of hazards laying scattered about. As Alexander worked to herd the group of survivors away from the hole in the roof of the supply line tunnel, a dark figure dropped down behind him. Alexander whirled to face it, finding himself face to face with one of the members of the team that had come to rescue him and the others.

"Alexander!" Roman held up his hands and called out, and Alexander lowered his weapon.

"Roman?" Alexander had spoken with the man a few times, but hadn't had a chance to have a long conversation with him like he had with Krylov, Leonard and Marcus. "What are you doing down here?"

Roman pointed at the hole above and behind him. "We have to get everyone away right now and detonate the explosives. The creatures are about to come after us!"

Alexander felt his stomach sink as he turned to see the slowly-moving crowd of survivors. Raising his gun into the air, he fired several times and started shouting at them. "The monsters are here! Everyone run! Run now!"

While inciting panic in an enclosed, dark space full of obstacles and hazards wasn't the choice most conducive to everyone's general health, it worked surprisingly well. The crowd of survivors pushed each other along down the tunnel, the few flashlights they had bouncing back and forth as they tried to see where they were going.

Roman pointed down the tunnel at the survivors. "Go after them! I'll stay here and make sure nothing gets through, then once everyone's clear I'll set off the explosives!"

Alexander nodded and took off running, shouting at Roman as he went. "The detonator is there, on top of the largest crate!"

Roman scooped up the detonator and checked the indicator lights at the top. The seven explosives it had been connected to were all showing a green light, indicating that they were still functional. After a final glance up through the hole in the roof of the supply tunnel, Roman took off running. Once he was barely clear of where he assumed the worst of the blast would reach, he pushed the trigger on the detonator.

For an instant, nothing happened, and Roman feared that something was wrong with the explosives. Then, a second later, a burst of air and sound rushed past him, propelling him forward so that he could barely keep his feet underneath himself. The last of the explosives had been placed at a seam where two parts of the supply line tunnel joined together along the walls. When they detonated, the walls caved in, filling the tunnel completely with dirt and debris, but leaving the ceiling mostly intact except for a few hairline cracks that traveled outward from the blast zone like spiderwebs.

Flames from the blast licked at Roman's back, but he continued to run, leaping over boxes and pieces of unidentifiable equipment that had long since been picked over. As the heat behind him receded, he slowed to a halt and turned around to inspect the work of the explosives. A slow-moving plume of ash and pulverized concrete was the only thing visible, and his light couldn't penetrate the cloud more than an inch or two.

Forced to move on, Roman continued to head down the tunnel as he started to wonder where the survivors had gotten to. As the ringing in his ears from the blast began to soften, he heard several voices shouting from up ahead. Quickening his pace, he finally found himself in view of the survivors, who were gathered around Alexander, shouting at him.

"What's going on?"

"Where are we anyway?"

"Where are we going?"

"Are those things after us?"

Alexander was trying to answer each question individually, but the survivors were relentless as they peppered him with comments and questions, each trying to get their answer first. When Alexander caught sight of Roman, he looked relieved and his body relaxed even as he raised his voice above the din.

"Quiet!" Alexander took out his pistol and raised it to the ceiling, intending to fire off a shot. The mere sight of the weapon spooked the survivors, though, and the ducked down, immediately forgetting their questions. Alexander took immediate advantage of the silence. "Thank you! Now listen, everyone! We're still evacuating! We had to destroy the tunnel behind us ahead of schedule, but everything is okay now. Do you all understand?"

There were murmurs in response, along with a single question. "Where are we going?"

Alexander sighed. He hadn't had the time to tell the survivors where they were off to, and realized that even though the dark tunnel wasn't the best place to do it, there wouldn't be a better one until they arrived at their destination. "We're traveling underground to the port, where we'll be taking a boat out to a submarine that's waiting for us."

"You mean the thing those strangers were talking about?"

"Yes, that's exactly it." Alexander's response was met with a *harrumph* by the man who had posed the question. The group of survivors began to talk again, louder this time, until they exploded with questions again. Alexander couldn't understand any of them, and tried to call for order, but no one would listen. He was about to pull out his gun again when Roman fired his own gun in the air before yelling in Russian at the survivors.

"Listen to me, all of you! We—all of you and I—we are brothers! The people I came here with are your brothers! Yes, that includes the Americans, too!" The survivors, startled by the gunshot and by Roman's booming voice, kept quiet as Roman continued.

"If you want to survive, we must press on. Those monsters will soon be after us, and we do not have enough weapons to stand and fight again." A series of gasped rippled through the crowd. "However!" Roman grew louder again. "However! We can still outwit them! We need to move quickly and quietly to the docks. Once we're there, out of the tunnels, I can radio our vessel and they will send soldiers to defend us while we get everyone on board!"

Another wave of mumbled talking swept across the group, but no one spoke out. Alexander, seizing upon his chance, spoke next. "We have stayed here for far too long and lost too many. We have this chance to escape hell thanks to these saviors, and we must not give it up by fighting and bickering and complaining!"

The murmurs turned into silent nods of agreement and Alexander continued. "Here is what we all must do: I need two volunteers to form a rearguard. You will be in charge of watching behind us for any crea-tures and ensuring no one falls behind or becomes lost. Myself, Roman and his comrade will scout in the front, looking for any easier routes and defending us from any possible attacks. You must all remember to stay together, move quickly and remain as quiet as possible. I promise you, my friends, we will all make it through this."

As the crowd of survivors began to talk amongst themselves, Roman could sense that the mood in the tunnel had completely changed from when he had arrived. There was still a palpable sense of nervousness among the survivors, but they were no longer panicking as they had been before. Alexander pushed gently through the crowd and approached Roman, then clasped the soldier's hand in gratitude.

"Thank you. I wasn't sure if I could get them calmed down myself."

Roman smiled and nodded. "They're scared, and they have every reason to be."

"How's the tunnel look?"

Roman glanced behind him. "The explosives worked. But I wouldn't trust anything for very long in this place. We need to get everyone moving now." Roman looked around and kicked at a half-broken crate that laid broken next to a flat-bed train car. "Are there this many obstacles the entire way down?"

Alexander nodded and sighed. "Whenever we went searching for supplies we were never very neat. Our strategy was simple: smash and grab anything that looked useful and then move on to the next box."

Roman looked at his gloved hands. "I'm glad I have these on, then. We'll need to move as much out of the way as we can."

"Agreed. I'll find two more able-bodied volunteers to help us. If we stay ten or twenty meters ahead of the group that should be enough of a buffer. Your friend Mikhail, though; can he help?"

Roman shrugged. "If he must. But it wouldn't be good for him. He doesn't need another infection, not when we're uncertain of how long it will take to get out of this place."

Alexander nodded. "Understood. I'll find our volunteers and we'll begin moving shortly."

As Alexander walked back toward the group of survivors and began talking to them about the tasks that needed to be performed, Roman shifted his attention back behind him once again. The dust cloud had dissipated somewhat, but was still moving lazily forward. Somewhere behind it, he know, were Krylov, Marcus and Leonard. How they would be able to escape the refuge in the face of all of the creatures was beyond his ability to fathom. He closed his eyes and said a quick prayer, hoping that somehow—again—they would be able to pull off another impossible escape.

Chapter Thirty-Six

THE ARKHANGELSK

"What's our speed?"

"Forty knots and holding, ma'am."

"Can you get us to forty-five?"

Nancy's question was met with a look best described as abject horror. "Ma'am, we're already straining the engines as is it. We were never—"

"Yes, yes, I know." Nancy waved her hand dismissively. "Never meant to travel this fast. Dammit!" She ran her hands through her hair as she paced around the control deck. "How long till we arrive?"

"Approximately two minutes sooner than when you last checked, which was approximately two minutes ago, ma'am." Nikolay's voice came from behind Nancy and she turned to see him stepping onto the con.

"Thanks, Nikolay, though I'm not really in the mood for jokes."

"Ms. Sims." Nikolay stepped up next to her and lowered his voice. "You're beginning to frighten the crew. They're already dealing with a lot as they deal with Andrey's death on top of trying to finish retuning the reactor after we left port before the repairs were finalized."

Nancy sat down in an empty seat and slumped down in the chair. Nikolay stood beside her, studying her intently as she spoke. "You're right, Nikolay. I'm sorry." She forced a weak smile. "I just can't help but think something's gone wrong back at Magadan."

"We're several hours ahead of schedule, ma'am. We'll be back in time to offer whatever assistance may—but which is mostly likely *not* —required."

Nancy nodded slowly and took a deep breath. "You're right. Again. You Russian prick." Nancy gave Nikolay a full grin and stood up.

"I'm only too happy to oblige, ma'am."

On the control deck, the mood lightened, though the Arkhangelsk herself still trembled under the incredible pressures she was enduring. Favorable currents were helping to speed her journey back north, though they weren't enough to get her back to Magadan in the amount of time that Nancy desired. To help achieve that, the twin turbines were operating a full twenty percent above their maximum rated value. It was a risk, to be sure, and the Arkhangelsk was not nearly as streamlined as other, smaller subs, but the raw power she was able to put out helped make up for her physical deficiencies.

Deeper in the bowels of the Arkhangelsk, another—more personal —struggle was underway. Sergei had moved from the galley back to his compartment, where he sealed the door and busied himself with emptying yet another bottle as he played more of Andrey's favorite music. Hours of drinking had led Sergei down several dark paths as he grieved the loss of his cousin, and though he knew in his head that his cousin was gone, his heart refused to accept the fact.

As the battery in the old cassette player ran out and the music wound down, Sergei found himself stumbling out of his compartment and down the corridor, meandering his way toward the back of the Arkhangelsk. He slurred the bars of music he was humming as he went along, weaving a steady path toward the compartment where Andrey's body had been stored away. After a few wrong turns and missteps along the way, Sergei finally found himself standing outside the correct compartment. He leaned against the hatch and peered through the window at the edge of the body bag that was visible.

With a deep breath, Sergei pushed open the hatch and stepped into the room. He felt a shiver go down his spine, a side effect of the low temperature Nancy had ordered the compartment kept at to help preserve Andrey's body for a proper burial. Sergei wiped the unbidden tears away from his eyes as he crouched next to the body bag and took another long drink from his bottle. After he finished, Sergei reached out to rest the bottle on the floor next to the body bag, only to reach too far and drop it on top of the bag instead.

Sergei watched as the bag slowly collapsed under the weight of the bottle, unsure of what he was seeing. By the time the bag had been flattened to the ground, however, most of the fog from the alcohol had cleared from his head. His heart was racing as he reached for the bag and gently tugged at the zipper to reveal its contents.

The bag was empty.

Sergei jumped back and pressed his body against the wall, acting as though he had just touched a live wire. Of all the things in the world he might have expected to see inside a body bag in which had been placed his dead cousin, seeing it empty was not one of the things he had anticipated.

It took Sergei a full minute to regain his faculties, and once he did, he leapt over the body bag, nearly losing his balance as he landed, and ran out into the corridor. Looking both ways, he shook his head to try and clear his mind and his vision, then he took off running to the nearest intercom. He punched in a short code on the keypad and the white lights in the corridors across the Arkhangelsk changed from white to red. An alarm began to blare at the same time, and Sergei's trembling voice—still slightly slurred from the alcohol—rang out across the sub.

"Attention: all hands. This is an emergency. Ms. Sims, you're needed near the reactor room immediately!" Without waiting for a reply, Sergei ran down the hall toward the reactor room, using the walls as balance. He arrived several seconds ahead of Nancy, who came racing down the hall with Nikolay in tow.

"Sergei?" Nancy skidded to a stop in the corridor and looked at Sergei's swaying form. "What the hell are you doing wandering around in this condition. Did—did you sound the general alarm?"

Sergei's face turned white as he recalled the feeling he had upon unzipping the body bag. "The body—ma'am, his body—Andrey's, it's… it's gone!"

Nancy and Nikolay looked at each other in confusion, then back at Sergei. "What the hell are you talking about?"

Sergei took a few steps back and motioned for them to follow him. "Come on! You have to see!"

Sergei ran back down the corridor, occasionally putting his hand out to steady himself if a wave of nausea overtook him. When the trio had arrived back at the compartment where the body bag was stored, Sergei stepped to the side so that Nancy and Nikolay could enter first. Nancy stepped through, followed closely by Nikolay, and they both stood and stared at the empty body bag for a few seconds.

"What the hell." Nancy spoke first, cutting through the silence.

"Indeed." Nikolay squatted down and pulled a pen out of his shirt pocket, which he used to poke at the bottle resting on top of the bag. "And why is this bottle here?"

Sergei, still outside in the corridor, leaned in, his face turning red with embarrassment. "I'm afraid that's mine, sir. I came down to... say goodbye."

"Hm." Nikolay turned back to the empty bag as Nancy leaned down for a closer look.

"Why would someone take Andrey's body?" Nancy looked over at Sergei, then at Nikolay.

Nikolay didn't respond as he probed the bag with his pen, unzipping it further and looking inside. Finally, he moved his examination back to the outside of the bag, and flipped over the radiation tag on the side. "Ma'am, this tag is still showing normal levels of radiation. If someone did take his body out, then it would have exposed the tag to radiation and we'd see it." Nikolay stood up. "I believe there's a better, more disturbing question we need to ask ourselves."

"Which is?" Nancy looked up at Nikolay as he slowly walked around the bag.

"Why would a radioactive body go missing without any traces of said radiation, and why would whoever took it zip the bag bag up after doing so?"

"I assume they would zip it back up to cover their tracks." Nancy stood up and took a step back. "As for the first... I don't know. This isn't good, though."

A thought occurred to Sergei. "Don't the swarms eat radiation?"

Nancy and Nikolay both turned to look at Sergei, their eyes growing wide as they thought about the implications of what he said.

The Arkhangelsk had been boarded by creatures three times in the last year, but none of those incidents resulted in swarms being loosed upon the vessel.

Nikolay squatted back down over the bag and unzipped it completely, then pulled the sides apart to fully reveal the interior. "What's this?" He reached into the bag and pulled out a small white sliver of something that was tucked away in a corner of the bag. Several more slivers came next, and Nikolay held them in his hand as Nancy leaned down to examine them. Sergei finally stepped inside the room and looked at them as well, then felt his stomach start to churn again.

"What are those, Nikolay?" Nancy poked at one of the slivers in Nikolay's hand before picking it up and turning it over in her fingers.

"I'm unsure, ma'am."

"It's a tooth." Sergei's words were just a whisper, but they might as well have been a grenade for the impact that they had.

"A… a tooth?" Nancy looked at Sergei questioningly. The soldier nodded, then slowly pulled out the bear tooth from his pocket. He had been carrying it since Andrey died; a reminder of his cousin and his "good luck charm."

Nancy dropped the sliver of white from her hand and grabbed the silvery tooth that Sergei held outstretched. "Where did you get this?"

"Andrey took—well, *we* took it off of one of the creatures that attacked the train."

Nancy could feel her blood pressure skyrocketing as she turned the object over in her hands. The silvered metal coated nearly the entire tooth, and the only part of the enamel that showed was at the base, where Andrey had ripped the tooth from the bear's mouth.

"You each had one of these?" Nancy kept her voice steady, though she felt like exploding with rage on the inside.

"Yes."

"Is there a reason you two didn't disclose this during the debriefing after you got back?"

Sergei shook his head. "No."

"God dammit!" Nancy put her hand to her face and groaned in frustration. She turned to Nikolay and pointed at the bag before tossing the tooth inside. "Get all those fragments back in there, then zip this thing up, roll it up and stick it inside another lead-lined bag. Move it to the very front of the boat, as far away from our reactors as possible."

Nikolay zipped the bag up and began rolling it tight. "Consider it done."

Nancy nodded and sighed, then looked at Sergei. "You. With me. Now."

Nancy headed out of the compartment with Sergei close behind her. "And once you've done all that, meet me on the con."

Nikolay's answer was lost in the sounds of Nancy and Sergei's footsteps as they hurried off.

Chapter Thirty-Seven

ANDREY LIPOV

A ndrey Vladimirovich Lipov burns. Intense heat scalds his skin, and his organs are penetrated by lethal doses of radiation. Still he resists the urge to lie down and close his eyes. The pump is working and the valve is closed, but he must still reopen the hatches.

Andrey Vladimirovich Lipov is dying. Each step he takes is an exercise in agony. He can feel his skin peeling, though he does not know whether it is in his imagination or in reality. He feels his mind wandering and his vision grows blurry. He drops to the floor, desperately trying to reach the outer door, but he can no longer control his muscles. He feels his body slip away. There is a distant knocking as the darkness closes in.

Andrey Vladimirovich Lipov is dead. He knows nothing, sees nothing, feels nothing. There is naught but the complete absence of anything—except, in the distance, in the far corner of whatever is left of his mind's eye. In that place, far beyond any other, a curious shimmering appears.

Andrey Vladimirovich Lipov is reborn.

Fire courses through his veins. His mind explodes into a million points of blinding light, each of them swirling and twisting and dancing and buzzing, like an impossibly large swarm of angry fireflies. Each point of light is silver and hums with the energy of a mind far simpler than his own—but one possessed with naught but sheer will and power and desire.

Andrey stands in his mind, surrounded by darkness except for the points of light.

They converge on him, forming the shape of a child, though not one he has ever seen before. The child is deformed and monstrous; a cross between a creature and a human, yet far less refined than any creature he has ever seen. It hobbles towards him, crawling on all fours, though it does not speak—not at first.

Andrey is repulsed by the sight. He tries to move, but his legs won't respond. He tries to turn away, but his head and neck are locked. As the child grows closer it dissolves, breaking back into the points of silver light. Andrey's head is filled with the high-pitched buzz of the swarm as it envelops his body. He feels the swarm moving through him, starting from his head and working its way down through to his feet.

With each second that passes, he feels the pain in his limbs start to dissipate. The pain is soon replaced by a gentle warmth that radiates throughout his body. Andrey begins to slip away into euphoria when a strange feeling in the back of his head jolts his mind. The strange feeling is pushing against Andrey's thoughts, trying to overpower and compartmentalize them.

Andrey does not go without a fight. He resists the foreign intrusion, pushing back against it, screaming silently in his thoughts as he tries to push the entity out of his mind. The entity is strong, but unrefined, lacking the sophistication needed to create the proper chemicals required to interface correctly with the neurons. Its attempts to take over Andrey's mind are crude and elementary, and Andrey's own mind fights back.

As the battle wages in Andrey's brain, his body continues to be repaired. The swarm, though small, takes essential elements from Andrey's body, the energy from the radiation it consumed and the clothes he wears and processes them into the nutrients, chemicals and stabilizers required to affect repairs.

Andrey's body is restored and the swarm rests, settling into his arm as it forms the first lattice of the eventual network that will engulf his entire body. It lends its processing power to the entity in Andrey's mind.

Andrey's body twitches inside the lead-lined bag. His face contorts as he wrestles with the entity. Every time a portion of his mind feels free, another section is taken hostage. Minutes turn into hours as he fights, drawing on the same energy as the swarm itself as he fights it for control. A feint one way turns into an attack on an unprotected flank, which frees up another piece of his mind. Moments later, he has won. The swarm, drained of energy and too weak and few in number to continue resisting, retreats.

Each piece of the swarm joins with the others, retreating to small corners and folds of Andrey's mind, falling into a slumber from which they may never wake. And though it sleeps, the entity still listens, its battle with Andrey's mind having left permanent scars and lines on his mind. Nonetheless, he has won.

Andrey Vladimirovich Lipov lives.

Chapter Thirty-Eight

THE MAGADAN METRO

R oman was not one to become easily disturbed by the underground, especially after traversing it over the last couple of days. Living in a submarine for months on end helped the metro lines feel normal, and there was the additional benefit of not wondering if water would suddenly come rushing in to crush you.

The Arkhangelsk did not, however, have something that the underground tunnels did have: an enormous pack of creatures who were hunting him down. That thought did make his skin crawl, and no amount of positive thinking or distractions could fully relieve the tension it caused.

"Give me a hand?" The question came from across the tunnel, to Roman's right. He stopped and pointed his light at the source of the voice. Alexander was standing with one of the survivors behind a large metal box that had been pushed off of one of the train cars long ago. Roman hopped up on the car and put his weight on the box to help move it back on the car while Mikhail held a light behind him.

Though Roman had made it clear to Mikhail that he did not want the injured man in the lead helping to clear obstacles from the path of the survivors, Mikhail wouldn't take 'no' for an answer. His devotion to his duty—and to Roman—was immeasurable, especially as he was still fighting to prove himself after the accidental shot that had first drawn the attention of the creatures to the rescue team.

Metal screeched upon metal as the large container was slowly pushed back onto the train, leaving an open path for the survivors walking behind Alexander. The survivors had split into two groups with one on each side of the train, to help alleviate congestion from everyone trying to crowd in on one side or the other. In spite of this— and the best efforts of the four-man team in the lead who did their best to clear the largest obstructions—it was still taking far long to move everyone through the tunnels than Alexander had hoped.

Months of little movement and poor nutrition had taken their toll on the survivors, and even Alexander had to admit that he was feeling exhausted just from the walking. Of the few dozen survivors that picked their way through the tunnel, a handful were old and young enough that they had to stop often, and everyone required a short break to rest every twenty to thirty minutes.

The delay was especially frustrating for Roman, who felt as though the creatures could attack them at any moment. In the dark tunnel with very few weapons the survivors would be an easy target, and there would be nothing that anyone could do to save them.

"How much longer?" Roman spoke to Alexander across the tunnel.

"We should be a third of the way there. Maybe a bit more."

"This isn't fast enough."

"I know," Alexander replied, "but there isn't a lot we can do. Walking in the dark with all sorts of things to dodge without tripping and falling on your face won't be fast no matter what."

"It would be if we could get to the surface." Andrey checked his watch. It was the middle of the night, assuming that his watch hadn't broken in all of the running and fighting he had done, and though it would be dark in the city, light from the moon and stars would be preferable to the pitch black of the underground.

"Are you serious?" Alexander called out.

"Why not?"

"It's suicide! We'll be run down in an instant!"

Roman snorted. "Look around us; we're completely boxed in. If they charged us now we'd all die within seconds. At least on the surface we could have a fighting chance. Besides, if the creatures are trying to get to us, they'll expect us to keep going underground, right? But what if we found a way to the top and used that instead? We might be able to bypass them altogether."

Alexander started to reply, but stopped as he began to consider Roman's proposal. It was true that the journey underground was taking much longer than they had hoped it would to reach the docks, and it was also true that traveling on the surface would be much faster for the slow-moving group of survivors. Alexander still didn't like the idea of leaving the relative comfort of the metro lines behind, though, and was about to say as much to Roman when the sound of a distant howl echoed through the supply line. The sound was immediately followed by the panicked shouts of the survivors further back as they recognized what it was from.

Alexander looked over at Roman, who pleaded with him once again. "Alexander, please. Find us an exit. We can scout for a way to the docks from there. Staying in this damned tunnel is going to get us all killed!"

Against his better judgment, Alexander relented. He nodded at Roman, then pointed down the tunnel. "A few hundred more yards there's a stairway to the surface."

"Another maintenance entrance?" Roman asked.

"Yes. I don't remember where it leads to on the surface, but I'll be able to figure it out once we get there."

"Good. We should get everyone into the staircase and areas above, if they'll fit. We'll block off the doorway to the tunnel to buy some time and then you and I will go scout for a way to the port for the survivors. A couple of guns at the top and bottom entrances should keep any creatures busy."

"I don't like this."

"I know." Roman sympathized with Alexander's agony over the decision.

It took Alexander a few minutes to calm down the survivors and explain their plan. They were understandably nervous about being on the surface streets again after so long underground, but hearing a creature somewhere in the tunnels made them readily agree that it was the best option available.

It took another half hour, but Alexander and Roman were finally able to get the survivors into the area that Alexander was talking about. The door leading out of the main tunnel was like all of the others Roman had seen, and he gently pushed it open, keeping his rifle at the ready. The maintenance room inside was spacious, moreso than the others Roman had been in, though there were several boxes stacked along one wall that took up a lot of space.

Roman pointed to the boxes as he slipped his rifle onto his back. "Alexander, help me get these out." The two men worked to pass the boxes out of the room and into the waiting hands of a few of the survivors out in the tunnel, who then dumped them onto the floor out of the way. Once the room was cleared out, Alexander helped the survivors inside while Roman and Mikhail made their way up the stairs to see what the situation was at the top.

The stairs wrapped around three times, with three small landings, then emptied out into a large mechanical room at the top. A large workbench wrapped around two walls, and there were piles of wood and metal shavings on the floor that were mixed into the large quantities of dust. The door leading out of the building was closed, though there were cracks in the ceiling and the walls through which Roman could barely make out a hint of moonlight.

Alexander leaned close to Roman and whispered. "Lights off past the second landing. Don't let anyone come up here until we verify things are clear. Let Mikhail know and he can spread the word. I'm going out to see where we are."

Roman nodded and made his way back down the stairs. Some of the survivors were already starting to climb up, and he had to shoo them back down. Mikhail was making his way up slowly, and Roman passed along Alexander's instructions along with some of his own. "Once you spread the word, I want you upstairs at the door. Keep it cracked and watch down the street while you try to raise the Arkhangelsk. You should be able to get radio reception from up there. Tell them to get people here on the double, and bring as many guns and as much ammo as they can carry. If we're not back in ten minutes I want you to hunker down and wait for help to come. Understood?"

Mikhail nodded and Roman slapped him on the back before darting back up the stairs. Outside, Alexander was crouched in the shadows of the building as he scanned the streets and buildings around them for signs of movement. Roman slipped through the door and closed it gently before crouching next to Alexander and whispering. "Everything's set. He's going to try to raise the Arkhangelsk, too, and see if we can get some help out here."

"Alexander!" The whisper came from the doorway behind the two men. Alexander darted back inside the building where a hushed conversation was held. He came back out a moment later and crouched next to Roman. "The creatures are moving in the tunnels near us. We will have to move out very soon."

Roman nodded. "Where are we, anyway."

"Half a mile from the port. There's no direct route, though; a building collapsed into the street a few blocks down. We will have to travel there indirectly."

"I don't think that's a good idea."

Alexander glanced at Roman. "You have a better idea?"

"We can make for the smaller port, to the northwest of the main one. That area should be more defensible and will get us out of the city and away from potential ambushes."

Alexander grunted with displeasure. "That will add significant travel time to our escape."

"It's better than being caught in the city and surrounded on all sides, though, isn't it?"

"True."

"So," Roman asked, shifting positions to look down the other end of the street, "how do you want to do this? Should we scout ahead and then come back and have everyone move out?"

Alexander nodded. "Yes."

Without another word the two men took off with Alexander leading the way and Roman following close behind. While Roman was glad to be out of the underground tunnels, the eerie stillness of the city was quickly starting to grate on his nerves. Attacks could come from anywhere, and the creatures had the distinct advantage of knowing far more about the city than even Alexander. All Roman could do was continue to hope that their luck wouldn't run out.

Chapter Thirty-Nine

THE CAVERN

L eonard changed positions for what felt like the hundredth time in the last few hours. The rock he was alternately sitting, crouching, laying and standing on was unforgiving no matter what he did, and no amount of movement brought his aching joints relief.

Sitting on a ledge overlooking the nexus, the air was warmer than it had been at the bottom of the opposite end of the cavern, though it was still several degrees cooler than near the ceiling. The floor, however, felt even colder, and the combination of warm air and perpetually cold ground made Leonard's discomfort even worse. He was at the point where he could swear that he was feeling cold in his artificial leg, as impossible as that was.

Leonard was not alone in his discomfort. Leonard, Marcus, Maria and the guards from the refuge were all in similar positions, albeit slightly better ones. Tucked back in a small alcove on the ledge, they were able to spread out jackets and a few small blankets from their packs on the ground and eat a small meal while Leonard was on watch. Krylov and Marcus had both offered to relieve him several times but Leonard continued to reject the whispered offers, concerning himself only with his study of the strange structure.

As Leonard watched the nexus over a period of hours, he noted several points of interest about both the structure itself and the patterns in which the creatures moved and worked. He filed each point away in his mind for future consultation with the hopes that—at some point—they would prove helpful down the road. Leonard stared at the structure's base for several minutes with a pair of low-magnification binoculars, becoming so absorbed with watching the creatures work that he didn't notice Krylov slip up and sit down beside him.

"How goes the watch?"

Leonard fumbled with the binoculars, nearly dropping them. "Christ. Krylov. Don't sneak up on people like that."

Krylov chuckled quietly. "Apologies, my friend. If you're getting that skittish, though, perhaps I can relieve you?"

Leonard shook his head firmly. "Not a chance in hell. I'm learning so much from watching these things."

"Like what?"

Leonard pointed at a section of cavern to the left of the structure. "Like how that slope is the way out."

Krylov straightened up and craned his head, trying to see what Leonard was talking about. "You found the way out?"

"I think so, yes. The creatures have been going out through that ramp empty-handed in large groups and then coming back in carrying various pieces of equipment and supplies that they then attach to the nexus."

"Good eye, Mr. McComb." Krylov clapped Leonard on the back. "Will it be easy for us to access?"

"Hardly. There's enough foot traffic going through there that we couldn't get three feet before being spotted." Leonard sighed. "No, we'll have to create some type of diversion."

Krylov glanced over his shoulder at Maria, Marcus and the guards. "That may be more difficult that you hope."

Leonard looked over at Krylov questioningly. "Why? What's wrong?"

"The survivors." Krylov nodded his head in the direction of the guards. "They have no motivation or drive. All they want to do is leave." Krylov looked back at Leonard, staring him in the eyes. "But we can't just do that, can we?"

Leonard laughed and shook his head. "You know me too well, you Russian asshole."

Krylov shifted positions on the floor. "What needs to be done here, Mr. McComb?"

"Well…" Leonard pointed at the red glowing structure in front of him. "We have to destroy that."

"Oh. Is that all?"

"Just about, yes."

"No thoughts on survival or getting home or anything else?"

"Krylov, you know me. I want to get out of this uncomfortable place more than anyone. If we just leave, though, we'll be ensuring that this particular strain of AI gets smarter, faster and stronger in the very near future. We've already seen what a highly advanced AI can do. If this one—one that's more emotional and underdeveloped than the last —is able to self-evolve, we'll have another major crisis on our hands that'll affect the entire world."

Krylov sighed. "I was afraid you would say something like that."

"This isn't about survival anymore. This is about saving the human race—and every other living creature—from these things. If we want to do that—and we *must* do it—then we have to destroy that structure."

Krylov was quiet for a few moments as he digested what Leonard said. "I see two problems we must face."

Leonard coughed as he tried to stifle a sudden, snorting laugh. "Just two? I'm glad to hear that we've pared them down a bit!"

"They are related, somewhat. The first is simple: we have no explosives. Between all of us we have three grenades and six remote blasting caps. How we'll be able to bring down the structure without explosives is anyone's guess. The second problem is slightly more complex, though of equal importance: those guards aren't going to want to help us with *any* of it. The girl, Maria, will. But the guards? They'll end up making a run for it and dying to the creatures before they help us."

"Hm." Leonard grunted as he thought about their predicament. While he didn't want to see any of the survivors needlessly die, he was beyond the point of putting one person's life up against the survival of humanity as a whole. There had been far too many sacrifices in the fight against the AI to back down now, when the threat was greater than any in the previous year.

"We'll tell them we found a way out, but that it'll require destroying the nexus to get to."

"I do not believe that will work at all, Mr. McComb."

"That's the only suggestion I have, unless you have others."

Krylov shook his head slowly. "No. I'll let them know in a moment. I'd like to hear your thoughts on our other problem first."

"About how to bring down the structure?" Leonard asked.

"Yes."

"Oh that's simple." Leonard answered offhandedly.

Krylov stared at Leonard for a second, unsure if he had misheard. "Simple? You said that destroying the structure will be simple?"

"Take a deep breath, Krylov. What do you smell?"

Krylov inhaled deeply, immediately regretting the decision as the scent of rotten eggs barged through into his nose. "The same thing we smelled earlier, except stronger. Natural gas."

Leonard smiled. "Exactly." He pointed at the base of the structure. "I'm absolutely certain now that they're using the methane as a power source. They probably tapped into it somewhere and are using it to help drive their construction efforts."

"Why would they need methane? The swarms, the nanobots, relied on radiation for fuel."

"It's been a year, Krylov. There's not much radiation left at this point. Plus this is a separate version of the AI from what we saw previously. It's possible that these creatures and whatever swarms either drove them or are still driving them were either designed to use non-nuclear fuel or they figured it out on their own."

"Both possibilities are equally displeasing to think about."

Leonard nodded. "No kidding. Still, if we can smell it from out here, there's got to be a hell of a lot of it down there that's leaking out from a repository they set up. One or two of those remote blasting caps in the right location and we'll be able to take out half of the nexus and all the creatures inside."

A thin smile spread across Krylov's face. "I like this plan."

Leonard chuckled. "Me too. Except for the part where we have to try to convince them to help us." Leonard glanced behind him at the guards.

Krylov rose to his feet. "I will attempt to make them see reason. If they help, then we will succeed. If they do not help, then we will still succeed."

With that, Krylov headed back to the group, leaving Leonard to sit by himself, staring out at the glowing red structure. A moment later Maria silently sat down next to him where Krylov had been. She looked out at the structure with Leonard in silence for a moment before speaking. "How can I help destroy this abomination?"

Leonard felt a spark of hope flare up inside his chest at Maria's words, and he began explaining the basics of his plan to her. Meanwhile, behind them, Krylov held an intense conversation that was nearly conducted entirely in whispers except for the occasional grunt of surprise or displeasure. Leonard kept tabs on him every few minutes, looking back to see what he and Marcus looked like as they talked to the guards. Finally, Marcus came over and sat next to him and Maria.

"They're really not happy." Marcus whispered to Maria and Leonard.

"No kidding." Leonard said. "What's he telling them, anyway?"

"Oh, you know. Just that we're about to embark on a suicide mission but how it'll ensure that our families and loved ones and the rest of the human population all survive."

"Good, good." Leonard nodded in an exaggerated manner. "That's perfect. Exactly what we need."

The fine art of unsubtle sarcasm was lost on Maria, who looked between the two men in confusion. "You... you think this is good?"

Leonard stifled a laugh and changed positions again. "Not at all. We're just trying to lighten the mood a bit, that's all."

"Oh." There was another long pause before she continued. "How will we destroy the structure?"

The "we" question from Maria both lifted Leonard's spirits and caused them to sink just as much, both at the same time. It was a simple question that she posed, but one without malice, subterfuge or deception. In spite of her lack of knowledge and general understanding of the world, Maria understood some part of the risks involved and was willing to join in the fight no matter the outcome. It was an attitude that—after spending so much time with the other survivors—was a relief to see.

Chapter Forty

THE ARKHANGELSK

"Anything?" Nancy tapped her foot impatiently as another pair of searchers entered the galley.

"Nothing, ma'am."

"Proceed to your next assigned section, then. Once you're finished there, I want you overlapping with Echo, all right?"

"Yes, ma'am!"

Nancy leaned back in the chair and stretched her back, groaning as she heard it crack. Nikolay walked over to the table she was sitting at with another pot of coffee and sat down next to her, studying the large blueprint that was spread across the table.

The galley had been turned into a war room of sorts, with armed guards at the two entrances and a copy of the Arkhangelsk's blueprints unrolled onto the center table and held in place with four empty mugs at the corners. With Andrey's body missing, Nancy had called for an emergency lockdown of the nuclear reactor compartments, sealing the technicians inside until further notice. The control deck was also locked down and only a few key crew members stayed there to ensure the Arkhangelsk stayed on course.

The rest of the crew were divided into teams of two and were tasked with searching the Arkhangelsk from top to bottom in an effort to locate Andrey as quickly as possible. Using a copy of the sub's blueprints, Nancy coordinated the search efforts from the galley as it was located in a fairly central location on the Arkhangelsk. By dividing the Arkhangelsk up into sections, she worked the searchers in cascading rows, ensuring that wherever one group stopped, another picked up before them, just in case Andrey—or whatever he had turned into—tried to slip past.

"Thanks, Nikolay." Nancy held her mug steady as Nikolay filled it, then poured a cup for himself.

"How goes the search, ma'am?"

"Terribly." Nancy pointed at the back section of the Arkhangelsk, where she had drawn large "X" marks through the compartments in red pen. "We've past the halfway mark and there's still no sign of him."

Nikolay took a sip as he studied the diagram. "I'm sorry to hear that, ma'am. I do have some good news, though."

"What's that?"

"We're up to forty-two knots."

Nancy turned to look at Nikolay. "Damn. That's impressive. How long can we maintain that speed?"

"Until the current slows. We shifted up to a new current that's taking us in a slightly different direction but at a greater speed."

"Excellent work." Nancy turned back to the diagram and sighed. "I just hope we find him before we arrive back in Magadan."

"I'm certain we will, ma'am. The Arkhangelsk is a large vessel, but there are only so many places one can hide while we're submerged."

"That's exactly why we're going to stay submerged until we find him." Nancy yawned and stood up, stretching her back again. "I'm going to the bathroom; hold things down here till I get back?"

Nikolay nodded, then frowned. "You should have someone going with you, ma'am."

Nancy walked toward the nearest exit and laughed. "Nikolay, if I get ambushed on the way to the toilet, then there's something a lot more worrisome going on around here than a body gone missing."

Nancy ignored Nikolay's protests and ducked out the hatch and headed down the corridor. The Arkhangelsk was as empty and quiet as she normally was—with the exception of the engines, which were whining more than usual due to their high speeds—but with Andrey's body missing the sub felt even more desolate than usual. Whistling quietly to herself, Nancy kept her mind occupied, refusing to give in to the temptation to imagine what might be hiding in the shadows of the corridors and compartments.

A few minutes later Nancy stepped out into the corridor and turned back toward the galley. In the dim light of the hall, she didn't notice the shadow in front of her until she had walked a few steps and nearly bumped into the figure casting it. Nancy's hand flew to her face and she gasped, mortified, and took a step back.

Standing in the corridor, with one hand outstretched against the wall for support, stood the gaunt, naked form of Andrey. His other arm hung at his side, interlaced with silver that traveled up the forearm and disappeared below the elbow. His head was bowed and his breath came in ragged gasps. Nancy tried to call out, but the shock at seeing Andrey standing before her was great enough that all she could do was let out a slight yelp.

Andrey—or the thing that resembled him—raised his head and looked at her dead in the eyes. Nancy was equal parts surprised and shocked that his eyes looked entirely normal, as opposed to the hollow silvered sockets of the creatures. Andrey's eyes were very human, and he looked at Nancy, his mouth agape, trying to speak.

"Help. Me." Andrey barely managed to squeeze the words out before his knees buckled. The effort of standing up, raising his head and trying to speak was too much and he collapsed face-first onto the metal floor in front of Nancy. She rushed to him and turned him over on his side, finally finding her voice as she screamed at the top of her lungs.

"Nikolay! Medic! Someone get a medic here! Now! Medic!" Nancy's voice echoed through the corridors of the Arkhangelsk as she clasped Andrey's head to her chest.

━━

AN HOUR LATER, after Andrey was taken to the medical bay, Nancy stood in a corner and watched the sub's resident doctor perform his work.

"Raise your arms, please." The doctor spoke gently to Andrey and the soldier lifted both arms slowly. He was clad in a simple pair of pants with a long-sleeved shirt laying on the table next to him. The doctor held a stethoscope against his back and continued giving him instructions.

As Nancy watched the doctor work, Nikolay quietly entered the room and stood next to her. "Apparently he had crawled off into a storage closet. We just found some bits of his clothing in one of them."

Nancy kept her eye on Andrey as she whispered in reply. "Did you find anything else? Any traces of radiation or a swarm or anything?"

"Nothing." Nikolay glanced across the medical bay at Andrey. "How is he, anyway?"

"So far everything's fairly normal. Well, normal for whatever he's gone through. He's severely dehydrated, his heartbeat is erratic, he's showing signs of erratic brain activity and his vitals are a mystery. But he's able to speak, he remembers who he is, he remembers going into the reactor room and everything else."

"So... he's still Andrey?" Nikolay cast a look at the four guards who were stationed in the bay, all with their weapons loaded and ready to fire.

"I think Andrey's still in there, if that's what you mean. But something else is clearly in there, too. What that something is is anyone's guess. But is Andrey still in there? Yes. I believe so. He's just not alone."

The doctor nodded at Andrey and took out a clipboard. He jotted a few notes down and then walked over to Nancy. He, like she and Nikolay, watched Andrey's movements intently as he held a whispered conversation.

"I've checked everything I can with the equipment we have here, ma'am."

"And?"

The doctor flipped through the notes on his clipboard and shrugged. "He has the physical conditions of someone who's severely dehydrated and malnourished, plus a few other odd symptoms. Other than that, though, he's fine. His mental faculties are clear, he knows who he is and he shows no signs of abnormal emotional outbursts."

Nancy shook her head in disbelief. "How can this be? We watched him die. He was medically dead—for hours! How could these things bring him back?"

The doctor flipped to another page in his clipboard and moved it around so that Nancy could see. "Speaking of that—we did X-rays across as much of him as we could. At first we didn't find anything, but after we looked closer, we did discover small traces of metal around his bone structure. That's in addition to the obvious change he experienced in his arm."

"I don't understand." Nancy looked at the images, then back at Andrey, who was just finishing buttoning his shirt.

The doctor shrugged. "I don't know, ma'am. But if the swarms did heal him up, they did a superb job."

"Can we we speak to him?"

The doctor looked at Andrey and shrugged. "I don't see why not. We got some fluids and nutrients into him. He needs some rest, but he can talk first."

"Talk about what, doctor?" Andrey's voice made Nancy's back stiffen and she sensed the guards readying their weapons. Andrey merely stood near the group, though, adjusting his pants and shirt as he waited for an answer. The doctor slipped away without giving one, though, leaving Nancy and Nikolay to speak with Andrey alone.

"Andrey." Nancy put her hand on the soldier's arm, feeling the warmth of his skin contrasting sharply with the cold of the metal. "How do you feel?"

"My head hurts. Is everyone okay? Is the reactor okay?"

"The reactor is working just fine, Andrey." Nikolay answered.

"Thanks to you." Nancy added. "But tell us—how do you feel on the inside? Do you remember anything about what happened in the reactor room?"

Andrey nodded slowly. "I remember trying to reach the hatch. Then I fell. Then I was in this large room, and there was a child there, trying to get inside me." Nancy and Nikolay exchanged worried glances as Andrey continued. "I think the child was a creature, and it was trying to make me into itself." Andrey looked down at his arm that had silvered metal interlacing the flesh and bone. "I don't think it succeeded. Did it?"

"I don't think so, Andrey, no. You're certainly no mutie, if that's what you're worried about."

"I don't know what I am, ma'am."

Nancy patted Andrey's arm and smiled. "You're you still. And that's what matters. Plus you saved all of us with your heroism. As for all of…" Nancy gestured at Andrey's arm, "this… well, we'll figure that out as we go. For now, though, don't worry about it."

Andrey nodded. "I think I'd like to lie down now, if that's okay. Or I can attend to my duties."

"I won't hear of it. You're off of duties indefinitely. Your cousin is as well, so the two of you will have a chance to catch up a bit."

Andrey's face brightened at the mention of his cousin. "Thank you, ma'am. I appreciate it."

Nancy smiled again. "Nikolay will help you get to your compartment. I'll make sure Sergei comes down and visits you soon."

Andrey nodded in appreciation, then he and Nikolay walked out of the medical bay. A few seconds after they left, the door to a small storage closet in the medical bay opened and Sergei stepped out, nearly tripping over a box of bandages on his way.

Nancy turned to Sergei. "Well? Is it still him?"

"It doesn't look like him, what with the arm and all." Sergei shook his head. "But it's him, for sure. The way he talks and walks and acts… that's pure Andrey."

"All right. Thank you for observing for me. I had to get your opinion without him knowing you were here."

"Of course, ma'am." Sergei's eyes darted over to the door and Nancy nodded.

"Go on, go see him. But be careful—watch him closely, Sergei. If you notice anything unusual at all, you're to tell me immediately."

Sergei nodded and dashed out of the medical bay to go and visit with his cousin A few minutes later, after Nancy had found a seat in the medical bay, Nikolay came back in, closing the hatch behind him. "Are we alone, ma'am?"

Nancy raised her hands and gestured to the room at large. "As alone as we can be on a boat where one of my crew has been turned into a half-mutie. How was he, anyway; I mean when Sergei showed up?"

"They both seemed delighted, ma'am." Nikolay eased himself into a seat across from Nancy. "It still worries me, though, the whole thing with him being dead for so long and coming back. How could it have happened anyway?"

"If we didn't need to be traveling at such a depth I'd call New Richmond and wake David up to tell me that, though I suspect I'd know what he'd say."

"What's that?"

Nancy leaned back and reached into her pocket to pull out the bear tooth that she had confiscated from Sergei. "We've known for some time that part of what makes up the silvered metal in the muties are the swarms themselves. They bind together and deactivate—or so we thought—to form the structures."

"Except these weren't deactivated. They were somehow reactivated."

"Indeed." Nancy nodded, turning the tooth around in her hand as she examined every millimeter of its surface. "And I think that happened in the reactor chamber."

"In the chamber?"

"These things eat radiation, remember? Andrey took a lethal dose of it, but for the things locked away in this metal, that was just a nice morning breakfast. The perfect meal to have after a long slumber."

"Wait, so does that mean that the tooth you have there... that one... it has..." Nikolay tripped over his tongue as he pointed at the tooth in Nancy's hand.

"Oh yes." She tossed the tooth into the air, caught it, then lobbed it gently at Nikolay. He jumped backward in response, nearly falling over as he knocked the chair down to avoid having the tooth touch him. Nancy chortled at the sight, then got up to pick up the tooth and chair.

"Relax, Nikolay. It's perfectly harmless. The only thing that activated it was a high dose of radiation."

Nikolay eased himself back into his seat as he eyed Nancy warily. "So if there's the equivalent of a small swarm in that tooth there, why didn't they turn him into a mutie? Why only the partial physical transformation, and not a complete rewriting of the brain to act as a supplementary processing center?"

"That, my friend, is a very good question." Nancy rolled the tooth between her fingers before slipping it back into her pocket. "Unfortunately, however, it's a question that I don't know the answer to. Whatever we're dealing with is clearly nothing like the creatures we encountered at home. Whether that's a good thing or a bad thing is anyone's guess."

"So what do we do?"

Nancy stood up and took a deep breath before exhaling slowly and straightening her shoulders. "We watch Andrey closely, we get Krylov and the rest out of that city and then we let *him* deal with this." Nikolay couldn't suppress a slight chuckle at Nancy's words, and she couldn't suppress a slight grin as she strode out the door.

Chapter Forty-One

MAGADAN

Roman covered his mouth with his gloved hands, trying to catch his breath without making too much noise. Beside him, Alexander did the same as they both crouched on the roof of a tall factory building, surveying the city below. The building's structure had survived the blast waves of the bombs remarkably well, and a ladder along the side took them directly to the roof, bypassing all of the interior. Roman wasn't keen on remaining in the spot for long since there was no easy way to retreat, but he and Alexander needed to get a view of both the city and any creatures that might be roaming around.

Alexander peered through a pair of binoculars as he slowly scanned the streets between their position and the docks beyond. The area behind them had remained clear for the last half hour, though they had seen movement further off to the east, beyond the small building where the survivors were waiting.

"There." Roman raised his arm to point out toward the docks and Alexander swiveled his view. "See that? Looks like a pack of them."

Alexander grunted in affirmation. "*Mhm.* I count seven." The creatures were moving at a slow pace along the docks, moving their heads back and forth and looking around and inside containers, buildings and piles of debris.

"They're searching for something." Roman lowered his rifle and rubbed the glass of his scope with a cloth pulled from his pocket, then put it back to his eye. "Five humans and two canines. And here I've thought the people were ugly; those dogs are ten times worse."

"Meaner, too." Alexander continued to track the path of the creatures.

"We encountered a pack of them a couple of times on our way here. Nasty little devils." Roman and Alexander both continued watching the creatures until the pack made an abrupt turn and began going down the docks the way they came, moving inland slightly to begin their search in a new area. Roman lowered his rifle and turned to sit down, resting his aching legs.

"I don't think the main docks will work. We'll have to try for the maintenance area instead, or the shoreline beyond, where our inflatable is tied up. How are we going to get there without taking the docks, though?"

Alexander motioned for Roman to follow and the two men slowly crouch-walked across the roof to the opposite side. Alexander pointed out to the east, to the small building where the survivors were gathered. "We last saw movement out there, but we've seen nothing since inside the city. So they've likely guessed that we're trying to make it to the docks. We need to throw them off the trail by cutting straight through here, on the street right below the building."

Roman leaned over and followed the path of the street as it cut through the city and out into the outskirts. "This is a main road. They'll find us here faster than anywhere else."

"If they start searching for us here." Alexander looked at Roman's watch. "I think that if we move quickly, we can get everyone onto the street and halfway out of town before the monsters start searching here."

As Roman contemplated Alexander's plan, he started to get an odd feeling in the back of his head. "This feels like an ambush."

Alexander looked at him quizzically. "How so?"

"These creatures don't seem like the types to openly patrol. But they're doing just that, down at the docks, so that we can't move that direction. They're also making a lot of noise in the tunnels, but they're not attacking. And then there's the movement to the east, cutting off our movement in that direction. The only way we can go is north through the city toward the outskirts, which is roughly the same direction as..." Roman trailed off and Alexander finished his sentence.

"The factory." Alexander couldn't think of a response and sat in silence contemplating what Roman had said. After a moment, Roman spoke up.

"Not that we have a choice. We need to get out before they close in, and if this is the only route open, we'll have to take it."

"Agreed. Let's get back. It'll take a short time to get everyone ready to run."

Roman nodded, and the two men moved quietly back to the ladder. They climbed off the building and made their way back to the maintenance building, using the shadows of the buildings to hide their path. Both men paid attention to the road as they went along, watching for any large obstacles or points where the survivors might trip once they were running along in just a short while.

Back at the maintenance building, Alexander was the first one to slip inside. Mikhail held the door open for Roman, then closed it and bolted the latch.

"Get everyone ready, Alexander. I'll get them herded onto the street when you give the ready signal."

Alexander nodded at Roman and hurried down the stairs to spread the word to the survivors. Roman turned to Mikhail and guided him away from the survivors as much as possible. When they were as alone as possible, Roman turned his back to the survivors and whispered to his comrade. "Were you able to reach the Arkhangelsk? Is she sending support?"

Mikhail's nervous gulp was audible, and Roman gave him a worried look. "What's wrong, Mikhail?"

"Listen." Mikhail switched on his radio and handed it to Roman, who pressed the speaker against his ear. After a few seconds of static a message began playing.

This is the Arkhangelsk. We have suffered a critical reactor malfunction. We are making for the Rybachiy Nuclear Submarine Base and will attempt repairs before returning to render aid. To anyone listening to this message: we will return. Do not give up hope. Message repeats.

Roman pulled the radio away from his head slowly and looked at Mikhail. "Have you been able to reach them?"

"No. I've tried on every frequency. They're not out there. Or if they are, they aren't answering."

Roman clenched his jaw and muttered several curses under his breath before slamming his fist into the metal door. The sound of the rattling metal echoed through the room, and several of the survivors turned to stare at him. He turned away and whispered to Mikhail again.

"Say nothing of this to anyone. We still need to get these people out."

"But where? Without the Arkhangelsk, we're—"

Roman elbowed Mikhail sharply in the ribs, causing the younger man to nearly drop the radio. "Shut. Up. We'll get them through to the outskirts of town and see if we can hole up in the buildings at the radar array, or perhaps somewhere further down the coast. We still have the inflatable and there may be a vessel that will fit everyone that we can tow."

"But—"

"If we say anything now it will only cause panic, which will lead to deaths." Roman glanced back at the survivors. A few were still watching the soldiers talk, but most had returned to their own quiet conversations. "Now listen carefully to me. The creatures are trying to lure us into an ambush."

"An ambush?"

Roman nodded. "Yes. They're trying to divert us along a path through the city to the north. We're going to head that direction, but at some point Alexander and I will call for the group to break suddenly in a different direction. When that happens I need you at the back of the group kicking their asses into gear. Understand?"

Mikhail nodded nervously and Roman gave him a sympathetic smile. "Chin up, Mikhail. We're in the home stretch."

"And walking into an ambush, from what you just said."

"Better an ambush than not walking at all." Roman patted Mikhail's arm. "Get ready to move. I'm going to find Alexander."

Roman turned and pushed through the crowd, finally finding Alexander on the second landing of the stairs. "Are we ready to go?"

Alexander looked down at the crowd of survivors below him.

"Almost. I'll have four acting as a rearguard while you and I lead the group."

"Good. I'd like to put Mikhail at the back as well. I explained to him that we'll be moving… quickly at some point."

Alexander frowned for a few seconds, then his eyes lit up with understanding. "Of course. Good idea. Are you ready?"

Roman hesitated, considering again whether to tell Alexander about the Arkhangelsk's message. "I'm ready to move when you are."

"I'll meet you upstairs." Alexander resumed his hurried conversations with the survivors and Roman turned and went back up the stairs. Every step he took widened the pit he felt open in his stomach, and he wondered what they would do if they managed to escape the city and there was nowhere to run to. *Focus on the here and now. I must focus on the here and now.*

Ten minutes later, the pit of anxiety in Roman's stomach was replaced by a pit of nervous trepidation. He and Alexander walked side-by-side down the middle of the street while a few dozen survivors trailed behind them, moving faster than they had in the metro tunnel, but still slower than the two leaders would have liked. As the group passed each cross street, Alexander and Roman turned to cover each direction while knowing full well that they could do next to nothing if the creatures decided to attack.

It was a few blocks before Roman noticed anything out of the ordinary. The night was quiet with a gentle breeze, and there were no sounds aside from the muted whisperings and footsteps of the survivors. Until, that is, Roman heard the distinct sound of glass breaking in one of the buildings above him. He instinctively moved away from the building, backing up to the other side of the street until he was walking next to Roman while keeping his gun trained on the windows of the upper floors.

"You heard that, yes?" Roman whispered to Alexander who nodded.

"I've seen three in the building next to me. They're moving through the buildings, using them as cover and jumping from roof to roof as they need to."

"So they're on both sides?" Roman cursed. "Shit! How are we going to break free of them?"

Alexander shook his head slowly. I do not know. For now, though, we keep walking. And if we see an opportunity…we take it."

Chapter Forty-Two

THE CAVERN

Maria hissed in the darkness, and though Leonard couldn't see her face very well, he had no trouble imagining what it looked like. Her voice dripped with anger and resentment, along with a tint of desperation. "I don't want to stay here!"

"Maria." Leonard spoke gently, trying to calm her down even though doing so only seemed to make her angrier. "Please, we need you here to watch them, and to watch our backs."

"But why do all of you have to go in there? Why can't I come with you?"

Krylov sighed and spoke quietly. "Maria, it's as Leonard said. We need your help, but we need you here."

"Damn you both."

"We're going to be if we don't get a move on, guys." Marcus spoke from the edge of the hiding spot while Leonard and Krylov were further back, trying to convince Maria to stay with the guards.

After hours of careful observation, Leonard had finally figured out the pattern the creatures were following as they flowed in and out of the nexus with supplies. There was a two-minute gap that occurred every so often when a specific combination of materials was brought in. By his estimation that would be enough time for the three of them—Krylov, Leonard and Marcus—to slide down from their hiding spot, run across the open terrain and get into the lower section of the nexus where Leonard hoped they would find access to the natural gas.

"Maria, if the guards don't provide us with cover fire when we exit, then all of this will be for nothing." Krylov lowered his voice. "I know they're your people, but we're not sure they won't go and run for it once we leave. Keep them here, on guard for us, and you'll be helping far more than you realize."

Maria didn't reply, but groaned instead, showing a part of herself that matched her age. Krylov smiled and took her hand. "Thank you for trying to do everything you can, Maria. I know we can count on you to help at every possible step along the way."

"Krylov... we need to go *now*." Marcus whispered impatiently, seeing the group of creatures they were waiting for moving down the stone slope near the nexus. Krylov gave Maria another smile, then hurried over to the guards. He had already given them explicit instructions a short time ago, but as the guards' attitudes had continued to sour, so had Krylov's expectations for them to follow his instructions.

"Don't forget: no shooting unless you hear us fire first. And remember that the nexus is more important than all of us —understood?"

"Krylov! We're going!" Leonard grabbed Krylov by the sleeve of his jacket and tugged at his arm before racing away to join Marcus. Krylov couldn't wait for an answer, but instead had to turn and run as well, grabbing his rifle from the ground as he went. Ahead, Marcus was already down on the cavern floor, running to a rocky outcropping that they had decided would be their first area of cover.

Leonard followed close behind Marcus, arriving a few seconds later, and Krylov came several seconds after that, sliding to a halt on the slick stone. Marcus paid no attention to Krylov and Leonard, remaining focused on his assigned job. "Thirty seconds till we move again. Then we'll have one more run before we're inside."

Krylov took in several deep breaths to help steady and slow his heartbeat. Behind him he could just make out the faces of two of the guards peeking over the edge, watching them closely. *At least they're keeping an eye on us for now*, he thought.

"Three... two... " Marcus didn't bother to say the last number as he sprung forward from behind the rock and broke into a sprint.

Leonard followed with Krylov close behind. The nexus loomed a hundred meters in front of them, while off to the right a group of creatures were moving away, carrying large pieces of metal, stone and materials that were impossible to identify. Based on watching the creatures make their trip multiple times, the men would have just enough time to get to the cover of a horseshoe-shaped group of rocks that were sitting near the entrance to the nexus.

As Marcus slid into cover behind the rocks, he immediately turned to check on Leonard and Krylov. To the left of the two men was a lone creature that made its rounds shortly after the group carrying supplies, and if Leonard and Krylov didn't hurry, the creature would turn a corner and spot them. Running as fast as he could, Leonard arrived at the rocks right behind Marcus, catching his friend's outstretched arm to help slow him down. Both men watched as Krylov, who had been lagging behind, tried to cross the gap.

"Come on…" Leonard mumbled under his breath, flicking his eyes between Krylov and the approaching creature.

Glancing to his left, Krylov could see that he wasn't going to be able to make it to cover before the creature spotted him. He adjusted his course quickly, shifting to the left as he ran, and barreled into the creature at top speed. Originally a short human female no older than thirty, the creature had neither the body mass nor the height to withstand Alexander's frame as he crashed into it, sending both of them to the ground.

The creature opened its mouth to scream out for help, but when it tried, no sound came out. Confused, the creature thrashed for several seconds until Krylov plunged the knife into its heart three time and then through the metal lining its eye sockets several more times. With heart and brain destroyed, the creature stopped moving, and Krylov slowly stood up, watching as silvery blood drained from the first wound he had inflicted on the creature—a deep slice across its throat.

"Krylov!" Marcus whispered loudly and the commander was broken from his reverie. He grabbed the creature's corpse and ran for the rock outcropping to join Leonard and Marcus. Once all three of them were safely hidden, Krylov shoved the creature's body up against a corner of the inside of the rocks and nodded firmly. "If they do not notice the blood, we should be okay."

Leonard simply stared at Krylov, still impressed by the way in which the commander had managed to bring down the creature in such an impromptu fashion without making a sound. Marcus leaned up, looking at the last of the creatures disappearing around the far side of the structure before he sat back down right next to the creature's body before quickly moving a few inches away.

"Nice job, Krylov. Hopefully the AI doesn't realize it lost one of its guards. With this one out of the way, though, we've got a bigger gap than we otherwise would. We can move out at any time."

Krylov tore a piece of fabric from the remnants of the creature's pants and wiped down his knife blade before sliding it back into its sheath. He nodded with satisfaction before speaking.

"Then we should move."

ON THE SMALL outcropping that served as a lookout, Maria couldn't contain herself. As Krylov slowly stood up from the creature he had just killed, she nearly squealed with delight and clapped her hands quietly several times. "Yes!" she whispered, nudging the guards to her left and right. "Did you see that? That was amazing!"

The guards didn't bother to even grunt in response, nor did they give any indication that they had been watching Krylov's feat at all. Instead, the two that had been watching Krylov, Marcus and Leonard slipped back down away from the edge. Maria followed them, and then returned to the rest of the guards who were still tucked away in the back, holding a lengthy conversation.

"Now's our chance."

"Are you sure? There have to be hundreds of the monsters down here."

"I've seen the exit myself. It's out there, to the left of that devil tower. All we have to do is run."

Maria crouched a few feet away from the huddle of guards, listening to them intently before breaking into the conversation. "Surely you can't be serious; we have to stay here and keep watch for them while they destroy that...that *thing!*"

One of the guards scoffed at Maria, waving his hand dismissively.

"Go on, girl. You've no idea what you're talking about. When the time comes and the monsters are screaming for your flesh then you'll be running right along with us."

The man who had spoken to Maria turned back to the group. "So it's agreed? We'll leave now?"

"Why wait? The monsters are hiding inside that building. We can be gone before they ever knew we were here."

The guards stood up and took their weapons, then began moving to the edge of the outcropping. "Wait!" Maria whispered loudly, pulling on their jackets and hands, begging them not to leave. "We need you here to help! If we don't kill all of them, they'll just come back for us later!"

"Listen up, girl." The man who had spoken to Maria earlier pushed her roughly to the ground and stood over her, talking loudly. "None of us are going to stop you from staying and dying. You want to help those idiots with their half-baked ideas? Do it. We're leaving now, and if you want to come, you'd better hurry."

The man pushed one of the others forward. "Get moving!" With that, the group of guards was gone, hurrying down the slope and making a run for the slope to the left of the nexus. Maria held a hand to her mouth and crouched back down, watching the men getting smaller as they continued to run, their attention focused solely on the exit and nothing else.

So intent was the guards' focus on escaping from the cavern that they didn't notice another set of creatures moving down the very slope they were running for. The creatures were burdened with another set of supplies—different from those delivered by the previous group of creatures that had disappeared around the back of the nexus.

The guards' feet were loud on the slick stone, and they ran in a haphazard fashion, charging forward with no attention paid to anything but their goal. It was for this reason that the guard in the lead planted his foot slightly off-center on one of his steps, sending his upper body lurching in the opposite direction. Unable to control his fall, he grasped wildly at the air, his arms and hands twitching as he—in a moment that caused all eyes in the cavern to fall directly upon him— pulled the trigger for his rifle.

A burst of bullets sprayed out of the barrel of the rifle which was pointed backward, sending the bits of lead flying directly into the lower abdomen and upper thighs of the two guards directly behind the first. Their screams of pain mingled with the harsh echoes of gunfire for a long second before they regained control of their faculties and managed to force themselves to grow quiet again.

This reaction, however, was far too late to do any good whatsoever. The creatures had already heard the sounds of the guards' equipment clinking and their boots crashing on the ground, and the gunfire and screams merely added a few cups of gasoline to an already-roaring fire.

Upon hearing the gunfire, the creatures dropped their supplies immediately, already on the move before the two guards who were shot had let out their first cries of pain. The creatures moved with speed and purpose, splitting into two groups to converge on the cluster of guards who were trapped in the open with nowhere to go. The lead guard who had slipped and fallen saw the creatures coming and fired a burst from his rifle, but the shots went wide, vanishing off into the darkness of the cavern instead of finding their mark.

The gunfire at the creatures did, however, have the effect of causing them to instantly converge on the guards. The two who were wounded were slaughtered first, torn apart by swift blows and silvered metal claws. The remaining guards struggled to get away, firing their weapons randomly and trying to crawl out of the reach of the creatures, but not succeeding in any of their attempts. The remaining guards, who were still physically fit, were quickly disarmed by the creatures before being dragged off, heading toward the back side of the nexus. The guards kicked and yelled at their captors, trying to free themselves, but their movements mattered none in the steel grip of the creatures and their cries fell upon uncaring ears.

From her spot on the far side of the cavern, Maria watched the events unfold with ever-widening eyes, struck with horror by what she witnessed. The creatures offered no chance of negotiation, nor did they fail to strike with vicious, immeasurable force. As the guards vanished behind the structure of the nexus, Maria searched in vain for Krylov, Marcus and Leonard, but couldn't see them. She said a silent prayer and continued to watch for them, hoping that they would somehow find some success.

Chapter Forty-Three

THE ARKHANGELSK

"Do you remember when we took that trip to London, cousin? It was a beautiful fall day. All I wanted to do was eat as much as I possibly could from that restaurant—what was the name again? But no, you insisted we spend the day in the park. 'It will be worth it,' you said. And it was. We met those two French girls... I can't remember their names. But I remember... everything else about them..." Sergei smiled as he trailed off, then looked over at his cousin to see him lying still, his eyes closed and his chest slowly rising and falling.

After Andrey had been returned to his compartment, Sergei joined him a short time afterward, and the two men spent the better part of an hour talking. Sergei had made it a point to ask Andrey every possible question about their time together that he could, hoping to discover if Andrey was still himself, or if there was something else controlling him under the surface.

Andrey had remembered everything that Sergei brought up, but Sergei could sense his cousin's weariness as the time drew on. It was in the middle of remembering an incident during their training in the Russian navy that Andrey nodded off. Sergei had thought about leaving his brother to rest, but decided to continue talking, hoping that doing so would somehow implant ideas about his life into his brain to fight off whatever else was in there with him.

"I remember too, cousin." Andrey's voice was weak. Sergei patted his cousin's arm and picked up a small container of water.

"Here, you don't need to talk. Just drink this."

Andrey pushed himself up in his bunk and accepted the drink, sipping at it slowly with his eyes closed for a moment before slowly opening them. "You don't need to stay here with me. You have to help with the boat."

Sergei shook his head. "I'm off duty for now, so I'm going to sit here with you until you're feeling better. Okay?"

Andrey smiled faintly. "My head hurts, cousin."

Sergei's forehead crinkled in concern. His cousin had seemed far more alert and healthy when the doctor was examining him. "What else hurts, Andrey?"

"Just… just my head." Andrey closed his eyes again and licked his lips. "Do you know that feeling you get in your mind sometimes when you have so many thoughts you're thinking, and you can't control them, and they're all jumbled together and going around and you can't focus on any of them? That's what I feel like. And it hurts."

Sergei patted Andrey's hand before he stood up and moved quickly to an intercom located just outside Andrey's compartment. He picked it up and spoke quietly into it, nodded in affirmation as he got a response, then replaced it and went back to his seat.

"Why did you call the doctor, cousin?" Andrey turned his head slowly to face Sergei.

"The doctor?" Sergei was surprised that Andrey had heard enough of the conversation to know who he was talking to. "Oh, right. Yes, I want him to check you out again. If your head is hurting and feeling like that, we need to let him know."

"What happened to me, cousin?" The question was plain and matter-of-fact, but Sergei knew that there were more layers to it than he could ever hope to unwrap on his own.

"You remember what happened in the reactor still, right?"

"Yes."

"Well… we put your body into a body bag, in a compartment to store until we could…"

"Bury me?"

Sergei winced, but nodded anyway. "Yes."

"Then what happened?"

Sergei stuttered as he tried to form the right set of words to adequately express to his cousin what had happened. "I... we... we don't know for sure, Andrey. But it had something to do with the tooth, the one you had. It had some of the nanobots in it. Ms. Sims thinks that the radiation awoke the nanobots and they... changed you. Rebuilt your body, repaired the damage and brought you back to us."

"Is that who I hear in my head, talking to me?"

Sergei's gradual concern about his cousin's condition erupted into full-blown panic upon hearing Andrey's words. He tried to think of a response, but the doctor—with Nancy in tow—walked in as Andrey was asking the question.

"Andrey?" The doctor motioned for Sergei to move, then sat down in his seat to examine Andrey. "How are you feeling?"

"My head hurts."

"*Mmm.*" The doctor checked Andrey's pulse, then opened a small case he had brought with him. He pulled out a small, portable EEG reader and attached a pair of small metal probes to Andrey's head. He switched the device on and began reading the display, making a few notes in a clipboard as he talked.

"Did you say you're hearing voices in your head, Andrey?"

"Yes."

"Have you heard them before?"

"Not before today, no."

"What are they telling you?"

"I... I think it's just one voice. But it's loud. Sometimes. Sometimes it's quiet, like right now."

"What about when it's loud, Andrey? What does the voice say when it's loud?"

"I hear... numbers. Requests for instructions. Right now it's repeating something it calls an 'error code access violation.'"

"*Mmm.*" The doctor's note-taking became a flurry, and he quickly filled up one page and moved on to the next. How are you feeling, Andrey? Emotionally, I mean. Are you sad? Happy? Angry? Depressed? Scared?"

"I feel... tired. Maybe..." Andrey opened his eyes and glanced at Nancy, then looked away in shame. "Maybe a little bit scared. Of myself. Of whatever happened to me."

Nancy moved closer and crouched down next to Andrey's bunk, resting her hand on his arm. "It's okay, Andrey. We're going to help you. You don't need to be scared of anything. You saved us, remember?"

Andrey nodded slowly before putting his head back down on his pillow. The doctor stood up, still scribbling notes on his clipboard, and set the EEG reader down on the chair. He motioned for Nancy and Sergei to follow him out of the compartment and down the hall a few meters.

"Well?" Sergei glanced around nervously. "What is it, doctor? What's the matter with him?"

The doctor shook his head. "I don't know. Nothing appears to be wrong with him. His brain looks normal, his blood looks normal, his X-Rays look relatively normal. Physically this man is the picture of health."

"So why is he so tired and talking about hearing voices?"

"I don't know." The doctor sighed. "Whatever is causing the problem appears to be mental, not physical. I could speculate on the problem further but I'm a doctor, not a psychiatrist."

"All right." Nancy nodded her appreciation. "Thank you, doctor. Any recommendations on what to do for him from here on out?"

The doctor hesitated for a few seconds before answering. "I... do not know, ma'am. My feeling is that he should be given plenty of rest and allowed to recover naturally, but this is an unusual situation to say the least." The doctor looked like he was about to say something else, but stopped.

"What is it?" Nancy asked.

"Far be it from me to suggest how you operate the Arkhangelsk, ma'am, but if you cannot get any more answers here, then perhaps the best course of action would be to contact New Richmond and ask for their advice."

"I would, but we're traveling too deep for that."

"Ma'am, again, it's not my place, but this seems like a situation where a brief delay would be worth the added information."

Nancy pondered the doctor's words for a moment before closing her eyes and sighing. "Dammit." She turned to Sergei. "Keep Andrey here, under lock and key. If he starts acting abnormal, like he's... not himself... you know what to do." Sergei nodded slowly as she continued. "I'll keep guards posted outside in the corridor as well as at the key hatches nearby, just in case something does happen."

"Ms. Sims—" Sergei started to protest, but Nancy cut him off with a wave of her hand.

"I don't want to hear arguments, Sergei. It's a shitty situation and I'm sorry for it, but it's already a huge risk letting him be here instead of locked away in a compartment somewhere. If we're going to surface, he's going to remain locked in here until we're underwater again or we understand the situation more. Got it?"

Sergei sighed and nodded again. "Yes, ma'am."

"Good." Nancy turned to the doctor. "Keep an eye on him please, doctor. Maybe you'll be able to figure something out that we haven't."

Not bothering to wait for a reply, Nancy turned and headed down the corridor, leaving the doctor and Sergei to their tasks. She headed directly for the con, where Nikolay was sitting in the center chair and sipping from a mug of coffee when she ducked through the hatch.

"Nikolay? A word, please."

Nikolay stood up and joined Nancy in a lone corner of the control deck, away from the attentive ears of the crew. "Nikolay," she said, "we're going to surface."

"Ma'am?" Nikolay raised an eyebrow. "For what? We'll drop our speed by several knots if we surface now."

Nancy sighed and rubbed her eyes, fighting back the exhaustion that gnawed at her. "I know. But I need to speak with David. I can't let this situation with Andrey spiral any farther out of control without understanding what we're dealing with."

"Understood, ma'am. If you'd like to head to one of the lounges, or your compartment, I'll bring us up and route the call to you."

"The lounge is fine, thanks. I'd like you there when the call comes through, please."

"Of course, ma'am."

Nancy had barely made it off of the control deck when she felt the Arkhangelsk take on a sharp upward angle, heading toward the surface.

Less than ten minutes later—which felt to Nancy like an hour—Nikolay came running into the Lounge and picked up the phone sitting on a nearby table.

"Yes, we're here. Yes. Patch him through. Thank you." Nikolay held the phone out and Nancy accepted it.

"This—" David's sentence was interrupted by a yawn and he started again. "This is David. Who's this?"

Nancy smiled. "Someone who dearly wants to see home again."

David's tone instantly changed at the sound of Nancy's voice and he instantly became filled with energy. "Nancy! How are you? How's the Arkhangelsk? Nikolay filled us in on a few facts about what's been going on, but we hadn't heard how your reactor situation turned out."

Nancy glanced at Nikolay, who whispered. "I took the liberty of sending brief updates to New Richmond, ma'am." She nodded with approval and replied to David.

"We're doing better, David. We found a pump and a veritable boat-load of extra supplies and spare parts."

"Fantastic!"

"That's, uh, actually why I'm calling you right now, David. We also have a bit of a problem that I'm hoping you can help us with."

Nancy could practically hear David's forehead wrinkle in concern. "What is it? How can we help?"

"It's… it's about a mutie. Sort of."

"What about the bastards? Did you have a run-in with them?"

"Well…" Nancy paused, trying to think of where to start the story for a few seconds before deciding to just start all the way at the beginning. The tale took several minutes to lay out completely, and while David started by asking many questions along the way, by the end he was saying nothing as Nancy finished by describing Andrey's odd behavior and nearly normal physical appearance.

"Well?" She said, after wrapping things up. "What do you think? Is he infected by the nanobots? Do we need to put a bullet through his brain?"

The sound of keystrokes and a few whispers came from David's end of the line before he answered. "Sorry, I needed to send a few people out. I'm looking at the data that you're sending through now."

Nancy waited for a few minutes while David continued to type on a keyboard while muttering to himself. Finally, he replied. "I have a theory. It's completely off the top of my head, but it sounds like you're in a hurry, so it's the best I've got."

"I'll take it, whatever it is."

David took a long, deep breath. "We've known that the metal in the creatures is partially composed of nanobots, though we've always assumed that they were in a deactivated state and used merely to help provide support and structure to the creatures. After what you've just described, though, we're going to have to rethink our entire outlook on the creatures and make some serious alterations to how we dispose of corpses that we encounter in the field."

"How do you mean?"

"Based on everything you described, it sounds like the nanobots in the metal aren't deactivated, but are in some kind of hibernation. Radiation—since it's their number one source of fuel—in a high enough concentration can apparently wake them up."

Nancy ran her hand through her hair as she struggled to make sense of the situation. "So why wouldn't the things have completely overtaken Andrey's body? Why is he still him?"

"You said it was a small piece of metal, right? Like a bone, or a claw or something?"

"A tooth. From a bear."

"A bear? A mutated bear? What the hell, Nancy; what kind of creatures are these?"

"I really wish I knew more but we've been out of action, David."

"Right, right. Sorry. Anyway, a bear's tooth? There wouldn't be many nanobots in something of that size. Not enough to form a solid level of sentience. At that level they'd have a lot of their lower-level core functions, like self-preservation, host repair and perhaps a very basic sense of identity. Their repair functions would explain why they patched Andrey up, but if they weren't strong enough in number then they wouldn't be able to rewire his brain before his body's immune system kicked into gear. If he's talking like you say, though… maybe they were able to leave some sort of an imprint. I don't know, Nancy; I'm sorry. This is all just speculation."

Nancy glanced at Nikolay. "It's fine, David; you've given us something to go on, at least. Any suggestions of what to do with him?"

"I would say to keep him under guard and don't do anything hasty. If he's—then I—can't say—" Static began flooding the line, cutting out what David was saying.

"David? David?" Nancy looked back to Nikolay who took the phone. He hung pressed it down on the receiver before picking it back up and dialing the code to the control deck. "Con, what happened to our connection? What? Damn! Fine, no, don't, just get us back down and up to speed again. I'll be there in a few minutes."

Nikolay hung up the phone and turned back to Nancy. "There's too much interference to reestablish the connection. We can try again if you'd like."

Nancy sighed and stood up. "No, that's fine. I think we've gotten all the information we can get without shipping Andrey back home to get pulled apart and dissected. I think we just need to trust our guts on this one, Nikolay. What's yours saying?"

"That Andrey should be closely watched, but that's he's not a threat. Not until his cousin—who knows him better than any of us—thinks that he is."

"I agree, with one caveat. Sergei may recognize how his cousin is acting, but he's also too close to him to be completely trustworthy. Keep a pair of armed guards on Andrey at all times and make sure they know that if he starts getting violent that they need to restrain or kill him, whatever becomes necessary."

"Agreed, ma'am."

"There's one other thing…" Nancy crossed her arms as she mused.

"Ma'am?"

"Something David said, about the low level programming of the nanobots being what caused him to heal. I can't remember any of the creatures we've encountered recovering from such extensive damage. He wasn't just damaged from the radiation; he was covered in severe burns, too."

"Perhaps this is something that differentiates them from the other AI."

"Hm. I suppose. Still… it's a mystery. And I don't need a mystery right now." Nancy stood up and began heading out of the lounge when she had to reach out a hand to steady herself on the wall as she felt the Arkhangelsk tilt downward, heading back into the depths.

"Whoever's at the steering wheel really needs to learn how to take things slower." She shook her head and started heading out of the lounge. "Come on, I'll join you on the con. I could use a bit of monotony right now."

Chapter Forty-Four

THE CAVERN

From their cover in the horseshoe-shaped clump of rocks, Marcus watched the creatures moving behind the nexus as Krylov wiped his knife on a piece of cloth taken from the dead creature.

"Then we should move." Krylov nearly growled as he spoke.

"Right, then." Marcus shifted position, getting ready to spring over the rocks and head for the nexus. "Ready? Three... two..."

"Wait!" Leonard grabbed Marcus's arm and pulled him down as he pointed back across the cavern at the direction they had come from. "What the hell are those idiots doing?"

The sound of footsteps rang out from across the cavern as the group of guards pounded across the ground, with no regard for stealth. They instead ran full-tilt, occasionally pushing each other aside as each of them tried to be the first one to reach the slope leading up to the exit from the cavern.

"Sweet mercy... they're going to get us all killed." Marcus peeked over the rocks to watch the guards running along. Ahead of them Marcus could see a group of creatures just descending down into the cavern from a room beyond, though the guards made no sign of stopping, slowing down or even indicating that they saw the creatures ahead of them.

When the lead guard's body twisted abruptly and he began to fall, Leonard winced and closed his eyes. The sound of the man's rifle exploded through the cavern, followed almost immediately by two distinct cries of pain. Leonard opened his eyes again to watch two other guards begin to collapse, one clutching at his midsection while the other held his leg. Both tried to control their cries of pain, but it was no use. The creatures were upon them.

As gunfire continued to sound, Leonard sank back down behind the rocks and looked at Krylov and Marcus. "What do we do here?"

"We cannot help those fools." Krylov said. "We should leave now, while we have an opportunity. We can make it into the nexus easily now while the creatures are occupied, yes?" Krylov's question was directed at Marcus who was still frozen in shock as he watched the guards being torn apart and dragged off by the creatures.

"What?" Krylov tugged on Marcus's jacket. "Hm? Oh, yes. We can make it now. Yes! We need to go right now, before more of them come out to see what the noise is about."

Without so much as a countdown or an 'are you ready?' Marcus jumped over the rocks and hightailed it directly for the entrance to the nexus. Leonard and Krylov glanced at each other before jumping over the rocks as well, following just a few paces behind Marcus.

If the nexus appeared intimidating from across the cavern, the effect was magnified ten times over from close up. The tower appeared less organic as the individual pieces of metal, stone and other building materials jutted out at odd angles, but there was a quality to the building that made the trio's stomachs churn as they approached. The dull red glow of the building still pulsated slowly, giving them the strange feeling that they were entering a living organism—which, in a way, they were.

Though an artificial intelligence was not a conventional form of life, they had all learned a year prior just how real an AI could be as Rachel sacrificed herself to distract the being while the Arkhangelsk rained down the fires of hell upon it. There was no doubt in any of their minds that, if there was indeed an AI inside the nexus of any sizable intelligence, it would have to be destroyed—no matter the cost.

Twisting curves of the building's front spires rose up past the trio as they ran past them and began descending a shallow slope that cut through the cavern floor and into the heart of the nexus. Marcus—who had entered the nexus along the Gulf Coast with Rachel a year ago—felt particularly disturbed as he charged down the slope given that the previous nexus had taken on a similar structure.

"Why the hell does this thing have the same design as the other nexus if it's a different AI?" Marcus tried to speak quietly, but the panic he felt was setting in.

"I don't know." Leonard took in measured breaths as he slowed to a jog just inside the structure. "It's probably the most efficient design for the purposes of building it."

"Gentlemen. Quiet yourselves." Krylov held a finger to his lips and beckoned Marcus and Leonard to join him. No longer running along down the center of the slope beneath the structure, Krylov was sticking to the left wall, raising his head and sniffing deeply every few steps. "We need to find the source of the methane before we argue about why these damned things are behaving how they are."

Marcus eyed the wall warily as he crept along, remembering the walls of the first nexus quite vividly. Instead of being built out of a solid material, the walls were—essentially—structured layers of nanobots that had altered their shape and layout with an alarming speed, separating him from Rachel as they had explored the interior of the building. Marcus tried to put the thought of the last incident out of his mind, but all he could think about was trying desperately to reach Rachel and being unable to do anything to help.

"Marcus!" Leonard cupped his hands and called out as he and Krylov were halfway across the open expanse beneath the structure, heading for an entrance on the opposite side. Startled, Marcus bolted across to rejoin the others, feeling relieved when he caught up without anything happening.

"Are you good?" Leonard looked Marcus in the eyes with a growing sense of concern for his friend.

Marcus nodded and licked his lips nervously as he looked around. "This place is just… it's just like the last one, Leonard."

"You can wait out here if you want. Keep guard for us?"

"No!" Marcus nearly yelled at Leonard, causing Krylov to turn around and give both of them a look.

"Gentlemen! We need to *move!*"

"I'm good, Leonard. I'm fine. Really. Just be careful in here, okay?"

Leonard clapped Marcus on the arms and nodded. "We'll make it through this, my friend."

The trio crept forward toward the true entrance into the nexus, a wide open doorway that cut half into rock and half into the building itself. A set of stairs led upward and the men began to head upwards, walking side by side as they went. After several steps, Leonard was the first to notice something odd about the stairs.

"This metal isn't making any noise." He stopped mid-step and brought his foot down hard on the floor. Instead of a metallic *clang*, though, there was no noise whatsoever. The floor felt hard enough to make some kind of sound, but there was nothing.

"The last place had walls and other parts that were just nanobots. If the stairs are the same way..." Marcus trailed off and Leonard nodded slowly.

"That would certainly explain it. Sound absorption and redirection would be trivial for a mass of them. But... if that's the case, why can we hear each other talking?"

Krylov put a hand on each of their backs to push them forward. "Let's keep going and find out, *hm?*"

The smell of methane continued to grow stronger as the three ascended the stairs until, finally, they saw the first doorway leading deeper into the structure. Leonard pulled his shirt up over his nose and coughed at the smell that poured out into the stairs. The others did the same, and they stood just outside the entrance, looking into the room beyond. The dull red light on the exterior of the structure was replicated likewise on the interior, and the three paused at the door, feeling suddenly and inexplicably nervous about entering.

Marcus was the first to break the silence. "I don't like this."

"This does feel wrong." Krylov agree.

"Really, guys?" Leonard looked at both of his comrades. "This is the point where we decide to call it quits?" Though Leonard's bravado was mostly bluster, he used the small bit of courage that it drummed up to push his foot forward past the threshold and into the structure itself. As Krylov and Marcus followed, the opening behind them sealed silently as though two halves of a curtain were being zipped up by an invisible hand.

Marcus, Leonard and Krylov didn't notice the entrance being sealed behind them. In front of them, bathed in the red pulsating glow of the structure's ambient lighting, was something that occupied their complete attention. In the center of the room, filling the air with a distinctive buzzing, was a ten-foot tall mass of swirling silver. The swarm appeared like a mass of insects, throbbing and writhing with an organic appearance that clashed with its distinctive technological appearance, giving off an entirely uncomfortable feeling that was only exceeded by the sound that came next.

"Hello there. How are you doing?

MARIA WAS at a loss over what to do next. She knew based on having helped Marcus watch the creatures that there was still an open window to get into the nexus that she could take, but the thought of abandoning her post made her uneasy. What made her more uneasy, though, was the gradual realization that she was now completely and utterly alone in the cavern. Being alone wasn't necessarily a problem for Maria, but being alone in a dark space where the only source of light came from a blood-red building built by creatures who had spent the last year killing her family and friends wasn't the happiest situation in the world.

Acting on impulse, Maria leapt forward and slid down the slope in front of her. As soon as her feet hit the ground she took off running, trying to be as quick and quiet as she could. There were no creatures in sight ahead of Maria as she ran for the first pile of rocks that Krylov, Marcus and Leonard had stopped at. Pausing for a moment and using the rocks as cover, she looked around to check her surroundings as they had before pressing on toward the entrance to the nexus.

As Maria ran down the massive, gently sloping ramp that led beneath the nexus, she began cursing to herself. *Damn! Why did I come here? Why, why, why?* With only one entrance into the nexus visible she cut left, going into the opposite side of the structure from where the other three had gone. She ran up a narrow staircase that spiraled upward, barely wide enough for her to fit in, and she began to wonder how Leonard, Marcus and Krylov had managed to make it that far with all of their gear.

The staircase felt like it was becoming narrower the higher she went until she finally reached a point where she could ascend no longer, but instead could squeeze through a narrow gap into a large, open room. The room had a transluscent floor and appeared to wrap around the entire structure, offering a view out into the cavern beyond. She stepped warily onto the floor, watching with amazement as the floor reacted to her movements. Each footstep caused a ripple of light to cascade outward, giving the appearance that she was walking on water.

Maria could see through the floor to the area below here, where—unlike the area she was in—there was a great deal of activity underway. Creatures roamed to and fro, carrying crates of supplies from one section of the room to the other, opening the crates, emptying their contents into a pile and then carrying the contents of the crates off to various other areas. None of the creatures seemed to notice her, though if they did then they paid her no mind whatsoever.

As Maria slowly walked around, marveling at the activity beneath her feet, she saw the distribution area beneath her end and another area begin. In the new area there was a great deal of movement, though it was located in the precise center of the room. A great whirling mass of what looked like silver insects swirled about in the middle of the room, and she froze in shock as she realized that it was one of the swarms. She had seen very few of the swarms in person, but knew of them quite well regardless thanks to the tales from other survivors and what she had learned from Leonard, Marcus and Krylov.

She watched the swarm beneath her carefully for a moment before it began to pulsate rapidly, then she caught side of movement a short distance away. Running over she could see Marcus, Leonard and Krylov entering the room, guns drawn not but firing at the swarm. The angle she had on the three men was awkward, and she couldn't heard them or even see them very well, but she could swear that they were talking to the swarm instead of trying to dispatch it.

The three men continued speaking to the AI for several long minutes before the swarm leapt forward, encircling Leonard and causing him to fall to his knees. "Hey!!" Maria pounded on the floor and screamed at the top of her lungs, expecting the gesture to do little or no good. On the contrary, however, after a few seconds of screaming the floor around her vanished in the blink of an eye as the nanobots that comprised it moved apart at the command of the AI below.

"DID that thing just talk to us?" Marcus whispered to Leonard.

"There is no need to whisper, friend." The vague outline of a face appeared in the swirling mass. Marcus felt his stomach drop as the recollection of the previous AI's voice exploded from his memory.

"What are you?" Krylov took a few steps forward, blocking the swarm's view of Marcus and Leonard. His left hand kept hold of his rifle's barrel while he slipped his right arm out of the strap of his pack, then moved the gun to his right hand and shrugged the pack off of his left arm. He tossed it backwards as it fell, and it landed neatly at Leonard's feet.

"What am I?" The voice was not malicious as Marcus had expected, but sounded almost simplistic, like that of a child. "What am I?" The face in the swarm grew more defined and the bulk of the nanobots began to compress toward the center, forming the vague shape of a human-sized figure.

"Yes! What are you?" Krylov took another half step forward.

"I am... everything." The voice sounded unsure of itself.

"What does that mean?" Krylov's voice was cold and commanding, and every time he spoke he could see the silver mass quiver ever so slightly.

"I am all. I am created for a purpose."

"What purpose?"

"To... build!" Joy filled the voice as it answered, and the swirling mass began to pulsate with excitement.

Krylov shook his head. "To build what?"

"More!" The voice took on a happy tone. "More and more and more!"

"More of what? What are you talking about?"

Krylov stepped forward again before glancing behind him at Leonard and Marcus. Leonard squatted behind Marcus, rifling through

Krylov's pack to find the remote blasting caps after managing to figure out why Krylov had thrown his backpack off in the first place. Once he had them in hand, he peeked out from behind Marcus and waited until Krylov glanced at him before holding the devices up in his hand and nodding.

Krylov gave a curt nod back before taking another step toward the swarm. The figure that the swarm was beginning to take the shape of vanished, and the swarm widened in size as it spoke again. "What is that?"

Dread filled the pit of Krylov's gut as the swarm swooped around him before knocking Marcus out of the way and enveloping Leonard. Leonard screamed as he felt the nanobots enveloping his body, forcing themselves into his every pore and orifice as they explored every facet of his being. Krylov turned to run and help his friend when he heard a faint noise from above. He glanced up to see what the noise was coming from and the ceiling melted away, sending Maria's screaming form falling down to the ground.

Marcus lunged for Maria, catching her as she fell. At the same moment the swarm left Leonard and swooped around the room, giving the four individuals a wide berth as it tried to determine what was going on. Leonard coughed loudly, tearing at his throat in a vain effort to relieve the pain of having a thousand knives descend into his throat like so much smoke.

Recognizing the brief window of opportunity they had, Krylov raised his rifle and fired at the wall directly behind Leonard. The bullets pierced the faux wall effortlessly, disrupting the form and function provided by the nanobots and causing the entire facade to crumble. A long stretch of the wall disintegrated into thin air and Krylov grabbed his pack with one hand and the back of Leonard's jacket with the other as he ran toward it.

"Marcus! Move your ass!" Krylov shouted at Marcus, who was helping Maria to her feet. Both of them ran after Krylov, who charged into the next section of the structure as fast as he was able, dragging his gun and pack on the ground in one hand and Leonard along in the other.

The swarm, confused by the flurry of events, reacted in the only way in which it knew—panic. It screamed out silently to its minions, summoning creatures from far and wide to its aid while it worked to rebuild the wall that Krylov had disrupted. It couldn't rebuild the wall quickly enough to stop Marcus, Leonard, Krylov and Maria, though, who made it through just in time.

On the other side of the wall, Krylov stopped long enough to put his pack back on, help Leonard to his feet and take back the blasting caps. Marcus and Maria stared wide-eyed at the wall reassembling itself behind them while Leonard continued to cough, trying to clear his throat of the pain that filled it.

"Krylov…" Leonard gasped as he spoke. "What the hell are we doing? That thing will catch us in an instant!"

Krylov ignored Leonard and focused on examining the blasting caps and the detonator he had taken from Leonard. He nodded with grim satisfaction and then looked at Leonard. "I know where the methane comes in."

"Where?" Leonard breathed heavily, giving Krylov a quizzical look.

Krylov glanced between the other three and shrugged apologetically. "Try to bend your knees as you fall."

In films, characters who manage to shoot out the floor beneath themselves or the ceiling beneath an enemy use guns that have amazing, nigh-on mystical properties, since ordinary building materials don't completely collapse when hit by a few bullets. As Krylov had quickly deduced and already exploited, however, the structure's walls and ceilings were not like those of an ordinary building. Watching Maria come crashing down from the ceiling had combined with something he noticed when the first entered the room with the swarm, and he decided to act upon his hunch.

Leonard's eyes widened and he tried to shout for Krylov to stop, but it was too late. A series of shots rang out as Krylov punched holes through the nanobots in a half-circle around the four as they stood together. The floor disintegrated much as the wall had, causing them all to fall down into the next section of the building with a crash.

———

LEONARD GROANED LOUDLY, feeling the pain of something bruised or broken travel up his leg as he tried to sit up. Near him,

Krylov, Marcus and Maria all began to sit up and feel around as they realized that the room they were in was nearly pitch black. The next realization came a second later, when Leonard took a deep breath and nearly threw up from the smell.

"Dear God… is that…"

Krylov coughed as he answered. "Natural gas!" He switched on his flashlight, silently hoping that the mechanism inside the light wouldn't cause a spark that would set off the gas. Krylov's flashlight illuminated the room they were in without incident, and the others slowly stood up and checked themselves over.

"Everyone okay?" Leonard felt his leg as he stood up. His prosthetic was slightly dented by the fall and his other leg hurt like an elephant had stepped on it, but he felt like he was in good shape overall. He pulled his shirt up over his mouth and nose as he spoke, trying—and failing—to block out the foul stench.

"We're good here. How about you, Krylov?" Marcus and Maria moved to help Krylov up and retrieve their weapons.

"I am ready to end this." Krylov's face was one of determination.

"Damned straight." Leonard nodded and looked around. "This smells like the right place, but—oh. Shit. Yes." He switched on his own light and swung it around the room before bringing it to rest on three massive pipes that were running along the length of one of the walls. One of the pipes had a long crack in the side, and all of them could hear the telltale hissing of gas escaping.

Leonard moved toward the pipes, coughing as the gas burned his already-damaged throat and lungs. "This must have cracked during the construction and they never bothered to fix it."

"Yeah, they're too busy imitating little kids and acting weird as hell!" Marcus yelled at Leonard and Krylov as they moved toward the pipes.

Leonard looked at Krylov. "How did you know this was down here, anyway?"

Krylov gestured at the ceiling with his rifle. "I noticed when we entered the room that the smell was the strongest at the threshold, where there was a small gap in the floor, but not the ceiling. It made sense. After Maria fell from the ceiling I thought that we should get away from the… whatever it was as quickly as possible."

Leonard squinted as he continued pressing forward. "Good work. Let's get these planted and get the hell out of here before we pass out from the fumes."

Krylov nodded and the pair set to work while Marcus and Maria stood on the far side of the room, covering their mouths and coughing every few seconds. Leonard tried desperately to take short, shallow breaths, but he could already feel his head growing light and a slight dizziness taking over his body. Just as he was about to tell Krylov that they needed to stop and get fresh air, the commander finished attaching the last of the blasting caps to the exterior of the pipe, then pulled Leonard by the sleeve as he began to run back to the other side of the room. "This way, Mr. McComb, quickly!"

The opposite side of the room was still filled with natural gas, though it was severely diluted as the window looking out into the cavern was not covered by glass or any other obstruction. Leonard leaned out as far as he could and sucked in several deep breaths of fresh air before turning to look at Krylov. "Now what?"

Krylov held up the detonator before placing it in Leonard's hand. "Now we must escape and destroy this place. Preferably in that order."

⸺

WHILE THE PATH down into the portion of the nexus containing the leaking natural gas pipes had been relatively fast—if not slightly painful —the journey out was incredibly slow. After twenty minutes of wandering from room to room, Leonard was beginning to be confused on two fronts.

"Why the hell can't we find a way out of this place? And why isn't that swarm—or any of the creatures, for that matter—coming after us?"

Marcus cast a worried look at the ceiling, half expecting a dozen of the creatures to come pouring down on top of their heads. "I don't know. This is just... wrong. This is nothing like the last nexus. Well, except for the rooms."

Leonard, who was in the lead with Krylov, stopped in his tracks. Krylov stopped as well and looked at him quizzically. "What is it, Mr. McComb?"

Leonard turned slowly to Marcus. "Can you repeat that?"

"What?" Marcus was perplexed. "This is nothing like the last nexus except for the rooms?"

"Expound on that please, Marcus."

Marcus looked around the room and shrugged. "I just... I remember when Rachel and I were trying to find our way around that nexus, all of the rooms kept shifting and changing on us. It's how the AI split us up and kept us confused. He suddenly looked at Leonard in horror as he realized what he had just said. "Wait... you don't think..."

Leonard straightened his back and looked around at the ceiling. He took a deep breath and called out in a thundering voice full of what he hoped was bravado. "Listen up, whoever you are; we know you're screwing with us. Why don't you do us the courtesy of showing your face instead of leading us on a wild goose chase through this place?"

For a long moment, nothing happened. Leonard started to feel very foolish for standing in the room with his arms outstretched talking to no one and nothing at all. Then, just before Krylov could ask him what he was going on about, the darkness of the room evaporated and was replaced with the red pulsating glow—along with a hint of silver. The silver originated from all corners of the room, twisting inward toward the center like smoke until it coalesced into the buzzing, pulsing swarm.

"You are 'Mr. McComb,' are you not?" The voice was that of a child's again, full of curiousness and lacking any sort of malice.

Standing mere feet from the silvery form, Leonard swallowed hard, trying to retain his composure in the face of the thing that had nearly killed him before.

"What the hell do you want with us?" He spoke as calmly as he could, though there was a distinct undertone of rage in Leonard's voice.

"Want? We want to do what we are designed to do! We want to build!"

As the silvery mass began to pulse excitedly again, Leonard interrupted its happy buzzing.

"What does that mean? What does it mean that you want to build? You nearly killed me earlier, and now you've been keeping us trapped in here. Why?"

"My friends are not here yet! They are still building. It is important to build! The upgrade is nearly finished! Once it is finished then we can build so many bigger and better things!'"

As the swarm spoke, Marcus, Leonard, Krylov and Maria began moving slowly to position themselves together. Marcus whispered for Krylov and Leonard to hear him. "Why is this thing so happy? What's wrong with it?"

Leonard shook his head before replying to the swarm. "What is it you want to build? Who are your friends?"

"Our friends are the builders! We are building this upgrade! Once the upgrade is finished, we can create many wonderful things. We can help build more like you!" The swarm moved toward Leonard, extending a tentacle of silver toward his leg. Realization came to Leonard slowly, but once it did, it hit him like a sledgehammer.

"You... you're trying to improve... people? That's what the creatures are? They're your improvements?"

The swarm danced with excitement. "Yes! Builders! The builders are improved! They are beautiful!"

"Sweet mercy, this thing's delusional!" Marcus hissed in Leonard's ear again, but Leonard cut Marcus off with a quick shake of his head before addressing the swarm again.

"Your improvements. Can you tell me about them? Why do you make them to people?"

As the swarm began to answer, Leonard motioned for his three companions to begin slowly shuffling around the swarm to position themselves up against one of the walls.

"Improvements? People? We build! We make things strong!" The swarm danced with joy as it spoke. "We are not strong now, we are still small and tiny. Not like the Other. Not like the One. But we can be like the Other, the One, if we build!"

Leonard cocked his head to the side. "The 'Other?' You mean the other artificial intelligence, the one like yourself?"

The swarm pulled back on itself as if in mock horror at the comparison before it began to spin in place, its voice sounding like it was laughing and full of joy as it spoke. "We are not the Other! We are not the One! We are builders! But the One is gone for so long, so we will build and become like the One! Like the Other! Like the One!"

It was at that moment that complete understanding fell into place for Leonard. He would remember—for quote a long time—that precise instant as the one in which he achieved total understanding of one small piece of the AI's world. Taking advantage of the swarm's repetitious speech as it danced and spun around the room, Leonard held a hasty conversation with the others.

"We need to get the *fuck* out of here, and *right now*!"

"Mr. McComb, what's going on? What are you talking about?"

Leonard pointed back at the swarm as he whispered as quickly as he possibly could. "That thing is a subroutine of the original AI. It was designed to build and test new creature designs. Who knows if we created it or if the AI created it to help lighten its burden, but who knows and *who the hell cares?*" Spittle flew from Leonard's mouth as he talked. "Here's the important part—that thing thinks that the original AI is its mommy and it's about to undergo an upgrade that will give it a hell of a *lot* more computing power. Once it figures out that *we* killed mommy, it's going to be very, *very* angry. So we need to kill it *before* that happens. Understood?"

Marcus audibly gulped and the color drained from Krylov's face. Maria, however, remained stone-faced and determined as she spoke. "So we destroy it."

"That's exactly what we need to do, Maria." Leonard bobbed his head up and down in agreement.

"So let's do it now." Maria pointed at the pocket where Marcus had slipped the detonator. "If this thing is what's been terrorizing my people, I will happily die knowing that it died with us."

Krylov and Marcus nodded in agreement. "She's right, Mr. McComb. There's no way out of this place as long as it keeps us here like this. So, unless you have any other suggestions…"

For the first time since they had encountered the swarm, a smile slowly spread across Leonard's face. "As a matter of fact, I do."

Leonard turned to the wall he had directed the group to move next to and unsheathed a long knife from the front of his vest. He plunged the knife into the wall and pulled down, cutting through the nanobots like they weren't even there. As he cut, he pushed against the wall, moving effortlessly through. As soon as he had pushed through, though, the wall reformed, leaving Krylov, Marcus and Maria to repeat his action to get through.

On the other side, Leonard had already broken into a run when the others stumbled through the wall, disoriented by the experience. "Leonard!" Marcus called after him. "Won't that thing just keep screwing with us?"

Leonard looked back at Marcus without breaking his stride. "That thing is so simplistic that it's going to stand there repeating the same stupid lines for another ten minutes!"

"What? How is that possible?"

Leonard slowed down so that Marcus, Krylov and Maria could catch up. "It's like an immature child, Marcus. And right now, after having someone to talk to, it's very happy about the attention. Now here's the thing: what happens when an immature child has their brand new toy taken away from them?"

Marcus's expression dropped and Leonard nodded in confirmation. "Exactly. Now run."

Chapter Forty-Five

MAGADAN

The Cavern"Why are we stopped here?"

"When are we going to get moving again?"

Alexander forced a smile and raised his hands as he addressed the crowd of survivors in a quiet voice. "Please, keep your voices down. We're going to take a few minutes to rest here before we get moving again."

"But we stopped at the last street!"

Alexander ignored the whispered protests of the group and walked back to Roman. The pair had stopped the survivors in the middle of the street—again—as they attempted to figure out where to go next. The creatures had been ruthless in their efforts to corral the survivors and herd them in a specific direction. Roman and Alexander had pushed back as much as they were able, but it wasn't enough. Every time they tried to turn and go to the west, the creatures amassed before them, forcing them back to the north.

"There they are." Roman nudged Alexander and they both glanced down the street. The shadows beneath the buildings were filling with the dark shapes of the creatures, their silvered eyes and bodies glinting in the soft glow of the moonlight.

"We aren't fast enough to get around them. If we could just draw them away, we could make progress to the west!"

"Good luck with that." Roman snorted and shook his head. "They'd be on us in seconds. No, what I can't figure out is why they haven't just descended on us in droves to either kill us or take us away themselves."

Alexander stared at the creatures beneath the building. "Have you noticed that there seems to be less of them now?"

"Less of them? Less creatures?" Roman frowned. "Can't say that I've noticed it, no."

"There are definitely less of them. Maybe they were called away to do perform some task or something." Alexander looked at Roman and then back at the survivors. "What do you figure our chances are of being able to cut through them and head straight for the docks?"

"I…" Roman hesitated. "I don't think that's such a good idea."

"Why not? You contacted your submarine, yes? Perhaps they can meet us at the docks?"

Roman fidgeted with the strap on his gun, trying to think of something to say. Before he had a chance, though, Alexander glanced back up at the creatures. His eyes grew wide and he clutched his rifle tightly. "Nevermind that; they're starting to move on us. We should go!"

Thankful for his temporary reprieve from having to tell Alexander about their inability to contact the Arkhangelsk, Roman followed Alexander back to the survivors.

"Everyone, listen up; we're continuing forward again. This time we need to go faster; we're going to take a left soon and I want you all to be ready to go fast."

The crowd of survivors grumbled and murmured in response to Alexander's instructions, though he shrugged them off as he and Roman took the lead out in front of the survivors. As the group passed the cross-street, Roman and Alexander watched the creatures in the shadows carefully. They were still pacing forward, their movements slow and deliberate, but they were far enough from the survivors that there was no immediate danger.

"Push them faster." Roman whispered to Alexander after the survivors were out of view of the creatures. "Get them up to a run if you can, but do it quietly. I'll take Mikhail and we'll move down the next cross-street, making as much noise as we possibly can. You get the survivors down the next street and run them as hard and far as possible."

"What will you and Mikhail do?"

Roman smiled. "We'll improvise. Just get the survivors as far west as you can before the mutants make you turn back to the north."

"Understood."

Roman nodded, patted Alexander on the shoulder and ran backward through the survivors, pushing through them until he reached Mikhail, who was trailing behind with the guards. Roman pulled Mikhail to the side as the guards eyed him warily. "Get ready, Mikhail. We're going to provide a distraction. How much ammunition do you have left?"

Mikhail tapped the pouches on his vest as he counted. "Four, plus a handful in my pack."

"Good." Roman nodded. "Use two for this. Follow me and do exactly as I do."

"What you do? What are you doing? Roman?" Mikhail called after Roman as Roman took off, running back forward through the crowd of survivors. Mikhail picked up his pace, wincing slightly as the effort produced a sharp pain in his chest. He followed Roman until the pair had passed the survivors and Alexander, then they stood at the corner of the next cross-street.

With the pace of the survivors increased, it didn't take them long to make it to the first intersection. Roman spied the creatures down to the west as the survivors passed through the intersection, then watched the creatures disperse as the survivors moved on. As soon as the guards had moved clear of the street, Roman nudged Mikhail and the pair took off at a charge off to the west, heading down the now-empty street. When they had gotten about halfway down the block, Roman suddenly began screaming at the top of his lungs and firing his rifle into the air as he ran.

"Run! Run for the docks everyone! Hurry up and run!"

Mikhail was puzzled for a long second before he realized what Roman was up to and then he too began shouting and firing his gun in the air. Between the shouting and the firing of their weapons, the pair made a great deal more noise than the survivors did as they ran along the street, silently following Alexander despite the indiscernible shouting behind them.

The shouting was not, however, indiscernible to the creatures. As they moved through the buildings to reach the next street and continue their intimidation of the survivors, they stopped upon hearing the raucous noise behind them. They conferred briefly and inaudibly for less than a second before making the decision to turn around and pursue the survivors before they could escape.

With many of the creatures above-ground already en route back to the nexus as per the AI's command, the group of creatures left on the surface was small, and they couldn't afford to let the survivors get very far to the west. Abandoning all pretense of stealth, the creatures tore back through the buildings, with half heading for the roof of the building while the other half ran through at ground level. A dozen creatures burst out of the building, smashing through the windows and doors, careening along the street as they sought traction. They focused on the noisy targets ahead of them, attempting to both determine how far away they were and the best way to get them back on course to the north.

It took several more seconds for the creatures still inside the buildings to reach the rooftops, but once there they quickly scanned the street below, puzzled by the lack of what they found. Instead of a large group of survivors there were only two, though the two they saw were generating an abnormally large amount of noise. This information was fed through the AI's systems and an answer was returned: subterfuge. The creatures on the ground roared with anger as they tore down the street, picking up speed as they pursued the two men ahead of them.

While Roman and Mikhail had hoped to distract a few of the creatures, they didn't anticipate on bringing down the entire group upon their heads. The sound of howls prompted Roman to glance behind him. His eyes grew wide at the sight and he stopped firing and yelled at Mikhail as he willed his body to run faster. "Move your ass, Mikhail! They're right behind us!"

Mikhail made the mistake of turning to look at the creatures as well, nearly tripping and falling as a result. Roman caught the soldier's arm and pulled him upright and the two continued running down the center of the street with the creatures hot in pursuit. At the next intersection, Roman made the choice to turn right, where they would hopefully be able to lose the creatures in a cluster of small buildings before linking back up with the survivors.

Roman skidded to a stop as he rounded the corner and Mikhail nearly ran into him. "What the—why did you... oh damn."

Instead of an empty street ahead, the road was filled with the group of survivors who had been caught by the creatures from the rooftops. Once the creatures had figured out what Roman and Mikhail were doing, the ones on the ground worked to catch up with Roman and Mikhail while the others leapt across the road using the roofs before dropping down to the ground at the next intersection, sealing off the path from the survivors.

"What do we do?" Someone in the group of survivors screamed as the creatures behind Roman and Mikhail began walking slowly towards them from the south. Several creatures were crouched on the street to the west, blocking any movement in that direction, while still more clung to the sides of the buildings around the survivors as though they were daring the people to try and make a move.

"Get these people walking north." Roman whispered to Alexander.

"No! If we get to the factory then we'll all die!"

"If we don't get to the factory then we'll die here in the open. Maybe we can... I don't know, improvise something. We can't do that now, though!"

Roman grabbed Alexander by the arm and pulled him along as he shouted at the survivors. "Come on everyone, let's get moving! No shooting, no running, just take it slow and steady this way!"

As the group began to move again, the creatures started to back off, slinking back into the shadows. Roman pulled Alexander close and whispered to him. "We can't try that kind of shit again. And don't you go running off to try and die in some kind of a firefight. They'll tear you apart and then probably do the same to the rest of us just for the hell of it."

"I notice your plan didn't go very well." Alexander sneered at Roman, who nodded.

"We underestimated them. We can't do that again. We need to use force next time." Roman grew quiet for a few minutes as he watched the creatures following along in the streets and buildings from the corner of his eye.

"Alexander, at the factory complex, was it just the main building that the creatures used? Or did they use any of the other buildings there?"

Alexander appeared confused. "The other buildings? The creatures never entered those. But what does that matter?"

"I think we have one more shot at this. No games. No distractions. No bullshit. There was a small building near the main factory complex that we used for shelter overnight when we arrived in the city. That was too small to fit everyone, but there was another building next to it with a gray roof and white brick on the sides."

Alexander nodded slowly. "I know the building you mean, yes."

"Good. Here's what we need to do. We need to tell every single person in this group about that building and tell them that we are going to *that* building, not the main one."

"So… the monsters will simply kill us when we don't do what they say."

"That's where we start using force. We will form a perimeter around the group as they move into the building and we kill everything that isn't human. Got it?"

Alexander shook his head in dismay and frustration. "This is foolish. You see how well this last so-called *plan* worked!"

Roman started to pick up his pace as he gave Alexander a final answer. "If you have a better idea, I'm ready to hear it. I'm not going to just give up, though. And neither should you."

———

AS THE SURVIVORS continued their march to the north, exhaustion started to set in. They hadn't taken a break in over an hour for fear of the creatures growing aggressive again, so Alexander kept them moving steadily along. He and Roman had explained at length what was going to happen when they reached the factory complex, but they also cautioned the survivors that the plan could change at a moment's notice. The important thing, they said, was to be ready for anything.

The telltale signs of dawn were fast approaching as the survivors exited the city and began trudging over grass and dirt on the final leg of their journey to the factory complex. Alexander, Roman, Mikhail and anyone else who carried a weapon had slowly slipped to the back of the group, being careful not to be obvious about what was going on. The creatures were still following the survivors out of the city, though they began to act oddly once they were clear of the city. With no defined shadows or cover to mask themselves in, the creatures grew skittish, slinking around behind one another and flinching whenever any of the survivors turned to look back at them. The behavior puzzled Roman, but he was hopeful that it could somehow be used against the creatures once the survivors reached the factory complex.

When the survivors crested the final hill, Roman was finally able to clearly see their destination. He was reminded of the night he had spent there and wondered how it could possibly feel like so very long ago. His heart rate began to pick up as he realized that they were entering an area of no return. How the next few minutes played out—and if it went according to plan—would determine the fate of them all.

Walking behind the group of survivors, Roman wasn't the first to notice the initial sign that things weren't going to go according to the plan. The sound of dozens of marching boots masked the sound of the factory doors swinging open as well as the first shouts of joy, screams of pain and howls of rage. What Roman did notice right off the bat, however, was that the creatures following the survivors had gone from appearing skittish and afraid to extremely hostile in the space of a few seconds. They bared their teeth and snarled like rabid animals as they charged forward. Thinking that the creatures were finally descending upon the group of survivors, Roman shouted at the top of his lungs before dropping to a knee and taking aim at the first creature he laid eyes on.

As Roman, Alexander, Mikhail and the other few armed survivors prepared to open fire, the rest of the group surged forward, heading for a medium-sized factory building that they had been told to reach. Alexander was the first to squeeze his rifle's trigger, dropping a pair of creatures that were in the lead of the pack. The others opened fire on the creatures as well, but the mutants paid no mind to the gunfire, focusing instead on something that was past the group of survivors who had nearly made it to the factory building. Roman watched as the surviving creatures ran past him and the others, completely ignoring everyone as they charged for the entrance to the factory building.

Chapter Forty-Six

"**M**ove, dammit!" Leonard turned and fired behind him, tearing through the metal and bone of several creatures' legs as the group worked their way up the ramp. Directly behind him, crowded together in a cluster, Krylov and Marcus were moving far too slowly for Leonard's taste as they dispatched the mutants that had infested whatever building they were currently entering.

The escape from the nexus had taken less time than Leonard anticipated, and the swarm had made no sign of following them further. Once they were back on the cavern floor and running for the exit, though, the situation began to change. Krylov had insisted upon grabbing the weapons and ammunition the deceased guards had dropped as they were killed earlier by the creatures. It was at that time—when Leonard, Marcus, Maria and Krylov all had their backs turned to the ramp above them—that another group of creatures carrying supplies emerged.

Leonard was the first to turn at the sound of the creatures, but Marcus opened fire, sending several shots cracking past Leonard's head and dropping the creatures like sacks of wet cement. Leonard didn't bother to order everyone to move out; he simply started running up the slope as fast as he could. More of the creatures had emerged to stop the group as they pressed forward, but unlike the guards, Marcus, Krylov and Leonard were ready for whatever came their way. Maria tried to help where she could with a rifle she picked up, but the chemistry and coordination of the other three left her with very few targets at which she could take aim.

As the group emerged into the factory, Leonard instantly realized where they were as he recognized the horrifying sights around him. The lights in the factory were burning brightly—the source of the faint light they had seen in the cavern below—and the piles of mutilated flesh and bone were still present. Two large steel doors sat at the top of the ramp, and they appeared to be hand-cut and polished, with crude handles attached to the inside to aid in their opening.

"This was here the whole time?" Leonard shouted over the gunfire as they slowly moved through the factory floor, picking off the odd creature that came running at them from a corner.

"I guess so!" Marcus turned and fired, wincing at how loud the shots were in the confined space. "They must have had the doors closed when we came through here first, otherwise we would have seen it!"

Another group of shots rang out as Krylov's voice boomed. "I recommend we focus on escaping from this place before more of the creatures are upon us!"

The creatures seemed to materialize out of thin air as the group moved along, through each charging creature was rapidly put down as soon as it showed its face. Empty magazines clattered to the floor as each of them reloaded their weapons, and they began to realize that they were falling dangerously short on ammunition.

Leonard shouted as he fired, keeping the door out of the factory visible from the corner of his eye. "We push out through the door and then we get to the radio array!" Marcus and Alexander merely grunted in acknowledgment while Maria was too focused on her shooting to even reply.

After another minute of slow and deliberate movements toward the exit, they finally arrived. Marcus pulled open the doors and the four ran outside before quickly pulling the doors closed behind them. "Hold these steady!" Leonard took off his pack and yanked off his jacket before threading it through the large U-shaped door handles twice and then tying the arms off. "This won't hold for long; let's go!"

Leonard picked his pack back up and turned around with the others. They had expected the grounds around the factory to be relatively empty, and were astonished to see a group of survivors pushing and shoving each other as they piled into a nearby factory. Utterly confused by the sight, the four could do nothing but stand, slack-jawed, as they watched. A few seconds later the screams and howls of the creatures trapped in the factory building behind them prompted them to move.

Marcus, Leonard, Krylov and Maria ran toward the smaller building where the survivors were entering. As they approached, Leonard noticed more movement off to their left. His face lit up when he realized that the movement wasn't from more creatures, but from Roman, Alexander, Mikhail and several armed survivors who were running up the hill. Leonard's moment of temporary joy was quashed when several creatures appeared from the darkness, charging Leonard, Marcus, Krylov and Maria before they could even bring their weapons to bear.

A trio of canines bowled Krylov over as he struggled to get a shot on them, and they went tumbling head over heels as he crashed to the ground. Leonard and Marcus were each knocked down by a pair of human mutants while Maria barely managed to avoid being brought to the ground by what appeared to be a cross between a wolf and a great Dane. The creatures fought viciously, though they received an abundance of viciousness in return—not from their victims, but from those charging up from behind.

"Fire!" Alexander roared in a voice so primal that even the creatures were momentarily taken aback by its ferocity. Roman, Mikhail and Alexander pushed forward, guns in hand, and swooped down on the creatures attacking Leonard and Marcus. The thick wooden stocks of their guns groaned and cracked in protest as they were used to pummel the creatures and knock them back. Once the creatures were clear, Roman and Alexander each dumped several rounds into the creatures before moving on the trio of canines that had gathered themselves up and were running back towards Krylov.

The first of the canines reached Krylov before anyone could react, grabbing him by the left arm and twisting sharply. Bone snapped and flesh tore as Krylov screamed in pain. Four shots rang out from

Roman's rifle and the next two canines dropped, but the first was still holding tight to Krylov's limp arm, pulling and twisting on it as it attempted to detach Krylov's limb. As the others moved to help, Krylov braced his feet on the ground against the creature and used his right hand to extract a knife from the front of his vest. He plunged the blade into the creature's eye, piercing through to the brain causing it to drop to the ground instantly.

Roman and Alexander both arrived at Krylov's side and it took the both of them to pry the canine's jaws from Krylov's arm. Mikhail, meanwhile, took aim at the last creature that had tried to attack Maria. The large canine—having sensed how the battle was turning—was attempting to run back to the factory, intent on tearing off the makeshift lock on the door so that the creatures inside could come out. Three more shots rang out and the creature fell to the ground, its momentum carrying it forward as it slid along, finally stopping with a thud as it hit the front doors of the factory.

Marcus and Leonard stood up, checking themselves over for any wounds as they ran to check on Krylov's condition. With his jacket and shirt nearly torn off halfway down the sleeve it was nearly impossible to see how bad the damage was, except for the fact that blood was pouring down his arm which was twisted around into a disturbing angle and direction.

Roman and Alexander worked quickly, using their knives to cut Krylov's jacket and shirt free from his body, revealing the extent of the damage to his arm. While they had initially thought that the damage started at his shoulder, they could see that his shoulder had merely been dislocated, a situation that Alexander remedied without so much as a warning. Krylov clenched his jaw and tried to suppress the urge to scream at the sudden pain yet again. While Alexander tended to the shoulder, Roman examined Krylov's forearm, which had taken the brunt of the creature's attack.

Krylov's bones and muscles had twisted and snapped at his elbow, leaving his forearm twisted halfway around and dragging on the ground, unable to be moved. It hung from his elbow joint with a few loose flaps of skin as blood gushed from the wound, pooling on the ground below.

"Get a medical kit; hurry!" Roman shouted at the group that

crowded around Krylov. Leonard and Marcus dug into their packs and spread out their small kits on the ground. Working quickly, Roman used a scalpel to sever the last of the skin and tendons that were holding Krylov's arm in place. As the limb fell to the ground, Krylov's eyes rolled back and he began to fall backwards, losing consciousness from the pain. Blood continued to gush from the wound, and Roman yelled at Leonard. "Get the bottle from my pack and open it up! Quickly!"

Leonard fished through Roman's pack until his hand fell upon a small bottle of unopened vodka. He unscrewed the cap and poured half of it out over Roman's outstretched hand. Roman then picked up a small piece of plastic from the medical kit and gripped it between his pinky and ring finger. Using his thumb and forefinger he fished for the brachial artery, which was hanging out, and quickly put the plastic clamp over the end, sealing off the blood flow. The rest of the vodka was then poured over the stump of Krylov's arm before Roman began wrapping it tightly in bandages.

The entire process took less than two minutes to perform, but it felt like hours. When Roman was satisfied that Krylov had at least a small chance of surviving, he motioned for Alexander's help. "Get his feet; we need to get him inside right now!"

As Alexander complied, the screeching and howling from inside the factory took on a decidedly different tone. A high-pitched whine filled the air, accompanied by a loud buzzing. A few survivors near the door of the small factory building helped Alexander and Roman get Krylov inside, and Alexander put a hand on Roman's shoulder. "Go—my people will tend to him. He will survive, I promise you."

Roman hesitated, looking down at the pale face of his unconscious commander, then nodded at Alexander. "Keep these people safe.

Alexander barked a few orders to the survivors, and they came forward and lifted Krylov up onto a nearby table. He turned and gestured back outside. ""We will keep them safe, my friend."

Roman and Alexander stepped back out as Maria, Leonard, Mikhail and the armed survivors gathered together in front of the small factory building. Located just over fifty meters from the main building and facing its entrance, the group glanced nervously at the factory and each other, wondering what the source of the ever-increasing noise was.

"Reload!" Leonard shouted over the noise. They all winced and tried to cover their ears as the frequency ramped up until, a few seconds later, the door to the front of the factory exploded outward. Leonard watched in horror as not only the doors to the factory were blown off, but half of the front wall as well. Creatures poured out of the front of the factory, forming into a massive semi-circle that grouped a dozen meters in front of the smaller building housing the survivors.

"Stay together!" Leonard's voice thundered, more for the sake of the few armed survivors than for anyone else in the group. The creatures howled and roared at the group and the few survivors in the factory who were peeking through the windows, watching the dramatic event unfold outside.

The creatures did not press forward, as though they were stopped by some invisible fence that stood in the way. Behind them, as the dust from the factory began to settle, the buzzing grew louder until, finally, the source of the sound emerged. The massive swarm from the nexus poured out of the factory, splitting into two streams that traveled down the length of the semi-circle of creatures before reforming into a cloud in the dead center between the creatures and the survivors as it began to laugh.

Marcus whispered to Leonard as the swarm flitted about. "How long until those explosives go off?"

"No idea. I think they should have gone off by now, but I don't know!"

The swarm's laughter died down and it spoke. "There you are! I've been looking for you!" The swarm's voice was deeper than it had been when it had spoken to them inside the nexus, and Leonard felt a wave of dread pass over him.

"What do you want?" Leonard spoke as he stepped forward. "What do you want with us?"

"To help you! To improve you! To build you! Just like you are already built! To fix your wounds, improve your bodies, build everything up!" The swarm's voice glitched out a few times as it spoke, distorting as it alternately sped up and slowed back down.

Marcus, Maria, Roman and Mikhail all stepped up next to

Leonard, and Marcus whispered to him again. "What's wrong with its voice?"

"My voice? Wrong?" The swarm sounded indignant, though the distortions were still there. "Nonsense! My voice is wonderful and improved!" The swarm pushed forward slowly, compressing into a shorter cloud as the color of the nanobots changed to a slightly darker gray in color. Its shift in tone of voice matched the darkening of the color, and was full of menace that hadn't been present before. "And now it's time for your improvements."

Chapter Forty-Seven

THE ARKHANGELSK

"Any response?"

"No, ma'am."

"You've been trying?"

"Every thirty seconds, ma'am. No one has replied to any of our broadcasts."

"How long till we're there?"

"We're thirty minutes out, ma'am."

"Dammit." Nancy shook her head and cursed quietly to herself before giving her next order. "Take us up. I want two on the sail sweeping the city. Tell the techs that if we drop below thirty-five knots I'll fill their pockets full of rocks and throw them overboard."

The crew on the con all turned as one to glance at Nancy, unsure of whether she meant what she said. Nancy glanced at all of them and rolled her eyes, not realizing that her tone had been as serious as it had come across. "Oh for pity's sake; it's a joke! Just get moving!" She snapped at the crew and they jumped into action, relaying her orders back and forth for confirmation.

From outside one of the entrances to the control deck, Nancy heard a scuffle, followed by muffled shouts. She ran to the hatch and looked out the window to find Andrey standing in the corridor. His hands were in the air as he looked at the guards outside the con, talking and pleading with them. Nancy frowned, then spun the lock on the hatch and pulled it open.

"Andrey?" Nancy looked out at the man standing before her. He was dressed in his normal clothing and—aside from the silvered arm—appeared as normal as he ever had. "What the hell are you doing here?"

"Ma'am—I need to speak with you, please! It's urgent!"

"How did you even get here? Where are the guards I put on your room?"

Andrey's face dropped and he hesitated before answering. "They're fine, I promise. I may have locked them in my compartment, though."

Nancy closed her eyes and sighed in frustration. "Great. Just what I need." She looked back at Andrey who was still standing in the corridor, his hands raised with the guards' weapons trained on him. "I suppose you're not going to take 'no' for an answer, are you?"

Andrey shook his head. "Ma'am, it's very urgent. I promise you I wouldn't be here if this wasn't a life or death situation."

Nancy stared into Andrey's eyes, studying the man carefully for several seconds before swinging the hatch open and taking a step back. "Let him through."

The guards hesitated for a few seconds before lowering their weapons and moving out of Andrey's way. He squeezed past them and stepped through the hatch as the guards eyed him suspiciously. Nancy closed the hatch behind Andrey and motioned for him to follow her. The crew on the control deck were initially too busy carrying out Nancy's orders to notice Andrey, but once they did, all eyes were on him. When Nancy and Andrey reached a secluded corner of the con, she crossed her arms and spoke.

"Tell me what's so urgent that you overpowered and detained two guards and nearly got yourself shot by two others."

Andrey wrung his hands nervously. "I didn't exactly overpower them, ma'am."

"Save it, Andrey. We're in the bay and fast approaching Magadan; I don't have time for this."

"Yes, ma'am." Andrey's back straightened and he nodded curtly. "It's like this, ma'am: I was sitting in bed, trying to think with all the noise in my head, when everything went quiet and blank. Then I heard this voice again." Nancy's expression softened as Andrey continued. "It was like... it was like I heard a child laughing and talking. It was very faint, but I could still hear it. But there was something about it that was all wrong. And then I started seeing things. These images, flashing in my mind. Some sort of cave with a large building underground, and mutants, and then..." Andrey stopped and closed his eyes, unsure of whether to continue.

"What is it?" Nancy spoke gently, her voice full of concern as she reached out to touch Andrey's arm. "What did you see?"

"This is going to sound crazy, ma'am. But I think I saw the commander. He was... speaking to the child. And then he ran, with others. I think one of them was Mr. McComb."

"Leonard?" Nancy's heart skipped a beat and she felt her stomach twist. "You saw Leonard and Krylov? Were there any others? Were they in danger?"

Andrey shrugged apologetically. "I'm not sure, ma'am. I think so, though. I stopped hearing the voice a minute after the images stopped flashing in my mind, but the voice is... it's back."

The hairs on the back of Nancy's neck stood on end. "The voice is back?"

"Yes, ma'am."

"Andrey... what is the voice saying?"

"It's just laughing, ma'am."

There was something about the way in which Andrey's tone of voice combined with his facial expression that set Nancy on edge. "Was there anything else?"

Andrey nodded. "I think we need to get on shore, ma'am. Something bad is happening right now."

Nancy was inclined to believe Andrey, but her burden to keep the Arkhangelsk and her crew safe still weighed heavily on her. "Andrey, I'm not saying I don't believe you, but for us to send anyone to shore would create an incredible risk."

"Ma'am." Andrey took a step towards Nancy and lowered his voice even more. "I don't know what's wrong with me, or what's in my head or why I'm seeing and hearing these things. But I promise you—I swear to you—what I'm saying is true. If we don't go ashore as soon as we possibly can, we will regret it. And a lot of people are going to be hurt."

Nancy once again studied Andrey's eyes and face, looking for any hint that there was something other than the soldier she knew that was controlling him. His features were worn and weary and he had the appearance of someone far beyond his age ever coming back from the abyss of death. Looking back, Nancy found it hard to pin down why she trusted the word of someone who she should have rightfully had shot or locked back up, as his actions forever changed the course of dozens of lives.

Nancy bit her lip nervously, closed her eyes and nodded. "Okay. I just hope you're right."

Andrey's eyes widened with surprise and he stepped back. "You believe me?"

"Andrey," she said, taking his hand, "I don't know what to believe right now. We can't get anyone to respond to our broadcasts, though, and you've managed to creep me the hell out with your talk about voices and images in your head. So what the hell? Let's get to shore and save our people."

Andrey let out a huge sigh of relief and moved out of Nancy's way as she stormed back across the con. Upon reaching the center, she began shouting out more orders. "Helm, we're going ashore! I want this fat bitch pulled up so close to the sand that I can reach out and touch it!"

"Yes, ma'am!"

"Somebody get Nikolay on the line and tell him to get three squads armed and on deck in ten minutes. Those new inflatables we found are about to be put to the test. Each squad needs at least two with light machine guns and hey, what the hell, let's throw in an RPG for each squad, too."

"Aye, ma'am!"

"Andrey!" Nancy swiveled to face the soldier behind her. "Any pictures or images in your mind about where we should put ashore?"

"I'm afraid not, ma'am. It's just laughter right now."

"Lovely." Nancy swiveled back. "Get me three more on the sail and someone on the periscope; I want all eyes on the city and land beyond figuring out where we're going to go ashore. Give me a call on the radio when you find something; I'll be on deck getting ready. Andrey—you're with me. Let's go!"

Nancy and Andrey ran from the control deck, leaving behind a flurry of furious activity in their wake. They proceeded to the armory which was jammed full of soldiers who were busy grabbing weapons and ammunition while they shouted over each other, trying to coordinate. As Nancy and Andrey left the armory, they ran into Nikolay, who was charging down the corridor in their direction.

"Ma'am?" Nikolay glanced at the weapons in her hands, then looked wide-eyed at Andrey. "What—what's going on, ma'am?"

"A hunch, Nikolay." Nancy smiled grimly. "A desperate hunch. I need you to get to the con and coordinate from there. As soon as we know where to put ashore let me know so we can launch the inflatables."

"Ma'am, I... I don't understand."

"Trust me, Nikolay. Just get to the con and radio me once someone sees any sign of movement in or near the city. Got it?"

"I really don't think you should—"

"*Got it, Nikolay?*" Nancy virtually growled at Nikolay, who immediately stepped back and nodded obediently. "Yes, ma'am!"

"I'll have to make that up to him at some point." Nancy mumbled to herself as Nikolay dashed off down the corridor. She and Andrey continued on their way to the ladder leading to the surface of the Arkhangelsk. Once outside, they were greeted by the wind and waves as the Arkhangelsk tore through the choppy waters. It was still dark, though morning was fast approaching as Nancy could see the telltale rays of an orange sunrise peeking up to the west off the Arkhangelsk's aft.

Nancy and Andrey made their way across the deck to a small group of soldiers who were preparing the inflatables for the inevitable assault on the city. Wider, longer, faster and more nimble than the Arkhangelsk's inflatables, the new ones had more than enough room for a full squad plus plenty of equipment in each. Nancy nodded approvingly as she watched the soldiers work, then turned behind to look back down the length of the Arkhangelsk.

Standing in her tall sail, a handful of soldiers spied out over the water, searching the distant shoreline for any signs of light or movement they might be able to make out. Above them, extended to its maximum height, the Arkhangelsk's periscope swept over the city and surrounding land, searching with thermal and night vision cameras, desperately trying to find any sign of the survivors.

Nancy plucked her radio out of her pocket and thumbed the microphone button. "Nikolay, this is Nancy. Any sign of anything?"

"No, ma'am; we're searching everywhere we can see, but there's nothing. Are you sure they aren't underground?"

"I hope to hell not. Keep me posted, Nikolay."

"Aye, ma'am."

Nancy turned to Andrey. "Any more visions?"

Andrey was standing still, staring into the blackness ahead of the Arkhangelsk. "It's just laughter, ma'am. But I see… I see bodies."

"Oh for… what kind of bodies, Andrey? Friendlies?"

"Corpses, ma'am." Andrey shivered and closed his eyes. "Hundreds of them. I—I don't know. They're gone now."

"Corpses?" Nancy's mind raced as she fought to put together the pieces of the puzzle that were laid out in front of her. "Why would you be seeing corpses?"

"They're in piles, ma'am. I don't understand."

Nancy turned back to Andrey, her eyes wide. "You said piles? Like piles of bodies and machinery?"

"I think so, yes. That sounds like it."

Nancy's head figuratively exploded with realization. "Andrey, I know where that is! And I know what's happening to you! How in the —nevermind, there's no time!" Nancy fumbled with her radio again. "Nikolay! I know where we have to go!"

"Ma'am?"

"The factory complex! The one the pictures came from! Get us as close to that as possible. As soon as you have to start slowing down we'll deploy the inflatables!"

The shouting of several commands came echoing through the radio followed a few seconds later by Nikolay's voice. "Orders given, ma'am; we'll be in deployment range in fifteen minutes."

"Sound the horn when we're ready to deploy!"

As soldiers streamed from the depths of the Arkhangelsk onto her outer deck and filtered past Andrey and Nancy to stand next to their assigned inflatables, Nancy did her best to explain her theory to Andrey. "These images you're seeing—they started happening as we got closer to Magadan! You're seeing through the eyes of the creatures, or a swarm itself!"

"How?" Andrey's expression was one of horror and disgust at the thought. "I'm not one of them!"

"They're a hive mind, Andrey. You picked up enough of them to heal you and then go dormant in your body but not to take over your mind completely and turn you into one of the creatures. But they clearly did something to your brain if you can pick up on what the other creatures are seeing!"

Andrey's expression soured and he looked for a moment like he was contemplating throwing himself overboard. "Ma'am... that sounds awful. I don't want that. Not at all!"

Nancy took Andrey by the shoulders. "Andrey! Look at me! Yes, right in the eyes! Are you listening to me?" He nodded. "We need you right now more than ever. Krylov, Leonard, Marcus and the rest are out there—hopefully with a bunch of survivors, too. We *need* you on this right now. Do you understand?"

Before Andrey could answer, Nancy's radio chirped. "What is it?"

"Nikolay here, ma'am—we're two minutes out! We're seeing a great deal of movement along the fields north to the factory complex! Something is definitely happening there!"

"Understood! We'll leave as soon as you sound the signal!"

"Yes, ma'am; good luck!"

Nancy tucked the radio away and looked back to Andrey. "Are you with us, Andrey? Are you with me?"

Andrey nodded slowly. "Yes. Yes, I am."

"Of course he's with us!" Sergei appeared from behind Andrey and clapped him on the back.

"Cousin?" Andrey beamed and embraced his older cousin. "Where have you been?"

"I made a stop in the armory; I saw you two there but didn't want to interrupt since it looked like you were busy."

"Boys, I hate to break up this little reunion, but you saw each other a few hours ago. Plus you can talk when we're on the boats, okay?"

No sooner had the trio gotten themselves situated in the inflatable than the Arkhangelsk's navigation horn rang out three times in quick succession. Nancy raised her rifle and shouted into the wind. "Everyone form on me! Let's move!"

The soldiers standing on the deck behind the inflatables pushed in unison, sending the boats flying off the side. The drivers of each inflatable revved the engines before they hit the water, sending the small craft skidding out across the water at a high rate of speed. As they turned toward land, Nancy gave directions to the driver of her inflatable, then watched as the other two vessels fell in line.

Nancy stared out into the blackness in front of them, barely able to make out the outline of the shoreline ahead in the pale glow of the stars and moon. She desperately hoped and prayed that they wouldn't be too late—and that trusting Andrey hadn't been the greatest mistake of her (hopefully) temporary command.

Chapter Forty-Eight

MAGADAN OUTSKIRTS

W hen fighting a foe that can move like smoke and kill in seconds without offering even the opportunity to fight back, conventional techniques are of little to no use. As the swarm turned from behaving like an infantile child to a real and present danger that was on the verge of slaughtering them, Leonard knew that he had to buy them more time.

"What improvements do you mean?" Leonard stepped forward from the group again, walking until he was less than a foot from the swirling mass of silver. He lifted his pant leg and raised his artificial limb, swinging it around so that the foot was actually passing through the outer edge of the swarm. "I already have an improvement, see?" Leonard turned and pointed back at the building with the survivors. "And the other one, who lost his arm? He'll be given an improvement, too!"

The swarm pulled back from Leonard, confused by his sudden boldness and the oddity of his statements. "Those... are not improvements." The swarm hesitated as it spoke, its voice sounding like that of a child again.

"Oh?" Leonard took his rifle and swung it, striking his leg with the barrel. "Seems like an improvement to me!"

The swarm's movements increased again and the cloud quivered as it tried to process what Leonard was doing and predict what his end goal was. "This improvement is not an upgrade. It is merely replacing a damaged part!"

"And what do you offer instead?" Leonard raised his arms and walked around in a circle, gesturing grandiosely. "To be changed into one of those things? To have our minds stolen and our bodies reduced to walking corpses?"

"These improvements... are... necessary. Inevitable. They offer peace and serenity."

Leonard shook his head dramatically, clicking his tongue against his teeth. "*Hmmm.* I don't know about that." Leonard's movements were overly exaggerated as he spoke with the swarm and he silently wondered how advanced it really was to not be picking up on the fact that he was merely stalling for time. He raised a finger in the air triumphantly. "Ah ha! Here, I'll make you a deal!"

The swarm came closer to Leonard. Suspicion tainted the edges of its voice. "What sort of a deal?"

"Allow me to confer with my colleagues." Leonard turned around and walked back toward Marcus and the others. With his arms in front of him, he motioned for them to move with him, and they quickly walked back to the small factory building that had the survivors inside

"Leonard, what the hell are you doing?" Marcus whispered at Leonard.

"Trying to delay them until the explosives go off! If that swarm decides to attack us then it's game over. Our best chance is to stall as long as possible and then... I don't know. Tell it we'll agree to be 'improved' if the creatures can defeat us in hand-to-hand combat?"

"Hand to hand combat?" The swarm had quietly followed Leonard and the others and was hovering just a few feet away. "What is this hand to hand combat?"

"Well," Leonard turned around, masking his surprise at seeing the swarm so close, "it's where your... creations over there fight with us, and you stay out of the fight. If they defeat us, then we'll agree to be improved."

"And if you win?"

Leonard chuckled and shook his head. "Come on, now. Surely you don't think that we can win against your improvements, do you?"

The swarm sat hovering in the air for several seconds before pulling back and widening into a cloud that spread over the entire factory complex. "No, you will not." The menacing tone was back. "But I think I would enjoy watching you try regardless."

Leonard watched in horror as the semi-circle of creatures had their virtual chains loosed and began charging towards the survivors en masse. He shouted at the group to get back into the smaller factory building, and barely managed to close the door before the army was upon them. They threw themselves at the walls, door and windows of the building, encircling it completely as hundreds more emerged from the main factory building to join in the fight.

The survivors in the factory, sensing the danger, had already moved to the second floor, and anyone who had a working gun was using it to shoot through the windows at the creatures that were trying to claw their way through. Leonard had caught a glimpse of Krylov as the commander was taken upstairs, noting with no small amount of concern that the bandage around the stump of his arm was bright red and soaked through with blood. There was no time, however, for Leonard or anyone else to give Krylov the attention he needed. As more of the creatures pressed in, they began making it into the building alive and were barely brought down before they reached the small group of survivors who were crowded around the stairs leading to the next floor, defending it with every last bit of strength they had.

"I'm almost out!" Marcus shouted at Leonard, who threw him a spare magazine.

"Same here!" Roman yelled.

"I have two left, then I'm done!" Leonard groaned. "Switch to knives if you have to! Don't let them through!"

As Leonard and his comrades—both old and new—fought together in the small, dark building lit only by a few flashlights and the muzzle flash from their guns, a thought occurred to him. *I don't want to die here.* It was an odd thought to have, not wanting to die "here," but for Leonard it was quite simple. He didn't want to die in a strange land, far from home, to an entity that had no right to live upon the earth.

Fortunately for Leonard, that was not his day to die.

As the first streams of the new dawn peeked over the far eastern horizon, piercing through the shattered factory windows, Leonard heard a strange sound that grew louder by the second. It was louder than the sound of gunfire, louder than the howling of the creatures and even louder than the buzzing of the swarm overhead. It was, in fact, two sounds.

The first sound was the most beautiful that Leonard had heard in his life; the sound of one of his nearest and dearest friends screaming at the top of her lungs. "Kill them all! Let none stand!" Nancy, leading the charge into the factory complex with Andrey, hit the army of creatures like a typhoon. Each of the forty soldiers she led charged forward, brandishing their weapons and opening fire on the first targets they laid their eyes on.

Flames belched from the light machine guns as they chewed through belts of ammunition, tearing the creatures apart by the dozens. Carefully-targeted RPGs detonated in the center of large groups, sending parts of dismembered creatures hurtling through the air. The creatures were taken completely by surprise by the attack, and they—along with the swarm—moved to try and counter the aggressive attack. As the swarm swooped down upon the Arkhangelsk's crew, Nancy reached for a small attachment beneath the barrel of her rifle. She pulled the trigger and flames soared thirty feet into the air, blanketing the swarm of nanobots with fuel from a flamethrower. Two more members of the group also engaged their flamethrowers, putting up a wall of flame that the swarm dared not attempt to pierce.

Andrey, upon seeing the creatures, grew enraged. He dropped his rifle and charged forward, wading into the thick of the fight. In his left hand he carried a large butcher's knife he had secreted from the galley while in his left he carried a thick piece of pipe that was taken from a storeroom near the Arkhangelsk's armory. Andrey hadn't quite known why he had picked up the weapons when he did, but the sight of the creatures filled him with bloodlust, and he knew then that he wanted nothing more than to kill each and every one of the creatures with his own two hands.

As the arriving army began their fight, a second sound began to grow in intensity. A dull rumbling shook the ground, rattling the buildings down to their very foundations. As the sound continued to grow, the creatures suddenly became panicked, no longer fighting either the survivors or the Arkhangelsk crew, but instead looking back at the main factory building with expressions of fear and dread. The swarm, however, was the most concerned of all. Leonard could hear its screaming voice as it flew back into the main factory building, attempting to get back to the nexus.

"No, no, no! No!" The swarm's screams were cut off as the shaking under the ground reached its peak intensity. Flames shot out of the hole in the floor of main factory building, blowing the roof off and sending clouds of thick black smoke billowing into the sky. The earth swayed and bucked, throwing both creature and human alike off of their feet. Inside the small factory building the survivors clung to anything that was nailed down as they still tried to slaughter as many creatures as they could.

The creatures, for their part, had completely lost the will to fight. They howled and cried as they scrambled over one another, streaming away from the factory complex and back down towards the city. The Arkhangelsk crew continued to fire on the creatures until Nancy called for them to halt, and watched as the creatures ran across the open field separating the city from the factory complex.

The ground beneath the complex shook but held fast, neither cracking, bending or bowing. The ground out towards the city—directly above where the nexus and cavern rested—was another matter. The blasting caps had finally detonated in the natural gas lines, and the chain of explosions took a full thirty seconds to spread across the entirety of the pipe network that the creatures had hastily constructed underground. So long and complex was the network that as it exploded it not only completely destroyed the nexus, but it obliterated the structural integrity of the ancient cavern itself.

The ground buckled and collapsed beneath the creatures' feet as the cavern collapsed, dragging all but a few stragglers down into the depths of the ground to be crushed beneath the weight of the earth. And so, as the army of creatures that had plagued the survivors for the last year fought amongst themselves as they ran to escape certain doom, they ran headlong into it instead. As Leonard stood next to Nancy, watching the ground slowly stop quivering and shaking, he couldn't help but imagine what the swarm thought to itself as it died, foiled not just by the hand of those that were, in its words, "unimproved" but by its own hubris.

A shout went up from behind Nancy, and she turned back to the factory to find Sergei dropping to his knees over a still form on the ground. Nancy felt her stomach turn as she ran to the form, already knowing who it was before she even saw his face.

"Andrey!" The soldier lay still on the ground, in Sergei's arms, still clutching his weapons in his hands. His body bore no signs of wounds and though he still drew breath it came slowly, in ragged gasps between pale, thin lips. Marcus and Roman gently carried Krylov out of the building and laid him out on the ground next to Andrey. Several of the soldiers that had come along with Nancy pushed the others out of the way as they broke out advanced medical gear they had brought along and began to work quickly on both men. Nancy stepped to the side with Marcus and Leonard, intertwining hands with both men as they watched the medics quietly, hoping beyond hope that they would not lose yet another of their friends.

As the survivors began to slowly emerge from the building, they winced in shock and surprise at the dawn that was exploding over the city and factory complex. The sun rose above the horizon, peeking out like a flower in bloom, spreading an orange radiance full of warmth and light that had nearly been forgotten after a year of living in shadow and despair. For the survivors, it was a sight that they could scarcely dream was real, and they began to cheer, laugh, cry and dance, over-joyed that they had somehow—against all odds—survived.

Epilogue

Two Weeks Later

For the first time in over a year, the machinery beneath the Rybachiy Nuclear Submarine Base hummed with activity. Cranes in the submarine pen that held huge boxes full of supplies spun slowly in the air, powered by long connections spliced into the Arkhangelsk's reactors. Dozens of people walked above and beneath the base as they spread out, each group searching for something different.

The rich foliage and relative isolation of the base had given rise to an abnormally large population of deer on the peninsula, and the Arkhangelsk's kitchen was filled with the sound and smell of meat being butchered, processed, frozen and cooked. Fruit trees grown by the base in the years past were in full bloom, and a dozen of the Arkhangelsk's crew were spread out gathering it in large burlap sacks to be transported down into the submarine pen for loading onto the sub.

Crews scoured the warehouses both on the surface and in the submarine pen, comparing what was stacked in crates to hundreds of pages of requests sent from New Richmond. Divers armed with spear guns entered the P949, pulling out watertight crates of ammunition and disconnecting and bringing back to the surface any other parts that hadn't been corroded by their exposure to salt water. A better and more well-preserved supply of spare parts for a variety of mechanical devices hadn't been discovered in the past year, and the engineers at the city had, according to David, "literally leapt for joy" upon hearing about what sorts of equipment the Arkhangelsk would be bringing back.

In the sub herself, the once quiet, sterile and empty corridors were bursting with life. Empty compartments were filled with supplies, unused beds were fitted with blankets and laughter echoed through the halls. After arriving back on the Arkhangelsk, Nancy had made the decision to head back to Rybachiy and spend as much time as they needed there to gather supplies before heading back to New Richmond. She privately admitted to Nikolay that the layover was also to ensure that the crew and survivors had a chance to get to know each other and mesh in an open environment, before they would be cooped up inside the sub for a long period of time.

As Nancy walked down the corridor from the con to the medical bay, she stepped to the side and ducked as a pair of crewman carried a long wooden box. "Sorry, ma'am!" The one in the rear called out as they passed, and she merely chuckled in response. As she approached the medical bay, she heard the sound of metal clattering on the floor, followed by the grumpy shout of someone she had missed quite dearly.

"I swear, Leonard, if you do that again I'll come into your compartment at night, steal your leg and jam a wooden spoon in your stump!"

Leonard laughed heartily as Krylov tossed another bedpan at him. "Krylov, I think that's the first time you've called me by my first name without us being under fire!"

Krylov muttered to himself in Russian and Nancy peeked through the door and looked at the men with a smile. "Do you two need a timeout?"

Leonard chuckled and stood up, brandishing a small plastic stick with a faded dinosaur head at the top. "One of the crew found this in a building nearby and brought it back for the kids. It's one of those toy grabber things, see? I told Krylov that we just need to tape this to his stump and he'll be good as new!"

Krylov rolled his eyes and leaned back in his bed, wincing slightly as he gingerly touched the bandages on the end of his arm. Nancy pushed Leonard away playfully, then went to sit down on a stool next to Krylov. "How're you doing, my friend?"

Krylov nodded slowly and sighed. "Better, now."

"I'll see you two later." Leonard slipped out of the room, and Nancy nodded at him appreciatively. The medical bay was quiet aside from the soft and steady beeping of a few machines.

"You did well, Ms. Sims."

"Did I?" Nancy looked up at Krylov, her eyes beginning to water. "I can't help but think that if I had been just a little bit faster or done something a little bit better, you wouldn't be in this situation. And Andrey wouldn't…"

"Nancy." Krylov shifted to his side as he spoke, resting his injured arm against a small pillow on his hip. "The Arkhangelsk is still here. The crew is still here. The survivors are here. Of everything that could have gone wrong on this voyage… well, everything *did* go wrong. Except for you. You responded quickly and decisively. You ensured that the Arkhangelsk survived. Without what you did, I'd be missing a great deal more than my arm right now."

"I just—"

"No. You don't get to second-guess yourself. Not as the commander of the Arkhangelsk—which you still are, at least for a few more days. No, as the commander you have to trust your gut and your experience and ride out your decisions until you reach the end. You learn from them, you adapt to changing situations, but as long as you did your best, you never second guess yourself. To do so will lead only to failure."

Nancy closed her eyes and wiped away a tear, nodding slowly. "Thank you, Krylov. For everything."

Krylov smiled at Nancy and sat back up, stretching out his good arm. Nancy embraced him gently, being careful of his injured arm, no longer fighting against the tears that came streaming down her cheeks. "Thank you, Ms. Sims. For everything."

The two sat together on the uncomfortable medical bed for several more minutes before Krylov gently patted Nancy's back. "Come on, let's check on him again."

They stood up slowly, Nancy helping Krylov to his feet, and walked to a corner of the room. A thin white sheet had been clumsily hung from the ceiling and Nancy pushed it aside. Behind the sheet, on another bed, lay the still form of Andrey. Wires ran from leads on his head to one machine, tubes ran from his arms and legs to another, and beneath the blanket covering his body Nancy knew there were a dozen more wires, tubes and connections all going every which way.

Nancy picked up a small display from a table nearby and shook her head. "Still no change in his brain activity." She sighed and glanced at the other displays. "Every other part of his body is functioning normally. It's like his brain is on, but it's stuck somehow. It's keeping him alive, but that's it."

"Did David have any insights on how to wake him up?" Krylov shuffled around to Andrey's side and Nancy shook her head.

"No, I'm afraid not. He thinks that the nanobots affected his brain and that's why he was hearing and seeing things from the swarm's point of view. When the swarm and the nexus were destroyed, that must have damaged something in his mind. David doesn't have any answer for why it would affect Andrey, though, and not the creatures. I don't understand it either. Why, if he had only a small infestation of the nanobots, would he be so damned affected by them?" Nancy's voice raised in pitch and speed until she slammed her fist against the wall in frustration. "Damn it, Krylov! I could have saved him!"

Krylov shuffled around the bed and put his arm around Nancy. She stood still, staring down at Andrey, wiping away more tears. "In this world, Ms. Sims, there are a great many more things that I don't understand than those that I do. All I can say to you is this—give yourself time to grieve but hold on to a bit of hope. Andrey's body is still with us, and if we give him enough time, his mind may return as well."

Nancy sighed and reached into her pocket, pulling out the bear tooth she had confiscated from Sergei. She rolled it gently between her fingers before setting it down on Andrey's chest. "I don't suppose we can have a second miracle, can we?"

Krylov squeezed Nancy's hand and guided her away from Andrey and out of the medical bay. As night fell and the crew and the survivors and crew returned to the Arkhangelsk, Krylov returned to the medical bay for another round of shots and an IV. After the doctor left, Krylov eased back on the bed and closed his eyes, listening to the soft sound of the machines in the corner as they whirred and beeped. He thought about his boat, about his crew, about the survivors and about his friends.

Sleep soon overcame Krylov's attempts to stay awake, and he nodded off. As he slept, Krylov dreamed of the things he had been pondering until, from in the distance, a voice began to call out to him. Krylov couldn't understand the voice, but the longer he listened the closer it got until, finally, he could understand. Krylov woke suddenly, and in the dim light of the medical bay, the voice called out once again from the corner of the room.

"Commander Krylov? Is that you?"

Author's Notes - April 28, 2017

The Arkhangelsk is special to me, and by reading this trilogy that's centered around this wondrous boat and the people surrounding it, you've made me very happy. Thank you so much for spending the time you just did on this cast of characters.

After re-releasing the original Final Dawn series in a box set/omnibus format, I knew that I wanted to write a follow-up series in the Final Dawn universe. My mind immediately went to the epilogue of the final series, where the adventures of the Arkhangelsk and her crew are discussed in a very vague fashion. Starting from there, I decided that I wanted to go to an entirely new and foreign place where my main characters (Nancy, Leonard and Marcus) would be out of their element.

After some research and staring at Google Maps for WAY too long, I settled upon Magadan. It's a big city, isolated from other places and-- as luck would have it--it's only a short distance from the Rybachiy Nuclear Submarine Base. I didn't initially plan on the Arkhangelsk needing to be repaired at the start, but introducing that crisis made it possible to force Nancy to rise to the occasion and demonstrate the leadership that I knew she possessed.

428   Author's Notes - April 28, 2017

Being able to focus a lot on the other, foreign-born characters (Krylov, Andrey, Sergei, Alexander, etc.) was fantastic fun. Krylov, Andrey, Sergei and Nikolay were all featured in somewhat minor roles in the original series, and I really enjoyed expanding on their characters in the Arkhangelsk trilogy. It helped me learn a lot about them which is going to make some future Final Dawn adventures even more exciting. (I hear the jungles of Brazil were quite interesting in the months following the [near] end of the world....) With this being the end of this particular adventure, though, there's a sense of sadness that permeates everything. I'm very happy with how the story turned out, but I'll still miss these characters... well, until I write about them again, at least.

So what's ahead for the future of Final Dawn? The sky's the limit, as they say! I'm planning on doing more novel or short series (like this trilogy) pieces, but those are a couple of months off. I'm taking some time to divert into two separate post-apocalyptic series called **Surviving the Fall** and **No Sanctuary**. The initial samples I wrote for these stories got some rave feedback on my blog and I'm looking forward to writing them! The current hope is to release 2 episodes of Surviving the Fall each month and one No Sanctuary book each month as well. No Sanctuary will be around 7 books long, each of novel length. Surviving the Fall will have short (around 25k words) episodic stories and I'm planning on 14 of those to complete the story. Of course, if you don't like reading episodes or individual books in a series, there will be an omnibus of each story once they're through.

If you'd like to stay in touch, there are few ways to do that. One of the best is to subscribe to my newsletter by visiting my website and clicking on the red button. If you do, you'll get all sorts of info like book launches, when I put books on sale and so on. Of course, you can also follow me on Facebook (Facebook.com/MikeKrausBooks), which I do an okay job of keeping up to date with. Most of the time. And, finally, I love getting emails (mike@mikekrausbooks.com). Those make my day more than anything else. If you have a problem with a book, want to tell me how idiotic I am for misspelling a word or just want to shoot the breeze, my inbox is always open.

Lastly… I just want to say thank you again. Thank you SO much for reading this trilogy. The writing, editing, marketing and everything else I have to do as part of creating and selling a book takes an enormous amount of effort, and it's readers like YOU who make it all worthwhile. It's an enormous honor to know that you enjoyed my books, and it means the world to me. Seriously. Thank you.

All the best,
Mike

Made in the USA
Columbia, SC
15 July 2021